IF WE COULD TURN BACK TIME

SIÂN O'GORMAN

B
Boldwood

First published in Great Britain in 2025 by Boldwood Books Ltd.

Copyright © Siân O'Gorman, 2025

Cover Design by Head Design Ltd

Cover Images: Shutterstock and iStock

The moral right of Siân O'Gorman to be identified as the author of this work has been asserted in accordance with the Copyright, Designs and Patents Act 1988.

All rights reserved. No part of this book may be reproduced in any form or by any electronic or mechanical means, including information storage and retrieval systems, without written permission from the author, except for the use of brief quotations in a book review. This book is a work of fiction and, except in the case of historical fact, any resemblance to actual persons, living or dead, is purely coincidental.

Every effort has been made to obtain the necessary permissions with reference to copyright material, both illustrative and quoted. We apologise for any omissions in this respect and will be pleased to make the appropriate acknowledgements in any future edition.

A CIP catalogue record for this book is available from the British Library.

Paperback ISBN 978-1-80415-703-9

Large Print ISBN 978-1-80415-702-2

Hardback ISBN 978-1-80415-701-5

Ebook ISBN 978-1-80415-704-6

Kindle ISBN 978-1-80415-705-3

Audio CD ISBN 978-1-80415-696-4

MP3 CD ISBN 978-1-80415-697-1

Digital audio download ISBN 978-1-80415-699-5

This book is printed on certified sustainable paper. Boldwood Books is dedicated to putting sustainability at the heart of our business. For more information please visit https://www.boldwoodbooks.com/about-us/sustainability/

Boldwood Books Ltd, 23 Bowerdean Street, London, SW6 3TN

www.boldwoodbooks.com

For my amazing friend, Sarah McNulty

"We are all in the gutter, but some of us are looking at the stars..."

— OSCAR WILDE

1

ALICE

Despite being squashed in the middle of a row of three on the plane from Perth, heading for Dublin, thirty-year-old Alice Murphy finally allowed herself to begin to feel excited. She didn't even mind the fact that on one side of her was a man who'd been watching episodes of *Friends* for the last eight hours, the volume of his headphones turned up so high she could hear every word. And she had ceased to be bothered by the practically passed-out woman on the other side, whose head repeatedly kept rolling onto Alice's shoulder.

She stared at the screen in front of her, watching a tiny, animated plane make its valiant journey across the world. They were catching up on time, she thought. Or, perhaps, they were ahead of it? But she knew her home village of Sandycove, perched on Dublin's rocky coastline, its feet in the sea, was at the end of this long journey.

It had been curiously liberating when she'd first arrived in Australia on a work visa ten years earlier. The sunshine had seemed endless, and she adored the freedom of life lived outdoors, from her morning coffee to glasses of wine basking in the evening sun, her feet in the warm sand. Instead of hunkering down for seven months of the year, and the other five spent looking at the sky or at weather apps, the threat of rain dictating everything, life was much freer, the world, bigger.

She had never seen herself getting old in Australia or doing mundane things such as pensions and healthcare or throwing one foot onto the property ladder. She had a gloriously unencumbered existence, almost as though she only half-existed in the real world. Neither did she collect belongings – her rented room had few personal items, just a teetering pile of books, and a few clothes. Being so unembedded in the world made her feel completely free, as though she could go anywhere, at a moment's notice. Worrying about growing older was something other people did.

When she first arrived in Perth, she liked the anonymity of not being just Eva Murphy's granddaughter or Ciara Murphy's daughter. Sometimes she thought that her need to be away was something to do with her long-lost, absentee non-father father. Did she have the running-away gene just like him? Was that why she lived so far from home, despite missing her mother and grandmother so much? Maybe coming back felt a bit like giving up, and she didn't want to be that kind of person. Not yet. She wanted to show the world that she could stand on her own two feet, that she was strong and resilient. But still. Homesickness was a killer. Warm sand and shark-infested waters were all very well, but she had missed the rain-soaked island of Ireland more than she admitted out loud.

She followed every Sandycove account on social media; the hanging baskets in bloom, the different festivals, or lost dogs or new businesses – there was even a new microbrewery – and these glimpses of village life stemmed the flood of homesickness. Whenever she'd been back in Sandycove, she'd soaked everything up but after a few weeks, she'd felt that twitch to be on the move again. However, this time, there was an urgency to her return, as though her soul were telling her that this was what she needed to quench her existential angst.

The reason why she'd gone and why she'd stayed wasn't something she could remember clearly. Was it the lack of her father who rejected her before she was even born? Over the last year, the idea of freedom, of the world stretching out in front of her, was beginning to wane. The sense of excitement was gone, and if that was gone, what did she have left? A month in Ireland would surely remind her, and she'd be desperate to return to a life where few people knew her, and no one would be wondering when she might start to grow up.

However, her thirtieth had triggered a pang or two of introspection. And for the first time in her life, she wondered what it would be like to have more than a few books to her name, to be someone who was part of a community and whose job might develop over time into a career. Perhaps even someone who had a child and who was in a relationship with someone who wanted the same things as she did.

It was the beginning of August and a whole month in Ireland stretched ahead. Having turned thirty just a month before, she'd suddenly been struck by the realisation that she was living her whole life on the other side of the world, far away from her two most beloved people – her mother and her grandmother. And for the first time, she wasn't sure if she was remotely okay with this. It was, she told herself, just your usual existential crisis, but sometimes a feeling of a kind of panicked nausea swirled inside her. Her flatmate, Grace, had looked concerned. 'Could you have an intolerance? An allergy? Gluten? Pollen...?'

She knew it was homesickness, the need to be with her

people. She'd met travellers over the years who'd been felled by it, immediately needing a cure of long video calls home or an emergency flight back to Ireland. She hoped this trip would quell her own symptoms. And by the time she returned to Perth, she'd be able for it again. Over the last decade, Alice could even add up how many days she had spent with Ciara and Eva. Five trips home in ten years.

She was lucky – this month wasn't even meant to happen. She worked as a classroom assistant but when a new building at school had led to delays upon delays, and with the water shut off and a JCB in the playground, a decision had been made to close the school and teach the children online until everything was up and running again. Before Alice even knew what she was doing, her fingers were tapping away on her keyboard and she was booking a flight home. She had had just enough time to tell her mother and text her best friend, Becca, before throwing her toothbrush and a few presents in a bag and heading to the airport.

The timing was perfect. After ending a relationship with her surfer boyfriend, Sebastian, she had nothing too pressing in Perth. Long-haired, bronzed of bod, and more than a little vain, Sebastian had immediately hooked up with a perma-bikinied goddess called Goldi, and his so-swift-it-was-practically-indecent ability to get over their break-up was almost impressive. But then again, the fact that Alice was so unbothered by his unbotherment was another reminder that she hadn't loved him very deeply at all.

She felt the panic rise up inside again, and tried to breathe deeply, her eyes fixed on the little graphic of the plane on the screen above her. They were now on the edges of Europe and she began to feel excited but scared all over again.

Excitement was really building now, thinking of her

mother, Ciara, who would be waiting for her at the airport, and her grandmother, Eva, who would be back home in Sandycove. They ran the family grocer's, Murphy's, on Sandycove's Church Street. It had been founded by Alice's great-grandfather a century earlier. Ciara was in charge of the shop these days, Eva helping out when she wasn't always out and about, waking early to make soda bread or swimming in the sea for her 'morning baptismal'.

Alice, changing planes in London, relieved to stretch her legs and realising that *Friends* was now ruined for her, texted her mother while waiting for the connecting flight.

ALICE
We're in the same hemisphere!

CIARA
YES! All very excited here. Gran was just in and said that you are to go and see her first thing in the morning.

ALICE
Can't wait to see her too. Will land at 10.35 p.m.

CIARA
Love you! See you soon!

ALICE
Love you too.

It had only ever been the three of them: Alice, Ciara and Eva. Her father was long gone, disappearing before she was born. His name was Lorcan Kennedy, her mother had told her. She'd met him only once, when she was eight years old, and Ciara had stood stiffly, holding Alice's hand, as this man who smelled of strange cigarettes asked her daughter perfunctory questions. There was a coldness and an oddness about him which was confusing because fathers were meant to be nice.

Finally, after almost a day since Alice left Australia, the plane landed in Ireland and despite it being after 10 p.m. and staggering under the weight of her rucksack, Alice sped through the airport, dodging the stragglers.

She handed her passport to the immigration officer.

'Welcome home,' he said.

She almost cried.

Walking as fast as she could, she headed towards Arrivals, out of the main door. It was dark, but the lights shone on the waiting cars, as she searched for that one face.

'Alice!'

And there she was. Her mother, Ciara, was standing beside her car, waving her arms and grinning wildly. Her hair was shorter than last time, and she was wearing a striped jumper tied around her shoulders, a pair of faded tracksuit bottoms, Birkenstocks and no socks.

Alice broke into a run and, before she'd even managed to slip her rucksack off her back, her mother's arms were around her and Alice sank into her, soaking up warmth and love from her favourite person ever.

Ciara stroked Alice's hair, tucking a strand behind her ear. 'You look beautiful,' she said gently. 'As always.'

'You too.' Alice hugged her again. 'It's so good to be home.'

'Oh my God,' said Ciara with a laugh. 'It's *so* good that you're home.'

Ciara wrested the rucksack out of Alice's hands and flipped it onto her back, making her legs buckle for a moment before steadying herself like a Sherpa, and then they both leant on the door of the boot to squeeze the bag in and then, they hopped in and they were off. Next stop, Sandycove.

On the journey, they caught up as much as possible with each other's news.

'And tell me, how is Sebastian?' asked Ciara, smiling across at Alice.

'Sebastian and I have split up,' said Alice with a shrug. 'He's fine about it. He seemed more bothered that his surfboard was stolen. His meditation practice was just too loud...'

'I didn't realise meditation could ever be loud...'

'Well, it can be. Humming and ahhing and making a kind of throaty sound as though he had a hairball.'

Ciara laughed as Alice changed the subject.

'How's Gran?'

'Her usual fine fettle. Still walking up the hill. Sea swimming with Angela and Dorrie every morning. Still managing to talk to everyone in the village and return full of news.'

'And the shop?'

'Thriving. We've a few new products. Nice new cheeses, and a new wine supplier. And...' Ciara paused for a moment, perhaps concentrating on moving to the outside lane. 'We're even stocking a range of beer made by a new local brewery called The Forty Foot.'

'I saw! So, the micro-beer craze has even come to Sandycove,' laughed Alice. 'Who owns it? Anyone I know?'

'Well, actually, Becca might have mentioned him to you. He's her new boyfriend...'

'Conal?'

Becca had told Alice about him in their long FaceTime calls. 'She just said he was lovely and it was early days.'

'He's Paddy Blake's son...' Ciara was staring straight ahead at the road. 'You know, from Blake's Beer?'

Alice nodded. Blake's products were in most pubs and bars across Ireland and the family lived in a beautiful house by the sea on Shankill Road. 'I love their house,' said Alice. 'You know the one? With the hawthorn trees at the entrance and its own harbour? Landfall, it's called.'

Ciara was expressionless, as though she hadn't heard. 'We're nearly home,' she said. 'You must be exhausted.'

'I am. Can't wait to get into bed.'

They turned onto their road, a couple of streets from the village, and the familiar sight of their small, two-bedroomed house, with the crab apple tree in the front garden and the rose which scrambled up outside the front wall, the white of the flowers shining in the moonlight, soothed her after her journey. A calm descended on Alice. *I'm home*, she thought. *For now.*

2

CIARA

It was dawn on Tuesday morning and time to be up for the day, but Ciara lingered in bed. Deliveries to the shop would already have begun, fresh milk and bread, the fruit and vegetables from the wholesalers, the yogurts and dairy would be stacked on the front step of the shop, ready for her to sort through and put out for sale. Today was a wonderful day. Alice was home.

She smiled in the half-light of her bedroom. For the next few weeks, she would just be able to be with her daughter again, hear her voice, see her face and reach out and touch her. Australia was too far, video calls weren't enough, and life was moving too fast. Not that Ciara would ever tell Alice just how much she missed her. Alice, after all, had her own life to live, it was just Ciara felt as though her own was running out of steam. She was fifty last birthday and instead of holding a party and celebrating, she hadn't even met her best friend Mary-Marg for a drink and had gone to bed early. She had thought that by this age, she would have been living her best life. But she couldn't summon up enthusiasm for anything. Even the shop needed a fresh injection of energy and ideas, both of which she was long out of.

It was light outside, the birds already in full song. Summer was easy, but how many winter mornings had she steeled herself, hauling herself out of bed, frozen, feeling for her slippers in the dark? There was barely a glance in the mirror, just enough to make sure that she was clean, her hair wasn't too bad and she'd remembered her bra. When had she stopped caring about anything beyond the shop, and whether they should open on the bank holiday, or why wasn't that artisan cheese selling, or how would she get more of that truffle salami which was flying out the door? And when would she manage to get to the hairdresser's for a trim?

Murphy's had begun life as a small grocer's selling fruit, vegetables and a few special items that her father had spotted at trade fairs or wholesalers'. Over the years, it had grown and developed, and now it was a very nice general store, selling everything from takeaway coffee and buns to wine and posh snacks, from olive oil and cheese to salamis. Ciara couldn't make enough ham, cheese and coleslaw sandwiches for the starving lunchtime hordes.

She and Alice had stayed up chatting over a succession of pots of tea into the early hours. Hearing her daughter's news of life so far away had inevitably made her wonder. Her own life seemed so small in comparison. She had been a mother for all her adult life, and her only career had been in Murphy's, the family shop. Being a mother had been a pleasure, she and Alice had grown up together, under the ever watchful, loving eye of Eva, but she was tired and was coasting towards old age. A decent social life had long since been jettisoned, never mind anything romantic. There had been a few brief liaisons over the years, but nothing worth giving up her evenings for. She socialised occasionally with her best friend, Mary-Marg, for walks and glasses of wine, and sometimes she joined her mother, Eva, at the Forty Foot for a swim but, really, her life was the shop. She'd grown up in Murphy's and had gone from helping her mother behind the counter and running errands for her father, George, to serving customers. When her father had died long ago, the year Alice was born, the running of the shop had fallen to Eva, and then, when she retired, Ciara took over. And she loved it – the way the days just flew, and the chat and craic you could have with people.

When she'd become pregnant with Alice, all those years ago, she'd been terrified of the future and worried about what everyone in the village would say – a young woman, unmarried, not even out of her teens, pregnant, and the man responsible having left the country. But when Alice was born, tucked up in her Moses basket behind the counter, being minded by either Ciara or Eva, the counter felt like a protection, the shop, a safe haven, and the gossip and the judgement never materialised.

Instead, the castigation and judgement came from within, Ciara berating herself for being so naive about everything that had happened. She hadn't blamed herself for a long time now and the pain of those years had receded just enough... but memories clung on. She'd never done any of that travelling she and Mary-Marg always planned to do when they were growing up. Nor had she even been to Perth to visit Alice, and she also understood why Alice had chosen to live on the other side of the world. Village life could be a little stultifying. God knows she'd wanted to run away herself a few times over the years.

All of Ciara's peers seemed to be on the cusp of massive life changes. Rachel Jordan had left her husband because, as she'd explained to Ciara the other week while buying sauerkraut ('my gut health is off the scale'), she had realised that she couldn't listen to him talk about rugby for a single second longer – especially as he talked with his mouth full of Weetabix. She was last seen boarding a flight to Delhi to find herself. Lily O'Houlihan had taken up ballet and could be seen in the queue in the post office in first – or was it second? – position, her hair in a slicked-back bun. And there was post-divorce Dessie Desmond who channelled his emotions into golf and had just returned from Portugal with a huge winner's seniors cup. Even Mona McCullough was on husband number four and she was only fifty-nine. Second chances and new beginnings were at least possible.

Mona had been in the shop only yesterday. 'Remember that disco you and Mary-Marg used to have when we were in school?' she'd asked, a dreamy look in her eye.

'Vaguely,' Ciara had said, wrapping up Mona's sourdough.

But *of course*, she remembered. How would she ever forget See The Stars, the disco they organised every Friday night, multiple lifetimes ago? Held in the old clubhouse on Sea Road, those Friday nights were the highlight of their young lives. Mary-Marg in charge of the music, playing records on two old turntables, Ciara front-of-house, greeting everyone, selling tickets, arranging the promotion, the lighting, the themes... God knows how any of them had got through their exams, because the disco had been their life. It was so much fun and there was that sense that anything and everything was possible. She and Mary-Marg were saving the money to go travelling in their year off before university, but then she became pregnant and Mary-Marg headed off to Limerick to do engineering and the old gang and their old lives dissipated.

'You should bring it back,' Mona had said. 'We need something like that now we're all in our fifties. A bit of fun.'

But Ciara knew there was no way Mary-Marg would want to go dancing again. A disco?! She had nearly laughed. Mary-Marg had her own problems and had recently begged her to join her on a retreat in West Cork called 'Making the menopause magical'. 'Don't make me go on my own!' she had wailed. But Ciara had chickened out, claiming she couldn't leave the shop – which was her perennial excuse when it came to weekends away or even nights out. She had tried to explain how tired she was.

Mary-Marg was feeling rudderless because her life – i.e. her eighteen-year-old twins, Jake and Josh – had just finished their Leaving Cert and would be off to university soon – results dependent. The last two years had been the worst of Mary-Marg's life, she had told Ciara, 'worse than the IVF years,' because she had worried about the boys' exams far more than they had. It was as though she were taking them herself, hovering over their revision, reading the textbooks, filling out all their college applications and driving them to and from every exam. Coupled with hot sweats, sleepless nights, palpitations and a sudden fear of heights, it had been an intense time. Going on the magical menopause retreat was part of her desperation to recover.

She'd returned pale-faced and shaken. 'It was as bad as I feared,' she'd told Ciara. 'You were right not to come. Chanting, humming, lentils. Being barefoot. But... apart from those horrors, I may – just may – have sensed a glimmer of the old me.' And Mary-Marg's eyes had begun to gleam in a way Ciara hadn't seen for decades.

'I've decided tiredness is a state of mind,' said Mary-Marg. 'We're *all* tired. At that terrible magical menopause retreat, every woman there said all they wanted was to be left alone in a pile of leaves in a forest like a squirrel and never be bothered again. I mean, we're all tired... goes with the territory...'

'But I'm not just tired-tired,' said Ciara. 'I'm tired of life... I just want to eat toast and watch TV...'

'You're flagging, that's all. And we all *flag* from time to time, feel a bit droopy, find it hard to haul ourselves from the depths of the duvet. Believe me, I have been flagging big *tiempo* for the last five years. But I have found my pep in my step again. Call it HRT, call it a ridiculous retreat, call it the will to survive in the jungle of life. But we can't give up. We need to get out there and live. Yes to discos and hanging out with friends, and no to uncomfortable clothes and making food for others. This is our time. Okay?' She fixed Ciara with that look. 'And promise me, when you start to flag, you will say something equally rousing to me?'

Ciara nodded, feeling buoyed by the pep talk. 'I promise.'

'And anyway, I need to talk to you about something... remember our...?' But they had been disturbed by a customer looking for a jar of jalapeños and whatever she was going to say was put on hold.

It was bright outside. Six eleven a.m. Ciara really should get up.

3

ALICE

From downstairs, there was a rattle of the letter box. And then the voice of Eva, her grandmother, calling from outside. 'Alice? Are you awake?'

Quickly, Alice launched herself out of bed, pulled on her old dressing gown and ran down the stairs. Through the glass of the front door, she could see a small, very familiar figure.

'Coming!'

And there was Eva, looking her usual magnificent self. Small, her hair grey and wiry, eyes bright blue, she was dressed in navy trousers, a sunshine-yellow cardigan, red socks and walking sandals. She was a beacon of warmth and wisdom, a safe harbour, the one person, along with Alice's mother, who had always been there, to comfort and advise, and whose love was the kind you took for granted. But Alice never had.

She flung her arms around her grandmother, knowing exactly what she would feel like, and they stood for a moment, recharging. And then, after peeling away, they studied each other for signs of change.

Eva smiled at her. 'You made it then. Half a world away. And you've cut your hair...'

'Just a trim.'

'It looks very well on you.' Eva nodded approvingly.

'You look the same.'

'Ah no,' said Eva. 'I do not. Ancient, I look. Like Methuselah. Every time I catch myself in the mirror, I think: *why is my grandmother here when she's been gone more than half a century?*'

Alice laughed. 'Well, she was beautiful... I've seen the photograph.'

'Yes, she was,' said Eva. 'And I have her soda bread with me...' Eva held up her bag.

'I've been dreaming of it...' When Alice was young, she'd help Eva with the bread-making, the stirring of the flour, the sprinkle of the oats, the swirling in of the buttermilk, the all-important pinch of soda, but when she'd tried in Australia to recreate it, it hadn't been quite the same.

'I thought you would be. And it's my grandmother's recipe and her grandmother's recipe and hers... ancient it is. But I always say, you can't improve on perfection... and with this, you can't go wrong...'

'You can,' said Alice. 'I've tried so many times...'

'I think it has to be made here. Our buttermilk is the best. And the flour. And you need Irish hands...'

'I've the Irish hands but the buttermilk was hard to find...'

'It would be,' said Eva, leading the way into the kitchen. 'My grandmother's recipe was to die for, you really would. My grandfather, that's *all* he would eat. When he was very old and ailing, he'd say, in a quavery voice, *Just a slice of Mary's bread...* We said it was going to cure him, so we urged her to make more. She was making three loaves a day. One for breakfast, one for lunch, one for dinner. *More,* we kept saying, *Grandfather needs his bread!* We used his illness just so we would have more bread.' Eva laughed. 'My poor old grandmother was worn out making it all.'

'It's the best breakfast,' said Alice, feeling intensely happy now she was back with her grandmother.

'Your mother said the flight was on time,' Eva said, turning to smile at her. 'You must be exhausted. You'll have to put your feet up and have a rest while you're home.'

'Well, actually,' Alice began, 'I thought I could help Mum in the shop while I'm here.'

'Ah, she'd love that,' said Eva, beginning to unpack her cloth bag on the kitchen table. 'I've brought butter as well. *Irish* butter. You can't get *that* either in Australia. We had our own cow, you know, when I was little. Blaithín – little flower.'

Alice said, 'Go on, tell me...' She loved all the stories, of life in the village and of her grandfather, George, who'd died before she was born. And she'd heard lots about Blaithín the cow and how it had lived in the field behind the house Eva had grown up in.

'Ah, she was a great cow, she was,' said Eva, slicing the bread. 'The sweetest cow, and so intelligent. She'd know it was me doing the milking and she'd be as good as gold. Quiet as a mouse she'd be, and as still as though she were in Mass. No kicking the bucket, like she did for my brother. He was the clever one, because it meant that it was only me who was sent down to milk her. But it was her eyelashes that we were all mad for.' She paused. 'Someone I used to know was desperate for Blaithín's eyelashes. She'd put on mascara – this was when we were teenagers, of course – and when poor old Blaithín the cow was long gone, the memory of her eyelashes was remembered by us all. And she'd say, the mascara painted on as thick as creosote, *Are my eyelashes Blaithín-long?* And of course, they never were.'

'We'd all like eyelashes like that...' Alice smiled at Eva. Listening to her stories – and surely she'd heard all of them by now? – was the very essence of home.

'And I have a jar of Dorrie O'Flanagan's raspberry jam. She made sure to drop it in to me yesterday, knowing you were on your way. She was tracking your flight, you know. Her grandson showed her how to do it. Rang me to say you'd landed in Dubai and then rang again when you took off for London...'

Alice made tea while Eva generously buttered the bread, and then she sat back for their breakfast. Eva admired the aboriginal bowl which Alice had brought home for her.

'The colours are tremendous,' Eva said, inspecting them. 'And the yellow is *my* yellow...'

'Your favourite colour,' said Alice, smiling at her. 'I knew you'd like it.'

'Sure, why would you want any other colour?' Eva always looked perplexed on the subject of colours. 'It's the colour of the sun, and eggs, and butter. The colour of an Irish breakfast.'

'The bread is so light and... just so tasty,' Alice said, buttering another slice. 'Fresh soda bread for breakfast, there's nothing like it.'

Eva smiled, satisfied, before setting her blue beady gaze on Alice. 'Now, tell me about this Sebastian. Are you going to settle down and marry the fella?'

'We're over,' Alice said. 'He moved on to someone far better-looking than me.'

'Impossible,' said Eva, quickly, and then, 'Was she your friend?'

Alice shook her head, wondering why Eva had thought she might be. 'No... I *knew* her, but we didn't hang out.'

'That's a relief,' said Eva. 'I always thought that there's enough men in the world, without having to go after someone's boyfriend.' Alice felt she was about to say something else when she suddenly began wrapping up the bread. 'We don't want this to go stale, do we? You'll want it for later...'

Perhaps Eva wanted Alice to settle down? But such a thing looked increasingly remote, despite how much Alice liked children. Working as a classroom assistant had only made her realise quite how wonderful and funny they were. She told Eva about the children in her school, and how she had followed one group from kindergarten to sixth class, and had said goodbye to them earlier in the summer as they left for secondary school. One little boy, Davey Hogan, had lost his mum to cancer and to see him coming in every day, eyes streaked with tears, and the way the other kids minded him, was so moving. And now, four years on, every time he'd laughed, she would cheer inside. And then there was another little girl, Willow Nguyen, an incredible miniature pianist prodigy, and the class had gone to a recital at the concert hall to see Willow perform, and Alice had seen the pride in the faces of her classmates as they'd clapped and cheered and jumped up and down. It took every ounce of self-control for Alice not to start sobbing uncontrollably.

Eva seemed to understand. 'You were disarmed by them,' she said, nodding.

'Totally,' said Alice. 'And I felt I couldn't let them down because they were giving all of themselves to the world. Does that make sense?'

Eva nodded again. 'Indeed it does. I saw Becca yesterday,' said Eva. 'She was wondering when you were landing. I told her to check in with Dorrie O'Flanagan.'

'I'm seeing her tonight,' said Alice, smiling. 'She's going to introduce me to her new boyfriend.' She stopped for a moment. 'He makes beer, apparently.'

'Is that right?' Eva gazed back at her.

'He's Conal Blake. You know Blake's Beer?'

Eva looked vague, but she knew *everyone* in the village, every family network and who was married to whom, their backstories, what happened when and where, down to the day, month and year. So why, wondered Alice, was she acting as though she'd never heard of Blake's Beer?

'Not really,' Eva said, abruptly changing the subject. 'Now let me know if you want any more of my bread. I could make a loaf every morning while you're home, if you like? I used to make a dozen every day to sell in the shop in the old days, so it's no bother. May as well make the most of me while you're here. And by the way...' Eva found her purse in her bag and rummaged around for a moment, before producing a fifty euro note. 'Here's something to keep you going for a while...'

'I don't need money, Gran,' said Alice.

'Ireland's getting very expensive,' warned Eva. 'And I want the opportunity to treat you. You're my precious one and only.'

'Put your purse away. I'm thirty. I earn my own money. I should be giving *you* money.'

'Oh, I'd like to see that,' said Eva, laughing. 'Now, shall we go to the shop and see your mother? She'll want to show you all the changes she's made.'

4

CIARA

Situated halfway along Sandycove's Church Street, Murphy's sat between the dusty old bookshop and the modern bakery which sold sourdough and spelt breads and provided all the celebratory cakes for miles around. The doorway split into two – one entrance leading to the shop, and the other up to Eva's flat. The outside was painted navy blue, with a hand-painted gold 'Murphy's' above. And below it, in smaller writing, 'Food and Wine Emporium'.

'Emporium is very grand,' Eva had said when Ciara had first come up with a way to describe the shop, years ago.

'I like it,' Alice had said. 'It deserves a grand word.'

Eva had laughed. 'Grand is grand with me, so,' she had said.

Ciara always spent time on the displays and had a selection of props stored in the back. At Christmas, she always brought out a vintage toy train which had belonged to her father and had found someone who got it chugging again. Now, in summer, she had placed a selection of olive oil bottles in a vintage-looking crate, some on their sides, others in a pool of their own oil. Inside was a counter running along the back, in front of shelves, and then there were more shelves running full-height on both sides of the shop, and fridges for the cheese and dairy.

The bell above the door rang and Ciara looked up to see Dee Maguire stepping inside. Dee had been in the same class at school as Ciara all those years ago and now ran a small craft shop in the village.

'Morning, Ciara,' she said. 'I hear that your Alice is home. Becca O'Hara will be pleased to see her... And isn't Becca going out with Conal Blake, Paddy's son?'

'She is,' said Ciara, fixing on a smile. 'As far as I know... I've seen them going into The Island a couple of times.'

'He's a handsome young man, don't you think?' Dee was one of those people who sniffed out mysteries and secrets. She had a nose for them. 'Seems very pleasant. Just like his father.'

Ciara nodded and fixed on another facial expression, this time a half-smile of vague interest. You had to be a Mrs Potato Head and change your expression all the time. But talking about Paddy Blake was always difficult because they'd been so close once upon a time, and he'd been part of Ciara and Mary-Marg's gang, growing up. There was never a romantic connection because she'd been obsessed with Lorcan in those days, and when she'd got pregnant and Lorcan had left, Paddy had retreated into his world and she into hers. Obviously, they exchanged pleasantries when they passed each other in the street or if he called into the shop for something, but she had never talked to him properly and longed to ask him what he knew of everything that had happened back then? But no one knew as much as she knew – it was just that sometimes, she wished she had someone who might understand, and she guessed that if anyone did understand, it would be Paddy. And now Paddy's son was all grown up and they hardly knew him.

'Conal was in my shop the other day,' Dee was saying. 'Needed a present for his *awful* grandmother. Impossible to buy for. I felt for the lad, I really did. Steered him towards one of the hand-painted Sandycove mugs.' She paused. 'She was a difficult woman, was she not? That Dol Blake. Now, she *liked* money. Married into it, obviously, but she flashed it about. That car she used to drive! A red thing, it was... no roof, remember? None of our mothers would *ever* drive something like that...'

'I can't remember,' said Ciara, 'it was so long ago...'

'Ah, it wasn't *that* long ago, Ciara,' said Dee. 'Conal looks nothing like his mother, though, does he? Breda. She was a strange fish, wasn't she? Never very friendly to any of us and I always wondered what Paddy saw in her because he was always so nice.'

Ciara nodded. 'He was... Still is, I think...'

'Do you think he was forced to marry Breda? Was she pregnant, do you think? I've always wondered what the truth was. Wouldn't have put them together at all. And then she left him! The cheek of her, leaving a good man like Paddy Blake. And all his money. I know she had family money herself, but still. And worst of all, leaving Paddy to bring up Conal on his own. Some people don't know they are born.'

'No...' It was at times like this that Ciara hated being trapped behind the counter. But she knew the history and the story of the Blake family far better than Dee did – or ever could – and she managed to nod and smile.

Paddy's father, Patrick Senior, had inherited Blake's Beer, which had once employed hundreds of people, and although he was a handsome, charming and affable man, he not very successfully tried to hide his drinking problem. The irony of an alcoholic running a brewery wasn't lost on any of the villagers. They'd see him slinking into a pub in Dún Laoghaire, hoping not to be spotted. Eventually, illness caught up with him, and he died when Paddy was still only a teenager. Paddy had then inherited the company, whether he liked it or not.

'They were a strange family, though. Poor Paddy. He seemed *drowned* by them all. His father's drinking, his mother and her desperate need to be the centre of attention, and then Breda leaving. And now Dol having a stroke and being in Honeysuckle Lodge. It's a lot for Paddy to take, I would say. But he's done such a good job with Conal. And you're stocking his beer, I see...' She looked towards the stand of Forty Foot beer. 'Is it selling well?'

Ciara nodded. 'Really well. He came in a few months ago to see if I would stock it.'

Conal had reminded her of Paddy all those years ago, and therefore how could she refuse to stock his beer, but Conal seemed a more serious and solicitous version of his father, whereas she remembered Paddy as always laughing and joking. He'd always been such great *craic*.

Dee was examining one of Conal's bottles. 'Banshee's Howl... I'm not a beer drinker, but Brendan is... I'll take a bottle for him, and I will let you know his verdict. He was remembering our first date at your old disco. Remember? The one you and Mary-Marg used to organise. My mother would make me go. "It's the only way you'll ever meet a nice young man, Deirdre," she used to say. And I did. My Brendan was drinking a TK Lemonade in the corner of the clubhouse. Behind the stacked chairs...'

The bell jangled and in walked Jimbo McAlister, the local postman, wearing his An Post uniform of cargo shorts and shirt, a pair of worn-down runners on his feet, his face and arms tanned.

'Ladies,' he said, 'how's it going?'

If We Could Turn Back Time

'Grand, thanks Jimbo,' said Ciara.

Dee put down the beer. 'Oh, *good* morning, Jimbo,' she said. 'Isn't it a beautiful day? How was your delivery this morning? Any vicious dogs?'

'Just the usual. The small ones are the worst. I keep a supply of dog treats handy...' He patted one of the pockets on the leg of his shorts. 'I have been known to fling a handful along with the post.' He smiled at Ciara. 'Sandwich, please, Ciara. One of the ham and mustard,' he said, as she reached for the bread and began buttering it. She knew practically every villager's coffee and sandwich order and who liked no butter, or extra mustard, or who liked lots of milk or a double shot.

'Jimbo,' said Dee, 'you must remember Ciara and Mary-Marg's discos?'

'I surely do,' said Jimbo. 'I've never forgotten those Friday nights. Sometimes I hear a song and I'm brought right back there. All of us dancing in the middle of the clubhouse... the doors open onto the darkness outside, the lights... and the anticipation!' He smiled. 'Magic, it was...'

Dee was nodding. 'Mary-Marg was such a good DJ, wasn't she? Always played the best songs. And you were so good, Ciara, making sure everyone was happy, that it all ran smoothly... I remember once Paddy Blake having to fix the generator, though. All the electricity went off and he clambered onto the roof, all the smokers holding up their lighters trying to brighten his way...'

Jimbo laughed. 'He stood on the top of the building and shouted ONE! TWO...! And we all screamed THREE! And the lights and the music were back on.'

Dee was smiling, as Ciara had attached a new expression, one which she hoped evoked dreamy reminiscence.

'Now, Jimbo, tell me this and tell me no more,' said Dee.

'Have you spoken to Paddy recently? We were just talking about him, saying what a marvellous job he has done bringing Conal up on his own. And now his mother being in the nursing home... so sad.' She looked at Jimbo. 'So tell us, how is poor Paddy doing?'

'Well...' Jimbo shrugged. 'I don't see much of him. He gave money when I was fundraising for the hospice. Always was very generous. But I don't see him in The Island having a pint. Or... well, anywhere much. I think he plays golf occasionally...' Jimbo shrugged again. 'But he doesn't look as though he's having much fun. But then, who is?'

Dee thought for a moment. 'No...' she admitted, 'no one is. Brendan's sciatica dominates our lives. He can only sleep sitting up. And...' She dropped her voice. 'I think I might have social anxiety. Comes with age, apparently. I thought you got more confident as you got older but it's not always the case.'

'I'm a bit like that,' admitted Ciara.

'Me three,' said Jimbo. 'I like to go home after my shift and *stay* home.'

'That's what I do,' said Ciara, wrapping up Jimbo's sandwich. 'I watch Scandi-noir...'

'I like those home-improvement shows,' said Jimbo. 'You know, when they begin with an unrealistically small budget, go years over schedule, and are shadows of their former selves by the end. But at least they have a fancy kitchen.' He took the sandwich from Ciara. 'See you, ladies. Don't get into any trouble, now, will you?' He laughed. 'Except that's exactly what we *should* be doing?'

Ciara laughed. 'Chance would be a fine thing.' One day, she thought, she'd be off having an exciting life. She just had to get off her arse and do something about it.

5

ALICE

Alice knew every inch of the shop, inside and out; from the granite step which had been softened by thousands of feet over the century, to the particular jingle of the bell above the door which, when she was tiny, she imagined was Tinkerbell paying them a visit.

'It's just nice to be back in the shop again,' Alice said. 'It feels like home.'

'It *is* home,' said Eva. 'Your grandfather was born in the flat upstairs. He grew up here, and it was to Murphy's he brought me when we were first married. And I'd already spent my youth in and out of the shop running errands for my grandmother, buying potatoes and flour, whatever she needed. Delivering her bread to be sold here.'

'And now you're back in the flat...'

'I couldn't be happier,' said Eva. 'It's full of happy memories. Now, talking of which, I'll leave you for now because it's time for a little gander of the paper.' She smiled at Alice, patting her arm. 'We love having you home, where you belong.'

Alice nodded. It was strange knowing that she belonged in

Sandycove but lived so far away. She didn't quite understand this need to travel, as though she were trying to prove something. Perhaps it was to do with her father, the man who couldn't even stay around long enough to see her born, who only returned that one time because he had his aunt's will to sort out, and who hadn't cared about her mother. It was so hard to understand.

She smiled at her grandmother. 'I'd better see how Mum is getting on.'

Inside Murphy's, not a huge amount had changed since her last visit. There was the long counter running along the back of the shop, smoothed from a century of use. The tall shelves behind were filled with bottles and jars. The round table in the middle, stacked high with what Ciara called the 'specialties' – chocolates, biscuits and sweets, the kind bought as gifts. Ciara was beaming at her from behind the counter.

'You're up!' she said. 'I thought you'd have a nice lie-in. How is the jet lag?'

'Grand. I might need a sleep later, but Gran brought some of her soda bread and how could I stay in bed and miss that?'

Ciara smiled at her. 'Your favourite.'

Alice nodded. 'It's just not the same in Australia. The buttermilk is wrong, the flour is different. It just doesn't have that same taste.'

'Well, make the most of it while you're here.'

Alice had a look around. The shop was warm and welcoming but compared to the small, artisan shops of Perth, it seemed too much of a jumble, a little faded, in need of a slight tweak to keep up with the times. Ciara had made so many changes over the years, transforming it from an old-fashioned grocer's to a posh deli, but perhaps she'd run out of energy to keep up the momentum? Whatever it was, it was good to be back. 'It looks even better than last time,' she said. 'A bigger cheese selection...'

'You can never have enough cheese,' said Ciara.

'True.' Alice stopped at a pile of vintage beer crates which were stocked with bottles of Old Seadog and Banshee's Howl, made by The Forty Foot Brewing Company. 'Here's that Forty Foot beer you were telling me about.'

Ciara looked blankly at her, as though she hadn't heard her.

'Becca's new boyfriend's beer,' prompted Alice. 'You told me about it? Maybe *you* have jet lag?'

Ciara laughed. 'Sorry...'

'Local brew. Very trendy. All the hipsters will be in.'

Ciara smiled. 'They have been... hipsters of all ages. Fintan Leahy is mad for it.'

'While I'm here,' said Alice, ducking behind the counter to join her mother, 'I thought I could work in the shop as much as possible, give you a break...'

'Ah, there's no need,' said Ciara. 'You're meant to be on holiday... you need to rest...'

Holiday. Alice hadn't thought of it like that. If you went home, were you on holiday? And if you were, did that make it less of a home? 'I want to work,' she said firmly. 'I want *you* to have a holiday.'

The bell above the door rang again and a young man entered the shop. Max was around Alice's age, with dark hair which was so thick it formed a kind of halo, wore chinos and a striped cotton shirt, the sleeves rolled up, and a pair of red-framed glasses and battered Converse.

'Ah, Max!' Ciara said. 'Finally, you get to meet Alice. Alice, this is Max who has taken over the bookshop next door. Max, this is Alice.' She smiled at her daughter. 'Max knows all about you,' she went on. 'Because I don't stop talking about her, do I, Max?'

'And very interesting it is,' said Max, holding out his hand and shaking Alice's. 'Your mother and I have quite the chats every morning when I come in for my coffee and *pain au chocolat*. It's amazing what you can discuss in five minutes.'

'That's the art of the shopkeeper,' said Ciara, turning around to the large, chrome Italian coffee machine. 'People have only a few minutes to exchange greetings. Some don't want even to make eye contact, but most want to speak to you and many want to confide in you. The stories I've heard in here... You'll get to know your customers, Max. Give it a few months.'

Max nodded. 'I already am,' he said. 'I talked to a retired gentleman about how he met his wife. He had left the priesthood and he plucked up the courage to go to a dance and it was Ladies' Choice. And there was a tap on his shoulder and there was this most beautiful woman asking him to dance. Turns out she was a former nun. And they were married for forty years. He was looking for a copy of Seamus Heaney poems,' said Max, above the sound of the steaming machine. '"Scaffolding". You know it?'

'It's my favourite poem,' said Alice.

'Well, I had a perfect edition and he went back to his wife, very happy indeed.'

Ciara handed him his coffee. 'Extra strong and your usual foamy top.' She turned to Alice. 'Max can't work without his morning coffee.'

'It's true,' he admitted, taking the cup. 'I am nothing without coffee. Like a farmer without a dog or Oscar Wilde without his wit.'

'When did you take over the bookshop?' asked Alice.

'A year ago. It was actually owned by my great-uncle Peter. It was either I took it over or it was sold. And I was taking too long to finish my PhD because the real world was just too damn distracting. My mother, in her eternal wisdom, told me that Uncle Peter's lease was up and did I want to do anything with the shop? I'd just spent a decade in a library and was seriously in danger of developing rickets or turning into Gollum from lack of light, and so it made perfect sense.'

Alice laughed. 'I've been in Australia for ten years. I think I've actually had *too* much light. I quite like the idea of dark libraries.'

'Alice's boyfriend is a surfer,' said Ciara. 'She's fully embraced the Antipodean lifestyle.'

'Ex-boyfriend,' Alice corrected her.

Max smiled at her. 'Well, you're very welcome home.' He gave her a lopsided smile which for some reason made her laugh. 'Now, I must return to my den of iniquity...' He pulled another face.

'It's a bookshop,' she said, still laughing. 'Hardly a den of iniquity...'

'A den of...' He paused to think. 'What's the opposite of den of iniquity? What even *is* a den of iniquity?'

'I wouldn't mind going to a den of iniquity,' said Ciara, looking over at them. 'Just to... I don't know... have fun.'

'You mean you don't have fun in this den of food delights, this gourmet palace?' asked Max.

'Not fun, exactly,' Ciara said. 'It's work... I mean, I love it... but it's the same, every day.'

Max nodded. 'The hamster wheel of retail...'

'I don't mind it,' said Ciara, hastily. 'I'm not complaining... it's just that...'

'...you would like a little iniquity from time to time,' said

Max. 'And who would argue with that? My particular evils are pub quizzes and reading detective novels into the early hours, eschewing sleep to discover if the bad guy wins.' He paused. 'Spoiler: he *never* does. Why is that? But in life, the good guy never seems to be appreciated enough.'

Alice was looking at Ciara who had a look on her face as though she were thinking of something else.

'I'll see you both soon,' said Max, turning to go. 'Good to meet you, Alice.'

'You too, Max.'

He closed the door behind him, the bell jangling, and Alice turned to Ciara.

'Is everything okay? What's this about dens of iniquity...?'

'It was obviously a joke... I just meant... I don't know... fun. That's all.'

'You're not having fun?'

'No... not really...' Ciara brightened. 'But it's not to say that I am not happy. Which of course I am. I mean, who needs fun? It's not exactly water or oxygen. Anyway, how do you think the shop is looking?'

Alice didn't hesitate. 'Wonderful,' she said. 'It's lovely. I like the new brands. The beer, all those cheeses...'

'Mainly Irish cheese,' said Ciara. 'There are so many producers making such wonderful cheese now... and business is going well. Early mornings are quiet enough, just people coming in for the odd coffee or tea. But the lunchtime sandwich crowd is busy. And...' She looked around. 'I don't think I can do any more. Sometimes, I wonder if it isn't time to sell...'

'No!' Alice was aghast. They could never sell the shop. It had been founded by her great-grandfather who borrowed £300 to lease this building, and he'd begun with flour in sacks and earthy potatoes in barrels. There was even fresh fish and crab every morning, brought up from Bullock Harbour. She'd seen the photographs, leafed through the old ledgers which were still stacked in the back of the shop.

'I won't, though,' said Ciara. 'Of course I won't. Now... let me show you the new coffee machine. State of the art. What this machine can't do... and I'm thinking of a gourmet frozen yogurt machine next. Whippy frozen yogurt... there's another young entrepreneur who makes his own...'

As her mother spoke, Alice felt a rustle of paper in her pocket and pulled out a crisp fifty euro note. She smiled at the kindness of her grandmother. It really was good to be home.

6

CIARA

Ciara and Mary-Marg were powering along the seafront. 'Walking is the only way to socialise these days,' Mary-Marg was saying, arms pumping. 'If I didn't force myself out every evening, I would just have to stare at Brian. And, my God, I've just noticed after twenty-three years of marriage how long his face is. And it's only getting longer. Faces are like ears and eyebrows. They keep growing.'

'Brian is only fifty-two,' said Ciara. 'He's not exactly elderly.'

'That's my point!' said Mary-Marg. 'Imagine how long his face is going to be when he's eighty. It'll be touching the floor. Just like my facial hair these days. Honestly, it's so luxuriant, I'll soon be able to tout myself as the bearded lady and snarl at people from a cage.' She paused. 'Which is kind of what I do these days. Poor Brian. He has the patience of a saint. I don't know why I'm so awful to him. Fecking menopause.'

'Is this why we're walking?'

'It's meant to be one of the best ways of managing symptoms,' said Mary-Marg. 'That and a good night's sleep. God, I'd give my firstborn twins to have a good night's sleep. I'm so fed up with flaxseed on everything, and spending the same amount on vitamins I spent on a deposit for my first house.'

On the other side of the road, dressed in black loose running shorts and a T-shirt, was Paddy Blake. Ciara felt herself – as she always did when she saw him – look away.

'There's Paddy Blake again,' said Mary-Marg, nudging her. 'All he does is run these days. Up and down Killiney Hill, along the seafront... I sometimes see him at Booterstown and towards Sandymount, following the coast. He doesn't stop.'

'He must enjoy it,' said Ciara blandly, looking intently at a yacht in the harbour. 'Is that Tom Curley's new boat? He said he had a new one...'

'Of course he doesn't *enjoy* running,' insisted Mary-Marg, with the lofty air of a mental health expert. 'No one enjoys it. It's not a fun activity. *Fun run* is an oxymoron. People do it for self-flagellatory reasons, to atone for past crimes and misdemeanours... or if they have general trauma. Personal demons. Running away from pain, usually.'

'Or perhaps just to get fit?' Ciara laughed. 'Are you suggesting everyone who runs 10K and marathons or park runs or whatever is traumatised?'

'Well, why not? Running is better than drinking your head off. And apparently, it's a great head-clearer. Although I prefer drinking my head off. Not that I've even done *that* since my sentence in parental prison began. I live like a bloody nun these days. Not a Blue Nun, unfortunately. I was thinking that it's time to reintroduce alcohol. Just a little. Not too much. But remember my garden drinks on Saturday evening. Now Alice is home to help, you have no excuse. I think I might make it a bottomless brunch...'

'A what?'

'A bottomless brunch. They're all the rage. Basically, food and drinks... but there's no limit.'

'Sounds dangerous.'

'Sounds irresponsible,' agreed Mary-Marg, 'but I'm just trying to introduce a bit of risk, a bit of living carelessly. And yes, a bit of danger... is that so wrong? But I know us, and we'll get a bit tipsy and we'll all still be home in bed for 9 p.m.'

'That late?' said Ciara, her eyes wide with horror.

'Eight thirty then. Final offer.'

'Then I'm in.' Ciara paused. 'But how can it be brunch if it's the afternoon and evening?'

'Bottomless lunch and tea, then. Tunch.'

'I like the sound of a tunch.' And at least she'd be in bed when it was still light outside.

They carried on, along the seafront to the cafe which was once the old swimming baths, a Victorian lido which filled with seawater at high tide, but had lain derelict for years until refurbished by the council. There was now a posh cafe which sold scones and tea to people sitting on the terrace, gazing out to sea. On wet, windy days – which were the more common – they gazed at the sea from behind the large plate glass windows as the rain lashed and seawater crashed against it.

'Can you believe we all used to be friends?' Mary-Marg said suddenly.

Ciara knew exactly about whom she was talking, but pretended not to. 'Who? Elaine?'

'No! Paddy!' Mary-Marg shrugged. 'Was it Breda? Would she not allow him to be friends with any of us? Maybe he never liked us in the first place and just ditched us?'

'Maybe he just entered a bottomless brunch and couldn't get out...'

Mary-Marg laughed. 'Let's hope that doesn't happen to us.'

She paused. 'But it was a bit strange, though, don't you think? A bit sad, really.'

'People do that though,' said Ciara. 'They move on. Find other friends.'

'I invited him and Breda to my wedding,' said Mary-Marg. 'They didn't come...'

'No...'

'I've become all nostalgic since the big 5-0,' went on Mary-Marg. 'I mean, I was too busy trying to get pregnant, and then all that bloody IVF and then the twins arriving and they were a nightmare, and continue to be one... but... where did the years go? Oh, I don't know...'

'You're just getting sentimental in your dotage.'

At the cafe, people were sitting out, facing the morning sun.

'Dotage! You're older than me.'

'By one week...'

'It's still *older*.'

They smiled at each other.

Five minutes later, they were seated on a bench, their backs to the wall of the cafe, their coffees in their hands, a slice of carrot cake on a plate between them, with two forks.

'Not as good as yours,' said Mary-Marg loyally.

'It's just nice to be out of the shop, drinking coffee I haven't made.'

'Even if it is inferior...'

Ciara laughed. Mary-Marg had been making her feel better about herself ever since they'd first met, aged six.

'Which brings me to my great idea.' Mary-Marg's glint was back in her eye. 'We're bringing back our disco...'

Ciara felt safe in the knowledge that there would be no disco. Their old club night was safely buried along with all their other youthful follies. 'We're fifty,' she said. 'And I can't dance. Not any more.'

'See The Stars,' said Mary-Marg. 'It was a great name for a nightclub...'

'It was hardly a nightclub,' said Ciara. 'It was a disco in the Gaelic football hall. There were markings on the floor. You used to have your record player by the goal...'

'No one said it was ever glamorous. It wasn't Studio 54 or Manumission or whatever...' Mary-Marg stopped. 'Look, I was chatting to the new owner of The Sandycove Arms today... Killian Walsh. Exceedingly nice man. And he was saying that they have just redone the function room upstairs...' She smiled at Ciara. 'And I was just thinking... that, perhaps, you know, you and me... and because Alice is home, you'll have more time on your hands...' She fixed Ciara with a look. 'You *do*. Don't give me that. Make the most of having your very able daughter around. Well, I was thinking we should have a bit of fun. Break out our old dance moves, a bit of DJ-ing... strictly over-fifties. Maybe over-forty-fives, if I'm feeling generous. A few drinks. Come on! It's exactly what the young middle-aged of Sandycove are crying out for.'

Ciara was silent for a moment, appalled. She wanted to say that they were too old, too uncool... too *tired* for a disco. But Mary-Marg looked deadly serious.

'But how...?' She began.

'We organise it. Just like we used to. Make a list of jobs to be done and get on with it.' Mary-Marg could see that Ciara was struggling with the concept. 'Look,' she said, 'we've done it before. We just have to find our old dancing pants and put them on. Metaphorically and literally.'

'But what about music? Are you our DJ again?'

Mary-Marg nodded. 'I mean... I *used* to be able to do it and

Brian *still* hasn't bought me anything for my fiftieth. He wants me to choose boring jewellery or a pair of fecking shoes, but I've ordered myself a set of DJ decks. I've asked the shop to invoice him. They're arriving on Monday.'

This was getting serious, thought Ciara. 'It's all changed a lot, though,' she warned, feeling nervous. Club nights these days, as far as she could tell, were nothing like a disco in an old sports hall. Back then, running their own weekly disco was so easy because the two of them were so confident and felt they could do anything.

'I'm going to get lessons,' said Mary-Marg. 'I have a contact in the biz. Well, he's in the boys' class at school, but he DJs locally.'

'But what...' Ciara faltered. 'What on *earth* are we going to wear?'

Neither of them had been cool for years and neither had the first clue about how to go about attaining it.

'I have no idea,' said Mary-Marg with a hopeless shrug. 'None whatsoever. But I was hoping that *that* would fall into place once we've organised everything else.'

'But...' Ciara began.

'Look,' said Mary-Marg, 'on that retreat I went to, they said that everyone's menopause journey is as unique as a snowflake. Well, this is what *my* menopause journey-stroke-crisis looks like. So, the question is, do you want to come on this trip with me?'

Ciara had been trying and failing to say 'no' to Mary-Marg for most of her life. 'But...' she tried uselessly as Mary-Marg's eyes gleamed, sensing victory.

'What about next Friday, the 11th? Is that too soon? That gives us nine days. Strike while the iron is hot – not that I have ironed anything in a very long time.'

Mary-Marg looked as scared as Ciara felt, but she couldn't let her do it alone. Obviously it was going to be a disaster, but they would face the disaster together.

'I'm in,' she said. 'Book me a place on your menopause journey.'

Mary-Marg smiled at her. 'Right. We'd better get cracking. Do you know something? I feel better already. For the first time in eighteen months, I'm not either sweating or exhausted or both. I feel...' She stopped.

'You feel what?' asked Ciara.

'I feel like dancing.' Mary-Marg grinned. 'What about you?'

'Me too,' said Ciara, smiling back at her.

They clinked their coffee cups, both suddenly excited.

7

ALICE

BECCA
Did you arrive or are you still up in the clouds?

ALICE
YES! Made it in last night. How are you? Can't wait to see you!

BECCA
YAAAAAYYYYY! Drink this evening? In The Island? You can meet Conal??!!

ALICE
OF COURSE! Can't wait to meet him!

Becca was a woman transformed. Glowing and radiating an aura that could only be attained by those who had consumed porridge for breakfast or the newly in love. In Becca's case, it was the latter. Alice had last seen her the previous winter in Perth and Becca had arrived, a hastily assembled suitcase of mismatched clothes, her moneybelt lost somewhere when she had changed planes in Dubai, having not eaten since a stale croissant in Dublin airport. Her lack of appetite and tear-streaked face was a result of her heartbreak after ending it all with Julian, her old-before-his-time boyfriend.

Julian hadn't taken it well, disappearing with a bottle of Jameson and a wild look in his eyes. When Becca had told Alice about it, over a flat white at The Beach Shack in Perth, Alice had thought it was probably the most exciting thing Julian had ever done. Almost Byronic in its intensity. But then, days later, when Becca had spoken to Julian's mother, it turned out that the whiskey had just been a threat and he'd instead spent the evening at her house, where he drank three strong coffees in succession and then couldn't sleep. 'He was grand,' Julian's mother had reassured Becca. 'He needed the kick up the backside and he got one. Fair play to you. I'd have dumped his sorry arse too.'

Becca's trip to Perth was a triumph. The moneybelt had turned up at the bottom of her ridiculously capacious tote bag, the mismatched clothes didn't even matter because Becca just wore shorts and a top, and her heartbreak miraculously was cured. By the time she had left, she'd gone native: tanned, flip-flopped, her hair braided and wearing denim cut-offs. She'd also had a brief dalliance with one of Sebastian's pals, Raffi, who told them – seriously – that he didn't believe Ireland was real and had always thought it was a mythical land, like Atlantis. Becca didn't seem to mind. 'I'm never going home,' she had declared recklessly. 'Ever.'

But real-life commitments were a consideration and Becca had her own business at home, a dog-minding service called Happy Paws, and Alice had brought her to the airport, now *both* tear-streaked as they had sadly hugged goodbye. Becca had been that blast of home she had so badly needed. And now, all these months later, as Alice stepped inside The Island pub in

Sandycove, there was Becca rushing towards her, arms stretched out. 'Alice!'

Becca was looking beautiful, the denim cut-offs now swapped for a floral yellow sundress and white Converse. Her hair, which was slightly orangey, hung around her shoulders, framing her pretty face, with brown eyes and long eyelashes, and she squashed Alice against her.

'Oh my God! You're home,' Becca said, releasing her and stepping back to look at Alice. 'You look amazing. Love the hair. Mine is a disaster. I put lemon juice in it for home-made highlights, you know, like I did in Australia, but obviously here in Ireland we have a completely different sun. It really doesn't work the same way. My hair went orange, like I'd done it with a felt-tip marker. I had to try to wash it out before Conal saw it and thought I was completely insane. He already did when I put freckles on my face with eyeliner and they rubbed off. I had to tell him I just wasn't very precise with my eyeliner. I don't want him to think I'm doolally.' She glanced at a man standing at the bar who was – Alice guessed – Conal, and beside him was that really nice man from the bookshop, Max. Becca turned around to them. 'Conal, come and meet my best friend in the whole world, Alice Murphy...'

Conal was the same height as Becca, with a floppy blonde fringe, blue eyes and freckles on his nose. He had a boyish, clean-shaven face and was wearing cargo shorts, sandals and a loose checked shirt, but it was his face which looked familiar. Perhaps Alice knew him from some summer camp or from the shop.

'Finally,' he said, shaking Alice's hand. 'I've heard so much about you.'

'And Alice,' went on Becca, her hand linked possessively around Conal's arm, 'this is Max Williams who—'

'We've already met,' said Max, shaking Alice's hand again. 'We're shop-neighbours. We're battling big capitalism one sale at a time. Or, in my case, one book at a time.'

'Max and Conal are old school friends,' said Becca, nudging Alice. 'Just like us! And Alice's mother stocks Forty Foot beer in Murphy's.'

'I know,' said Conal, smiling at Alice. 'I couldn't believe she would. I always thought how much I would love Murphy's to stock it and then I went in on the off-chance, thinking she would say no, but she said yes immediately.'

'Al, you have to taste it,' said Becca. 'The Forty Foot beer is *delicious*. I like Old Seadog. Very fruity. And Banshee's Howl! Exquisite!' Alice knew Becca hated *all* types of beer, but she'd obviously made an exception for Conal's.

He was laughing. 'Becca's my number one fan.'

'Oh, I am,' said Becca fervently.

'And I am hers,' said Conal, as they gazed into each other's eyes for a moment.

Max and Alice looked at each other, Max with an amused expression on his face.

'Conal comes from a family business,' Becca went on, once she'd roused herself. 'Just like Murphy's.'

'Except Blake's is *slightly* bigger than Murphy's,' said Alice.

'Blake's is slightly bigger than most companies,' said Max.

'But you've done your own thing,' said Alice to Conal, 'you didn't want to join Blake's?'

Conal shook his head. 'No, never. I grew up surrounded by the business, no one talked about anything else... well, apart from... well... Anyway. But the thing is, Dad would bring me down to the office. Just to get me away from my Nintendo.'

'His dad was a single father,' said Becca, her head on one side, as though Conal were a tiny, injured puppy.

'It was grand...' said Conal with a shrug. 'It's no biggie. My mother left us when I was eight or so and it was just me and my dad, but we're so close. Always were. He *wanted* me to join the business... but I've seen what it has done to him... I don't know... negativity and all that. My grandmother...' He stopped again. 'I didn't want her interfering in my life. So... I did business in college and was looking around for something. I had this idea about a coat you wear after swimming in the sea to keep you warm...'

'Conal's a sea swimmer,' said Becca proudly.

He shrugged. 'I don't go in the winter,' he said. 'Too much of a coward for that. I've tried to get Max to join me but...'

Max was shaking his head. 'Terrible things happen in the sea. Have you read *Jaws*? Do you know what happened to Shelley?'

'Who's she?' said Conal.

'I think she's an Instagrammer,' said Becca with a shrug.

'Anyway,' went on Conal, 'there was no way I wanted to go into beer, but the more I thought about it, the more I realised it was what I was passionate about. I thought I could improve on a few things...' He paused for a moment. 'Dad was a bit sad I didn't join the *family* business... I don't know... it's complicated.' He stopped talking as though relieved that he had explained himself the best he could. There was something sweet and almost vulnerable about Conal, as though he wanted the world to understand who he was, or rather to help him figure it out because he wasn't quite sure himself, yet.

'All families are,' said Becca, as though she understood very well, but she hailed from an exceptionally uncomplicated family where no one argued or harboured dark secrets. 'You were going to ask Alice to come on Saturday...'

Conal nodded. 'Are you free? We'd love you to come,' he said, smiling at Alice.

'It's Conal's thirtieth birthday party. It's at *Landfall*...' said Becca, making a face that only Alice could see. 'It's *massive*,' she mouthed.

Conal had looked away at the sound of a rowdy group at the back of the bar.

'It's the pub quizzers,' said Max, referring to the noisy crowd. 'We just finished our quiz night and I think too many sherries have been had.'

Conal laughed. 'I don't know how we're friends. I wouldn't have a clue about some of those questions. So did you win?'

'It's an aggregate,' explained Max. 'My team is at the top of the leader board and there'll be a final the week after next... Anyway, let's go outside to the courtyard. I'll get the round in – what does everyone want?'

With their drinks in front of them, they sat at a corner table, in the shade of a large fern, and as Conal and Becca held hands on one side of the table, Alice sat next to Max. Conal and Becca were discussing Conal's birthday party and whether Conal should wear a tie. 'I mean, I'm not a tie guy,' he was saying. 'But it might look cool... what do you think?'

Becca took the conundrum very seriously. 'What about a bow tie? Are you a bow-tie guy?'

'I might be,' said Conal. 'I mean, it's a personality type I have never tried out.' He turned to Max. 'Bow tie or not bow tie...'

'That is the question,' said Max, making Alice laugh again.

'What?' said Conal, confused.

'I think it depends on the tie,' said Max. 'And no one apart from Fozzie Bear can carry off a bow tie...'

'Good advice,' said Conal. 'Thanks, Max.'

Becca and Conal began discussing the playlist, the drinks, and if there should be more food on offer than just crisps. 'I don't think you can go wrong with a sausage on a stick,' Becca was saying.

'But crisps are food of the gods,' said Conal.

'They are *snacks* of the gods,' said Becca.

And with that, Alice realised Becca and Conal were perfect for each other and Becca had finally met a man who deserved her. It was as though the last ten years Alice had been away and only back for short visits was no time at all. Becca was still the same, the most lovable, loving and loyal of people. If you were Becca's friend, you were it for life. If she liked you, then she really liked you, and was almost too loving and loyal – she allowed people to walk over her a little. With her ex-boyfriend, the dreaded Julian, she had let him dictate everything, even what she read. He once threw her Jilly Cooper into the recycling bin because he said it wasn't intellectually demanding enough, and another time he ate the Easter egg she had been given by her parents because he said she should lose a few pounds. Hopefully, Conal returned all of Becca's enthusiasm and passion.

Alice left Conal and Becca to their serious discussion about crisps and turned to Max. 'Good day in the shop today?'

'Another day in paradise,' he said, making her laugh. 'No, I'm serious. I am *in love* with my shop. I adore it. It's like being in charge of a sweet shop, except better. It's books!' His whole face was one of joy. 'I mean, is there anything more wonderful? All those stories, everything you would ever need to know about humans and the world, about how to live a good life...' He looked overawed by the very idea of books. 'The other day a woman came in looking for a book set in Sandycove that she'd written years ago and had been out of print for thirty years. I knew I'd seen it in an old box, which belonged to Conal's grandmother, actually. Paddy had dropped it in when she went to live in Honeysuckle Lodge.' He lowered his voice slightly. 'Have you met the infamous Dol Blake?'

'Infamous?' Alice raised her eyebrows.

'I mean...' He shrugged. 'Legendary... imposing. She's not like my grandmother, who had her own book-printing works and still found time to build me a tree-house in the garden and made an incredible five-layer chocolate cake. Dol Blake is actually scary. Anyway, I haven't gone through the whole box yet. But that was on the top. The customer was delighted.' He smiled at her. 'So, enough about me. Why do you stay in Perth when you could be home in this haven of culture and civilisation?'

Alice opened her mouth to answer, and was about to say something about being free and loving the lifestyle and the weather and being able to go to the beach for most of the year, but Conal was standing up. 'Same again?'

They all nodded and when he left, Becca turned to Alice. 'How are the gang in Perth? So Sebastian is no more.' She looked at Max. 'Alice dumped her surfer boyfriend, despite the fact he looked like a hot Jesus.'

'More like Judas,' said Alice, making Max laugh. 'He was over-impressed with his own hair,' she explained.

Max patted his own. 'I'm not impressed by mine,' he said. 'It's like it's not connected to me. I mean it is, physically. But emotionally it does its own thing.'

'And how is *Raffi*?' said Becca.

'Raffi's moved to Sydney to start college. He's doing geography.'

'Really?' Becca looked surprised. 'But he'd never heard of Ireland. How on earth did he get in?'

'A surfing scholarship,' said Alice and they both laughed.

'Anyway,' said Becca, 'I only have eyes for Conal now...'

'How did you meet?' asked Alice.

'Well...' Becca beamed. 'I was on the seafront walking some of the dogs. I think I had five with me that day, including the dachshund brother and sister who are terribly behaved. And Conal was going swimming at the Forty Foot... and Dinky wrapped his lead around Conal's legs and almost toppled him. And after I'd untangled us all and Dinky was sulking, Conal and I began chatting and he invited me to a beer-tasting that evening he was holding for a few people here in The Island. You were at it, weren't you, Max? And so... that was it.' She smiled at Alice. 'He's nice... *really* nice.'

'Well,' said Max, 'I've never seen Conal so happy. He's met his match.'

'Really?' said Becca, glowing. 'Because... well, I've never been so happy either. He's the nicest person I've ever met.'

Max and Alice met each other's eye for a moment and smiled, both equally happy for their friends.

'What about you, Alice?' asked Max casually. 'Anyone in your life after the hot Jesus?'

'Oh no,' she said. 'I am just enjoying being single at the moment. You?'

'Me too,' he said, loftily. 'Urrgh. I couldn't think of anything worse than meeting the love of my life and being happy ever after.'

It was the way he said it that made Alice laugh. This may not be Shiraz on the beach, but a Thursday evening in Sandycove was, in so many ways, much better.

8

CIARA

It was Friday lunchtime in the shop and Alice had been back for a couple of days which Ciara had adored, rushing home to see her in the evening or delighted when Alice called into Murphy's. Today, jet lag had caught up with Alice and she was back at home, resting. Ciara was in the middle of the usual lunch-making whirr and blur. Whenever she could, Eva would pop down from her flat to lend a hand buttering bread and slicing tomatoes. They would weave in and out of each other, in a well-practised dance, making teas and coffees, wrapping sandwiches in parchment and popping brownies into paper bags. Eventually, by 2 p.m., the rush was magically all over.

Behind the counter, Ciara perched on a small stepladder and Eva on an old wooden stool, and they ate their own lunch. It had been a lovely few days with Alice. She'd been in and out of the shop, had met Becca for walks, and already Ciara was used to having her around, as though she were always with them. *Don't let it go by too fast*, she kept thinking to herself, knowing this was the usual pattern of a homecoming and how much of a shock and wrench it was when it was time to say goodbye again, all of them in tears.

'Sometimes,' said Eva, her cheese and tomato sandwich on her lap, 'I think how much George and Alice would have got on. Like a house on fire, wouldn't they?'

Ciara nodded. 'They would have. Same sense of humour.'

'Pity he never even got to meet her. Missed her by...'

'Six months. I was three months pregnant when he died...'

Eva nodded. 'He would have loved to be a grandfather,' said Eva firmly. 'He was a good man. I was glad I married him, he was the right one for me.'

'Well, you were lucky,' said Ciara. 'It was all simpler in your day. You met someone and you married him. None of this messing about. No apps or dating...'

'It may seem simpler,' said Eva, 'but we managed to make our own complications...'

'I always liked the story of him carrying you over the threshold of the shop...'

On Eva's mantelpiece, there was a large, framed picture of Eva and George standing outside Murphy's on their wedding day. George gazing at Eva with a near-rapturous expression on his face, and Eva laughing for the camera, dressed in a white mini dress, the epitome of swinging sixties Sandycove, both so young and looking so happy.

Ciara could imagine the rest of the scene; her kind, lovely father scooping up Eva and them laughing.

'He wanted to show us off to the shop girls. In those days, we had Maisie and Maureen...'

'I remember them...'

Maisie and Maureen had both left at different stages to get married and Eva and George ran the shop with just a succession of delivery boys. One of whom was...

Ciara stopped. She didn't want to think about *him*. She'd much prefer to think about her father. George had been ill for a few years – what he said were just aches and pains turned out to be something far more serious. When Eva eventually managed to get him to go to the doctor's, it was too late, and he declined faster than they could have imagined. He died the week after Ciara's nineteenth birthday, just when she'd discovered she was pregnant with Alice.

At his funeral, she was gripped by hundreds of hands as people told her what a fine man he'd been, but she had just spent a week with Eva at his bedside, knowing she was pregnant and wondering what she was going to do. Having Alice home brought back memories of that dreadful time, and then going to that house and how everything had unravelled. It was only in the last few years that she was any closer to processing what had happened. But although the pain was gone, the heartbreak near-neutralised, she could sometimes still feel the shock reverberating through her, like a bell.

Eva was talking away. 'Maisie and Maureen had organised a little tea party,' she said. 'I'll never forget it. They'd borrowed some proper china teacups and Maisie had asked her mam to make some of her cherry scones. Maureen had brought a bottle of Babycham...' Eva's smile dropped when she saw Ciara's face. 'What's wrong? Are you feeling all right?'

'I'm grand,' insisted Ciara. 'It's just nice to have Alice home.'

'She's looking well,' said Eva. 'As always. Looks just like you when you were her age.'

'She's thirty,' mused Ciara. 'Can you believe it?'

'I can and I can't,' said Eva in her inimitable way.

All Ciara knew for sure was that being a mother was like letting your heart roam free out in the world, all on its own, and there wasn't much you could do about it. But Alice was living her dreams and exploring the world and who was Ciara to ever try to stop her? She was living the life of freedom that Ciara never got the chance to have.

'I'm glad she and the boyfriend are no more,' said Eva. 'Means she won't be settling down there anytime soon. There's still a chance she'll come back to us.'

'You never know.' Ciara didn't even tell Eva quite how much she missed Alice, but she didn't need to, it was just understood between them. 'Do you remember her first day of school?'

'How could I forget?' Eva smiled at her. 'I've never seen a child more excited. Couldn't wait to get there, wouldn't hold your hand. She was a big girl, even at the age of five...'

Ciara smiled, thinking of that little version of Alice, who hadn't changed so very much. Still independent but also desperate to belong. That first day, Alice had marched ahead of her along the road to the Star of the Sea junior school, outsized backpack, shiny white sandals, her hair clipped to one side. 'Come on,' Alice had ordered. 'We'll be late.'

But as soon as they had arrived in the playground, Alice had hesitated, suddenly overwhelmed by the noise and the fact that she would soon be saying goodbye to Ciara, as though she hadn't quite thought this bit through.

The junior infants' teacher was standing at the door, among children racked with huge sobs, clutching their mothers. 'Best to just go,' the teacher was saying to the parents. 'And we're all going to have a lovely morning, aren't we?'

Ciara had leant down to kiss Alice. 'Have a good day, okay?' she'd urged, holding her two hands and looking into that face which refused to meet her eyes, her mouth clamped shut, her little fists clenched. 'I'll see you soon.'

The teacher had gently pulled Alice to one side and there was nothing else Ciara could do except walk away.

At the edge of the playground, she had looked back, hoping to see Alice playing or talking to another child, but Alice's sorrowful eyes were fixed on her. The look in her eyes was saying, *You've got better things to be doing? Like what. Tell me.*

I haven't, Ciara wanted to say. *I don't have anything better to do than to be with you.*

Their eyes were locked, she and this tiny girl. *I love you,* Ciara thought. *That other love – the one I thought was everything – was nothing compared to this.*

'She seems happy and that's the main thing,' said Eva.

'And healthy,' said Ciara.

'And at least she's home for a good stretch...'

'Yes, it's going to be lovely. She said she would help out in the shop while she's here.'

'You should make the most of her.'

Ciara nodded. 'And it's nice for her to catch up with her friends.'

They looked at each other again, this time not exactly sure, thought Ciara, of what the other was thinking, as though they were uncertain of what the other *knew*.

'Now, where are those biscuits?' she said to Eva, standing up. 'You get them out and I'll make the tea.'

9

ALICE

At first, it had been quite a struggle for Alice to persuade Ciara to leave her solely in charge of the shop so she could go to Mary-Marg's bottomless tunch.

'Look, I'll be here all afternoon and close up later. Becca's going to call for me and we're going to Conal's birthday party.'

Ciara didn't say anything.

'When was the last time you went out?' Alice persisted.

Ciara shrugged helplessly. 'I went for a walk last night...'

'Walks don't count. Walking is like breathing. You don't have a choice. And look, the more times you leave me, you can go and do things. Even just read a book...' She paused. 'When was the last time you read a book, by the way?'

'I don't know... can't remember.'

'Well, then. Or you could swim in the sea like Gran does...'

'I suppose... in the summer.'

'It *is* the summer! Honestly, you have no hobbies. None at all.'

'I'm too busy to have hobbies,' said Ciara, finally defeated and untying her apron, folding it and placing it on the counter of the shop to reveal her outfit of a spotted blouse, jeans and a pair of Birkenstocks.

'You're wearing that?' said Alice.

'What's wrong with it?'

'Nothing... it's just it's not very going-outy.'

'But we're staying in... it's in her house.'

'Look, put on my blazer,' said Alice, slipping it off. 'It will just smarten you up, rather than a cardigan.'

Ciara put it on and immediately, thought Alice, looked better. Ciara glanced at herself in the mirror. 'I look,' she said, 'as though I am meaning to leave the house, rather than just doing it accidentally.'

Alice laughed. 'You mean, as opposed to just falling into some clothes and finding yourself outside...'

Ciara nodded. 'That's my usual approach. This takes more effort but at least I look more presentable. I won't be shunned by polite society.' She smiled at Alice. 'Thank you. Now, you're happy to be in charge in the shop. And you can close up later?'

Alice nodded. 'Of course... Becca's calling for me so we can walk to Conal's party together...'

'So you know about the new till,' Ciara said briskly. 'It's complicated. You need to scan everything...'

'I know...'

'And the coffee machine... there's a knack...'

Alice gave her mother a look. 'I know how to use it.'

'And lock up when you finish. The keys are in beside the till, and you know the code for the alarm...?' Ciara looked around, as though trying to find other impediments to her leaving, or why no one else could ensure Murphy's remained unburgled.

'I know everything,' Alice assured her. 'I used to work here, remember? And I can always call Gran.'

Ciara left the shop and gave one last wave from outside the front window, as though she were leaving a child in the crèche for the first time.

But once she was gone, Alice began to enjoy herself. She served customers, chatted about the weather, asked after them and family members she knew, all while making coffee, wrapping up their purchases, advising on olive oils and recommending wine or cheese. Finally, at 7 p.m., she began locking up, sweeping the floor, wiping down the fridges and counter and turning off the lights.

Becca knocked on the glass window. 'Ready?' she mouthed.

Alice grabbed her bag, locked the front door behind her, set the alarm, and they walked out of the village and along the coast to where the big houses – the ones with sweeping lawns and gravelly driveways, multiple cars, manicured lawns and swishy swathes of lavender – were.

And, finally, there it was – Landfall.

They stood for a moment at the gate. Close up, the house was even more beautiful. It was a large, double-fronted building behind a high wall and black-painted gates with the name etched into a smooth granite block. A perfect oval lawn hugged the gravel driveway that continued around the side of the house, beyond which you could see the garden, where the edge of a white summer house peeked out, before the garden slipped into the sea which sparkled in the summer evening sunshine.

'It's been in the family for years,' said Becca as they walked along the driveway. 'It belonged to Patrick Senior and Dolores – Conal's grandparents. Everyone calls her Dol. His grandfather is long-gone now. But then Conal's mother left when he was young and...' She lowered her voice. 'I get the impression Landfall wasn't a particularly happy place to grow up. Conal's grandmother is in Honeysuckle Lodge after her stroke last year. You know, the nursing home?'

Alice looked at the house again. Landfall was lovely but soulless; a house to be admired, not a home. She thought of Eva's little courtyard behind the shop with her terracotta pots of red and salmon-pink geraniums, and Ciara's small patch of daisied lawn with her leaning cherry blossom tree, and how *homely* they were.

'Ah! Becca! How are you?' A tall, handsome man stepped out, dangling car keys, wearing jeans and a blue shirt; his hair was grey and cut short, the front pushed to one side. He looked curiously at Alice, smiling at her.

'Hello, Paddy,' Becca said. 'This is Alice, a friend of mine... Alice, this is Conal's father. Paddy Blake.'

He smiled at her. 'I know your mother. We used to be friends, back in the old days...'

'Were you?' Alice was surprised. Ciara had never mentioned it.

He nodded. 'We used to hang around together. And then... well, we all drifted, I suppose,' he said. 'I was working in the brewery and Ciara had you... and... I was busy... and... well, it was a long time ago.' He smiled at Alice again. 'I'm going to collect my mother from Honeysuckle Lodge and bring her to the party. She's always been very keen on a party, you know. Her time to shine.' He waved as he climbed into his car. 'See you later, girls.'

'Bye, Paddy,' said Becca. 'Don't drive too fast!'

As they watched the car disappear out of the gates, Becca covered her face with her hands. 'Why?' she shouted. 'Why do I say such ridiculous things?'

'It's a nice thing to say,' said Alice, laughing. 'I mean, it's not as if you told him to drive carelessly and have an accident.'

'But I'm trying to impress these people and all I do is make a fool of myself,' said Becca. 'I don't fit in with this family. They are all so charming, and here I am probably covered in dog hairs and smelling of terrier, and I'm sure I have rabies which is yet to manifest and by the end of the evening, I will be frothing and snarling...' She sighed. 'I'm just not like Conal's previous girlfriends. They're all, as far as I can tell, the perfect types, you know? Nice, straight hair. Ditto teeth. Ditto personalities.'

'You have nice hair and teeth. And personality.'

'Yes, but my teeth are only straight because of seriously hard work. Those braces were on for seven years... those girls are effortless.'

Alice laughed again. 'I prefer you and your dog hairs – far more charming, to be honest. They are lucky to have you.'

Becca didn't look sure. 'Come on,' she said. 'Let's go in and say hello. See if Conal still likes me.'

They could hear the music from outside, and they walked on to the large porch, and then into the entrance area. They were suddenly in the middle of a crowd – some of the faces were recognisable to Alice. There was a DJ in the corner of the room, a pair of headphones half on his head, and a small sign propped up in front of him, saying 'MC Dub-Dub iz in da house'. He looked as though he was still in school, but the music he was playing was really good, some old house tunes mixed with some new disco.

Conal immediately weaved his way through the huge crowd to hug Becca. 'I'm so glad to see you,' he said, raising his voice over the music and kissing her on the lips.

'Happy birthday,' Alice said, handing Conal a bottle of wine and a gift bag. 'It's just something small,' she said as he took it from her.

'You shouldn't have...' He pulled out one of the bowls she'd brought with her from Australia. 'It's gorgeous,' he said, examining it. 'The colours... the shapes...'

Alice smiled at him. 'It's just to say welcome to the Big 3-0 Club.'

He grinned at her. 'God, I feel ancient...'

'I've been thirty for ages now,' said Becca. 'You get used to it. Being in your twenties now sounds ridiculously young. I *love* being old.'

Conal laughed and turned to Alice. 'What about you? When did you turn thirty?'

She nodded. 'Three months ago. No party. Just a few drinks with friends...'

'Dad insisted that I have this party,' said Conal. 'Although he's not much into parties himself. The only one who ever liked a party was my grandmother. She always had a Christmas one and one for her birthday, right up to her stroke. The house would be filled with people none of us had ever met before.' He shrugged. 'But my friends all like parties and maybe it's time to start enjoying them.'

'Maybe...' Alice smiled at him.

'I love parties,' said Becca. 'Even bad ones. And I have hosted a few bad parties in my time. There was the one where someone got hummus all over the curtains and I had to hire a steam cleaner before the landlord found out. Or the time when Julian complained because the music was too loud and ended up calling the Gardaí.'

'Your own boyfriend called the *police* on you?' asked Conal, shocked.

'He was very particular,' explained Becca matter-of-factly. 'And he knew the law. Music had to be off by 11.30 p.m. and it was 11.32 p.m....'

'What did the Gardaí say?' asked Alice.

'They asked to speak to me and Julian handed over the phone, thinking they were going to tell me off, and it turned out to be a friend of my cousin's, Tommy O'Sullivan. They played on the same hurling team. So he said, *How's it going, Bec*? And I said, *Grand, sorry about the music, I've just turned it off.* And he said, *Don't worry about that, just turn it down, and have a good evening.* Julian was furious. Wrote to our local politician about Gardaí corruption.' She turned to Conal. 'But in a massive house like this, noise isn't a problem.'

Conal nodded. 'It's too big... sometimes I wish we hadn't moved into Landfall. It made sense, I suppose, for us all to live in the same house. But it was always my grandmother's house and that must have been difficult for my mother. And it's been just me and my dad since my grandmother's stroke.' Conal stopped. 'I sometimes wonder if that was why my mum left. She didn't like my grandmother. And my dad is too nice to say anything to her... it's like she's got this power over him. Over *all* of us.'

His grandmother sounded truly terrifying, thought Alice. '*My* grandmother isn't into parties,' she said. 'Likes her own company or just one or two people she knows really well. She goes swimming every morning with her friends and she does all her catching up, and then she's done for the day. My mother isn't into parties either, so we never had them...'

'Well, then, you're *owed* a party,' he said. 'You can share this one. Now, let me get you both a drink... I'll be back in a sec.'

'Alice, hi!' It was Louise Fitzgerald from school, who had got the top marks in their year for their Leaving Cert. And there was Fran Egan, who once was a Rose of Tralee – a peculiarly Irish beauty pageant – and had never let anyone forget it ever since. Alice hugged them both and they began asking the latest news, who was where, doing what, when a silence suddenly descended on the room. Alice looked around. A woman was leaning on the arm of Conal's father.

'Here she is,' said Fran. 'Dol Blake herself.'

The room fell silent and even MC Dub-Dub had stopped the music.

Dol Blake was dressed immaculately in a cream jumper and trousers, a string of pearls around her neck, her snow-white hair perfectly set. She carried a black walking stick, with a crystal-eyed cat's head on the top, her nails were painted blood-red. And even though her mouth was slightly drooped at one side from her recent stroke, she still exuded an aura of power. Longevity had not withered her charisma and she was still beautiful, with a sharp bone structure and delicate features. But her ice-grey eyes darted like a cobra assessing its prey.

'Hello, Mrs Blake...' Fran had rushed across. 'Now, don't you look lovely? So elegant. I might ask to borrow that walking stick of yours, you know?' She let out a tinkly laugh as Dol gazed through her.

Conal had reappeared, carrying a bottle of sparkling wine and two glasses, but his sunny expression faded like an eclipse.

'You made it, Dol,' Conal said, swiftly handing the wine to Becca and heading straight for his grandmother. He bent quickly and kissed close to the side of her cheek. 'It's so good of you to come. How is everyone in Honeysuckle Lodge? I'll be in this week...' His easy smile didn't seem quite so easy now.

People had begun talking again, and MC Dub-Dub had resumed the music, albeit at a much lower volume.

'I'll bring Mother into the living room,' Paddy said. 'And a nice sherry, is that right, Mother?'

Dol turned her head up to look at him. 'You make me sound like a woman who has lost her marbles,' she said. 'I can assure you, Paddy, I am very much all there. I will have a very *strong* gin and tonic, please. Ice and lemon. And do you have any smoked salmon?'

'Of course,' said Paddy.

Leaning on her son's arm, Dol moved like an elderly Cleopatra across the hall, past the grandfather clock and towards the living room. But she stopped, as though she had remembered something. 'And where is the girl?' said Dol, looking around.

Alice nudged Becca, who stepped forward.

'I'm Becca,' she said, almost dropping into a curtsey. 'We met before, remember...?'

Dol looked at her, aghast. 'No, not you... the other girl.' She looked at Paddy. 'Where is she? You told me she was here.'

10

CIARA

The blazer was slightly tight on the arms, but Ciara did feel a little better, a little more put together. Alice was right. She had to make more of an effort. Getting dressed up had been one of the pleasures of her young life. Except she was no longer young and she rarely went out. As she stood on Mary-Marg's doorstep, she thought about the disco and her stomach sank again. No one was going to come, and anyway, she had nothing to wear. Years ago, she and Mary-Marg had been obsessed with clothes and dressing up. It was the real reason, initially, they had started the disco. There wasn't anything like that in Sandycove and, fuelled by the confidence of youth, they had just gone and done it.

It was strange to think of herself thirty years ago. For that whole year, maybe much, much longer, she'd been in shock. It was as though she'd landed on another planet and would never be the same, and she had almost had to learn who she was again. It was Eva who would gently take a crying Alice from her arms and soothe her to sleep, or would make a stew and scoop out bowls of it, placing them in front of Ciara, and encourage her to eat.

Ciara suddenly remembered the last day of school, when they had a leavers' ball at The Sandycove Arms, when it was still a shabby, run-down, old-fashioned hotel. Ciara had brought along Lorcan, who had refused to wear black tie but instead turned up in a Velvet Underground T-shirt and baggy jeans. Mary-Marg had come with Paddy Blake, and later, when everyone had drifted home, they had gone down to the Forty Foot and in only their underwear, had all swum in the sea in the pitch dark, the sea calm and warm, like a bath, the light from the houses on the shore their only light, except for the phosphorescence in the water. It was as though when they moved through the water, they were part of some incredible magic show. Ciara remembered being overawed by the gifts of nature; she had already met the love of her life and even the sea was illuminated, as though the universe were conspiring with her.

Lorcan – who wasn't a good swimmer – had paddled up to her, his long fringe plastered to his head. He'd looked funny like this, all his usual swagger and confidence diluted by the sea. If it had been anyone else, she would have said something to make them laugh. But Lorcan didn't ever laugh at himself. Instead, he quoted poetry. '...To an isle in the water... with her would I go,' he'd said, his hands flapping under the surface, his chin held up as high as possible.

'W.B. Yeats,' Ciara had said to Lorcan. 'I had to write an entire essay on him in my Leaving Cert exam.'

Lorcan was looking at her, with that strange intensity again, as though he were thinking of her and something else with the same kind of focus. She'd never seen it with anyone before – the ability to think, very intently, about two things at once.

Normally, people were distracted when talking to you, or perhaps they were hyper-focused and couldn't think of other things, but with Lorcan, he was very present and totally absent at the exact same time. It was intriguing and unsettling. But mostly she found it intriguing.

'To an isle in the water,' he'd said again, 'with her would I fly.'

'Would you though?' she'd said, her legs cycling below her, the sea a shimmering light show. 'Would you go or would you fly?'

'I would fly,' Lorcan had said.

'But you wouldn't go...' Mary-Marg had said, swimming towards them, drunk enough to act as though it were a perfectly normal conversation.

'No, I would go...' Lorcan had said.

Mary-Marg had laughed. 'Well, I would skedaddle.' She had turned in the water to Paddy. 'Would you go, or fly, or skedaddle, or something else?'

Paddy had thought for a moment, his shoulders shining in the moonlight. 'I would go.' He paused. 'Of course.' He'd turned to Ciara. 'What about you?' He'd spoken in that gentle way he had. Lorcan wasn't gentle, he was hard with his words, the poetry he spouted seemed odd in his mouth, and it was only now, all these years later, she realised that he was no poet and that just because someone tells you something, it doesn't mean it is true. Paddy, she knew now, was much more of a poet, the way he thought about life, the things he wanted. He wanted to go to university and study Classical Civilisations. He always said his dream life was travelling around Italy and thinking about the Romans. Instead, he was forced to do commerce and then had to join the family business.

'I would...' she'd begun. 'I would...' She'd spread her arms in the water – scooping all this life, these glowing organisms, this magic – and clutched it close to her. 'I would bottle all of this, like a bottle of Blake's Beer, and keep it forever...' She had looked over at Lorcan and he wasn't even listening. He was already back on the rocks and scrambling up, his Velvet Underground T-shirt, which he'd refused to remove, plastered to his skinny body. And it was only then, for the briefest of moments, that she wondered who he really was.

Now, older and wiser, she knocked on Mary-Marg's door for the tunch. Mary-Marg was dressed in leather trousers and a black silk shirt. 'Thank God you're early,' she said. 'I've been having a wardrobe crisis.'

'Me too,' said Ciara.

'Well, you look good,' said Mary-Marg. 'Jacket is very nice. You look like a very smart...' She hesitated.

'Clerical officer?' suggested Ciara.

'That's it! A very smart clerical officer. Which is a good thing. The world needs clerical officers. Otherwise, who would cleric the offices?'

The two of them began to giggle. 'I know I look boring,' said Ciara. 'But it's better than looking like I have rolled out of bed, which was the other look I contemplated.'

'Well, I,' said Mary-Marg, 'have gone too far the other way. Brian said I looked like Tom Jones, the Las Vegas years.'

Ciara laughed. 'Well, Brian is wrong. I think Mary-Margaret, in her prime. The Sandycove years.' She hugged her. 'You look gorgeous. Very sexy.'

'But I don't want to look sexy,' said Mary-Marg, in a low voice, so the twins wouldn't hear. 'I just want to look *nice*. And maybe a tiny bit cool. Why is that so hard these days? I don't know what my style is, what I like, what suits me. When did it get so difficult?'

Ciara shrugged. 'I've got the same problem. I borrowed this from Alice.'

Mary-Marg smiled at her. 'What happened to us? Why is it now such a big deal when we dress up or make an effort? I feel like my grandfather in drag.'

'Wait, those aren't *his* leather trousers, are they?'

They began to laugh again.

'No,' said Mary-Marg, 'but I did buy them for twenty euros from Grainne O'Flaherty who was decluttering her wardrobe and said she'd never worn them. And I can see why. It's like wearing a squeaky leather couch. I'm changing, I've decided. I don't want to *squeak*. I want to look like me, but better. Is that too much to ask? I'm going to go and change. Put on my trusty jeans. The twins are in the kitchen. They are under strict instructions to look after you. LADS!' she shouted. 'Pour Ciara a glass of prosecco.'

Ciara was very fond of Jake and Josh, Mary-Marg's large and lumbering twins. Even after all these years, Ciara still found it hard to distinguish between the two of them, something she could never admit to Mary-Marg who was always shocked when others confessed they couldn't tell them apart. 'Josh has softer features,' she would say, as though that made all the difference. 'Jake's nose is bigger.'

'Mam said to get the prosecco,' said Josh or Jake. 'It's in the fridge.'

'That sounds perfect,' said Ciara as Josh ambled over to fetch the wine, while Jake pushed a bowl of crisps towards her on the kitchen island.

'Crisp? Take two.' He seemed quite proud of his generosity.

'I will,' she said. 'Thank you.'

It was so hard being eighteen, thought Ciara. You are so young and know so little about the world, and yet adults expect so much of you. When she was eighteen, she thought she was in love with someone who couldn't have been less deserving of her affection.

'Boys...' Mary-Marg was coming through the living room towards them. 'I hope you are looking after our VIP.' She was back in the jeans she'd worn a million times and her white T-shirt, and a blazer just like Ciara was wearing. It was almost like the old days where they used to dress the same.

'We are,' said Josh. 'Just like you said.'

'And have you been asking Ciara how she is? *Making conversation*?'

Jake and Josh looked at Ciara, as though hoping she would verify that they weren't Neanderthals.

'They've been lovely,' said Ciara. 'Prosecco and crisps...'

'My favourite pairing,' said Mary-Marg, ruffling the hair of Jake and then Josh. 'Apart from these two, of course. *They're* the best pairing.'

The boys looked pleased but pretended to be embarrassed. '*Mam*, I just put gel on,' said Jake, squirming away.

The doorbell rang and then there was the rush of door-answering and squeals of hellos as the other guests arrived, and then more prosecco was opened and poured, and the women went out into the garden.

11

ALICE

Why on earth did Conal's grandmother want to meet her? Alice couldn't work it out. She glanced at Paddy, who shrugged apologetically, as Alice swallowed and stepped forward. Perhaps Dol had her mixed up with someone else? 'Hello, Mrs Blake... it's good to meet you. What a lovely party...'

'Parties are usually full of dull people,' said Dol, glancing quickly at Paddy. 'I thought I said a Gordon's and tonic and some smoked salmon?' She turned back to Alice, taking her in again, those ice-grey eyes travelling over Alice's face. 'You're very like your grandmother,' she said. 'In the eyes. Her smile.'

Everyone knew Eva, particularly those of Dol's age. She must know her from the shop.

Dol kept her eyes on Alice. 'How is she?'

'Who?'

'Eva! Eva Murphy...'

'My grandmother?'

'Yes, of *course,* your grandmother...'

'She's very well,' said Alice, glancing at Becca, who gave a tiny, helpless shrug.

'Oh! She's never mentioned me!' Dol had a smile which was more like a sneer on her lips. 'Isn't that funny? Oh, to be forgotten... to be expunged from someone's life like that.'

Eva wasn't the kind of person who expunged people, thought Alice. She had a small group of lifelong friends. She and Angela Flaherty, her swimming buddy, had grown up together. There were also Dorrie O'Flanagan and Maeve O'Driscoll, whom Eva went on walking weekends to Kerry with every year. Eva didn't fall out with people or bear grudges, but Dol had had a stroke and perhaps this was part of some kind of lasting damage and she was confusing Eva – whom perhaps she remembered from the shop – with someone else.

'My grandmother is *Eva Murphy*,' said Alice, in a loud, clear voice. 'She used to run *Murphy's* in Sandycove...'

'Yes...' Dol was beginning to look bored. 'Yes, Eva Murphy. We used to be friends. Like sisters. Grew up next to each other. In and out of each other's houses all day long. Her kitchen was my kitchen. Her world was my world. I was part of her family. She was part of mine. Although, who would want to be part of mine? Not me, anyway. We shared everything... *everything*.'

Alice had thought she knew all there was to know about Eva's life, about growing up on Pearse Terrace in Sandycove, about her school, about her friends. But she had never mentioned Dolores Blake. 'Really?' said Alice, looking at Paddy, hoping he might help. 'You and my grandmother were *friends*?'

Dol was nodding. 'That's right. Eva Murphy. My best and closest friend. Past tense, however. She wants nothing to do with me.'

Alice was conscious that people were listening in. Fran Egan was looking wide-eyed, fascinated. Becca and Conal were both shifting awkwardly.

Paddy tried to intervene. 'Mum,' he said, 'Alice doesn't need all this now. She's here for Conal's party...'

Dol silenced him with a look.

'I'll pass on your best wishes,' said Alice.

Dol laughed. 'Oh, don't bother,' she said. 'They won't be accepted. Now, Alice, if you will assist me to the living room. My living room. This was my house, you know. When I married Patrick Senior, he asked me where I wanted to live and I said the house by the sea, the one with the crenellated wall. The one with the summer house... I dreamed of that summer house, as a girl. Eva and I would come down and look through the gate, wishing we had grown up in such splendour.'

As they walked into the living room, Alice could feel Dol's hand on her arm, like a bird's claw.

'I can assist, Dol,' Conal said, dashing ahead of them and rearranging the cushions on the biggest and most comfortable-looking armchair, upholstered in a cream, striped damask. 'Here we go,' he said, patting the back of the chair. 'Right, there you are...' He took Dol's other arm and tried to manoeuvre her into it.

'I am not infirm or incapable, Conal,' she said witheringly.

Conal drew back, but Dol's claw-like hands were still holding onto Alice as she sat down. There was the sound of a clinking glass as Paddy returned, carrying a small tray with a large, frosted glass of gin and tonic.

'Ah, here he is.' Dol almost rolled her eyes. 'My son and heir. Is there enough ice in it? You know I can't stand a warm gin and tonic. Is there lemon on the salmon?'

'It's all there, Mother.' Paddy's smile was perfunctory.

'Well, then,' Dol said. 'You may leave.'

Alice turned to retreat, along with Conal and Becca, but Dol spoke again.

'You can stay and tell me all about your grandmother. I want to know how she spends her time.' She used her stick to point at a small, upholstered footstool. 'Bring that over and sit down and talk to me.'

Alice was relieved to see Paddy had stayed, along with Conal and Becca who hovered on the edge.

'Well, she's... very well.' Alice smiled at Dol, hoping that she might soften a little into someone easier to talk to. 'She walks a lot, up and down Killiney Hill, and she swims in the sea first thing every morning, even in the winter.'

'I can well believe it.' Dol showed no signs of softening. In fact, her hardness was almost being sharpened by the exchange, as though she needed this as some kind of fuel. 'She used to swim when we were young as well. Now... friends? Who does she see?'

'She's got her swimming friends... and there's her best friend, Angela Flaherty.'

'*Angela...*' Dol's face darkened.

'And Dorrie O'Flanagan and Maeve O'Driscoll...'

Dol's face darkened even more.

'She's just very busy.' Alice had realised that it was best to keep the conversation light on details.

'And your mother?' asked Paddy. 'How is she?'

'She's really well. Working hard, you know...'

He nodded. 'Life slips by so quickly. And one day, you wake up and you wonder where all those days have gone that we once spent hanging about... wasting those minutes and seconds... because we felt we had just so much *time*.' He looked at Alice, a sad smile on his face. 'And then, at some point it all speeds up and it's like you're in a rocket, hurtling through your life... and everything is a blur and you barely look up to breathe or to enjoy the ride.'

'What are you going on about?' said Dol, with a roll of her eyes. She was drinking her gin and tonic, like a toddler with its sippy-cup, both bird's claws wrapped around the glass. She met Alice's eyes. 'You may come and visit me at Honeysuckle Lodge,' she said. 'Visiting hours are from 10 a.m. to 8 p.m. every day. Patrick never misses it, do you, Patrick?'

Paddy shook his head. 'Never.' He smiled at Alice. 'It's lovely to meet you. And you look just like your mother. *Exactly* like her, to be honest. As she was. As she *is*.'

'Well, goodbye,' said Alice, still feeling a little unsettled after the encounter. 'Enjoy your...' She couldn't think what to say. 'Enjoy your drink.'

Dol threw her a look as Alice escaped, Becca and Conal on her heels.

'Sorry about that,' said Conal. 'She's a bit intense at times...' He shrugged. 'I hope you didn't mind.'

'Of course not,' said Alice. 'She seems to have known Gran when they were younger... but Gran has never mentioned her.'

'Perhaps they weren't all that close,' said Becca. 'Maybe Dol is misremembering. Is she...?' She glanced at Conal. 'Is she totally... you know... like, is she... has she... or could she have...?'

'She's sharp as a tack,' said Conal. 'In temperament as well as brainpower. The stroke hasn't affected her mind, just her ability to walk about and get dressed and all that.' He turned to Alice. 'I don't know why she was so intense with you though. She's just not that...' He searched for the right word.

Nice, thought Alice. *She's just not that nice.* Dol Blake was the last person Eva would ever have been friends with. Perhaps it was the stroke making her think she was friends with someone she definitely hadn't been. The encounter had mystified her, though. Why had this woman been so keen to talk to her? Even if she had known Eva, it didn't make sense why she had been so intense and so determined. All she knew was that she wasn't particularly keen to ever run into her again.

12

CIARA

They were in Mary-Marg's garden, sitting on her wicker lounge set. They'd all drunk a little too much, eaten a little too much, had had seconds of the strawberry pavlova and were now gently soaking up the evening sun, as well as the rosé to which they'd moved on.

'By the way, I saw Paddy Blake the other day,' said Eileen O'Connor. 'You know he plays squash with Tony every Thursday. Anyway, he's selling Landfall.'

'I can't believe he is selling that beautiful house,' said Monica O'Leary who, as the mother of six boys, was lying outstretched on the lounger, her eyes half-closed. Mary-Marg had given her a straw to make it easier to drink while supine.

'The views from the garden terrace are to die for,' said Siobhán McDonald. 'I was on it once when Dol Blake was still living there and it was stunning. The views across the bay are incredible.'

'He's never been the same since Breda left,' said Monica, as Mary-Marg topped up her glass. 'Paddy was a broken man.'

'He's at the same gym as Tony and never joins the boys on

the golf trips to Portugal,' said Eileen. 'He and the lads were such good friends at school and these days, he looks so serious.'

The Paddy Blake that Ciara and Mary-Marg used to be friends with always saw the joke. He was always laughing and finding humour everywhere. He even used to find a way of making gentle fun of his parents – the imposing father, Patrick Senior, and his terrifying mother, Dol. Patrick Senior may have been charming socially but was also a functioning alcoholic who, despite being financially very successful, would be seen in Dún Laoghaire and Sandycove's divier pubs. When he was drinking, he hid from life, and when out of that hole again, he would reappear sober and well-dressed, back to his salubrious self and life. As an inveterate social climber, Dol would have been horrified that anyone knew anything of the family's secrets. But, of course, everyone knew. There were no secrets left in Sandycove... well, not many anyway.

'Breda was hard as nails though,' said Siobhán. 'I tried to talk to her once at a mother and baby group. And she blanked me. Looked through me. Like I was a fecking ghost.'

'It's not easy being a new mother,' said Ciara.

'No, but you don't blank people,' said Eileen. 'Another time, I was parking at the back of SuperValu...' She looked over at Ciara. 'Hope you don't mind, Ciara. You know how much I love Murphy's. Anyway, this is years ago now... and I pulled out and I saw a car indicating to come in... some Mercedes. So, me being me, I roll down my window. "Do you want my parking ticket?" I say. "It's got forty minutes left." And anyway, it's Breda Blake. Stone face on her. Shakes her head. "Are you SURE?" says I, like a lunatic. I mean, who refuses a free parking ticket, Mercedes or no? Feeling like an eejit, off I go, embarrassed, and in she goes to my space. The one I just vacated. The one she could have got for free.'

'Perhaps she wanted to stay for longer than forty minutes?' suggested Ciara, but Eileen turned on her furiously.

'Perhaps she did! But that's no reason to refuse a free ticket. It's good manners, so it is, to accept it. It would be like me saying to someone, *Nice day, isn't it*? And them not commenting that it is indeed. Even if it *isn't* a nice day at all.'

They all nodded, being regularly in that same scenario of weather-related small talk themselves.

Mary-Marg tapped her wine glass with her fork. 'Announcement,' she said. 'I am now a DJ again. My decks have arrived and we're bringing back our See The Stars disco... I've already put a notice in the Newsletter and put up some posters.'

'Your old disco?' said Siobhán.

'Yes, remember it? It's very definitely happening, even if it's just me and Ciara. So, say hello to DJ Margarita.'

Ciara laughed.

'What?' said Mary-Marg. 'Does that sound silly?'

'What about DJ Mary-Margarita?' suggested Ciara.

'Well, I can work on my *nom de decks* later,' said Mary-Marg. 'So, who's going to come?'

'I remember your nightclub,' said Siobhán. 'I used to go every Friday night for the whole of fifth and sixth year. Oh, your disco nights were magical...'

'Yes,' said Mary-Marg. 'See The Stars...' She paused for dramatic effect. 'The return!'

'A *disco*?' Eileen looked appalled. 'Why on earth would you do such a thing?'

'As in dancing? Music? Those strobe light things?' Monica

shook her head. 'My dancing days are long gone. I can barely get out of bed in the morning. My hips are in bits these days.'

'And my plantar fasciitis is agony,' said Eileen, crossing her arms over her chest.

'But for young people, right?' said Monica. 'You're putting on a nightclub for young people. Not us.' She was beginning to slide down her seat – her sunglasses were wonky – as she drained her glass, looking for a top-up.

'It's for us, our age,' said Mary-Marg. 'In other words, young. From age forty-five... we don't want *children* at the event, after all. Just youthful people, in their prime.' She winked at Ciara.

'*Our* age?' said Eileen. 'No one is going to come. I hope you don't lose any money on this? What would be better is a Nordic walking club... or perhaps a local history group.'

'Or a book club,' suggested Monica. 'We could read nice books and talk about them. I read a lovely one about cat grooming the other day. Apparently cutting a cat's whiskers is the equivalent of castrating a human. It's that serious.' She drained her glass. 'You know,' she said, 'we should start a campaign, a campaign against whisker castration... it's a crime against cats.'

'I tell you what's a crime,' said Eileen, 'people who can't hold their drink. There was a time, Monica O'Leary, when you were able to remain upright after three bottles of wine. What's happened to you? I blame the menopause. It even robs us of our ability to absorb alcohol like a sponge.' She turned to Mary-Marg. 'But a nightclub, Mary-Marg? *Really*? Have you lost your mind? I mean, as Monica is proving in real time, we no longer have any ability to have fun without embarrassing ourselves. A nightclub is not age appropriate.'

'What will you be playing?' Siobhán sniggered. 'A bit of Elvis or "The Hucklebuck" or whatever?'

'No,' said Mary-Marg, 'music we all like. I still have my old records upstairs in the loft, and anyway, I wasn't too bad, was I, Ciara?'

'You were amazing...'

'The boys have this friend in school called MC Dub-Dub,' went on Mary-Marg. 'Real name Hugo Sinnot-Smyth. Mother's on the board of the Bank of Ireland, father something else high-flying in finance. Anyway. He's a bit of a DJ and I'm going to ask young Hugo, aka MC Dub-Dub, if he might give me a few lessons.'

There was that light again in Mary-Marg's eyes. It used to be on permanently but now only gleamed occasionally. It wasn't easy to keep the inner fire glowing and it needed friends to make sure that the lights never dimmed. Ciara was Team-Mary-Marg all the way, even if it meant social humiliation.

Ciara smiled back at everyone. 'It's going to be brilliant,' she said, sounding absurdly confident. 'Be there or be square.' But only Mary-Marg laughed – everyone else looked utterly horrified.

13

ALICE

It was Sunday morning and Ciara, Alice and Eva were eating breakfast in the courtyard at the back of the shop, which Eva had long ago transformed into a tangle of ferns and vines, clematis and honeysuckle and ivy, twisted around the three painted white brick walls; the floor was a bed of sea pebbles and there were all her geraniums. The sun was shining, the light dappling on the ground, the sound of birds who fluttered around the feeders, the robin who hopped around their feet looking for crumbs from Eva's soda bread. An old rattan lawn chair which had been there for as long as Alice could remember was where Eva sat, while Alice and Ciara perched on the bottom step of the fire escape which led to Eva's flat upstairs.

'More soda bread?' said Eva, passing over the wooden board where slices of buttered and jammed bread were laid.

'It's as good as ever, Gran,' said Alice, taking another slice.

'How many would I make, Ciara?' asked Eva.

'At least ten,' said Ciara, her mug of tea in her hands, the plate of buttered bread balanced on her knees. 'We'd have five in the oven at a time and then it was my job to cycle them down to the shop, still piping hot, and put them on the counter. And then I'd go to school.' She smiled at Alice. 'I can still smell them now, piled in the basket at the front of my bike. I would pedal in a kind of heady fume of bread.'

'Not a bad way to cycle,' said Alice. 'Better than breathing in car exhaust. So when did you stop?'

Alice and Eva glanced at each other. 'George hired someone else to do the delivering,' said Eva quickly. 'Ciara had exams and was too busy and then... well... after he died, I just stopped baking all that bread. When you took over the shop, you began to buy it in, didn't you, Ciara?'

Ciara nodded. 'Just took the pressure off,' she said, looking up from her phone which she had been staring at intently, scrolling through something. 'It wasn't the same, of course. Our customers were really disappointed, I remember. But it just meant that Mam wasn't up at dawn baking furiously.' She smiled at Eva.

'You should never bake furiously, though,' said Eva. 'Because people can taste the fury. My mother always told me that. You have to have a good heart when you bake...'

'Which is why I never bake,' said Ciara, again with a laugh, immediately returning to her phone.

'You have the best heart,' said Eva. 'You don't bake because you don't want to. You're already too busy... Now, this girl here...' She looked at Alice. 'She wants to learn properly how to make bread, don't you? I'll pass on my secrets. And my mother's secrets.'

'What are you doing?' Alice asked Ciara.

'I'm googling what do fifty-somethings wear to nightclubs?' said Ciara without looking up.

'You're going to a *nightclub*?' asked Alice.

'No, not going. Having one.' Ciara smiled at them both. 'Mary-Marg has convinced me that we should bring back our old disco...'

'Your old what?' asked Alice, amazed.

'Our old disco. We used to run our own club night.' Ciara shrugged, as though it were nothing. 'When we were still in school... before I had you, we used to run a kind of disco, I suppose, at the clubhouse down by the big field. Mary-Marg was the DJ...'

'Wait, Mary-Marg was the DJ?' Alice laughed at how preposterous this was. Mary-Marg was the least DJ-type of person she'd ever known. She didn't wear cool T-shirts or backwards baseball caps, or have sunglasses surgically attached to her face.

'Is that so hard to believe?' Ciara looked affronted. 'She was brilliant. She used to have two little record players and a speaker... her older sister was in her first year doing electronics at Limerick University and she set up the system. It was quite temperamental, but Mary-Marg was really good at taping wires together and practising cross-fades and beatmatching.'

Alice realised that perhaps there was a whole world belonging to her mother that she didn't know anything about. She thought she knew everything about her.

'It was called See The Stars disco...' Ciara went on, smiling at the memory. 'Our old junior school was...'

'Star of the Sea,' said Alice, smiling back. 'I went there too...'

'Of course,' said Ciara. 'Anyway, we ran See The Stars for the last two years of school and everyone came. Every Friday night we'd have around 200 or 300 teenagers in the clubhouse... Oh my God...' Her eyes were shining now, and Eva was listening, letting her speak, smiling at how happy Ciara was remembering. 'The place would be packed. We'd set up at 7 p.m. Doors opened at 8 p.m. And you'd hear them, the voices beginning as they made their way along the paths beside the pitches, the excitement building. And it hung in the air like this wonderful cloud... and the two of us, Mary-Marg and me... well, we were on cloud nine. And our other friends... they'd be hanging lights or on the door... and then... boom! 8 p.m. Doors open, and they'd flood in, cheering, and the music would be pumping, the whole place vibrating, the dancing, the singing... the craic!'

Alice felt almost stupefied at how alive Ciara seemed to be, as though she were right back there, those Friday evenings in Sandycove, seeing the stars.

'So why did it end?'

'Ah... well...' Again, Ciara glanced at Eva, who was looking utterly passive. 'Things always come to an end. Especially *nice* things. Life always gets in the way...'

'It doesn't have to,' said Alice. 'You don't have to give things up...'

'Everything changed after we'd left school. I'd taken a year out before university and was working in the shop,' Ciara was explaining. 'I found out I was pregnant with you... so that was a *lovely* thing...' She smiled at Alice, as though it was. And of course it was, but surely it wasn't ideal? Alice had never really thought of her mother as the very young woman whose youth had been cut short by *her*. 'Let's just say I was too busy to think about putting on discos, and Mary-Marg went off to Limerick to study engineering and... well, life got in the way.' Ciara laughed again. 'It was a busy time, wasn't it, Mam?'

Eva nodded. 'To put it mildly,' she said.

'By the way,' Alice said, 'you know Conal Blake, who is going out with Becca?'

Eva looked over at her – again that passive, unemotional expression. 'Oh, yes?'

'Well, I met his grandmother...'

Finally, there was a flicker on Eva's face. Ciara was brushing some crumbs off her legs.

'Dolores Blake... Dol... well, she says the two of you were friends. Best friends. Like sisters, she said.'

Eva gazed for a moment at Alice. 'We were friends...' she said quietly. 'Once. Many moons have passed since we were friends. Several lifetimes, in fact. We were different people back then. What do they say? "The past is another country"? This was another world, a whole new universe. Well, she was the same but...' Eva sighed and shook her head, her small lips pursed. 'She's never changed, but as you grow older, one's capacity for others diminishes. And there are certain things that you just can't accept.'

She and Alice locked eyes. Ciara was looking at Eva, listening.

'What kind of things?' said Alice gently.

'Things I can no longer remember or recall,' said Eva briskly. 'But suffice to say, I don't spend any time thinking of her.' She paused. 'How was she looking? She's had a stroke, I hear. She'll not enjoy being at Honeysuckle Lodge. But she's probably ruling the roost, terrifying the other residents. Like a fox in a henhouse, I would say. Ruffling a few feathers.'

'She's...' Alice couldn't quite think of the words to describe Dol Blake. 'She was intimidating. Bossed everyone around. Her son, Paddy. Conal seemed a bit scared of her. But she was determined to talk to me.'

Eva nodded. 'I bet she was. Best not to talk to her again. She'll eat you alive. Nothing stops her from getting what she wants.'

Alice felt a shiver down her spine. What on earth had happened? Had Dol Blake murdered anyone? How bad could it be? Eva's words left her slightly shaken. Whatever it was, it had made her sweet and lovely grandmother suddenly seem icy-cold. It had to be very bad indeed.

14

CIARA

Mid-morning on Monday, Ciara was making herself a coffee from her precious machine, the one she had to convince Eva was worth all that money when she imported it from Milan years before. It had been the first coffee machine in the village and everyone had flocked to the shop, queuing up for various sizes and coffee strengths, all admiring the froth and the foam and loving the shake of cocoa. It had brought in extra money and footfall and had been one of those many modernising decisions she'd made which had paid off. She'd gone on to gain the wine licence, introduce lunchtime sandwiches and cakes, but she had long run out of ideas. It was enough to be keeping the shop going and making sure she had the right stock. The beer was new, she supposed, but she was tired and couldn't quite understand why.

She tried to have one of those mindful moments she'd read about in a magazine. Something about breathing in the aroma and clearing your mind. How was she meant to do that? Ciara wondered. Her head was permanently full of everything she was yet to do, everything she had done, and everything she would never get around to doing.

When it all went wrong with Lorcan Kennedy, mindful moments were thin on the ground. Then, she was left searching for the next breath, her chest squeezing her lungs as though in a vice. There was a time when she thought she was never going to breathe again and that she was going to die on the street in front of everyone. But she got through it; she had Alice and the shop to concentrate on. A life, after all, had to be led.

When Lorcan had returned that one time, when Alice was perhaps eight, Ciara could barely make eye contact with him, but by that point she had few feelings left, even the bad ones, and she stood in The Sandycove Arms hotel watching as he talked briefly to Alice, wondering what exactly she had seen in him? Those thin lips, the wispy hair pushed to one side, the silly neckerchief, the cigarette dangling in his yellowed fingers. How could she have been so in love with this pretentious man who had impressed them all with his lines of poetry? He wasn't funny like Paddy and Mary-Marg. He never smiled, believing humour was a waste of time. When Paddy had been larking about, making them all laugh, or Mary-Marg doing something ridiculous, the whole gang rolling about the floor laughing, Lorcan would shake his head. 'What's wrong with you all?' he would say. 'It wasn't *that* funny.'

'I need one of those,' said Mary-Marg, entering the shop and nodding over at the coffee. 'Pronto!' She leant over the counter while Ciara heated the milk and filled the cup with the ground beans.

'Cappuccino?'

'As per usual, thank you...' Mary-Marg always slipped a few euro coins into the charity box on the counter. It was the deal they had come to years ago, when Ciara began making coffees for her every day. 'I am gasping,' Mary-Marg was saying. 'I've had quite a morning. The twins are refusing to get up even though I vacuumed noisily outside their bedroom at 8 a.m. They *still* haven't got a summer job. Brian is going to ask around to see if anyone has boxes to shift or buildings to construct. Hard labour, that's what they need.' She smiled at Ciara. 'Now, back to us. And the return of See The Stars. Now, good news. It's all organised. Killian at The Sandycove Arms is a yes. My decks have arrived and Hugo Dub-Dub is coming over later to go through all the buttons with me.' Mary-Marg looked just as terrified as Ciara felt. 'And the boys said that they could make some kind of website where people can buy tickets.'

The bell above the shop door rang again, and Ciara looked up, ready to smile and say hello... Except she froze.

It was Paddy Blake, looking a little surprised to see both Ciara and Mary-Marg. Was he really the boy who would do anything to make them laugh? The one who smuggled five crates of Blake's Beer in for one of their discos? Who dressed up as Santa Claus for the children's party in the church hall? The only teenager who used to volunteer for the homeless shelter in Dún Laoghaire? He was greying now, but still the same. Tall, handsome and wearing the kind of rugby shirt that costs serious money. The few times they had bumped into each other, they'd merely nodded and moved on. She now only ever saw him in his running gear, an expression of determination on his face which she never recognised from his younger self. They hadn't talked since it had all happened. It had been easier to disappear into the world of the shop with Eva and focus on minding Alice. But sometimes, when she passed Paddy in the car, as he powered up Killiney Hill, his face pressed into the rain, his jaw fixed, she wished she could talk to him. She would say, *How much do you know?* And, *Are you all right?*

Breda, Paddy's then-fiancée and later wife, had no interest in Paddy's old friends, especially Ciara and Mary-Marg. Paddy had brought Breda to the disco one evening, and Ciara had overheard Breda telling Paddy that she wanted to go home, that the place was 'tacky' and that his friends were 'infantile'. But Breda always looked so unhappy, and she just became unhappier and unhappier. Once, years later, Ciara was walking along the seafront and caught sight of Breda, wrapped up with a scarf and sunglasses. It was the way she held her mouth, her jaw slack, as though she were done, beaten, her skin grey. Ciara had walked over. 'Breda,' she'd begun. 'If you...' She'd wanted to say that whatever Breda was going through, she understood. A hand of friendship. But Breda had looked at her with absolute horror, as though she'd been accosted by a mass murderer. 'Get away,' she had said. 'Get away from me!' And she had turned and almost run back to her car. Poor Breda, she'd thought. What a mess it all was.

'Well... look who it is!' said Mary-Marg.

'I just wanted to say thank you for stocking Conal's beer,' Paddy was saying now.

'That's no problem,' Ciara said, remembering her Mrs Potato Head smile. 'He came in and asked... and gave me a taste... It's really good.'

'Well, I just wanted to say it was very kind of you...' He nodded at her, still not smiling. 'After everything.'

After *everything*? What exactly did he mean?

'It's grand,' she said. 'Glad to help out.'

'You know Ciara,' said Mary-Marg, 'always happy to support a fledging business. You're looking well, Paddy. It's all that running you do. Up and down Killiney Hill. Honestly, every time I drive up the hill, there you are. I feel tired just thinking about it.'

Paddy smiled. 'Sure, what else would I be doing with myself... clears my head...'

'Too true, Paddy,' said Mary-Marg. 'Except, I was recently at a retreat. Making the menopause magical. And anyway, I was lying there listening to the sounds of whales giving birth and I thought to myself, *If I ever get out of this place alive with my mental health intact, I promise to do more with my life*.'

Paddy half-laughed, as though unsure if he could fully laugh.

'And so, drum roll...' went on Mary-Marg, 'we're bringing back See The Stars night. Would you like to come? Strictly over-forty-fives. This Friday, The Sandycove Arms, from 9 p.m. Are you on?' Mary-Marg was smiling at him. 'You used to dance, if I remember rightly. We could never get you off the dance floor. You were quite the mover...' She pulled a face at Paddy, daring him to disagree, and for a moment, Paddy smiled, and he looked exactly like the Paddy of thirty years ago, the person who was always laughing and *always* up for having fun.

'Anyway, think about it,' said Mary-Marg. 'And do come along. We need numbers. It can't just be me and Ciara staring at each other...'

He was shaking his head. 'Maybe... I'll have to see...'

'I'll take that as a definite yes,' said Mary-Marg.

He hesitated for a moment, as though there were something else he wanted to say, but what could it be and why now?

'Can I help you with anything?' asked Ciara. 'Are you here to buy anything?'

'Yes... yes...' Paddy started looking around, as though trying to find something he could have been in to buy, but he'd never shopped in Murphy's since it all had happened. Before then, he was in all the time. After all, Lorcan worked in the shop and it was one of their gang's HQs, along with the old sports hall, as well as the summer house at Landfall. 'Olive oil,' he said, his eyes obviously alighting on the display. 'I need some olive oil...' He picked one up at random and turned back to Ciara and Mary-Marg.

'Is your Conal still living at home with you, Paddy?' asked Mary-Marg. 'Still under your feet?' She laughed again. 'And how's your mother getting on in Honeysuckle Lodge? I hear they have very nice little independent-living houses down there now. I bet she's lovely and comfortable. It can't be easy when you've had a stroke.'

'No,' he said. 'It isn't.' Paddy looked at his feet for a moment and then he looked back at Ciara. 'I've got to get back,' he said. 'I'll see you both... again... around.' He turned to leave.

'Bye, Paddy,' called Mary-Marg. 'See you at the disco!'

He nodded, as though he hadn't really heard, and was gone.

Ciara and Mary-Marg looked at each other, neither knowing quite what to say.

'He looks well,' said Mary-Marg. 'The jogging obviously suits him. He's had a rough ride, hasn't he?'

Ciara shrugged. 'I don't know any of the details.'

'None of us do,' said Mary-Marg, sighing. 'But hopefully he's doing better. There was a time he looked *so* unhappy. After Breda had gone... it was such a shame that we all lost contact. When I came back from college, I went up to see him and Breda told me that they were all too busy to see people. He shouldn't have married her and he should have gone to college. Remember he wanted to go and do Ancient Civilisations or whatever?'

Ciara nodded. 'Life got in the way...'

'Life has a habit of doing that,' said Mary-Marg. 'I always thought he was in love with you,' said Mary-Marg as they walked out into Church Street, the hanging baskets swaying in the breeze, the only sounds from The Island and people walking home. 'He always brightened up when he saw you. But you only ever had eyes for that *awful* Lorcan.'

'He *was* awful,' agreed Ciara.

'Do you remember when Paddy first brought Breda to meet us all and she was so strange? Just ignored us and wanted to leave.' Mary-Marg put on a posh, pinched voice. '"*Can we go now, Paddy? We'll be late for dinner with your parents...*" But why did she leave Paddy and Conal? I wonder, was she unwell?'

Ciara pretended to be thinking about something else and checked her phone to see what time it was, but Mary-Marg was obviously in a wistful mood.

'I used to fancy Paddy,' she said. 'But you could just tell he only had eyes for you. Ah, he was so sweet and funny, wasn't he? Remember that St Patrick's Day when he said everyone had to wear green to See The Stars and he turned up painted like The Incredible Hulk, in those tiny, ripped denim shorts...'

Even Ciara laughed at the memory. 'He looked amazing.' But she also felt sad for all he had been through. No one warned you when you were young that one wrong decision could change simply everything.

'He had the body as well... and now... All that running. If only Brian would take up running. Or anything, really, other than being obsessed with his new barbecue. Honestly, you'd think he was the only man who'd ever cooked on fire. He goes on about rubs, marinades, brining, as though he were Gordon Ramsay.' She paused. 'Although he did something with a sausage the other day that was quite magnificent. "Brian", I said, "you've got your mojo back".'

Ciara was barely listening, feeling terrible for everything that had happened to Paddy – he didn't deserve any of this. He'd been forced into it, she guessed. None of what was done would have been his idea and it had slowly been unravelling ever since. And soon it was going to be completely undone. Ciara wondered if Mary-Marg had guessed some of it. It was like being a detective in a Scandinavian drama, putting all the clues together, except there was no resolution here, no big denouement. You just had to be happy with the not-knowing. But it was the not-knowing that drove you mad.

15

ALICE

Alice was making changes in the shop. It was Tuesday and she'd been home nearly a week. All day, she'd been tweaking and rearranging things and had moved the wicker baskets to the other side of the front door, tidied up the area behind the till, throwing out old notebooks, stubby pencils and Ciara's pot of supposedly useful things which, once she'd been through it, consisted mainly of pen tops and elastic bands. Ciara seemed delighted to have a fresh eye and approved of every change. She and Mary-Marg were spending a great deal of time talking together, crossing off items on lists, making phone calls and giving out their debit card numbers. Alice had even caught Ciara watching a video on how to apply 'party-tastic make-up.' She had put down her phone, sighing heavily. 'It's all so much effort,' she said.

That morning, Alice disappeared into the back of the shop and returned dragging one of the old benches which were stacked in the storeroom. 'Will you give me a hand?' she said to Ciara. 'I'm going to put these outside...'

'In the garden?' said Ciara, standing up.

'No, in front of the shop. We're going to give people a nice little seating area outside...'

'So, people drink their coffees and teas outside?' said Ciara, picking up the end of the bench, helping Alice manoeuvre it around the counter, across the shop floor and down the granite step, to the front of the shop.

Alice nodded. 'If they want to... We're right in the sun for most of the day and... Wait a minute...'

Alice ran back into the shop and to the courtyard, and returned with two of Eva's smaller terracotta pots with geraniums spilling out of them.

'Do you think she'll mind?' she said to Ciara. 'I'll replace them,' promised Alice. 'This is just to see what it looks like.' She stood back and looked at her effort once she'd placed the pots on either end of the benches. 'What do you think?'

'What are you two up to?' Eva was looking down at them from the flat upstairs.

'I've stolen two of your pots, Gran,' called up Alice. 'Just to see what it looks like...'

Eva nodded approvingly. 'Looks lovely,' she said. 'Maybe we could put some more out...'

'But we're trying to sell food and drink,' said Ciara, looking up at Eva. 'We're not a garden shop, or a café...'

Eva gave Alice a wink. 'I think Alice knows what she's doing... Wait a minute, I'm coming down.'

While they waited for Eva, Alice dragged out another bench, which she and Ciara placed next to the first one, so the front of the shop was a long line of seating. Thinking back to the outlet in Perth that had cacti and jasmine which covered the front with its deeply scented flowers, Murphy's needed lightening up.

'Mum,' she said, 'I think we should paint the front of the shop. A really bright yellow.'

'It's fine,' said Ciara. 'I like the navy. Reminds me of my old school uniform...'

'It's a little boring,' said Alice, turning to Eva who was now standing beside them. 'What do you think? Would yellow work for the outside?'

Eva was nodding. 'When I first married your grandfather,' she said, 'the shop was yellow. Egg yolk, your grandfather called it. But I thought of it as mimosa yellow. It really stood out. And "Murphy's" was written in green. Maisie, Maureen and I would take it in turns to wash down the paintwork every few weeks and George liked to clean the windows himself. No one else could get rid of the streaks as well as he could. It's an art to have streak-free windows, but ours gleamed.' She paused. 'But the yellow is a good idea. Navy is a little too dark, don't you think?'

'It's two against one,' said Ciara. 'I'm beaten. So, yes, as long as I don't have to pick up a paintbrush...'

'I'll do it all,' said Alice quickly. 'Don't you worry...'

A customer was walking towards them and Ciara turned to her. 'Morning, Josephine,' she said. 'Lovely day, isn't it?' She followed the woman into the shop, the two of them chatting, just as Max appeared carrying a box of books.

'Oh, even *you* are going all al fresco,' he said. 'Just like everyone else. My customer book group is now a *walking* book group... just for the summer, where we walk while in deep discussion of the book.'

'You know,' Eva said to Max, 'you are the sixth shop to set up next door to us. I remember, when I first married my husband, there was a cobbler... Jerry One-Eye he was called because...'

'He had one eye?'

'No! He had *both* eyes... in full working order... No, he was called Jerry One-Eye because his name was Jeremiah and his mother was obsessed with people spelling it correctly. *"Jeremiah, with one i"* she used to say, *"not Jerimiah"*, which she thought made him sound more common and less Old Testament. And... let's see, who was after Jerry One-Eye? There was one man who set up a photographic studio... his name was Valentine Fox, I think. Wore huge ties and flares wide enough you could hang off them. The ladies loved him... he had an affair with Cassandra Douglas whose husband was the chairperson of the Sandycove Community and Business group... so Valentine was run out of the village. Poor Cassandra. She was stuck with her awful husband...' Eva paused. 'I always felt sorry for her. She took up walking along the seafront every night, up and down, like a mad thing, swinging her arms, just to be out of the house.'

'Sounds like my book group,' said Max, making Alice laugh again.

They lingered in front of Murphy's for a moment. 'Do you think,' said Alice, 'that the shop needs a bit of a spruce up? There's a gorgeous outlet in Perth called Sheila's, and it's a kind of deli, makes these amazing sandwiches which you need the jaws of a crocodile to eat they're so big, and there are seats outside, and inside is like walking into the most stylish kitchen pantry...'

'A crocodile, you say,' said Eva. 'We don't have any of those here.'

'It was painted the colour of crocodiles as well...' went on Alice. 'Green.'

'The shop used to be green,' Eva said. 'And I like the navy

your mother painted it, but I am looking forward to the yellow...'

Max was studying the front of the bookshop. 'Maybe I should paint mine... I don't want my shop looking shabby in comparison. What about a jungle green? Is that outdoors enough?'

Alice laughed again and Max smiled back at her, pleased he had amused her.

The door of the shop opened and Josephine appeared, holding a coffee cup and a bag with a pastry inside. 'I think I'll just sit outside,' she said, smiling at them. 'It's such a beautiful morning.'

'Of course!' Alice felt a surge of joy. Who knew that dragging out a bench could have such an effect? This customer was about to enjoy a few minutes of sun-drenched peace, get her requisite vitamin D. It was a lovely feeling to know that you had contributed in some tiny way to improving someone's day.

* * *

After lunch, Alice drove to the DIY shop. Eva sat like a little bird in the passenger seat, bolt upright, her hands in her lap, looking around at every junction as though she were on duty to make sure they didn't crash into another car. Eva always behaved as though driving and being driven was a two-person job.

'There's a bike,' said Eva. 'A nice one... George had a bike just like that.' Eva kept her eyes on the road ahead. 'Motorcycle,' she announced. 'Zebra crossing. Your grandfather's bike was a big blue thing, it was, and he'd tuck his trousers into his socks. He always said he preferred his pushbike to the car. I liked neither. I liked walking.' Eva's lips were pursed, her eyes scanning for a parking space. 'There's one,' she said. 'Beside the red van.'

Inside the shop, Alice manoeuvred a trolley to the paint section and they chose some paint and picked out some extras, including some fine bristly brushes, a gallon of white spirit, fluffy rollers and a few rolls of masking tape. Alice began pushing the trolley towards the till and almost careened into someone walking around the corner of an aisle. It was Paddy Blake.

He stopped, startled, and then collected himself. 'Ah, Alice,' he said. 'And Mrs Murphy. Haven't seen you for a while. Keeping well?'

Alice expected Eva to be as purse-lipped and magnificently disinterested as she had been when speaking of Dol Blake, but when faced with Dol's son, she was smiling, as though they were old friends and she were extremely fond of him.

'Ah, well, Paddy,' she said. 'Yes, haven't seen you for a fair while, now. And how are ye all?'

'Doing grand, Mrs Murphy,' he said, smiling down at her, and speaking in a quiet, gentle voice. 'Conal's spreading his wings. Has his own beer company. A rival we have.'

'A cuckoo in the nest,' said Eva, and for a moment, they both looked at each other.

'Indeed,' he said.

'And your mother?'

'She's doing well. She's at Honeysuckle Lodge these days, in their independent-living houses.'

'I heard that...'

'She never liked living alone,' he went on. 'You know how much she liked company.'

'I do,' said Eva. 'I do indeed.' And there was that look again.

'Bye, Paddy, mind yourself now, won't you? Give my regards to Conal.'

'Bye, Mrs Murphy,' said Paddy. 'Will do. Bye, Alice. Good to see you again.' And he disappeared around the corner, past the paint thinners, the fluffy rollers and the turpentine.

Once back in the car, their cans of paint and brand-new brushes in the boot, Eva and Alice both strapped in, Alice glanced at Eva, wondering why she had been so friendly to Paddy and yet was so reluctant to admit how well she'd known his mother. 'What happened between you and Dol Blake?'

'It's so long ago, I can barely remember.' Eva kept her eyes on the road ahead.

'I'm lucky to have you, and Conal is stuck with her...'

Eva didn't speak for a moment. 'Paddy has done well by him,' she said. 'He was fortunate that way.'

Alice gave up and changed the subject. 'Gran, would you be able to make six loaves of soda bread every morning?'

Eva turned to her. 'You've got a fierce appetite all of a sudden.'

Alice laughed. 'No, to sell in the shop. You make the best soda bread, and I want to sell slices of it with butter and jam every morning. An Irish breakfast, I'm going to call it... I thought while I'm here, I could do it. Mum doesn't have to continue it when I'm gone.'

'It's a lovely idea,' said Eva. 'And yes, of course I could make them. I had my kitchen certified by the health people. I like the idea of a takeaway breakfast. People like to eat here, there and everywhere these days. And better than that, I could show you how...'

'Would you? And what about your jam? How many jars do you have?'

'Let me see...' said Eva. 'Dorrie has a supply and I have my own. Dorrie makes the best.'

'Well, can I have them for the shop? For my Irish breakfasts? And could you and Dorrie make more?'

Eva nodded. 'Of course you can. And let me know when you want your first soda bread lesson.'

Alice smiled and nodded. 'Thank you, Gran.'

They drove in silence for a while and then Alice spoke. 'Do you think I'm doing the right thing?'

'In what? The breakfast idea?'

For a moment, Alice hesitated. She wanted to say in life. Do you think I am doing the right thing, am I right? Will it all work out? But she didn't want to worry Eva and let her know she had a granddaughter who wasn't exactly sure who she was and where she was going. What she also wanted to ask Eva was about her father, Lorcan.

'Do you think I'm doing the right thing painting the shop yellow?' she said instead.

Eva smiled, making her look like she was a young woman again, the one in the wedding photograph, in the mini dress. 'I think,' she said, 'that it's a wonderful idea. A golden shop, why didn't we think of it before?'

16

CIARA

Ciara was leaving Alice alone and in charge of the shop most days, now. It was just so freeing to have someone to rely on, and it meant she was less tired and had more energy for going out after work. She and Mary-Marg had been meeting every day in the shop to organise the disco, but then they had discovered that the place most conducive to meet was the wine bar, where they drank delicious wine and ate cheese and biscuits, the world becoming a little soft around the edges.

'Your usual table, ladies?' said Francisca, the manager of the wine bar, leading them to what she and Mary-Marg now considered their home away from home. 'Rosé, ladies?' asked Francisca. 'Or two glasses of the Montepulciano... it's very good...'

Mary-Marg and Ciara looked at each other, both making the decision telepathically. 'Rosé, I think,' said Ciara. 'Thank you, Francisca.'

Around the other tables in the wine bar gathered similarly small groups of women – on this Friday evening, all either talking intently or laughing uproariously. It was like, thought Ciara, being back in the real world again, the one *outside* the front door of Murphy's. And all thanks to the fact Alice was working in the shop so much. In fact, Alice was constantly helping out, even when Ciara was working, as though she loved being there. And with Eva upstairs in the flat, or coming down every morning before her swim with her piping hot loaves of soda bread, life seemed easier and far less of a slog.

She hadn't realised how much Mary-Marg also seemed to need these times. Since she'd had the twins, she too had been consumed by the demands of mothering and life, and Mary-Marg's mother who had needed minding after her dementia diagnosis. These meetings were far more than organising sessions – they were reclaiming their old selves, the ones which had been in hibernation.

She and Mary-Marg grinned at each other when they clinked their glasses, both excited to be together and to taste freedom after all these years. Obviously, they were privileged and so lucky with everything they had, but it was just nice to be out. One day, when she retired, she would go travelling and see more of the world, rather than just this little part of it.

'Do you remember our first ever See The Stars?' asked Ciara.

It had been Friday night in the autumn term of their fifth year in school, and at 7 p.m., the two of them had looked at each other worriedly. The room was totally empty apart from them.

'What are we going to do?' Mary-Marg had wailed.

'Right...' Ciara had taken charge. 'Turn the main lights off, I'll switch on the strobe, the mirror ball and those flashing things... and you... you start playing music. If no one comes, then we'll just have the place to ourselves.'

And that's exactly what they did.

Except everyone did come, the place was heaving, the tin walls of the clubhouse reverberating with the bass and the dancing.

But that was then. The world had changed unutterably. *They* had changed unutterably. Ciara still wasn't sure if this plan of Mary-Marg's was a good one, or why exactly she was going along with it if it wasn't.

'You know,' said Mary-Marg, 'who says our best days are behind us? I think they are still to come...'

Mary-Marg laid out her numerous notebooks, the spreadsheet, the lists of everything they needed to have done for the disco.

'Ticket sales have been robust,' she said. 'That's the word they use, isn't it? Robust. It's a very comforting word. I'm going to use it more often. Right, so it's a week to D-day. D for disco! Anyway, so... let's go through the list...' She picked up a black olive grissini which Francisca had left for them, dangling it with the insouciance of a 1950s Italian film star. 'Have you double-checked the lighting will be delivered?'

'Done,' said Ciara.

'Have you checked that the equipment, the speakers, et cetera will be delivered?'

'Done...'

Mary-Marg looked at her notebook. 'What else? I've done all the publicity, spoken to *The Sandycove Newsletter* and *The Dún Laoghaire Gazette* who are both going to run a feature on the night... and... well, my DJ lessons haven't been brilliant, but I think I'm getting the hang of it. There are just so many *buttons*. And flashing lights. Might add Migraleve to my list.' She smiled at Ciara. 'And the twins will be on duty to set everything up. They'll be on table and chair clearing, delivering my decks and anything else last minute.'

They checked everything again, had the same worried conversation about outfits and stared at a floor plan of The Sandycove Arms' first-floor function room. 'So everyone will enter here...' said Ciara.

'And the DJ area will be here...' Mary-Marg circled a corner of the room.

'Dancing all here...' Ciara gestured to the middle of the floor.

'And the bar area here,' said Mary-Marg. 'And there's a nice seating area on the first-floor landing if anyone is finding it too much.' She underlined Migraleve on her list. 'It might very well be me.'

'What about your set list... what have you decided on?'

'Still refining it,' said Mary-Marg. 'But MC Dub-Dub, my DJ tutor, is helping me with my transitions...'

'Ah, transitions...' said Ciara sagely.

'That's what they're called,' said Mary-Marg. 'I was reading *Mixmag* the other day...'

'*Mixmag*?'

Mary-Marg nodded. 'The library are ordering it in for me every month,' she said. 'Apparently a lot of people our age are buying decks and DJ equipment. Anyway, *Mixmag* was explaining the perfect transition.'

'But you really think people will come?'

'Well, we've sold thirty-eight tickets and word is spreading.' Mary-Marg picked up her glass.

'But what if they don't turn up?'

'Well, then, it will be a disaster... but at least we tried. Now, talking of trying something new. Do you fancy sharing that gorgonzola pizza?' Mary-Marg paused. 'But, seriously, if we fail, we fail, and there is no one I would rather fail with than you.'

'That's the most beautiful thing anyone has ever said to me,' said Ciara, and the two of them dissolved into giggles.

17

ALICE

Alice began painting the following afternoon, borrowing a ladder from the back of the shop, but as soon as she had applied the first brush-stroke, she recalled just how untalented she was. There had been that attempt to decorate her hall in the house in Perth after which she was left with patchy walls, as though she had applied a distressed technique beloved of pretentious interior designers and hated by everyone else, or the time she painted her shelves and ended up smearing the colour on with her hands, near tears. She soon realised the job was far more than just applying colour to surfaces and one of those jobs which, as soon as you began, you wished you'd never had the ridiculous idea of in the first place.

Arms aching, morale at an all-time low, Alice was losing the will to live and to paint when Max appeared, having just finished work.

'You've missed a bit...'

'Thank you,' she said, twisting around, trying not to fall.

'Very cheerful,' he said.

'Me or the colour?'

'The colour. You don't seem so cheerful...' He stood at the bottom of the ladder, looking up. 'Need a hand?'

'Yes...' She laughed. 'Do you know any decorators?'

'Yes, me...' He grinned up at her. 'Despite appearances, I'm actually quite handy with a brush. My grandmother taught me,' he said. 'She used to do all our DIY...' He smiled up, shielding his eyes with his hand. 'She tried to bring me up not to be useless, something I wrestle with every day. If you let me help you, then this would be a day of not being useless and I would sleep more soundly. I've given up my detective fiction and trying to sleep more like a normal person.'

Alice clambered down the ladder. 'How can I say no, then?'

Max had already placed his backpack against the bookshop and was rolling up his shirtsleeves, surveying the Sisyphean task to which they were now committed.

And so they began, carefully working their way up and down, painting slowly and steadily and as neatly as possible, making their way towards the door in the middle.

At 7 p.m., Ciara had appeared. 'I'm closing up now,' she'd said. 'I'm meeting Mary-Marg.' She had given Max a smile when she spotted him kneeling on the pavement, painting with the precision of Michelangelo. 'You're doing a good job there, Max. Aren't you afraid of getting yellow paint on your lovely shirt? Wait there...' Ciara disappeared into the shop, returning with a pile of aprons and an old overall that Alice could remember being in the back room for decades. 'Put this on,' she ordered. 'And then this on top.'

Max did as he was told, putting on the overall and then the apron.

Alice laughed. 'Next, we'll be seeing that on the catwalks of Milan,' she said.

'It's better than getting paint on his clothes,' said Ciara.

'Thank you, Ciara,' said Max. 'I shall studiously ignore Alice's fashion advice.' Max didn't seem to mind looking ridiculous. In fact, he played up to it, draping a tea towel over his head. 'I cannot have paint in my hair. The ignominy.'

Ciara headed back inside and returned with potato salad and cold chicken. Alice and Max sat on the bench outside the shop, yellow paint on their fingers and hair and freckling their faces as the sky darkened and the evening closed in.

'I think chicken and potato salad, eaten on a bench, outside a half-painted shop, is the only way I can eat from now on,' said Max loftily. 'I've been spoilt.'

Later, as it was starting to get too dark to paint and Alice's arms ached – more than that time she'd moved flat and thought she would never be able to lift her arms to brush her teeth or drink a cup of tea ever again – they stopped for the evening. She and Max stood back and surveyed their success.

'A work of genius,' said Max.

'A towering achievement of biblical proportions of brilliance,' said Alice.

'My mother and my grandmother would be so proud,' he said, taking out his phone. 'Will you take a photo of me in front of the shop? Caption: your useless offspring says hello.'

Alice snapped him in front of the shop, and then he put his arm around her neck and they took a selfie. 'Say cheese,' he said. 'Or, as they would say in Murphy's, say *local artisanal homespun sheep's milk made by moonlight cheese.*'

'Sheep's cheese,' said Alice, and he pressed the button.

They grinned at each other. It was amazing to think that only hours ago the shop had been navy and now was yellow. The only thing that needed changing was the Murphy's sign, but that was a professional job, not one for enthusiastic amateurs.

'Thank you for today,' said Alice. 'It looks surprisingly professional.'

'*Surprisingly?*' said Max, nudging her with his shoulder. 'How insulting.'

'Oh, I forgot, you're a professional painter slash bookshop owner...'

'Slash local superhero and...' He paused, musing. 'What else? Crossword completer? I make an amazing granola, as well.'

Alice turned back to the shop. 'I'll finish the last few bits tomorrow.'

'Same time tomorrow, then?' he asked.

'I can do it on my own,' she said firmly. Max had already given up too much of his time and she didn't want him to feel obliged to help again. 'I'll fly through it.'

'But I've got my costume now... my tea towel... Where is it?' He turned to pick it up from the ground and flicked it onto his head. 'There... back in the zone. Where's my paintbrush?'

Alice laughed again. 'No, really,' she said. 'I'll be fine. You've been amazing.'

He nodded. 'That's what they all say. But I'll help. Now, what about a drink and a bag of crisps for the workers?'

'I'd love that.'

* * *

The Island was quiet that evening and they took their drinks to a table in the corner of the small courtyard. Max picked up his pint of Guinness. 'Thanks for this.'

'It was the least I could do.'

'Cheers.'

Max smiled at her. 'So, tell me. Why the makeover? Every

time I come in, you are rearranging some shelf or display. There are the benches outside and now the yellow frontage...'

'I don't know,' she said, 'I just want it to look as nice as possible. It's just something I can do to help Mum, I suppose. Who wouldn't want to go into a yellow shop?'

'I am sure retail psychologists have something to say about the colour yellow,' said Max. 'Does it make you buy more cheese?'

Alice laughed. 'And lemons.'

'Bananas?'

'Of course. I have a few other ideas, things to make it a better business... You know you buy your coffee every morning...'

'Yes...'

'Why are we all obsessed with coffee? Why not tea? I was thinking of doing a breakfast takeaway. Irish tea, soda bread, butter and home-made jam. My grandmother...'

'The fabulous Eva.'

'Indeed. Her soda bread is incredible. As is her home-made jam. Her friend, Angela, has an allotment and gives her damsons and raspberries. I thought that would be nice. An Irish takeaway breakfast...'

'Very patriotic.'

'And... I thought of a Friday night kit... a cheese and meat board and a bottle of wine. No messing about. Who doesn't like cheese or wine?'

'Only people not worth knowing.'

Alice laughed again. The Guinness was delicious. It had been a long time since she'd had a proper pint. She sat back against the stone wall which felt cool on her back. Perth was not just half a world away, but another universe entirely. She smiled at Max. 'Have you always wanted to run a bookshop?'

'Always. My grandfather left school without being able to read... he taught himself at night school and he used to say to me that reading was the most empowering thing in the world. And I knew he was right... so imagine the power of a bookshop or a library...' He paused. 'I have a theory about Irish literature and that the reason why we have so many amazing writers is because of our weather. Writing is best done indoors with the rain on the roof, or by the fire while a storm rages outside. Rain is the ink with which a thousand great Irish books have been written.'

Alice laughed. 'Interesting theory...'

'It's just that I wouldn't let the weather put you off...'

'Put me off what?'

He shrugged. 'Oh, you know... being in Ireland. I mean, Australia is beautiful and all that, but you can't stay there forever...?'

She hesitated. 'I'm not sure... I've spent the last decade doing odd jobs. I worked in a lot of bars. And I did a stint on a sheep farm. And a whole year in this gorgeous wine bar on the beach. I'm now a classroom assistant, which is basically minding the kids, helping them do whatever needs to be done. And I really enjoy it. The children are lovely... but...' She hesitated. She didn't know the answer to if she was going to stay there. She supposed she would, but a future with no plan had lost its meaning. She realised now she wanted a plan and a purpose. The problem was, she didn't quite know what either was. 'I'd like to do something with my life,' she said. 'But I'm not sure what...'

For some reason Max looked quite pleased. 'I think Australia is overrated, personally,' he said. 'The spiders are ridiculously big. And did you know koalas aren't actually cuddly?'

Alice laughed again. 'They have claws,' she said.

'I used to have one,' said Max.

'A koala?'

He nodded. 'Kenny. A cuddly one. No claws. Slept with me every night until I lost him on the train to Galway. I still think of poor Kenny, endlessly hurtling between Galway and Dublin. Anyway, my point is, real koalas aren't all what they seem.'

'Hidden depths?'

He smiled. 'That's right...'

'It's funny,' she said, 'that's what I am looking for, I think.'

'A koala?' He pulled a face again.

'Hidden depths.' She smiled at him. 'At the beginning, working in a bar, or on the sheep station, nothing had much meaning. I was enjoying life in the now. I could leave the next day, if I wanted to. I had no ties. Nothing trapping me... which was exactly what I wanted. Except...' She paused.

'Except what?'

'I think I now want hidden depths. I want to be tied down. I want to have a plan for a month's time, a year's time... I want to have roots in a place...'

'You have them here, though?' Max spoke carefully.

'I know... but I don't know what I want exactly. I just know that the running away part of me is tired...'

'It's called getting old,' he said. 'Think of Kenny, forever on that train, running away permanently.'

Alice nodded. 'Poor Kenny. I used to think that all you needed in life was a bit of money and your passport...'

'And clean underwear...'

'Goes without saying.'

They smiled at each other and then Max raised his glass.

'Here's to being unencumbered by that with which you don't want to be encumbered,' he said. 'Such as this sentence, which is quite encumbering.' They clinked glasses. 'Here's to life,' said Max. 'Whatever is important to you.'

Alice thought travelling and freedom were important to her but she suddenly wished they weren't. It was as though, ironically, she'd trapped herself with her need for freedom. And perhaps freedom wasn't quite what she needed. Maybe there was something else?

18

CIARA

Since Alice had arrived home, Ciara was feeling a little lighter. Perhaps it was the handful of lie-ins or perhaps it was having someone who shared in the love and the care of the shop, but whatever the reason, she no longer felt a bone-dragging tiredness and desperate need to crawl onto the sofa. In fact, this Tuesday evening, she didn't immediately remove her bra and reach for the remote control. It was after 8 p.m. and the late summer sun was streaming through the window. There were only a few days left before the disco and she felt a kind of nervous energy that she needed to burn off.

Pulling on her old trainers, she left the house... and, for some reason, broke into a sort of run. Instead of turning right towards the seafront where she knew everyone in Sandycove would be parading their dogs and up for long chats and catch-ups, she turned left and jogged up towards Killiney Hill. The hill was large, and a very beautiful public park rose from grassy meadows to a forest. At the very top there were the most stunning views of Dublin and the sea and on the clearest days, you could see as far as the Mountains of Mourne in the north,

Wexford in the south, and if you had particularly sharp eyesight, you could even look across the sea to beautiful Wales.

Ciara kept going, placing one foot in front of the other and, somehow, found a rhythm. On she went, until she heard footsteps behind her. Someone was trying to get past her on the pavement.

'Oh, hello, Ciara...' It was Bernadette O'Hanlon, who was nearly seventy and was always heading off somewhere to take part in half-marathons or Ironwomen or desert treks. 'Lovely evening, isn't it?'

Bernadette sailed past, powering up the hill, towards the park. Ciara nearly stopped running. *Perhaps*, she thought, *I should rethink my marathon-running plans and go back to watching television from under a blanket.*

And then, just as she was about to cross the road to enter the park, she heard someone call her name.

'Ciara... how's it going?' Paddy Blake ran up behind her, pushing up his sunglasses.

'Hello, Paddy...' She was suddenly mortified, as though she had been caught doing something she shouldn't be, like stealing or feeling a bit sorry for England when Ireland had trounced them in rugby. Should she just turn back and run down the hill? Going down would surely be a lot easier.

'Are you going up the hill?' he said. 'We could run together?'

No. No. God, no. 'I'm not very good,' she said. 'I'm very slow. I was just overtaken by Bernadette O'Hanlon.'

'Ah, well, she's practically a professional. Got a personal best in the marathon last year. Under three hours, I think...' But he was smiling at her and she suddenly wished everything were different.

'Come on,' he said. 'We'll run together. Up to the top and see the view...' And there was that slightly sad smile again.

'Yes, okay,' she heard herself say. 'But you run ahead if I'm too slow.'

He nodded and off they set, but he stayed with her – as she knew he would – all the way.

'Use your arms less,' he said at one point. 'You'll expend too much energy like that on a long run like this...'

She did as she was told, but her legs were burning and there was a pain in her side that she'd last experienced during torturous school cross-country. But they kept going, crossing the meadow and past the trees that were in full leaf, and then following the path and up through the dark wood, where light streamed through gaps in the canopy.

She was about to say something when Paddy spoke.

'This always reminds me of your old discos,' he said.

She was lost for words for a moment – and, anyway, was too out of breath to speak properly. But Paddy took it to mean that she didn't understand what he was saying.

'It's stupid, really,' he said, trying to explain. 'But like a disco ball, the light coming through, the patterns on the ground, the way the leaves move...'

'I knew what you meant,' she said. 'I can see it too.'

On they went, over the disco forest floor. Her legs were really hurting now, her lungs on the verge of exploding, and she was ready to surrender, roll into a ball and let herself be gnawed on by woodland creatures.

But the forest began to thin, and in front of them was the top of the hill, the whole of Dublin bay spreading out below them, and on the other side of the hill, the Wicklow mountains, a swirl of purple heather and yolk-yellow gorse. There were yachts in the sea below and a warmth in the breeze that made you feel, on rare evenings like this, that there was literally nowhere else you'd like to be. Ireland on a summer's evening was glorious.

Ciara took all of this in *intellectually;* physically, however, she was on her knees, trying to breathe normally and not in huge, loud, worrying gasps, as though about to expire.

Paddy handed her his water bottle. 'Here we go.' He smiled at her.

'Thank you...' Her hands shook as she swallowed down the water. 'I'm not...' she said between swallows, '...used to it. That's all. I am... trying... I mean... I can't...'

'Come on,' he said. 'Let's sit on the benches.'

They sat on a bench and looked out to sea as Ciara's breathing began to slow, her lungs out of the danger zone.

'That was impressive,' he said. 'If that was your first time...'

'*Last* time,' said Ciara.

He laughed. 'Well, it was quite the inaugural run.'

'How long have you been running for now?'

'Years,' he said. 'It's been a great stress reliever. No fuss. You know? You just leave the house. And it gets me out. Otherwise, I think I would just stay indoors and never leave...'

'That's what I do,' said Ciara. 'The thought of socialising is overwhelming sometimes...'

He nodded, as though he understood. 'If I didn't run,' he said, 'I'd be in a much worse place. I know it.' He shrugged. 'It calms me now, helps me cope...'

He'd been a single father for all these years, just as she'd been a single mother. She should have contacted him, made sure he was all right. It was never easy, none of it. But the loneliness could be so hard.

'So how have you been?' she asked.

'Grand...'

'Paddy.' She looked at him. 'How *are* you?'

He didn't say anything for a moment, but she saw it all there in his eyes and understood.

'I know,' she said quietly.

'Sometimes,' he said, 'I realise I'm braced for the next calamity... you know? I know a storm or an earthquake or something else is going to happen and I have to be ready...'

'Maybe it won't, though?'

'I keep thinking of the people in Pompeii...'

Ciara laughed. 'The *Romans* of Pompeii?' She and Paddy used to talk like this, she recalled, about life, love and the universe and he had been obsessed with the Romans.

Paddy laughed too. 'Yes, the Romans. I keep thinking of them as this great disaster was about to unfold and I wish I could warn them... it's one of my fantasies.'

'But some of them did know,' she said. 'Many of them left...'

He nodded. 'They just seem so helpless, that's all. And that's how I feel...'

'Helpless?'

He nodded. 'Yeah, sometimes... but maybe that's getting older... Being aware of one's fallibility. Vulnerability, I suppose.'

'God, life is hard,' Ciara said, her back against the cool wall. 'Why doesn't it get easier?'

He shrugged. 'Hopefully, we get better equipped to deal with it.'

'Hopefully,' she said. 'But that's not a given.'

They sat for a moment in silence.

'You never met anyone since... you know...' he said.

'God, no. Who'd I meet? And how? I've no interest in any of that... too much trouble.' She paused. 'What about you?'

'Same,' he said. 'Too busy with Conal and the business.

And now, too old, too tired, too busy worrying about the citizens of Pompeii...'

Ciara laughed. 'You've a lot going on...'

He stood up. 'Shall we go? Downhill is a lot easier. And maybe, when you've recovered, we could go for another run sometime?'

'Maybe,' she said, refusing to commit but wanting to see him again.

The run down the hill with Paddy relied entirely on the laws of gravity and her legs somehow managed to keep her upright.

Outside her house, they stopped.

'Thanks for the company,' Paddy said. 'Say hello to Mary-Marg and Alice. She came to Conal's birthday party, by the way...' he smiled. 'She's beautiful... and lovely...'

'Yes, she is...'

'She reminds me of you. She's the cut of you when you were that age...'

'Oh God, don't be saying that,' said Ciara, embarrassed. 'She's a vast improvement. And Conal, by the way, he's a fine young man... brought up well, I can see that.'

He nodded. 'He is a fine young man... he's the best of us, he really is.'

When Ciara went inside, her head was full of Paddy and all the myriad opportunities that existed in the universe, except sometimes, for some people, like her and like Paddy, there was nothing you could do except keep your world as small as possible because it was the only way to cope.

19

ALICE

It had taken a while, but on Thursday morning, at last what had felt like a mammoth painting task was finally finished. Becca had also given a hand when Max had to return to the bookshop, but not being as neat as Max, her orangey hair looked much more yellowy than before.

Eventually, there was nothing left to paint, and the two of them drew to a halt.

'All I can see is yellow,' said Becca. 'I feel dazzled, like when you look at the sun for too long.'

'I feel dizzy from the fumes,' said Alice, but the dizziness may have helped because as she gazed up at the shop, the slightly wonky, wobbly painting bits were concealed and the shop not only looked transformed – it glowed.

Alice cleaned the last splash of paint off the windows, swept the pavement free of dust and dirt, replaced the benches and the geraniums – to which Eva had added more – and stood back again to admire her handiwork, although there was paint on the pavement and paint on Eva's geraniums. 'They'll wash off,' she told a worried Becca. 'Or *grow* off.'

'Oh, girls,' Ciara said, coming outside to have a look. 'It's wonderful... Oh, *well* done.' Ciara looked so pleased as she stood looking up at the shop, taking it all in. 'The Murphy's sign needs to be redone,' she went on. 'I'll call the sign-writer, see when he can fit us in.'

Max popped his head out of the bookshop. 'Did I hear you'd finished? Have the two Michelangelos of Sandycove finished their masterpiece?' He stepped out and looked up at the shop, nodding approvingly. 'You can do mine next,' he said, looking at Alice. 'Before you go back to Australia. I will pay you in books.'

'Now, *that* is a deal,' said Ciara. 'Being paid in books...'

'I'd like to be paid in chocolate bars,' said Becca. 'But money would be preferable.'

'We could pay people in cheese,' said Alice, laughing.

Ciara was smiling. 'I do remember your grandfather once accepting a dozen eggs from someone in exchange for flour. Years ago now, but people would run out of money and needed to put food on the table.'

Alice had a twinge in her neck which she rubbed.

'You need to go swimming,' said Ciara, looking at her. 'Your grandmother swears by the sea to soothe muscles. Get yourself down to the water.'

Alice looked at Becca. 'Do you fancy it?'

'I can't,' she said. 'I've got some dogs arriving to be minded.'

'Max?'

He hesitated. 'Is the sea heated?'

Alice shook her head. 'It's cold...'

'Then I can't. Something to do with being a massive coward,' he said. 'But I can be on hand to hold towels or administer hot drinks... or help with a post-swim rub-down...' He suddenly blushed then, as though what he'd said sounded wrong. 'I have to work... Sell books and...' His voice drifted away.

* * *

Later, when everything had been put away and the lids on the paint tins closed and the brushes and rollers washed and drying in the courtyard, and the shop looked resplendent, Alice walked down to the Forty Foot for a swim. It was late Thursday afternoon and the day had been warm, and there was quite a crowd gathering at the small rocky bathing place, and a space to change was at a premium. She found a corner and changed into her swimsuit, stowing her belongings under the bench. The sea sparkled and glittered, but she wondered just how cold it was. She was used to Australian water, and the sea there was like stepping into a warm lagoon.

'Hello...' Conal Blake was there, smiling down at her. 'I didn't know you were a sea swimmer.'

'I'm not,' she said. 'Well, not for years. But I've been painting the shop and feel as though the sea might help. My grandmother says it's like a free massage.' She paused. 'How cold is it?'

'Well... it's not *warm*,' he admitted. 'You have to brace yourself, get yourself in, and then wait... and *then* it feels amazing. Every time I'm getting in, I wonder why I am doing this, and then when I'm finished, I remember why.'

'You're putting me off,' she said. 'I like my gratification to be immediate. And I'm just back from Australia where the sea is much warmer.'

'What about the sauna?' He pointed to a black wooden shed which was just beside the steps, a few metres away. 'You go in for a few minutes and then race into the sea; do you want to give it a go?'

'It's an Irish solution to the cold sea,' said Alice. 'Make it a good thing.'

'Exactly. May as well make the most of our natural elements. Can't complain then.'

They walked over to the shed, opened the wooden door, crept through the hot mist, and squeezed in between some indiscernible bodies. They sat on the bench, wiping away the condensation on the window, through which they could see people running one by one from the sauna, along the rocks and jumping into the sea.

'I think we're cooked enough,' said Conal. 'Come on. It's our turn.'

They broke into a run, Conal launching himself in just moments before Alice flew through the air, slicing into the water and then dropping to the bottom of the sea. She felt the rocky bottom with her feet, as she pushed upwards, her body feeling something beyond cold, beyond hot, as though she'd been electrified. She felt invincible. She surfaced, laughing.

'What did you think?' Conal said, swimming up to her.

'Incredible... Shall we do it again?'

The two of them repeated the cycle another four times until, eventually, they floated on the water, Alice's toes pointing upwards, her face towards the sky.

'It's pretty nice here, isn't it?' Conal said, as they sculled their hands. 'I don't think Australia compares. I mean, this is more interesting, isn't? This makes you feel more alive?'

'Perhaps...' Alice felt relaxed and happy, as though her body were melting into the sea.

They floated peacefully around, sculling or slipping and twisting, before swimming out to the buoy and back until it was time to return to shore. Conal was so easy to be with, as though they had known each other forever. Eventually, they headed in. They changed quickly, gathering up their things.

'Shall we go and get a coffee?' said Conal. 'There's a food van at the harbour run by Rory, a friend of mine.'

They bought their coffees and sat up against the wall, their legs stretched out in front of them.

'I couldn't imagine living anywhere but Sandycove,' Conal said as they watched some teenagers dive off the pier into the sea. 'I think I'm the opposite of you. I'm not adventurous. I never want to be anywhere else.'

'I always knew I would leave,' said Alice, 'and when I could, I did.'

'But you're so close to your mother and your grandmother. Did you never worry about them?'

Alice nodded. 'Always. I know they are self-sufficient and both of them always encouraged me and never held me back. But it didn't stop me worrying. Especially now. Gran is getting older and Mum looks tired.' She thought about why she had planned on leaving and couldn't quite remember why. She had always wanted to live abroad and travel, but when did you call time on an adventure and come home? It was as though she had decided something about herself at an early age and had to live up to it. She saw Ciara who had never left home, who had wanted to travel but never had, and Alice had learned about her own father who had gone and only returned that once. What was she trying to prove, that she was having a life more than her mother? None of it made sense.

'I could never abandon Dad because he doesn't have anyone. I mean, at least your mum and your grandmother have each other. I don't think he's ever had anyone, except me. Mum leaving must have been hard for him...' He smiled at her.

'And you...'

'I suppose...'

She waited for him to say more but he didn't. 'What was your mum like?' she said instead. 'Were you close?'

He shook his head. 'Not really. She took care of me, but she wasn't affectionate... you know? Not into hugging or the *I love yous*, but she did her best. I missed her when she was gone but Dad's my best friend.'

'You're lucky...'

'I know...' He smiled at her. 'It's great to finally meet you properly... Becca's told me so many stories about the two of you.'

'It's really lovely to see her again... I feel like I am a different person in Perth. Over there, I am the Irish one, no one knows quite what to make of me... and here, I just blend in. I'm just me.'

They finished their coffees and began to walk back to the village, Conal pushing his bike. 'Have you ever thought what it would be like if there were still dinosaurs?' he asked.

Alice laughed. 'Never... you obviously have...'

'Every day.' He turned and grinned at her, one hand on the seat of his bike, the other gesticulating wildly. 'I was obsessed with dinosaurs when I was little. My room was decorated with dinosaur wallpaper, a duvet cover, every book I had was dinosaur-related. I knew every fact and I drove Mum and Dad mad talking about them. My mother would try to look interested, nodding away, a far-away look on her face... I must have been so incredibly boring. Dad was a little more involved, taking me to London when there was a big exhibition going on. I must have watched *Jurassic Park* a million times...'

'And you wish they weren't extinct?'

'Oh my God... don't you?' He looked at her excitedly. 'Imagine! Pterodactyls flying above us right now! I mean, obviously the human-eating ones wouldn't be ideal, but the herbivores could fit right in... Think of a brachiosaurus or a diplodocus or even a parasaurolophus...'

'A what?'

Conal laughed. 'A parasaurolophus. My favourite, actually. God, so cool. Anyway, my point is, why do things need to become extinct, why do all the wonderful things this beautiful planet has ever made have to go away...'

'Like the dodo?' Or mothers, she was thinking. Or fathers.

'Well, that was our fault,' he said. 'Humans are to blame for that. But to bring something back alive like Hammond did in *Jurassic Park*... I mean, why do things need to go?' He wasn't laughing any more, he was looking serious, his blue eyes, sad. 'I sometimes think that with everything we've achieved, the steam engine, humans to the moon, the pop-tart...' He paused. 'My breakfast of choice, by the way. But...' his speech slowed down, 'it would be nice if things didn't come to an end.'

Alice didn't know what to say. She wished she could find some words of comfort, but that wasn't what he was looking for. Conal was one of those people who needed you to know who he was. He was such a sweet, open-hearted person, the kind you would worry about. 'Your mother?' she said.

'Partly. I mean, totally, I suppose. Completely.' He shrugged. 'It didn't make sense. Still doesn't. I've seen her. Not so much recently. But our meetings never went well. Was she depressed?'

'Perhaps,' said Alice. 'It must have been so hard for you.' She wished she could make it better for him and hoped she had found the right words. But thankfully he was nodding.

'Yes, it was. It's the blank space. The nothingness. Like feeling around in the dark...'

'I know how that feels,' she said. 'I don't have a father. Well, I did. I didn't *know* him. But he died. And so there was never a chance to know him. And I feel like I am only half a person... half of me is in colour. All singing and dancing. And the rest of me is... nothing.'

She thought he would say she was being silly and how lucky she was to have Eva and Ciara, and to have come from a beautiful place like Sandycove. But she didn't fit in. Half a person didn't fit in. You had to be whole to fit in, and it sounded ridiculous and abstract, but it was how she felt. And perhaps if she kept moving, she might find the rest of herself one day. She sensed that perhaps Conal was the only person she'd ever met who might come even close to understanding.

'I think it's why I've stayed away,' she said. 'I always wished I were normal...'

'No one's normal,' he said.

They had stopped in the street, just across from the shop.

'My mother is normal,' Alice went on. 'Stayed in Sandycove all her life. So's my grandmother.'

'Are you saying you're a black sheep?' he said, smiling.

'The black dinosaur,' she said, and they both laughed. 'But I need to be okay with being the black dinosaur, I need to stop looking for my missing half.'

'Me too,' he said. 'Maybe that's what growing up is, you stop looking for the things you don't have. You accept not being normal.'

Alice smiled at him. 'Maybe I'm not ready for normal yet.'

He laughed. 'I'm definitely not ready. I don't think I'll ever be ready. Becca said you were easy to talk to. She was right.'

Alice smiled at him. 'I hope so,' she said. 'I would hate to be difficult to talk to.'

'You understand things,' said Conal. 'You get that life is

complicated. Most people just see things as black and white, good and bad, they don't understand motivations, why people do the things they do. My mother isn't a bad person. My grandmother used to say she was glad my mother had left and we were better off without her.'

'Knowing things are complicated doesn't mean you have any answers,' said Alice. 'It's more of a leap of faith, until you know the full truth, you just have to wait in limbo, and that's hard.'

He nodded. 'It really is... but...' He paused again. 'It's better than shutting yourself down, filing things into boxes labelled "Good" or "Bad". You must give people the chance to explain or redeem themselves.'

'But what if they *are* bad?' Alice was thinking of her father, the man who'd left before she was born.

Connel shrugged. 'Well, then they just are...' He smiled at her. 'We'll just have to be black dinosaurs together. Thanks for listening to me. Sometimes I have so much going on in my head and no one to talk to about it. I don't want Becca to think I'm mad and no one else would understand.'

'Maybe it's because you don't know me and I'm going back to Australia soon,' said Alice. 'I'm a safe vessel.'

'Yeah, maybe...' He turned to go. 'Let me know when you want to go for another swim? And next time, I promise not to be so introspective, okay?'

'Okay...' She shrugged. 'But I liked listening to you. It's helping me sort a few things out as well. While I'm here, I am happy to listen to your ramblings, if you will listen to mine.'

He grinned at her. 'Free counselling? Sign me up.' He began walking away from her. 'See you soon, Alice – my fellow black dinosaur!'

20

ALICE

Alice had worked in the shop all afternoon when Becca rang.

'Where are you?'

'The shop. Do you want to call in?'

'After you finish? We could go and grab something to eat?'

'That sounds lovely. I'll be done at 7 p.m. Mum's gone to her disco.'

With a few minutes to closing, Alice swept the floor and checked the fridges and tidied the displays, before she heard Becca coming in.

'Oh my God,' she was saying. 'Sometimes I wonder why I work with dogs. I mean, I love them, of course. More than most humans... but chihuahuas are the divas of the dog world. Like little dog despots...'

She came and pushed herself up onto the counter, her legs dangling, just as she used to do when they were teenagers and Alice was on shop duty.

'The chihuahua triplets are very demanding,' Becca went on. 'None of them is keen on walking. Nor do they like being on the ground. They insist on being picked up and carried everywhere, like toddlers or medieval queens.'

Alice laughed, putting down the broom with which she had been sweeping the floor. 'You carried all three at once?'

Becca nodded. 'If I put one down, it barked. They only stopped yapping if I carried them all. I kind of made a sling out of a blanket.' She sighed. 'Lily, Billy and Philly. If the owner didn't pay me double, I would have sent them back. She wants me to take them once a week from now on because she said she'd never seen them so attached to someone other than her.'

'That's because they were attached to you by a blanket.'

'Do you have something to remove some of their fur?' said Becca, brushing down her leggings.

Alice found a scrubbing brush and a roll of cellotape, and she and Becca began removing the chihuahua fluff.

'It might be easier to lick it off,' said Alice. 'It's like it's been sewn into the weave of your clothes.'

'Oh, I give up,' said Becca. 'I mean, I am practically half-chihuahua, so I might as well accept it. If there were a volcanic explosion and we were suddenly covered in molten lava and ash... or whatever it is we would be covered with... in thousands of years' time, these archaeologists would brush off our remains and put me through a microscope and declare they have discovered a half-human, half-dog person-thing.'

Alice laughed. 'Then please don't remove any more hair... we have to confound those future archeologists.'

Becca had grown thoughtful and was looking concerned. 'But being covered in dog hair all the time – which I am – isn't exactly attractive. Or alluring. I mean, Conal is pretty gorgeous, don't you think? And a little out of my league. Well, a *lot* out of my league...'

'Don't be ridiculous...' Alice began, but Becca carried on.

'He's not like Julian at all...'

'Thank God...'

'He's good-looking and really kind. He's nice to everyone and he's entrepreneurial...'

'So are you,' said Alice. 'You're all of those things. You have your own business. You're beautiful and nice and kind...'

'But...' Becca seemed at a loss how to explain it. 'But he's just *really* nice. He and his dad have both been through so much with Conal's mother leaving them like that. Conal doesn't really talk about it, but he said he woke up one morning and she'd just gone. Barely kept in touch...' Becca shrugged. 'And then the way the two of them deal with Paddy's mother...'

'Becca,' said Alice, 'you're going to have to just accept that Conal likes you and that you are worthy of being liked...'

'I know... but... Julian wasn't very attractive. I can say that now we're not together, but I never felt he was out of my league...'

'Why would you? He wasn't in any league...'

'But Conal...'

'He's lucky to have you, remember that.'

'I hope so...' Becca looked worried. 'It's just I never thought I would meet anyone nice. I just really like him, that's all...' She paused. 'Now, please be truthful. Don't lie to me, will you? Promise? Cross your heart? Hope to die? Stick a needle in your eye?'

Alice crossed her heart and mimed stabbing herself in the eye. 'Of course...'

'Do I smell of dog? I mean, just be honest. Because that's not very attractive... unless, of course, you're another dog.'

Alice leant in and sniffed at Becca's neck. 'You smell of soap and perfume...'

Becca looked relieved. 'Thank God.'

The floor was swept, the shop in a place of orderly calm. It looked gorgeous, thought Alice. Like a theatre stage, ready for a performance. 'Shall we eat here?' she suggested. 'I could put money in the till, and we could have some bread and cheese...'

'And some wine?' said Becca.

'Definitely. Would that be weird?'

'Not weird at all...'

Alice took some cheese from the fridge, while Becca opened a bottle of rosé, and then they sat by the counter and had their picnic.

There was a knock on the glass and Max was peering in. 'Just saying hello,' he called. 'And goodnight...'

'Join us!' called Alice, as Becca ran to the locked door to let him in. 'And give Conal a call to see if he will come as well?'

Conal arrived in under ten minutes and the four of them sat on either side of the shop counter, eating their cheese and drinking the wine.

'How was your day?' asked Max.

'I had those chihuahua triplets again today,' Becca said. 'Quite the literal handful.'

'That's not work,' said Conal, pulling her ponytail from behind. 'I know people who would do that for free.'

Becca laughed. 'Don't tell anyone, but I'd do the same,' she said, turning around to look at him. 'If people knew how much I enjoyed it, they wouldn't pay me.'

'What about you, Alice?' asked Max.

'My day was...' She thought for a moment. She'd spent the morning in the shop and there had been the lovely woman who came in asking for advice on what to cook for her vegan niece who was coming for dinner, and that gorgeous customer who wanted to put together a nice food hamper as a thank you present. There was that handsome man who came in for pasta and left with some of Conal's beers, two bottles of wine and some of the cheese. And all of the interactions felt meaningful in some way, as though she were actually doing some good in the world. But that couldn't be right, could it? Working in a shop, ringing through people's purchases, oiling the wheels of capitalism? But it had felt nice. 'My day was really good, thank you,' she said to Max. 'How was yours? Many customers?'

'Not too bad, actually,' he said. 'I've started a new section which I call "Max's Raves and Faves" which are my favourite books...'

'Genius,' said Conal, making everyone laugh.

'And I sold three copies of *Rebecca* just today. I was thinking of setting up a "books in the post" service, as well,' he said. 'A surprise book and a chocolate bar every week or month.'

'That's a gorgeous idea,' said Becca, turning to Alice. 'And you're coming up with innovations for Murphy's. And Conal with his beers. I'm surrounded by...' She paused.

'Captains of industry?' suggested Max. 'Capitalist titans?'

Becca laughed. 'If I knew what that was, I might agree. No, I was going to say, three amazing people. You're all very inspiring.'

Alice felt incredibly pleased. She hadn't felt inspiring for a long, long time but for a brief moment, as she basked in the glow of feeling she had a purpose in life, she felt good about herself. Except this was just temporary. Her return flight was booked and she would be back to her rootless free-spirited life.

21

CIARA

It was finally D-day, the return of See The Stars. Ciara had woken feeling the kind of nervous excitement she hadn't felt in years. Mid-morning, Mary-Marg waltzed into the shop. In fact, she wasn't waltzing, she was dancing... shuffling around the floor, exactly the way she used to back in the old days. She had a huge grin on her face. She found the broom and twirled it around. Ciara was laughing along; it was so lovely to see Mary-Marg looking happy.

'Did I hear you were seen buying a pair of silver jeans?' asked Ciara, turning to the machine to start making a fresh coffee.

Mary-Marg nodded. 'I look like a baked potato wrapped in aluminium foil,' she said, 'but I don't care. I *feel* amazing in them. I had forgotten all about the power of clothes. It's like dressing up to feel good. I've been wearing fleeces for the last twenty-something years. Like a sheep. But this sheep is ready to go to the ball. Or disco.'

'So *that's* what the jeans are for?' Ciara warmed up the milk in her metal jug, and then poured the hot coffee into

Mary-Marg's mug, jiggled in the foamy milk and handed it over.

'Brian thinks I've lost my mind.' Mary-Marg paused and leant across the counter in front of Ciara. 'I know I'm just being foolish and it's so hard not to feel like a fool these days. Wear the wrong thing and you're mutton dressed as lamb, say the perceived wrong thing and you're called awful names. Women can't do anything without being controlled and curtailed, and I just want to feel free of all that. You know? And perhaps a nightclub *is* a terrible idea...' Mary-Marg placed her cup down. 'But...' she turned to Ciara with a fire in her eyes, one she hadn't seen in a very long time. 'If I *don't* do it, I think I will just fade away to nothing. We'll just think that fun and frolics are behind us. We all need a good time and to be reminded that we not only *deserve* a bit of fun and dancing – a let-your-hair-down kind of night – we require it! For our health! For our minds, and bodies, and souls... because...' She looked deep into Ciara's eyes. 'We all need to reclaim those people we used to be. We need to do it before it's far too late. You know what I'm saying?'

Ciara nodded. She knew exactly what Mary-Marg was saying because she felt the same way. But despite their closeness, she'd had no idea Mary-Marg felt like this. Mary-Marg was the kind of woman who just cracked on with everything, never faltered, never stopped. But if they both felt like this, then maybe everyone else they knew did too, even the women at the bottomless tunch who'd dismissed their idea?

'Maybe Eileen, Siobhán and Monica are scared about what will happen if they grab their old selves back again?' she suggested.

'Of course they are!' Mary-Marg threw her arms out, nearly hitting the mug which Ciara had placed on the counter in front of her. 'Of course they are, all of us. Earlier, I couldn't even wear something that took me out of my sartorial comfort zone. I have worn jeans and a kind of tunic top and variations thereof for decades now. Definitely since the twins were born. So eighteen years wearing safe, comfortable clothing. I want to wear something unsafe and uncomfortable...' Mary-Marg suddenly grinned at Ciara. 'We're going to do this,' she said. 'We're going to make everyone in Sandycove over the age of forty-five very unsafe and very uncomfortable.'

Later that day, Ciara's bedroom was reminiscent of that of her teenage self. The floor was a heap of tried-on and discarded clothes, there were piles of jeans and tops, long dresses and short skirts, and everything – every single thing – made her look wrong for myriad reasons. Why couldn't she be one of those effortless women who just found it so easy to get dressed and accessorise, who wafted around on a cloud of Jo Malone with a jaunty scarf or statement shoe (singular), rather than finding it an absolute nightmare to wear anything?

However, even if tonight were a disaster, at least it was a distraction from normal life. Lately, she'd been consumed by thoughts of Paddy and everything that had happened all those years ago. Eva was right, secrets should stay that way unless they were hurting someone. But the problem was someone *had* been hurt and they were bound to find out sooner than later. Secrets rarely remained secret.

She wondered if Paddy would come to the disco or if he would stay away? His old school friends would be there, but he seemed such a loner these days. If only she could text him and ask how he was, or meet him for a coffee sometime... or... she didn't know what she could do, but she felt a longing deep inside for everything to be different, for all to be well. *We were all so young*, she thought. *None of us knew anything about the adult world and yet we were thrust into it.*

Oh well, there was nothing she could do, except finish getting ready. Tonight wasn't the night for dwelling on past mistakes.

On cue, at 6 p.m., Mary-Marg knocked on the front door, two large bags from the boutique in the village on the ground beside her, and she was clutching a bottle of sparkling wine. She took one look at Ciara who had one sock on, her dressing gown over a T-shirt and her hair in a towel. 'Hello, Cinderella,' she said. 'Fancy going to a ball?'

Ciara laughed. 'Do you have a magic wand?'

'No, but I have some tops from Nell's,' she said. 'Silvers, metallics, even lamé.'

Ciara felt immediately better. Having Mary-Marg beside you made everything easier. She helped her in with the bags and then brought down her full-length mirror to the front room.

'Right,' Mary-Marg was saying. 'Jake and Josh have dropped my decks off at the hotel and they have their lighting people setting things up. One man asked what the disco ball was...' She looked shocked. 'On a scale of one to ten,' said Mary-Marg, 'how scared are you?'

'Eleven and a half,' said Ciara.

Mary-Marg nodded. 'I'm ten and three-quarters... and I need some alcohol to get me down to nine and half...' She opened the bottle with the speed of a mother who had a feverish child opening a bottle of Calpol. 'Let's get a glass of this down us and then we can have a try-on.'

They sat beside each other on the sofa, Ciara cross-legged, Mary-Marg spread out as though she'd been washed up on shore.

'Whose idea was this?' she said. 'Who do we blame?'

Ciara laughed. 'I have no idea,' she said, 'but when I find

whoever that person was, I will make them explain themselves.'

'Next time I have an idea,' said Mary-Marg, 'tell me to shut up. Don't encourage me. I blame you, you're too nice to me. You need to be stricter with me.' She smiled at Ciara. 'Now, let's go through our roles again. You're the hostess, the meeter and greeter, the charming one, making sure people have drinks, introducing people – okay with you?'

Ciara knew she could do that; after all, it was pretty much what she did all day, game-face on, big smile, full of chats.

'And you're in charge of the music,' she said. 'Good dancey songs, nothing too hard-core...'

'Ciara, I'm a proudly middle-aged woman!' said Mary-Marg. 'I think I know what kind of music our peers want. Now, let's try on some of these outfits Jessica chose for us.'

There was a rule when two women tried on clothes: they must praise and validate each other, as though they were members of the French court at Versailles circa 1780. Ciara and Mary-Marg duly oohed and aahed at each other, while staring at themselves disconsolately in the mirror. Ciara ended up in a silver dress which was an inch shorter than she would have liked, Mary-Marg was in a pair of skinny black jeans and an artfully distressed T-shirt.

'I look like my mother going to Studio 54...' said Mary-Marg, gazing at herself mournfully.

'You look amazing,' said Ciara, meaning it.

Mary-Marg grabbed her by the arms. 'Babe,' she said, 'we both look fecking amazing. We rock. Now, let's go before we lose all our confidence again.'

'You're doing better than me,' said Ciara. 'My confidence isn't there to lose.'

'Will you shut it?' said Mary-Marg. 'Come on, once that disco ball is turning, it will all come back to you.'

* * *

At 8 p.m. they were in the hotel feeling anxious and getting under the feet of the bar staff, or dodging the guys fiddling with the lighting, or watching while Jake and Josh carried tables on their backs and dragged stacked chairs across the room. Mary-Marg was checking her equipment, making sure her records were in order and if her brand-new bottom-of-the-range DJ decks had been set up properly. To quell her nerves, Ciara repeatedly swept the floor with the giant broom. Even if no one came, she'd already had a fun evening with Mary-Marg during the wardrobe session and perhaps it would be better if no one came... because then they could pretend that it never happened. She looked at the time on her phone: 8.59 p.m. exactly. She was suddenly electrified by panic. 'Get on your decks!' she shouted.

Mary-Marg screamed, making Ciara laugh, the panic leaving her just as suddenly.

'Let's...' Ciara said.

Mary-Marg nodded. 'Get...' she said, rushing back to her decks and slipping on a record.

'This...' said Ciara, standing by the big doors.

'Party...' shouted Mary-Marg.

'STAAAAAAAARTED!' They screamed together, and just as Mary-Marg put the needle on the first record – the Beastie Boys' '(You Gotta) Fight For Your Right (To Party!)' – Ciara opened the door. And...

...No one walked in.

She turned back to Mary-Marg who merely shrugged and

began to dance behind her decks, so Ciara joined her and the two of them carried on dancing, laughing together and jumping around, until they looked around and realised they had been joined by eight people... No, nine, as someone else had come in, and then ten. Eleven. And there were Elaine, Monica and Siobhán... And Jimbo and his gang were coming in, all making their way to the bar or already dancing. And there were some more arriving.

In fact, there was a steady stream of the most fabulous-looking people, dressed in their finery, in feather boas, old band T-shirts, ripped jeans, runners, high heels, comfortable flats, metallics, sequins... faces that Ciara knew well or only to see. And best of all, they were all over-forty-five and they were all smiling, the room filling with laughter and talking, women dancing together or men in their groups, long-term couples segueing into well-practised moves, and a few shier types standing at the edge, building up confidence.

Exactly like the old days.

Mary-Marg lined up another song – 'Buffalo Stance' – and still more people were coming in. The bar was packed, people were shouting at one another above the music but, above all, on the floor which was lit by a billion sparkles from the glitter ball, they were dancing, the whole hotel moving in unison as the beautiful people of Sandycove danced their hearts out.

22

CIARA

At the See The Stars disco, as House of Pain's 'Jump Around' filled the air, everyone was doing as the song encouraged: jumping around. Long-married couples threw themselves wildly up and down. Rebecca O'Neill, who had been left by her philandering husband the year before, was now jumping up and down with her gang of old school friends, their long hair swirling in the air, all of them laughing and singing along. Peter O'Brien, who ran the car garage in the village, was out of his overalls and dressed in a clean pair of jeans and shirt, his face shaven – a look he hadn't sported practically since his holy communion – and was throwing himself around with abandon, singing lustily along. And there were Eileen, Siobhán and Monica doing what looked like some kind of synchronised dance, arms twisting in the air, feet tapping out. The See The Stars disco was a triumph.

Ciara turned to look around at the faces, the smiling, the laughing, the ocean of bodies moving as one. It was glorious. She had spent the night running about from group to group, as everyone wanted to shout in her ear about what an amazing time they were having. Jimbo McAlister even picked her up and squeezed her. 'I needed this!' he cried out as he swung her around. 'I fecking needed this! Haven't had it in years... my back hasn't twinged once.'

Mary-Marg picked up the microphone. 'Ladies, gentlemen... thank you for coming to the See The Stars disco... and now, it's nearly time for us Cinderellas to be in bed, so grab that man or woman and enjoy this last song of the evening...'

Everyone began to sway again, in anticipation of a slow song but, instead, the sound of 'Gett Off' by Prince filled the room and everybody started shrieking with delight, faces contorted with the sheer pleasure of being awake and out of the house at this unearthly hour. Peter O'Brien was punching the air, Rebecca and her friends were holding hands in a circle and Monica, Siobhán and Eileen were still doing their routines, looking happier than Ciara had ever seen them.

And then it was all over and Ciara had flicked the switch. Everyone in the function room of The Sandycove Arms blinked in the sudden light. Jimbo and Jessica were kissing right in the middle of the dance floor as the mirror ball stopped its stately rotation, and coats were retrieved from the cloakroom, bags and shoes were fished from under chairs and tables and the room began to clear.

Ciara and Mary-Marg hugged each other, the music still in their ears, the feeling of swaying bodies clinging to their bones.

'Now, *that* was a night,' said Mary-Marg. Neither of them had had a drink since they were getting ready, hours – a lifetime? – ago. 'Jake and Josh are collecting my decks in the morning. All we have to do is go home and have a drink...' She smiled at Ciara. 'And when I say drink, I mean *tea*. I'm gasping. Need to put my slippers on, take my bra off, and have a nice cuppa.'

'Oh, thank God!' said Ciara. 'I was worried you'd make us drink *alcohol*. I am desperate for a cup of tea and a sit-down. My feet are aching.' They took one look behind them, the disarray of the room, the music still pulsating in their ears. 'I can't believe we did it,' said Ciara. 'I feel like my eighteen-year-old self.' She paused. 'No, I don't feel like my eighteen-year-old self. I feel like me. My *fifty*-year-old self. But just happier.'

'Me too...' Mary-Marg slipped her arm through Ciara's as they began walking along the corridor towards the reception of the hotel.

The desk in the corner of the foyer was lit by a low lamp and behind it was a young man in a suit. 'Hugo!' said Mary-Marg. 'You're on night duty.'

'Hello, Ms O'Loughlin.' The young man looked back at them earnestly, blinking through his black-framed spectacles. 'Yes, I just do night shifts on a Friday and Saturday. It gives me a chance to get on with my pre-med revision.'

'Ciara,' said Mary-Marg, 'this is MC Dub-Dub.'

Ciara gave him a wave. 'Hello, MC Dub-Dub.'

'Safe,' he said, perplexingly. And then to Mary-Marg, 'So, like, how did it go?'

'It was amazing,' said Mary-Marg. 'I didn't do most of the things you showed me but kept it basic, just record to record, nothing crazy, good basic mixing. Thank you, Hugo.'

'No worries,' he said.

'Bye, Hugo!'

'Safe, Mrs O'Loughlin.'

Ciara and Mary-Marg walked through the village and back along Sea Road towards their houses. See The Stars night had been like time-travelling. At one point during the evening, Ciara had felt almost disorientated – the same music, the same lights, even the same faces, just a little older, that was all.

Otherwise, she and all of them could have been eighteen again... talking, dancing... and falling in love.

'We'll do it again,' said Mary-Marg. 'Next Friday. Just while Alice is here, and then we'll all go back to our boring ways again.' She squeezed Ciara's arm. 'Deal?'

'Deal.'

* * *

MARY-MARG 2.56 A.M.

> I can't sleep. Too much adrenaline. Going downstairs to take a Nighty Night.

MARY-MARG 3.23 A.M.

> Have just taken Nighty Night and sprayed myself liberally with my magnesium and lavender spray.

MARY-MARG 3.46 A.M.

> Brian is snoring loudly, as are Jake and Josh. About to bash my brains out with my magnesium and lavender spray.

MARY-MARG 4.06 A.M.

> It was a good night, though. Wasn't it?

CIARA 7.35 A.M.

> It was the best night ever. You are a superstar DJ. Next stop Ibiza! Love you!

23

ALICE

Murphy's Irish breakfast.

Start your day the patriotically delicious way with Irish tea and a slice of heavily buttered, home-made soda bread and jam – from the kitchen of Eva Murphy, available from 8 a.m. to 11 a.m. every morning from Murphy's, Church Street, Sandycove. Begins this Monday!

It was Sunday morning and Alice had posted on the newly launched 'Murphy's Sandycove' Instagram account. They already had one hundred followers in the first hour, which seemed surprising. But it was the weekend, and perhaps everyone was in bed, on their phones.

And then she rang Eva. 'I'm ready for my soda bread lesson now. Are you around?'

'Just back from my swim,' said Eva. 'Call up when you're ready.'

Eva was barefoot, her grey hair damp, wearing her towelling dressing gown.

'Gran, you look like a teenager,' said Alice, hugging her.

'It's amazing how shoes can make you seem more of a person,' said Eva. 'I think that's why the shoe was invented. To separate us from the animals. If you're wearing a shoe, you are civilised.'

'I think it's because walking on rocks all day is uncomfortable...'

'And ties,' went on Eva. 'The tie is another way of separating ourselves from the animals...'

'I suppose,' said Alice. 'Now, are you ready to make some soda bread? Teach me everything...'

They stood together in the kitchen, side by side, as they had done a thousand times before.

'So, about this much of flour, the same of wholemeal, a good drink of buttermilk, a teaspoon of bicarbonate, a scoop of honey...' Eva was saying, still in her dressing gown and bare feet. 'And give it a mix...'

Eva turned the dough out onto the work surface and began kneading it slightly. When Alice was little, she'd stand on a chair and help mix the bread or the cake, but this time, she took notes.

'I am now entrusting the family recipe to you,' said Eva. 'When I am gone, you need to keep making this because this is how my mother used to make it and hers before her...' She looked up at Alice, fixing her with those blue eyes. 'Promise me?'

'But you're not going anywhere...'

'Not quite yet...' There was that look again.

'Go on,' said Alice. 'What do you do now? You just shape it?'

She watched as Eva deftly formed the bread into a perfect round, sprinkling oats on the top.

Alice had watched and helped Eva make bread thousands of times, but it was just nice to spend time with her. She wanted to make the most of it. Soon, she'd be back in Australia and she'd miss this, just being with Eva, hearing her stories. Eva wasn't getting any younger and perhaps... one day... Alice stopped herself from thinking of a world without Eva in it.

'And now cut a cross into it and...' She slid the loaf into the oven and shut the door.

'And you can do six loaves for tomorrow morning at 8 a.m., for opening?' Alice's mind was already working. If they were ready for opening time, sliced with butter, jam or marmalade, and a cup of tea, perhaps some people would like it? Or if no one wanted it, it wasn't too much of a waste? Perhaps people wanted croissants and Danish pastries? Would customers want to go back to something more traditional and Irish? But she had spoken to plenty of Irish people while she was travelling and so many of them mentioned missing soda bread and proper Irish tea.

'I'm up at 5.30 a.m.,' said Eva confidently. 'I'll have everything ready.' She smiled at Alice. 'You know, I feel almost useful. George used to get me to bake my bread in the early days. I used to make twelve loaves every morning, so six is no bother... and then, people stopped wanting soda bread. They wanted a sliced pan, one made in a factory with all sorts added.'

'If they know what's good for them, they'll want soda bread, Gran,' said Alice, filling the kettle. 'You get dressed and I'll make us some tea.'

While the bread baked, they sat in the two armchairs in the big window which overlooked the street outside, and Eva began to read out clues from the crossword. But Alice's mind was elsewhere.

'Gran...?'

'Mmmm...' Eva didn't look up, the end of her pen in her mouth.

'Did you like Lorcan...?'

Eva's head was up. 'What did you say?'

'Lorcan. My father. Did you like him? He worked in the shop, didn't he?'

'It was a long time ago...' Eva watched Alice attentively, a strange look in her eye, as though she were wholly present but also thinking of something else entirely.

'Thirty years ago...' Alice smiled, hoping that if she kept the conversation light enough, Eva might tell her something – *anything* – about this man who had lived in the village, whom her mother had fallen in love with... and why he had left. No one ever talked about him and for years it hadn't mattered, but now it suddenly seemed important. Surely Eva might tell her *something*. Sometimes Alice felt like half a person, one side of her full of stories and generations going back, and the other side of her totally blank.

'George hired him,' said Eva, the newspaper in her lap. 'I didn't have anything to do with it.'

'How old was he?' Alice pressed, seeming more casual than she felt. 'You know, when he started working in the shop?'

'Oh, I don't know. Sixteen? Seventeen? He lived with his aunt in Sallynoggin and would cycle down to the shop and then George put him on deliveries.' She paused. 'He was a funny boy...'

'Funny?' Funny sounded good, thought Alice.

'Funny odd.'

Alice's heart sank a little. But at least Eva was telling her something about him. And odd, she supposed, could mean *interesting*.

'He wanted to be a poet,' Eva was saying. 'He would go

round reciting bits and pieces. You know, "Shall I compare thee" and all that...'

Alice nodded.

'He would read books aloud or sit in the back of the shop and talk to George about poetry. Talk *at* George, really. He was a great... what's the word? Pontificator.'

'Oh...' He sounded awful and pretentious. 'But was he nice? Kind? You know...'

'Nice? Well... George tolerated him well enough, and he was a great favourite of... some of the *female* customers.'

'Like who?'

'I couldn't possibly remember,' said Eva, clamming up again as she picked up her pen once more.

Alice realised that that was all she was going to get out of her.

The timer in the kitchen rang.

'The bread is calling,' said Eva, getting to her feet. 'It can't be a minute over or underdone... It has to be exact.'

Soon, they were sitting at the kitchen table, Alice buttering the piping hot bread and spooning on Eva's jam.

'So this is your new invention?' said Eva. 'The Irish breakfast?'

'Well, not an invention, but I just thought it would be nice... I think people are bored with coffee and a croissant...'

They chewed ruminantly. It was somehow sweet *and* savoury, The flavour was deeply resonant of days spent in warm kitchens, of grandmothers and childhood. More than anything, it was delicious, it all melted in your mouth, none of that clagginess of white bread.

'So, what do you think?' said Eva after a moment or two. 'Good enough to sell?'

'It's a triumph,' said Alice. 'And it tastes... It tastes of my childhood.'

Eva smiled. 'That's exactly what it's meant to taste like,' she said. 'It tastes of mine too.'

Alice felt inspired, all thoughts of oddball Lorcan dismissed. It was the shop she was most concerned for. 'Right,' she said, determined. 'Tomorrow we start!'

On her way home, she was stopped by Roz Sweetman, one of their regular customers.

'I read about the Irish breakfast on the old Instagram thing,' she said. 'I'll be in tomorrow, that is if I can haul myself out of bed. I like it in there too much. Becoming quite the hermit, just me and the dogs and not a man to be found. We wake early and I pop down and make a cup of tea and Enda and Kenny go outside, and then we all slink back upstairs again for tea and a snooze and a listen to the radio. Put me down for one of those Irish breakfasts in the morning, will you, Alice? And tell me, how was the disco? Pity I'm too young to go. I'm three months too young.'

24

CIARA

Monday was the inaugural day of the Irish breakfast and Ciara was carefully slicing the hot loaves which Eva had just delivered, still in her dressing gown. The heat radiated, the aroma filled the shop. Ciara had spent the previous day on the phone to everyone who had been to the disco, everyone sharing stories about the music, the atmosphere and how they felt the following day. All Alice could hear from Ciara was her laughing. 'I know, he didn't stop jumping. I thought the floor was going to cave in.' Or, 'it was inevitable that they would get together. They've had an eye on each other for thirty years.'

It was lovely to hear Ciara so giggly. Alice had never seen this side of her mother. And Mary-Marg had come round for dinner, bringing an array of sushi for them to have, and they filled Alice in on how the night had gone. Alice suspected that she wasn't told *everything* that had happened, but Ciara and Mary-Marg seemed so delighted.

'Everybody loved it, Alice,' Mary-Marg said, smiling. 'We're going to do it next Friday as well. The room's free. And everyone is up for it.'

'This brings me back,' Ciara said as she sliced the soda bread. 'I'm going to make sure we have some left over for us...'

Alice was feeling a bit nervous. She had enslaved her grandmother into making an incredible amount of bread, just to fulfil some silly idea she had to bring more revenue into the shop. Just when Eva should be taking it easy, she was putting her to work. And what if no one wanted it?

But Eva was already back down from the flat, this time dressed, with her swim bag over her shoulder, eagerly observing the preparations. 'It's not too crumbly, is it?' she said, peering over Ciara's shoulder.

'It's the perfect amount of crumbly,' said Ciara. 'There's the optimum amount of crumble.'

Eva nodded. 'Grand, so,' she said, heading for the back of the shop to leave from the courtyard. 'I'm off for my swim. I'll see you girls later.'

When she was gone, Alice turned to Ciara. 'If people really like soda bread and butter, then why are *French* pastries so popular?'

'We'll have to wait and see,' said Ciara. 'I've come up with so many ideas over the years and some have worked and some have failed. The shop is doing well, it really is. I can't complain... but sometimes, I think I'm running out of steam.'

'You only have visions of disco balls in your head,' said Alice.

At 7.55 a.m., five minutes to opening time, there was a knock on the front door. A face loomed through the glass, mouthing something.

'It's Aoife Dolan,' said Ciara, rushing forward to open the door. 'She's probably on her way back from the Forty Foot. She likes to be there before anyone else. She likes swimming in the dark.' She unlocked the door at the top and at the bottom and Aoife nearly tumbled in.

'...mmfffhhmssshhh breafffast...' was all that Alice managed to hear.

'Of course!' Ciara was saying, giving Alice a delighted look. 'It's all ready. It's raspberry jam on soda bread and a cup of Barry's tea... All right with you?'

Aoife was nodding. 'I saw the ad on the Instantgram last night and I went to bed, dreaming of it. I remember Eva's bread from when I was young... I try to make my own, but it's never as good as hers. It used to melt in my mouth...' Aoife's nose was twitching at the bready aroma.

'It still does,' said Ciara, slipping back behind the counter. 'Aoife, you remember Alice, don't you? She's home for a few weeks from Australia...'

'Ah, Alice!' said Aoife. 'Of course I remember Alice, although it's a long time since you've been back. Perth, isn't it? Well, you're very welcome home, now you're finally here... And isn't it great that your mother and grandmother are still so busy, the two of them. That's what had me so addled this morning, I was thinking, they are going to run out of those Irish breakfasts... so I thought I would rush down and try to be first...'

Just as she was speaking, someone else came in. 'Have you got those Irish breakfast things...?' the woman said, just as the bell above the door rang again.

'Irish breakfast, please...' It was a man, dressed in a suit.

'I'll make the teas,' said Ciara to Alice, 'you slice more bread.'

Alice buttered and jammed lavishly, wrapped them in greaseproof paper and then slid them into a paper bag, along with a couple of napkins. She handed them over, along with a tea each, as Ciara rang the money into the till.

And the customers kept coming, a queue which kept being added to, in an ever-evolving line. Ciara was doing everything so efficiently and swiftly, and she also managed to have a chat with everyone, making sure that they were all well taken care of.

'Don't be stinting on the butter, now, will you?' said one man. 'Need my sustenance.'

'If there's one person who doesn't need any more butter, 'tis you, Mikey Fitzpatrick,' said someone else, making everyone laugh.

And as people were coming in, they were leaving with more than just the Irish breakfast, they were adding a few things to their order, a packet of coffee here, a jar of olives or a bar of chocolate there. One woman even bought one of Conal's beers. 'For later this evening,' she assured them. 'I'm not one of *those*.'

For the next hour and a half, the door kept ringing as people came into the shop asking for the Irish breakfast, until all that was left were a slice or two and mainly crumbs, and the beginnings of repetitive strain injury for Alice from all the bread-slicing.

Finally, at 9 a.m., when the queue had dwindled, along with the bread supplies, Alice and Ciara looked at each other, delighted.

'Well, that was a successful first morning,' said Ciara. 'Shall we try it for the rest of the week, and then see if it's still popular?'

Alice nodded. 'I'm going to make the bread as well, so we can have twice as many. I'll make a few for the morning.'

'We'll keep it going until you leave,' said Ciara. 'It's a nice summer treat.'

They drank their tea behind the counter, Alice leaning against the back wall, Ciara sitting on the stepladder, and they discussed the world of retail, a topic which Alice was finding increasingly fascinating. By her bed were a pile of library books, one which was called *The Power of Shopping Local*, from which she was taking copious notes. She and Ciara talked earnestly about the importance of having the right stock and in the right amounts, the idea of the 'star product', as well as well-priced essentials.

'No one seems to want sliced pan any more,' Ciara was saying. 'People are coffee-obsessed. We can't sell enough of artisan, freshly ground, one estate, Ethiopian, Kenyan... whatever.'

Alice nodded, thinking about how tastes changed and what exactly influenced them. Her eye fell on the display of Conal's beer.

'Mum, what happened between Gran and Dol Blake?'

'I'm not sure...' There was an airy quality to Ciara's voice, as she too looked around the shop, as though her mind were elsewhere. 'There's a cobweb,' she said. 'In the corner... I'll need to go and get—'

'I've never heard Gran talk like that about someone,' pressed Alice. 'She made it out that Dol Blake was truly horrible... What do you think? Did you meet her? You were friends with Paddy...'

Ciara was reaching for the broom and began to poke it into the top corner of the shop, beside the high shelves on the right. 'No,' she said, clambering on top of the small stepladder. 'She's not *truly* horrible... just horrible.'

'You don't often meet people who don't care what you think of them,' said Alice. 'Most people want everyone to like them.

Even the not very nice ones manage to hide it for long enough. But she didn't care.'

'No,' said Ciara, the handle of the broom in her hands, the brush part swiping at the cobweb until it was hooked, and she stepped down. 'No, she doesn't care. Never did. Never will.'

'But Paddy and Conal... they're good people?'

Ciara nodded. 'Paddy definitely is,' she said, poking at the cobweb with the broom. 'Conal takes after him.'

'But what did Dol *do* to Gran?'

'Perhaps Gran just had enough of her,' said Ciara with a shrug. 'It's allowed, you know, you move on from friends. Maybe Gran preferred Maeve, Dorrie and Angela?'

She looked up as another customer arrived in. '...Breakfast?' he asked hopefully.

'We're all out,' Ciara said. 'Sorry. More tomorrow. Promise. It's been so popular...'

At 9.30 a.m., Eva returned from her morning swim. 'I'm here for my Irish breakfast,' she said brightly. 'I'm ravenous.'

Ciara was already reaching below the counter, producing a plate. 'I saved you some, Mam,' she said. 'Here we go. You sit here with us and I'll make you a cup of tea. How was the water this morning?'

'It's like winter, some days,' said Eva, sitting down on the old wooden chair, in the gap that led to the back room. 'But they say that's when it's best for you, and you have to take their word for it, don't you? Whoever "they" are. But there was a current which was like being grabbed and pulled down by a sea monster.'

'That sounds horrible, Gran,' said Alice, shuddering.

'Oh, it was wonderful,' said Eva, happily. 'I kicked it away and pulled up to the surface.' She took the plate and the cup from Ciara. 'Thank you, loveen,' she said.

'It's one of your best loaves, Mam,' said Ciara. 'I tasted it earlier. Melts in the mouth.'

'As it's meant to,' said Eva, taking a bite, and chewing it before nodding. 'Not bad. Not as good as my own mother's or my grandmother's, but then it never is. We can only do our best.'

'Alice said she was going to make a few loaves for tomorrow,' said Ciara. 'Pressure's on, Alice.'

'It won't be as good as Gran's,' Alice said.

'It might be,' said Eva, after drinking her tea. 'There's no reason why it wouldn't.'

Alice felt a warm glow quicken through her. Perhaps it was being with the two people she loved and trusted more than anyone else in the world? It was almost tangible how much they loved her and how much confidence they had in her, but more than anything it was because they wanted her to be better than they were. It was that generosity of spirit, that lack of ego, that they wanted her to shine, that made her feel so loved. And she loved them back. This shared enterprise of the Irish breakfast had them all invested, as though they were on a team together.

The bell jangled and Max walked in. 'Morning, Murphy ladies,' he said.

'Morning, Max,' they chorused as Ciara turned to the coffee machine.

'Usual, Max?' she asked over her shoulder.

'No,' he said, 'I'm here for the Irish breakfast...' He looked at their faces. 'No! Don't tell me, I'm too *late*?'

They all nodded.

'Apparently, it was a feeding frenzy,' said Eva. 'Like the sea lions in Dublin zoo.'

'Or piranhas,' said Ciara.

'It was the smell of Gran's bread,' said Alice. 'Drew them all in...'

Max looked crestfallen. 'I was really looking forward to it.'

'We'll keep some for you for in the morning,' promised Alice.

'Will you?' He looked delighted. 'Thank you, Alice.'

'Who would have thought people could be so enthused by soda bread, butter, jam and tea?' said Eva.

'Who wouldn't be?' said Max. 'It's the taste of home... My father's mother was pretty good at bread. Put caraway seeds in hers...' He paused. 'But isn't it great that Alice's plan worked?'

Ciara turned to Alice, smiling. 'Yes, she seems to have a head for business...'

'No, I don't! I just knew the one thing I missed more than anything living in Perth was Gran's bread.'

'Alice has lots of innovations,' went on Ciara. 'The cheese fridge now makes sense.'

Alice had organised it from strong to mild, from Cashel or Crozier Blue to crumbly Ardrahan, and she had also divided it between goat's, ewe's and cow's cheese. If somebody wanted a decent selection for a cheeseboard, they could just take one from each section. She'd even hung up a framed picture of the perfect cheeseboard.

Ciara smiled at Alice. 'I think you might have the grocer genes in you...'

'Maybe I do...' Again, that glowy feeling, as though the universe were trying to tell her something. Last year, Sebastian had discovered astrology and went on and on about the universe and how it had a plan for you. He delivered monologues about how we were all connected and how it was all written in the stars. What was written in the stars, decided

Alice, was that she and Sebastian would part company. But now, here in Murphy's, she felt an undeniable sense that all was well with the world.

'She takes after her grandfather,' said Eva. 'He was always coming up with new ideas. I tell you what used to go down very well with the local children, George came up with it. He called them surprise bags… they were only 2p at the time, but they might have had a balloon or a whistle and a paper twist of sweets. The children loved them because you never knew what you were going to get. Do you remember, Ciara? George used to make them up on a Friday night because most children, if they got pocket money, would come in on Saturday morning and ask for a surprise bag. There was one little boy who never got any pocket money, even though he was from a very well-to-do family, and George used to give him a free surprise bag. George was like that, heart of gold.'

Ciara was nodding as she placed the coffee on the counter in front of Max. 'He was… but who was the child without pocket money?'

'Oh, I can't remember his name now,' said Eva, airily. 'It was all so long ago…'

Max picked up his coffee and his paper-bagged croissant. 'Well, goodbye all… may business be brisk and the cash floweth liberally.'

Eva and Ciara both laughed. 'Same to you,' said Ciara.

'George used to say, *May the gods of commerce smile upon us once again*. And do you know something, they always did. Now, if you would excuse me, I think I will have a little potter at home and then do some gardening.'

The rest of the day was a succession of over-forty-fives who either had been to the disco – 'Best night I've had in years' – or those who'd missed out – 'I'm raging, so I am.' All, however, were already buying tickets for the next one. And all enquired about the Irish breakfast. Ciara and Alice grinned at each other. Whatever they were doing seemed to be working, and best of all, they were having fun.

25

ALICE

In the evening, Alice and Becca were in The Island, having a quiet drink, just the two of them.

'Conal's on a marketing trip,' Becca explained. 'He's gone to Galway and to Cork and Limerick, meeting with bars and shops.' She paused. 'I hope he's okay. He hasn't texted me today. Or yesterday.'

'He's just busy, I'm sure.'

Becca nodded. 'Yes…'

Alice told her about how well the Irish breakfast had gone. 'I'm going to be up really early to make the bread, so Gran doesn't have to make so much. And I have another idea. Friday night hampers. Wine tasting…' All these ideas were bubbling up inside her, nothing that would cost too much, but ways to bring more people into the shop. 'I thought we could have an evening. Get some kind of bow-tied wine genius in to explain about it all. Mum could recommend some cheeses…'

'And beer tasting,' said Becca, immediately. 'Conal could come along and tell everyone about his beer…'

Alice nodded. 'And I could do nibbles.' She felt quite excited. 'Even if just one or two people turned up, it would be nice...' She had thought of it earlier as she had rearranged some of the wine bottles. Ciara had organised them by country, but it was a bewildering mix of countries, grapes, colours. Perhaps, Alice had been thinking, it would be better to have far fewer wines and remove the decision-making pressure. Small and select. The same idea could be replicated with the cheese section. Make it more bespoke...

'I can assist, be in charge of the corkscrew, the slicing of the cheese... the...' Becca faltered as she couldn't quite think of what else the evening might consist of and therefore what assistance might be required. 'Catching the corks as they pop off?'

'I don't think we'll be doing champagne,' said Alice. 'Just inexpensive, drinkable wine...'

'And beer,' Becca reminded her.

'Who will be our wine expert?' said Alice. 'We can't have anyone pretentious. We don't want someone going on about grass in the nose...'

'Someone could have hay fever,' said Becca seriously. 'They wouldn't be able to drink any of it.' But then her face clouded over, suddenly.

'Everything all right?' asked Alice, worried.

Becca nodded and then shook her head. 'I am just feeling really insecure about Conal. He's been a little distracted lately. Just looking off into the distance. Not so chatty.' She looked at Alice. 'Has he said anything about me?'

'Like what?'

'Like if he's not interested.' Becca looked agonised. 'I just wondered if he had confided in you and said that he's gone off me, or was never on me, or... I don't know...'

'He hasn't said anything...'

Becca threw her hands up in the air. 'You see! That's the problem. He doesn't think of me. And he's thinking of me less than he did think of me, which wasn't very much thinking of me in the first place!' She dragged her hands down her face, pulling the flesh of her cheeks downwards as though in a German expressionist silent film. 'He hates me.'

'He doesn't! He likes you!'

'But he's gone quiet on me. I haven't heard from him for thirty-six hours...' She checked her phone. 'Thirty-six hours and forty-two minutes...'

'He's busy...'

'I *think* he likes me... but he's so busy with the business... and I know that I'm busy with Happy Paws, but it's just that I want to see him all the time. And he does other things. Like swimming at the Forty Foot.' She glanced at Alice, quickly. 'He's so different to Julian, who acted like he hated me but wanted me around all the time, and then Conal acts as though he likes me but doesn't see me all the time...'

'I think that sounds better than Julian...' Alice paused. 'Although Hannibal Lecter would be better than Julian. At least he knew his wine...'

But Becca wasn't listening. 'He's too nice for me... I don't know what to do with nice.'

'That's ridiculous... and impossible...'

'But I like him... *really* like him. Not only did I not *love* Julian...'

'Who could?'

'...I didn't even *like* him...'

Alice smiled at Becca. 'Conal seems to like you back, so I wouldn't worry.'

'I know my self-esteem is in need of an overhaul. I need to

go to some kind of weekend where you hug trees and bare your soul... It's just that—'

'You *should* have sky-high self-esteem,' interrupted Alice. 'You have your own business. You're beautiful. Intelligent. A nice person...'

Becca looked at Alice. 'Fran Egan said she saw you and Conal looking very happy at the Forty Foot... you were *laughing*, apparently... She said you looked – and I quote – "very cosy" together.'

'Becca, *nothing* is going on... I am not remotely interested in him in that way...'

'So he's not fanciable...?'

'Not to me, no. Becca, I can't believe you would listen to Fran Egan. Do you honestly think that anything would happen? I mean...' She was lost for words for a moment. 'Who do you take me for?'

'I know! I know! But Fran was so insistent.' Becca's eyes were filled with tears. 'She said I had to say something and that if it were her, she would be reading her boyfriend the riot act, but I don't even know what the riot act is...'

'I think you just rant and rail a bit,' said Alice. 'Look, I would have no interest in him in that way, but we get on well...'

'I *want* you to get on well!' said Becca.

'And I like him...'

'I *want* you to like him!'

'But I could *never* fancy him...'

'Why?' Becca looked outraged for a moment. 'What's *wrong* with him?'

'He's not my type.' Alice smiled at her. 'Not remotely. But it doesn't mean he isn't nice and good-looking... He's just right for you, not me.'

Becca was smiling again. 'I knew I shouldn't listen to Fran Egan.'

'Look, I went for a swim. I bumped into Conal. We had a really nice chat, he told me about his love of dinosaurs...'

'He's obsessed,' said Becca. 'I think he would marry one, if he could, rather than me...'

'You want to *marry* him?'

Becca was blushing. 'I might do...'

Alice laughed. 'Why didn't you just say, then? We have to make it happen!'

'But how? He's building a business, he's got a lot to think about...'

There was something so sweetly innocent about Conal and she sensed that he needed someone to talk to as though he still had things to work out and he wasn't ready to burden Becca with it all. 'I think he just needs to talk to someone, and maybe it's easier to talk to me, who doesn't know him.'

'Yeah... you're right.' Becca smiled at Alice. 'I'm sorry, okay? Why did I listen to that Fran Egan? Can we just forget about it?' said Becca. 'I'm sorry... I think I'm going crazy...'

'You've fallen in love,' said Alice. 'It's a nice thing. And I get it about Conal, I really do. I know it seems weird but I promise you, it's not. I wonder if it's because he lost a mother and I had something similar with my father? He seems to need people to talk to. But he's your boyfriend and I *promise* you...' She laughed at the absurdity of liking Conal more than a friend, 'he's not *remotely* my type.'

'That's true. You're into hot Jesus types like Sebastian.'

Alice shook her head. 'No, I think I might be into geeky men who have a quirky sense of humour...'

Becca thought hard for a moment. 'We need to find you one

of those. We'll put an ad in the Newsletter. Geeky, quirky type wanted.' She paused. 'God knows where we'd find one.'

'Yeah... they're thin on the ground,' said Alice, knowing exactly where one of those would be found and wishing she weren't going back to Australia quite so soon.

26

CIARA

In the evening, instead of staying in, Ciara put on her trainers and headed out. She didn't exactly power up Killiney Hill, but she kept a steady – if slow – pace, thinking about the Friday night and how much fun everyone seemed to have had.

Just as she was about to cross over to the grassy embankment and up to the meadow, she saw Paddy Blake running from the other direction, about to turn right into the park. He raised his hand and came towards her, removing his earbuds.

'How was the disco?' he said, not quite smiling. 'I heard it was a triumph.'

She nodded. 'It was great... you would have enjoyed yourself.'

'I'm glad it went well.' He was about to move on when she spoke again.

'We're having another one, this Friday... it's only a laugh... no pressure to be cool or anything like that...'

'Yeah, maybe...' He was looking at her, a slight smile on his face. 'You don't want to... you know... run together again? It's nice to have company...'

'I'd love to. But not fast. Okay?'

He laughed. 'As slow as you like.'

They jogged across the meadow, making straight for the top of the hill, not talking to each other, but just slowly and steadily making the climb. Even though she knew they must be going so much slower than his usual pace, Paddy didn't seem to mind. But that was the kind of person he'd always been. She remembered him being so nice to his mother, who was just the worst kind of person, always bossing everyone and giving out, griping and moaning. She'd look you up and down, see what you were wearing. But it wasn't done in a nice way. Dol looked at you as though you were competition.

The gang would go back to Paddy's because the summer house in the garden was the perfect hang-out. They'd drink, talk and mess around, they'd tell each other secrets. Once, Paddy told them that the only person in the world he was scared of was his mother.

'Nearly there,' said Paddy as they pushed on. If it weren't for Paddy, Ciara would have given up long ago, she would already have been back at home. And then, there it was. The view. All of Dublin and the coast spread out below them, people reduced to ants on the golden beach below, the yachts in the glittering bay now toy boats, the mountains, mere hills.

Ciara and Paddy flopped onto the bench, their backs against the wall, Ciara's lungs three times larger than when she'd started out, her breathing like that of a drowning woman.

Another memory. That time, outside Landfall, when she'd run to the road and her legs gave way, the world slipping into slow motion as she crumpled to her knees, trying to breathe. Her hands were on the pavement, she on all fours, trying to just get a breath in, wondering if she, at the age of nineteen, was going to die, right there, right then, with her unborn child inside her.

Oh God, it had been terrible. It was a hot afternoon, and the ground was warm and she had focused on a small ladybird which was walking along the ground beside her right hand. It was so small and so tiny... and so beautiful and perfectly formed. She had breathed in again, and this time it was deeper, and again deeper, and again a little more...

'Water?' Paddy passed over his water bottle.

'Thank you...'

'It's... it's good that we're talking and everything...' He was blushing a little and she immediately recognised the old Paddy, that gorgeous schoolboy who was both super confident and also someone who didn't quite know where he fitted in the world.

'It *is* good...' She wanted to say more. The longing inside her to make everything all right, to wish it all away, was like a deep twist within her. 'It's nice, actually.' She smiled at him.

'Yeah?' He looked surprised.

'Of course it is,' she said. 'I missed you... we were all such good friends. I didn't mean... I didn't want to lose a friend...'

'Nor did I... but it happened. It's been... it's been...' He cleared his throat. 'It's been a lonely enough old road.'

'For me too...' They looked at each other for a moment. Oh, poor Paddy. It had been worse for him with all that had happened, with Dol for a mother and Breda leaving.

'Has it?' he said.

She nodded. 'I always thought that when Alice left home I'd be able to do the things I hadn't had a chance to, but it turned out I'd lost any of the skills I thought I had. Socialising, for one.'

'Me too,' he said with feeling. 'I can barely talk to anyone.

Small talk is near impossible and talking about anything important is completely beyond me. That's why I run. Can't stop and chat...' He laughed.

'We're managing it all right, aren't we?'

He gave her a half-smile, looking into her face. 'Yeah... yeah... we are.'

She had always loved being with Paddy. Back in the old days, when they were young and free of worry and responsibility, he was the kind of person who made everything all right. One time, Lorcan had disappeared when he was meant to be meeting her and she couldn't find him, and it was Paddy who listened to her tearful worries about how he'd perhaps been run over, or attacked and left for dead. She had guessed where Lorcan had gone now, of course. But all those times, Paddy had been there, someone to talk to, to sort things out. He had taught her to drive because he was the first to get his licence and he once brought a few of them to Newgrange, and those were the days when you could park outside. On midsummer's day, the rising sun would suddenly hit the entrance, the shaft moving along the tunnel, and illuminate the inner chamber. It was one of the wonders of the world, one of those places which no one can quite explain but takes your breath away.

Lorcan stayed back in Sandycove and it was just Paddy, Mary-Marg and a couple of others who walked over the fields to the megalithic tomb and slipped through the stone entrance, and along the narrow tunnel until they arrived in the chamber. That day, it was pitch dark and for the first time in her life, Ciara thought she was going to have a panic attack. But just as she was trying to keep her breathing steady, she felt a soft, warm hand reach for hers, his fingers around hers, and her breathing slowed, her heart rate calmed and she stood in the dark, contemplating the wonder of that place, how thousands of years ago, people built this temple to the sun.

Wasn't that what we all wanted, she thought now, sitting here with Paddy, a way of capturing the sun? Didn't we all want our worlds to be full of light, even just for a moment?

'Do you remember Newgrange?' she said.

He nodded, smiling. 'Of course. What a place.'

'It really is.' She wondered if he remembered him holding her hand or if he'd ever thought about it, even at the time. He'd probably done it without thinking and hadn't given it another thought.

'We should...' He stopped abruptly and changed the subject. 'So you loved the disco?'

'Amazing. It was such good fun. Everyone was there...'

He looked away. 'Those were good days, weren't they?' he said.

'They were.'

'It's great for everyone to let their hair down.'

'We're just trying to bring back a bit of fun to the lives of the over-forty-fives in Sandycove... It's part of our midlife crisis.' She laughed.

'Beats buying a sports car or giving up on life.'

'Which are you?' Ciara tried to keep her voice light. 'The sports car or the giving up?'

'Well...' He paused. 'I don't drive a sports car...'

'No...' They looked at each other for a moment and again she thought of his hand reaching for hers in the dark. 'Are you going to come to the next See The Stars?' she asked, sounding brighter than she felt. 'It might be fun?'

'Maybe...' He smiled at her. 'You and Mary-Marg were always so great together. The two of you brought out the best in each other. I'm glad you're still so close.'

'I couldn't have done any of the last thirty years without her. And Mam, obviously.'

And then Ciara spoke, gently. 'Who was looking after you?'

He shook his head. 'It's different for men,' he said. 'We just get on with it.' He looked as though he were trying to work out how much to say or how much she knew. Perhaps they both knew all of it, thought Ciara.

'Do you?' she said.

'No... of course we don't. We just wish we did.' He sighed. 'Breda leaving. That was tough. I didn't blame her and I couldn't stop her. She was right to go.' He leant his head back against the wall and looked up at the sky. 'What about you, the shop? All going well?'

'I need a break... I just need something else, you know?'

He nodded. 'Tell me about it...'

'I don't know who I am any more... I know I've been so lucky. But I wouldn't mind something else... another chapter...'

Paddy was nodding. 'Me too,' he said. 'I'm fifty. What else is out there for me? I've felt trapped for so long...'

'Do you mean Conal?'

'Oh, not Conal...' He looked anguished for a moment. 'Never Conal. God, none of this is his fault... but I have to face up to my own part in all this...' Paddy seemed to be rambling a little.

'Would you sell Blake's Beer?' Ciara suggested gently. 'Or is there something else you need to do?'

'Oh, I don't know...' He looked at her then, and there was something in his eyes that made her grasp that something was going on, something darker and so much bigger than both of them. And in that moment, she was almost sure she now understood what it was. And she had known ever since that moment she was on that pavement, looking at that ladybird, trying to breathe.

'Do you want to talk to me about it?' she asked. 'Or whenever it suits you... you know where I am...' She gave a weird laugh. 'I'm not going anywhere. For now.'

'Thanks... I appreciate it.' He stood up. 'Shall we get back? I'll run you home.'

They smiled at each other, and she wondered if what she thought was true really was. And if she would ever be able to tell him what she knew.

* * *

Back home, Alice was in the living room, under Ciara's blanket, watching another episode of *Mörda*. 'Budge up,' Ciara said, squeezing onto the sofa next to her. 'This is such a good episode and I wouldn't mind watching it again.'

Alice tucked the blanket around Ciara, and Ciara slipped her arm through Alice's, and they snuggled down together.

Alice squeezed her arm. 'It's so nice to be home,' she said.

Ciara squeezed her back. 'It's so lovely having you home.' She paused. 'Even just for a short while.'

'I didn't realise how enjoyable working in the shop is.' She laughed. 'No offence.'

'No, I get it. And it is enjoyable. Running your own business, being your own boss, making your own rules... Don't get me wrong, it's hard work, it's stressful... but sometimes, when I am locking up the shop for the evening, I have this feeling inside me, this kind of glow...'

'I've been getting it!' said Alice excitedly.

Ciara smiled at Alice as she pressed 'play' again, her eyes

back on the screen, flinching as a body of a man was discovered in an industrial bin at the back of an Ikea store. 'It's brilliant,' she breathed, clutching Ciara's arm again. 'I can see why you're addicted.'

27

ALICE

The following afternoon, her phone buzzed. A text from Conal.

CONAL
> Heading down to the Forty Foot later. Do you fancy it?

ALICE
> Great! I could meet you there? 4 p.m.?

She understood that Becca had concerns, but she knew there was nothing between her and Conal. Despite them being of similar ages, he seemed so much younger than she was, and she knew he was struggling with a few things, as though he were trying – and failing – to gain an understanding or a perspective on his childhood and his mother's departure. It took time, Alice knew. She hadn't a clue what to think about her own father and why he had left too.

Just before 4 p.m., Alice left Ciara in the shop and, with her swim things in her bag, she walked down to the Forty Foot. The weather was bright and warm, the sky blue, but there was a crisp wind which buffeted the waves, making the world seem to roll and roil. The bathers in the water were being swashed around within the undulating swell.

Conal was sitting on the edge of the changing area, staring out to sea.

'Do we really want to get in there?' Alice asked as she walked towards him.

'It's definitely choppy,' he said. 'But it's a metaphor for life, isn't it?' He grinned at her.

'But I don't want to swim in metaphors...'

He laughed. 'It's bracing. Is that better? We don't live in the Maldives so this is as good as it's going to get. Come on, let's have a sauna first and then throw ourselves in. I need a swim. It's all been a bit manic lately. And I'm trying to renew my passport because I'm going to a trade fair in Paris for Irish food producers. But I can't get all my documents. I can't just renew my passport, it seems, but I don't know why. I spent all day yesterday on the phone to the Department of Foreign Affairs and they couldn't help me.'

Alice changed quickly and then, with her towel around her, they raced up to the sauna and crept in the door. Inside were some of the ladies who'd bought their Irish breakfast at Murphy's the last two mornings.

'Well hello, Alice,' said a voice through the steam. 'It's Alice Murphy,' she said. 'Eva Murphy's young one.'

'Ah Alice,' said another voice. Her face emerging from the mist like a tanker at dawn was Philomena Burke, and then her sister Sheila. 'How's it going? You'll have to make more bread every morning... I had the last slice yesterday.'

Alice peered at them. 'Oh, hello, Sheila... Philomena...'

'So you're a sea swimmer now, are you?' said Philomena. 'It's like a drug, isn't it, Sheila? The two of us like addicts, we are, like taking the *old cocaine*...'

Sheila nodded sagely. 'That's right,' she said. 'We need our swim, so we do. If we don't have it, we get fierce cranky. Philomena particularly.'

Philomena nodded proudly. 'It's getting worse as I get older. Sweet Mary and Joseph, being able to be cranky and not all sweetness and light is the best thing about being old. And people don't mind it... they *want* you to be cranky...'

Beside Alice, Conal had started to laugh. She could feel his body shaking as he slipped further down the pine-slatted benches to where the steam was heavier.

'And who's this with you?' Sheila leant closer to see Conal, who was now so low down that all that was visible were the curls on the top of his head.

'This is a friend of mine, Conal Blake,' said Alice, and Conal had to sit up and straighten his face.

'Now, would you be a Blake from Blake's Beer?' said Philomena. 'Anything to do with Dolores Blake?'

'She's my grandmother,' said Conal, who had calmed himself down a little.

'Is she now...?' The two women looked at each other and then Philomena turned back to Conal. 'And how is she, after the stroke and everything? We heard she was in a bad way. We knew her from school. She always had the best clothes, didn't she, Sheil? Like a model she was. Always dressed to the nines. Even for Mass. Although she wasn't much of a Mass goer, was she? Just Christmas and Easter.'

'She's doing okay,' said Conal. 'She's in Honeysuckle Lodge now...'

'Assisted living, they call it now,' said Sheila to Philomena. 'I like the sound of that... living with assistance. We do that, don't we, Phil. Live with a sister?' She cackled suddenly.

'I'm going to see her later,' said Conal. 'I can pass on your best wishes.'

'Oh, will you?' Philomena gave him a toothy smile. 'Tell her that Phil and Sheila Burke say hello.'

'Shall we go and get into the sea?' said Alice to Conal. 'Bye, ladies, see you for breakfast on Monday...'

'Bye, Alice, say hello to your grandmother as well,' said Sheila. 'She wasn't much of a Mass goer either. I don't recall ever seeing her there.'

'Not even on the big days,' said Philomena.

Once in the cool air, Conal and Alice raced along the rocks and just as they jumped in, Conal grabbed her hand and the two of them pushed up into the air and then curved into the sea, sploshing down. Again, there was no coldness, just this delicious, indescribable feeling and total and utter well-being. Alice plunged down and, for a moment, she felt the rocky floor beneath her feet and then she pushed up and surfaced, just beside Conal.

'Good, isn't it?' he said, shaking the water from his head.

'It's amazing.' They grinned at each other in the water and then spent a little while floating, allowing themselves to be carried up and down with the swells. She stared up at the sky, the sound of the people on the shore muffled, the seagulls overhead, and she thought how different beach life was here in Ireland, compared to Australia. Here was colder and you might think, worse. But there was something to be said for cold water on a warmish day, as opposed to warm water on a broiling day. It was just so much more invigorating, and to be invigorated was exciting.

Conal swam up to her. 'Do you want to come and see my grandmother with me? She took a real shine to you...'

'*Really?*'

He laughed. 'Okay, let me rephrase that. *Will* you come and see my grandmother with me? I need some moral support. I'm taking Becca out to dinner later but I just thought... if you were free, we might just quickly pop in to see Dol?'

Alice nodded, not minding that she was being used as a human shield, and as little as she desired to see Dol Blake, she felt strangely protective of Conal.

'Of course, I will,' she said. 'I'd love to.'

'You would?' He looked relieved. 'Come on, I'll drive.'

28

ALICE

The door of Honeysuckle Lodge was answered by a woman in a cerise trouser suit and matching lipstick, which was both on her lips and her teeth when she smiled.

'Ah, Conal,' she said, stepping aside so they could enter. 'You're so good, you are. Such a lovely grandson...'

'Not really,' said Conal, smiling back. 'Abigail, this is Alice Murphy...'

'Of course it is,' said the woman, taking Alice's hand and clutching it to her chest, 'don't we all know the Murphys. I went to school with your mam, Ciara. And my own father would have known your grandfather, George. My father was Paddy the milkman, used to always stop off and have a chat with George. Lovely man. Loved his wife, Dad used to say, couldn't do enough for her. I remember him telling me of the day he brought her home after their wedding. Had the whole shop decked out in bunting and everyone on the street, all the shopkeepers and workers, all stood and clapped. My dad was there and said he did a figure of eight in his old milk-cart in front of Murphy's. He had some stories about Sandycove in those days. Says everyone pulled together, more than now. Although people aren't too bad now, are they?' She released Alice's hand finally. 'Now, Conal,' she went on, 'you know your grandmother. Her mood is as cantankerous today...'

'When is it not?' said Conal.

'Oh, we love our more cantankerous residents,' said Abigail. 'I think they have earned the right to be cantankerous, don't you?' She smiled. 'I just think it's important to warn people about the reception they might be facing. Now, you know where you're going? Lovely to meet you, Alice. Say hello to your mother, will you?'

Alice followed Conal and they passed what looked like a day room, lined with books and filled with long sofas and easy chairs, and up a flight of stairs, and along the corridor where they stopped in front of a door.

Conal took in a deep breath, his hand about to knock. He seemed to be bracing himself for the Spanish Inquisition or, worse, for the job interviews on *The Apprentice*. 'Thanks for coming with me...' he whispered. 'It's easier with someone else...'

'So why do you come?' Alice whispered back.

'Because she's my grandmother. And if Dad and I don't come, no one will see her. I have to do it for Dad, to support him. He's given me everything. Minded me. Been nice to Dol, even though she treats him like he's nothing. When Mum left, Dad had to cope with everything. And so I come for him. And anyway, we're all Dol has got. The thought of her being on her own is awful...'

Alice nodded. Anyone on their own, however dreadful, would play on your conscience.

'I've always seen her like some kind of medieval queen,' he

went on, 'you know, she would hang, draw and quarter you at first light...'

'And tarring and feathering?'

'That too...' He was smiling now.

'And throw you to the lions? Throw boiling oil over you?'

'All of it. Definitely.'

'Come on,' she said. 'Let's go in. We're here now.'

He nodded and knocked on the door.

'Dol?' he said. 'She never wanted me to call her Grandmother,' he explained to Alice in a low voice. 'Dol?' he said again. 'It's me, Conal.'

There was a sound from inside the room. And then a little bell was rung. 'That means we are to go in,' he said to Alice. Gingerly, he pushed open the door and half-stepped inside. 'I've brought a friend of mine with me...' There was the sound of a voice, which Alice couldn't make out. 'It's Alice Murphy,' he said. 'You met her at my birthday, remember? You talked to her in the drawing room?' Dol spoke again and Conal turned to Alice. 'You're to come in.'

The room was a fair size, with two large nearly-floor-length windows, a walnut bed and matching wardrobe. There was also a small dining table and one chair, as well as silver-framed photographs on the mantelpiece. A half-open door led to what looked like an en suite, and there were some books on a small bookcase beside the armchair which faced one of the windows and where Dol Blake was sitting. She was dressed in a long blue dress, almost the kind you would wear to a dinner dance. Her white hair was held back with a diamanté clip and on her feet, she was wearing a pair of ballet slippers. It was a little bizarre, thought Alice, but she looked warm and comfortable, which was all that mattered.

Her manner was, as before and as Conal had predicted, less

than warm or comfortable. She allowed Conal to kiss her on the cheek before looking at Alice.

'Hello, Mrs Blake,' said Alice, holding out her hand to shake Dol's. It was as claw-like as before, and actually not like a bird's – it was bonier and scalier, like a pterodactyl's claw.

'Did your grandmother send you?' Dol asked.

'No,' said Alice as she and Conal stood a little awkwardly, 'I just came with Conal...'

'Shall we sit down, Dol?' said Conal. 'I'll pull over this chair. You take it, Alice...' He placed the dining chair in front of Dol's chair and unfolded a plastic chair from behind the door. 'So, how have you been, Dol?' said Conal with forced brightness. 'How is life in Honeysuckle Lodge?'

'Less than satisfactory.' Dol shrugged. 'The tea is always cold. All the others seem to do is sing. There's a dreadful choir. And I was invited to join in a game of bridge, which is really not for me.'

'I could bring in a kettle to make sure your tea was hot?' suggested Conal.

'You could.' Dol glanced at him. 'Thank you, Conal.'

'It's no problem.' He smiled at her, but she didn't smile back.

'I shouldn't have had this stroke,' she said. 'It was my fault. If I hadn't had it, I wouldn't be in this awful place.'

'The doctor said you were better off here...' said Conal.

'The doctor is about twelve.' Dol's eyes were back on Alice. 'Tell me some news. You said Eva is retired... Who runs the shop now?'

'My mother, Ciara...'

'Oh, Ciara.' Dol's eyes glittered for a moment. 'So she's a shopgirl now...'

'She enjoys it,' said Alice, defensively.

'It's easy to enjoy something when you have no choice in the matter,' said Dol. 'And your grandmother never wanted to work in a shop. She wanted *my* life.' Dol looked quite pleased with herself. 'Yes, she wanted my life, the one I had.'

'Dol!' Conal gave Alice a deeply apologetic look. 'Would you please not talk about people like that, especially Alice's grandmother? She is one of the nicest women I've ever met. Everyone loves her...'

'Of course, they do,' said Dol, now seemingly bored of the conversation. 'They always did. At the ballroom in Dún Laoghaire, she'd have a line of men asking her to dance. But mine was longer, obviously. Eva was jealous of me, I think.'

Conal was shaking his head at Alice, still trying to apologise. 'Is there anything we can get you?' he said in a firmer voice, beginning to stand up. 'Otherwise, we can get going? Or maybe ask Abigail to call me and I can drop anything you like in?' He began to fold up his chair, placing it back where he found it. 'Alice? We'd better go. We have to do *that thing*...'

Alice stood up and glanced at the mantelpiece again. She realised that the photo frames were empty, they just had the backing sheet that came with them. Dol didn't have a single photograph of her family.

'Good to see you again, Mrs Blake,' she said.

Dol Blake didn't say anything, just looked out of the window. But there was something about Dol that made Alice feel terribly sorry for her. What had gone wrong?

29

CIARA

Disco fever had gripped Sandycove's over-forty-fives. Whenever Ciara was out and about, it was the first thing people would mention to her. 'I've got my ticket,' they'd say, or, 'I haven't a clue what I'm wearing!' with that same panicked look in their eyes that she and Mary-Marg had. But the conversation soon slipped into reminiscences of the original disco, memories of hot nights in Sandycove's sweaty old clubhouse, the teenagers dancing like no one was watching, their arms in the air like they didn't care. Their future for the taking. And now, some of that excitement had returned.

Yvonne O'Callaghan's divorce had just come through, she told Ciara. 'Ten years, it's taken me,' she said, a hollow look in her eye. 'Ten whole fecking years and it nearly broke me. Financially... bodily... mentally. But it's my boys who convinced me to go to the disco. "Mam," they said, "you deserve a night out". And they bought me a ticket. I just want a drink or two and a dance and that's it. And obviously home by midnight.' She suddenly grasped Ciara's arm. 'It *does* finish by midnight, doesn't it? I need to be in bed by then or I'll never cope.'

Ciara reassured her that it was lights off, music off, and doors closed by midnight. 'Who wants to be out after midnight?' she agreed.

Yvonne shuddered. 'The very idea,' she said.

Ciara remembered Yvonne from years ago, that summer after their Leaving Cert, after their school prom. Yvonne didn't go to bed for forty-eight hours and on the Monday morning, was still in her ball gown which was trailing behind her, wet from the sea and filthy from the sand.

Another time, Dessie Desmond raced up. Another relatively recent divorcé, he'd thrown himself into the world of golf when Marian, his ex-wife, had left him for the man who fitted their new bathroom. 'It wouldn't be so bad,' Dessie had said, 'but I'd always wanted a power shower and once we finally got one, I had to move out.'

This time, he was still tanned from a recent Portuguese golf trip, and looked a million miles from that deflated, defeated person he'd been. 'Me and the lads will all be at the disco,' he said, referring to his gang of friends who were still as close as they'd been aged seventeen, just with a few more life wounds and scars. 'You know, Ciara,' he went on, 'I don't think any of us has been looking forward to something this much since Padraig Harrington cut the ribbon on the new golf club.' He paused. 'Except... what the feck am I going to wear? I can't wear *golfing* trousers or a polo top!'

Ciara laughed. 'Why not go and dig out your old band T-shirts?' she suggested. 'Weren't you always wearing them back in the day?'

'I was, Ciara!' His eyes gleamed. 'I will do just that! One thing she *didn't* want in the divorce was my old band T-shirts, so thanks be to *Christ* my collection is still intact. See you, Ciara!'

And as he walked off, Dessie jumped to one side and clicked his heels together and whooped.

She was still managing to run – still slowly, but she told herself as her legs ached and her breathing laboured that it was better than nothing. And if on her evening run Ciara didn't see Paddy, she missed him. And when she did and they ran together or walked, it was as though a much-needed balm were being applied to old wounds. It was Wednesday evening, two days before the second disco, just as she and Paddy walked in the cool, damp air, that he turned to her. 'Do you ever take a day off?'

'Why?'

'I have a few hours off tomorrow afternoon,' he said. 'And I thought of getting out of Sandycove...' He looked at her, shyly again.

'And go where?'

'Newgrange?' He looked so hopeful, it almost broke her heart. 'Or another day... I was thinking about it and... I haven't been for so long...'

'I was thinking about it too...'

'It's not the same these days. You have to book a tour and then take a mini-bus and listen to a guide...'

'I don't mind...'

'You don't?'

'I'd love to go tomorrow. What time? Alice can mind the shop for me.'

'Really?' He was smiling.

'Why not? I'm practically a lady of leisure these days with Alice around. And I may as well make the most of her while she's still here...'

'Okay.' He was still smiling. 'I'll pick you up at your house at 12 p.m. We could have lunch on the way?'

She was smiling back at him. Was she really this excited for a trip out of Dublin or was it something else?

Afterwards, she showered and changed and walked to the village to Mary-Marg in Francisca's wine bar. She decided not to tell her about tomorrow's trip to Newgrange, she wasn't ready for that look on Mary-Marg's face. It was just a trip, that's all. But she needn't have worried because all Mary-Marg wanted to talk about was See The Stars. 'I feel as though we've unleashed something,' she said. 'I have this theory, that teenage hormones don't ever go away. We just learn how to control them better. But I think they've been unleashed, like a hive of bees. Mark my words,' she went on, 'I bet everyone over the age of forty-five breaks out in acne.'

They were nibbling on a cheeseboard and drinking their Montepulciano.

'You know,' said Mary-Marg, balancing some gorgonzola on some bread, 'I think I have found my calling. I mean, I know I should go back to medical research but, my God, this is so much better. Meetings in wine bars, working with my best friend, playing music. Feeling alive again...'

'I feel alive again too,' agreed Ciara.

'Do you?' Mary-Marg looked pleased, despite finding it hard to speak due to trying to eat at the same time.

'And so does everyone else,' said Ciara. 'Everyone who comes in the shop...'

'The over-forty-fives...'

'Yes... well, they're all excited. Jessica in the boutique says people are coming in to buy new clothes for the disco. Everyone wants metallic this and that.'

'Disco fever has arrived.'

They giggled for a moment, grinning at each other.

'It's better than menopause fever, aka the hot flush,' said

Mary-Marg. 'This is far more fun. And less sweaty. And, I don't know, I've been sleeping well and waking up actually rested. It's as though having something so exciting to think about...'

'And inconsequential,' said Ciara. 'That's the key. It's just fun.'

'That's where we went wrong. We got too serious.' Mary-Marg began to pile more cheese on some bread, topping it with another black olive.

'So, what do we do differently with our second disco?'

'Might tweak the playlist,' said Mary-Marg.

'And I was thinking of a signature cocktail on the bar,' said Ciara, looking at her list.

'Something rummy,' said Mary-Marg. 'Piña coladas...'

'Everyone would be violently sick. You can't dance after drinking those.'

'True.'

They both put some serious thought into it.

'Margaritas? Named after yours truly?'

'Mojito? It's practically a health drink. With all that mint, it's basically a salad.'

'Mojito it is.'

Ciara wanted more, she thought. She wanted to have fun and not be so tired. She wanted to go to South America, where she used to so desperately want to go. She wanted to feel the sand between her toes – not the damp, gritty sand of Sandycove, but the silky-soft sand of somewhere tropical. She was definitely going to go to Perth, to see Alice.

'Do you remember we used to want to travel?' she said.

Mary-Marg sighed. 'Another dream never realised.'

'But we could!' said Ciara. 'Your boys have finished school...'

'And who would mind the shop?'

'I'd find someone,' said Ciara. 'I think I used the shop as an excuse to stay in my comfort zone. But surely I can find someone to mind the shop for a week...'

'Or two...'

They grinned at each other.

'It's not the *worst* existence...' said Mary-Marg. 'As existences go.'

'No...' Ciara smiled at her. 'It's not bad. But what if there were something else out there for me? Like... I don't know... whatever I could do... sometimes I fantasise about working for someone else, not having to make decisions. Being told when to turn up, what to do, let someone else worry about ordering stock or dealing with suppliers or making enough money to keep me and Mam fed.' She sighed. 'Just someone else to worry about everything.'

'Pity Alice is so determined to return to Australia,' said Mary-Marg. 'She could be your co-manager. She's shown quite the commercial skills, has she not?'

'She has,' agreed Ciara. 'She's been brilliant. I'm going to miss her.' But she was also thinking about her trip to Newgrange the following day. It was only an hour away but it may as well be on the other side of the world. She really had been closeted if, apart from the disco, a trip out of town and lunch on the way was the most exciting thing to happen to her in a long time, but it really was. 'Another bottle of Montepulciano, Mary-Marg?'

'Oh, we shouldn't...' said Mary-Marg. 'But I'm all about living dangerously these days.' She held up the empty bottle. 'Francisca!' she called. 'Another one of these unctuous things, please!'

30

ALICE

Weirdly, Alice was getting used to the alarm going off so early. Previously, she had no idea that the clock on her phone even went back that far. She'd stayed up way past 5.30 a.m. from time to time, but that was fun, knowing that she was soon going to bed and that she could stay there for as long as she liked. This was an altogether different proposal. She'd been getting up early enough, she thought, with her dawn starts to make the soda bread, but this was another realm entirely. Six thirty now seemed positively lazy.

She opened her eyes. It was still early. Not winter dark, but that grey summer dawn that creeps into this hemisphere, preparing to yank you into the day. Except this seemed altogether nicer and not as threatening as she thought it might be. Ciara had been awarded a lie-in because of the oldies disco the night before, and Alice was on duty.

She lay in the dark for a moment. It was nice to feel a sense of purpose, not just in helping out Ciara, but also knowing that the shop was a place where people would be coming today, that sense of villagers thinking to themselves – even right now –

that they would need to buy such and such and Murphy's would be sure to have it. And there were the people who came every day for the Irish breakfast, brand-new customers, Ciara had said – the commuters on their way to the train, the post-swimmers, the dog-walkers, all of them handing over their three euros for their takeaway Irish breakfast. And the area outside the shop with the bench and the geraniums looked beautiful, and some people couldn't get a spot on the bench, so they sat on the step of Murphy's and that of Max's bookshop.

Another bench, she thought, adding it to her to-do list.

It had only been a couple of weeks, really, but every morning she woke up with an inner glow, excited about what might happen that day. In a shop, anyone could walk through that door and it was your role to make sure that when they left, they felt happy and satisfied. She and Ciara had fallen into a pattern with Ciara on the early shifts and Alice heading down to Murphy's after breakfast when Ciara could go for a walk or meet Mary-Marg for a coffee or even go shopping. They would swap over in the afternoon, and then Alice would take over the last afternoon shift, when Ciara would go for her runs, returning fresh-faced – if a little sweaty – but invigorated, as though endorphins were real and not just something made up by fitness gurus.

It was Ciara who told her about Willie Williams who ran a small wine importing business. She said he would be perfect for her wine tasting idea.

'He's exactly what you're looking for,' said Ciara. '*Incredibly* pretentious about wine, takes it far too seriously, but I like him...'

Alice rang him immediately and arranged for him to come and see them that evening. Ciara was off with Mary-Marg, so just Alice and Eva met Willie who arrived at closing time. He seemed to be the very embodiment of a wine expert. Around Alice's age, Willie wore a yellow corduroy jacket and a red bow tie, his hair a halo of curls.

'Alice Murphy,' he said, walking straight into the shop, hand outstretched, 'I have been waiting to meet you ever since your mother told me about her free spirit daughter, the wanderer, the Odysseus of Sandycove, a will-o'-the-wisp...'

Alice shook his hand. 'Lovely to meet you,' she said a little uncertainly.

'The reason why I wanted to meet you is that I am in love with your grandmother and your mother... and to hear of another Murphy, well! It's like something out of Greek mythology. The Three Graces...'

Alice laughed. Willie turned to Eva and took her hand, grasping it in his own. 'And of course, the fantabulous Eva Murphy, the matriarch magnifica...' Willie suddenly flung himself onto the counter and sat up, legs swinging. 'I was thinking of your proposal for a wine tasting evening,' he went on. 'I thought of a beautiful Barolo... a Piazza Principe 2019... fresh, light... *perfecto* for your discerning clientele. And then, perhaps, a stunning Michel Flambert Flaurence... a 2022 would be nice, and then a dessert vino, a Moldovan, my own little discovery, but an absolutely lip-smacking 2016 Puy de Grasse Absolument.' He pulled a bottle of wine from the inside of his jacket. 'Let's try the Puy de Grasse,' he said.

And like a magician, he proceeded to pop out the cork and sloshed the wine into the glasses. 'Ladies,' he ordered, 'sniff and tell me what you detect...' With his long nose in the glass, eyes closed, he described it. 'Grass, obviously... but sunflowers... humus... and a note of petrol. What else?'

'Wine?' said Eva. 'Although I am no drinker. Prefer tea myself.'

'A noble drink,' agreed Willie. 'But I'm sensing lemons...' he went on, 'and oh yes... there it is... wet dog. Glorious!'

'Shall we taste now?' asked Alice uncertainly.

Willie nodded and sipped at his wine, masticating wildly before swallowing. 'I love it,' he declared. 'What do you think?'

Behind them, there was a knock on the shop door. It was Max.

'Ah! Maximilian,' said Willie. 'My nemesis!'

'We're cousins,' said Max. 'Last time I saw you was at our grandmother's eighty-fifth birthday. You left early.'

'I was in search of a decent bottle of wine. The sherry was beyond awful,' said Willie. He beamed. 'Now, shall we continue with our tasting? Max, will you imbibe?'

Max nodded. 'If you twist my arm...'

They pulled out one of the benches from the back of the shop where Eva, Max and Alice sat, and Willie on the counter, and while they sipped, they listened to Willie's lyrical wine waxing. He knew an infinite and almost interminable amount about grapes and harvests and soil.

'And I thought it was just a drink,' Alice said as Willie poured the last drops of the wine into her glass.

Willie looked genuinely horrified. 'Oh, Alice,' he said. 'You don't mean that! It is like saying that Mozart is just a piano player, or James Joyce, a mere scribbler.'

'You know,' said Max, 'I think I know all I need to know about wine. Three things. Red, white, and in between.'

Alice laughed. 'Willie,' she said, 'will you give a wine masterclass? When are you free?'

'Anytime,' he said. 'Now, I am at your service. Just say the date and I will be there. As long as it's not next Thursday as I have my monthly dinner with my father which is an evening I dread... or on a Sunday, which is my weekly audience with my mother. Ditto.' He looked at Max. 'If I could swap my parents for yours, I would. We got the money. You got the non-dysfunctional parents.'

Max shrugged. 'Non-dysfunctional parents are priceless.'

'Exactly,' said Willie, and he looked sad for a moment. Alice and Eva glanced at each other, worried. 'But I have wine,' he said, to their great relief. 'And all is well with the world.'

'What about the day after tomorrow? On Thursday?' suggested Alice. 'I'm only here for such a short time, and I could put the message out on social media and the Newsletter? It would be lovely just to get it all organised before I go back.'

'Consider it done,' said Willie. 'No time like the present, is there?'

Max caught Alice's attention, as they were clearing up the bottles of wine. 'By the way,' he said, 'the reason why I called in was to see if you...' He stopped. 'I'm on a pub quiz team and the final is tomorrow in The Island. Two of my team are busy. Well, one has some kind of stomach bug after eating a dodgy burger from a dodgy van at a festival. Another has decided he'd rather go to Dingle for a weekend with his girlfriend. So, I'm stuck and I need a team. Conal's going to come...'

'But I'm not good at quizzes,' said Alice.

'Of course you are,' said Eva, taking the sweeping brush from her. 'You used to be a demon at Trivial Pursuit.'

'I can't go on my own,' said Max, looking a little pleadingly at her. 'I'll never win. I'll only be able to answer questions on the life and work of JRR Tolkien, or the proper way to paint the exterior of a shop.'

'But I have zero general knowledge,' said Alice.

'What's the capital of Australia?' he said.

'I know that... but—'

'Where is Machu Picchu...?'

'I know that as well...'

'What is the ingredient in Irish soda bread that gives it its rise...'

'And that... but—'

Max was smiling at her. 'Please? You'd be doing me a big favour. And I thought Becca might come because Conal is going to be there. Well, he said he would only come if you two came.'

Alice had to nod. 'We're going to lose,' she said. 'Badly. Just warning you... we're going to crash and burn.'

Max shrugged. 'I don't care. It's the taking part. And you never know, you might have fun. I promise to buy the first round.'

Alice couldn't remember the last time she had had such a lovely day. Life, she thought, could be very simple.

31

CIARA

Earlier that day, Ciara had been looking nervously out of the window, waiting for Paddy's car. She felt as though she were jumping off a cliff, into the unknown, all on her own. What if they had nothing to say to each other? What if he was angry about the past and blamed her? But it was Paddy, she reminded herself. Lovely Paddy, her old friend. Finally, his car pulled up at just two minutes past 12 p.m., and she grabbed her bag and her cardigan and rushed outside, just as he was getting out of the car.

'You're ready, so,' he said. 'I didn't know if I would have to drag you from the shop, you saying that you couldn't leave your customers...'

'It's nice to be away for a day,' she said, as he opened the passenger door for her and she slipped inside the car. Paddy walked around and sat in the front seat. 'So, ready for our Newgrange adventure?'

She nodded, trying to seem calmer than she felt. 'Now, you're the expert,' she said. 'You were always into ancient civilisations and all that...'

'I was... I was...' He looked surprised as though he'd forgotten it himself, or that she had remembered. 'I loved all about the Romans and the Greeks... these who lived in Newgrange were older than all of them. We're going back thousands of years...'

'We can learn from the past,' said Ciara.

'It's the only thing we've got...'

They swept out of Sandycove in Paddy's very nice car. Even to Ciara's untrained eye, it seemed nicer and smoother and more comfortable than the usual cars she was in, and she began to relax as roads gave through to motorway, and then eventually the turn-off to smaller roads and passing fields of acid yellow rape, and of cows munching grass, and the rocky tumbrils of County Meath, the sparkling River Boyne snaking through this beautiful ancient valley. She listened while Paddy told her as much as he could remember about Newgrange and who the strange people were who rolled huge rocks across the country to build this structure and then, as they grew closer, she could see it from the road. A round grass-covered building, surrounded by tightly packed stones.

'Did you wish you'd gone to university?' she asked him. Any of the other questions which burned inside her were ones which might upset the gentle equilibrium of the day. Paddy, she sensed, was doing everything he could to remain light and cheerful, which is what she wanted as well. Perhaps they could ignore the past and just be here in the Boyne Valley, where the weight of history, of people from the past, from battles fought, hung and clung so heavily.

'I haven't thought of it,' he said. 'At the time, I wished I'd gone but I was working in the business at that stage and I used to tell myself that that was my university, learning about the way it worked… the university of life…' He glanced at her, smiling. 'But I was really pleased when Conal went.'

'He and Alice are friends,' said Ciara.

'I know…' He glanced at her again. 'They get on, I think.'

'They've been swimming together…'

'It's nice that they get on.' He paused. 'Like us.'

Her laugh somehow diffused the tension in the air. 'Yes, like us.' She smiled at him.

They stopped in the lovely village of Slane for lunch, with its wide main street, neat, brightly painted terraced houses, grey slate church and old coaching inn. 'That looks all right?' said Paddy. 'What do you think? Ready for the culinary delight of a toasted cheese sandwich?'

'My favourite…'

There was an open fire with two long sofas either side and Ciara and Paddy sat opposite each other. 'This isn't too bad,' he said, leaning back. 'You could while away a few hours here.'

Ciara was looking at the menu. 'Toasted cheese sandwich…' she read.

'Thank God. I would have had to leave if it weren't on the menu,' he said, making her laugh. 'Chips? Please say there are chips, or it's straight back to Dublin…'

She laughed again. 'Yes… three types. One of them is thrice-cooked…'

'Thrice-cooked? Surely once is enough. What does that say about a nation that it cooks its chips three times?'

'It says we have notions,' said Ciara, still laughing. Paddy was more relaxed than he'd ever been since they'd first reconnected and it was good to see him so happy.

The waiter came over to them.

'Two toasted cheese sandwiches and two thrice-cooked chips,' said Ciara. 'Paddy, what would you like to drink? A beer?' She winked at Paddy, before turning back to the waiter. 'Do you have Blake's Beer?'

'We do,' the waiter said, before Paddy interrupted.

'Just a lime and soda,' he said, smiling across at Ciara. 'I'm driving.'

'I'll have the same,' said Ciara.

'If you change your mind, we have Blake's on draft,' said the waiter. 'It's very popular...'

'Oh, I've had enough of it,' said Paddy, handing their menus back to the waiter. 'You know when you get bored of something? Well, I am bored of Blake's. I fancy a change.'

When the waiter had gone, he smiled at Ciara. 'I *have* had enough of it,' he said. 'I want something different in my life. And that's why this is so nice...' He shrugged. 'Just being away, even an hour up the road, you feel different, as though we were a million miles away.'

'It's as though you can see everything so much more clearly by just being out of Sandycove,' said Ciara. 'I should do more of these trips, getting away...' It was remarkable how much better she felt, sitting here on this comfortable sofa, the log fire crackling away beside them, her old friend Paddy stretched out in front of her, his arms resting out on the back of the sofa. 'I needed this,' she said. 'I've been feeling stuck...'

Paddy was listening, his eyes on her.

'Trapped, I suppose,' she went on. 'My world felt so small and it's amazing how much smaller it gets, the less you do. I was thinking it's like those Russian dolls, you keep removing something – like going out with friends, or that hobby you used to do, or travelling, or even reading books – and your world gets smaller and smaller, until all you're left with is the little doll in the middle.'

Paddy nodded. 'You have to force yourself to do things. I've been putting off running a marathon. There's one in the South of France that I keep wanting to sign up for but I always chicken out.'

'I never go away with friends,' said Ciara. 'But the disco has meant I've seen more of Mary-Marg socially than I had for years, really. She just used to come into the shop for a coffee, but recently we've been going out and drinking *wine*...'

'What? *Actual* wine?' He whistled. 'Talk about living dangerously.'

'I know! Talk about crazy...'

He laughed. 'You have always been one of my favourite people...' He coughed as though trying to swallow the compliment, as though he wished he could take it back. 'You and Mary-Marg... you were both always so funny...'

'We were?' She was about to ask him more when their drinks and food arrived, and then they were too busy trying the chips to see if the thrice-cooking had made any discernable difference. It hadn't.

In Newgrange, they took the tour and the mini-bus to the ancient site and followed the group into the narrow tunnel which was illuminated – thankfully – all the way. Finally, they arrived into the central chamber which was dry, warm and perfectly made. The handiwork and genius of their ancestors who'd made this magical and mystical place were visible in the meticulously layered, overlapping stones, and the carved swirls and circles. *Someone made this*, thought Ciara. *Our ancestors were here, making their mark, working away, creating this beautiful place.* It was like being in a cocoon, safe from harm and hidden from the world.

The tour guide was explaining about midsummer's day when, as the sun rises over the Boyne valley, just peeking above the hill over the river, a shaft of sunlight begins to edge along the passageway. Paddy and Ciara looked at each other, impressed and awed by the genius of these ancient people. 'And then, after seventeen minutes, the sun illuminates the whole of this chamber, the room is awash with what was most precious to these people – the sun. And then the light begins to slowly retreat again and we are plunged back into...' – there was the sound of a switch – '...darkness.' And the chamber went dark. There were sounds of gasps of shock as their tour huddled together in the pitch black, and then Ciara felt Paddy's hand find hers and their fingers linked and they stood for a moment just like that.

32

ALICE

Outside The Island, Conal waved when he saw them. 'Remembered your brains for Max's quiz?' he said smiling, as Alice and Becca drew closer.

'I've left mine at home,' said Alice. 'Knew I'd forgotten something.'

Conal grinned before going over to Becca and kissing her. 'How was your day? Any vicious dogs?'

Becca nodded. 'A Jack Russell who nearly took the hand off me... but he was just scared. Soon had him purring...'

'Do dogs purr?'

Becca nodded. 'Of course they do... they make all sorts of noises to communicate. Purring is just one of their love languages...'

'Talking of which...' Conal dug around in his jeans pocket and produced a packet of Rolos. 'You said you hadn't had one in years. And so I thought...'

Becca was speechless for a moment, as though he'd given her a diamond. 'Oh, Conal...' She stared at the Rolos and then kissed him. 'This is *literally* the best present I have ever received.'

He laughed, delighted with her reaction. 'I can buy more of those,' he said. 'I could shower you in them...'

'You could,' said Becca. She ripped open the packet. 'We all need a Rolo to get us through this pub quiz.'

They each took one and, chewing ruminatively, they went inside.

'The brainiacs are gathered yonder,' said Mick, the barman, when he saw Conal leading the way. 'I'll bring the drinks out. Old Seadog for you all?'

In the courtyard, Max was sitting next to a woman with long blonde plaits and disproportionally large blue spectacles. Max stood up to hug Becca and Alice and give Conal the back slap and hug they always did. 'Thank you for coming,' he said. 'I couldn't have dropped out...'

Alice smiled at Max. 'But what if we're terrible?' she said. 'What if we let you down?'

Max shrugged nonchalantly. 'I think it was a wise being who once said, "Winning is overrated".'

'And who was that wise being?'

'Snoopy,' he said. 'A long-time hero of mine.'

Alice laughed. 'My hero too,' she said. 'I used to have my own fluffy Snoopy... but I lost him...'

'Probably on the train with Kenny,' said Max, making Alice laugh again, just as the woman with the large glasses stood up and somehow managed to edge her body in between Alice and Max. 'Hello,' she said, holding out her hand to Alice. 'I'm Breedge. Max's *friend*.' She gave Alice a swift up and down with her eyes. 'Although, *Max*...' she said pointedly, 'I don't understand why you didn't call me if you were short of a quizzing brain. You *know* I was on the University Challenge team. We beat Mary Immaculate College in that nail-biting final, remember?'

Max shrugged. 'Sorry, Breedge,' he said apologetically. 'I just... well, it was easier if I...' – he made eye contact with Alice – 'Alice said she always wanted to be on a quiz team. And so... I had to ask her.'

Alice nodded. 'Yes, it's been my life's ambition,' she said. 'That and swimming with dolphins and scoring the winning goal in the All-Ireland.'

'No,' said Max, laughing, 'that's *my* life's ambition.'

Breedge curled her lip. 'Now I know you're joking,' she said. 'I don't think Max knows what the All-Ireland is. He probably thinks it's a car rally.'

'It's a baking competition, isn't it?' said Max, airily. 'Either that or something to do with cattle? Or tractors?'

Breedge rolled her eyes. 'Max, stop being annoying,' she said. 'God, honestly, anyone would think that you don't have a PhD.' She turned to Alice. 'That's how Max and I met. We were on the same course. Everyone used to call me Jo, because I was so like Jo from *Little Women*.' She laughed. 'I don't know why they thought we were so alike. So, I like to read books and I am independent of mind.' She smiled at Max. 'We used to have long conversations into the night about literature, life and everything in between. Didn't we, Max?'

'Did we?' Max looked a little confused.

'You came up with a game to see how many books we'd all read...'

'I sound insufferable.' Max looked slightly pained. 'I've matured since then... I hope.'

'Not too much,' said Breedge. 'You were always such craic. And then Jenny Boyle said that you'd opened up a bookshop and I thought I'd come and see how you were.' She smiled at him. 'And here you are... I spotted you coming in here, like a character from a Dickens novel. You never did manage to tame that hair of yours, did you?'

'It's got a mind of its own,' said Max. 'Anyway...' He tried to move the conversation on.

Becca came over, Conal just behind her.

'Rolo?' said Becca, offering the packet of toffees again. 'Breedge?'

'I can't,' she said, averting her eyes. 'I don't do sugar.'

'Max, the quiz is going to start,' said Conal. 'Someone said that we all had to take our places...'

Breedge hesitated. 'Perhaps I will come and see you again, Max,' she said. 'When you are not so engaged. Or I could join your quiz team.' She beamed at him.

'You know,' said Conal to Breedge, 'you really remind me of someone from a book I read when I was young. There were these really great pictures...'

'Oh, I know,' preened Breedge, 'everyone says it. We're so alike. I'm just one of those bookish types. Always reading.'

'I thought she liked cheese.'

'Jo?' said Breedge.

'No, *Heidi*,' said Conal.

Breedge turned to Max. 'I don't think you're going to win the quiz this evening,' she said. 'You should have called your clever friends.'

'I did,' said Max. 'And they are all here.' He popped a Rolo in his mouth.

'Look,' said Breedge, 'just give me a call next week. Jenny is having a book swap party and it's going to be such fun. I've got the most to give away, me, being such a bookworm.' She turned to go. 'See you, Max.'

Max nodded. 'See you, Breedge.' He smiled at Conal, Becca

and Alice. 'Right, are we ready? Do you see them over there?' he said, gesturing to a group on the table opposite them. 'Those are Sandycove's finest quizzers. They call themselves the Clever Coves and they take quizzing very, very seriously...'

'Well, we're hardly a match for them,' said Becca.

Max sighed. 'I have found in life that humiliation has to be normalised. If you fear it or try to avert it, then life is excruciating. Just accept it, like a zen master, and let it flow through you...'

'Are you thinking about Polly?' Conal asked him teasingly, as Mick carried their drinks towards them, setting the tray onto the table and dishing them out.

'Polly?' said Alice, taking her drink. Weirdly, she felt something stir within her, almost jealousy. It was a little strange seeing Max being pursued so doggedly by Breedge, and now this Polly.

'Polly wasn't her real name,' said Max. 'Her real name was Susan and she was very much into country and western, had the boots, the hat, worshipped at the altar of Dolly Parton, had gone to Dollywood...'

'Max was quite struck with her...' said Conal.

'I was,' he admitted with another sigh. 'She was just so different to all the other girls from school. Polly Darton, as she called herself when she performed...'

'She *performed*?'

Max nodded again. 'She had a Dolly Parton tribute act. She took it very seriously, as though she were actually Dolly herself.'

Even though she felt the stirrings of jealousy, Alice found herself laughing.

'Max was really keen on her,' said Conal.

'She was magnificent,' Max admitted. 'Or so I thought at

the time. Those rhinestones were blinding, the way those cowboy boots clattered about, the wigs... it was very exotic.'

'And where does the humiliation come in?' asked Alice, intrigued.

'So, one night,' went on Max, 'I drove her to a wedding venue, this big posh hotel where she was performing, and I was to wait and drive her home again.' He paused. 'Anyway, so there I am, reading in the foyer with a cup of tea...'

'One of the wild men of rock,' teased Conal.

'So, I'm there, with some big Russian novel...' said Max, 'and Polly rushed out. She was shouting, in her Southern accent, that I needed to dress up as Kenny Rogers and sing "Islands in the Stream". Obviously I began to protest, wielded to my Dostoyevsky until she prised my fingernails off the table and carried me in...'

'She was very strong,' said Conal.

'Did you do it?' asked Alice, laughing.

Max nodded. 'I had to... Let's just say that thankfully the guests were so drunk that that they completely accepted a bespectacled Kenny Rogers.'

'Ladies and gentlemen...' A woman with tight, grey curly hair, turquoise spectacles and dressed in a long kaftan was tapping a biro on a pint glass. 'Welcome, everyone...' she said. 'I'm Professor Pauline Moloney. Formerly of the Shackleton Centre for Engineering and Discovery in UCD and, as usual, I can see some of my former students here this evening.' She peered through the glasses. 'We are delighted,' she went on, 'to see so many intelligent faces here tonight... including the invincible Clever Coves!'

A self-satisfied rustle emanated from the group across from Alice, Max, Conal and Becca.

'I think you'll all have a job to beat them,' went on Professor

Pauline, 'but do not worry, taking part is the important thing, that's what they say, don't they? The ones who are never going to win anything, anyway!' She laughed, as Becca, Max, Alice and Conal all looked at one another.

'This is your fault,' Conal teased Max again.

'I'm sorry...' Max said. 'I really am.'

'Right, Kevin here is handing out sheets of paper and pencils. No shouting out answers, absolutely no consultations with the interweb thing, and write your answers down and Kevin will mark it all later. Now, let's begin... Everyone ready?'

Max held the pencil for the team and they all looked at one another nervously. 'Look, it's an hour of our time,' said Max. 'As I said, humiliation is a fact of life. Let it flow through you...'

'In one ear and out the other,' said Becca. 'Isn't that what the zen masters used to say?'

'Perhaps,' said Max. 'Depending on the particular zen master...'

'Shhh... the Prof's about to begin,' said Becca, as Max wrote their team name on the top of the sheet – The Old Seadogs.

'Right... our first round is not an easy one,' Professor Pauline said. 'It's Russian literature...'

Groans and audible sighs were released around the courtyard, except for Max, who suddenly looked alert.

'Pencils at the ready. Right, question number one. Anna and Vronsky are one love story, but what is the other love story in this famous novel...'

Max began writing.

'Next,' went on Professor Pauline, 'what is the full name of the novelist Pushkin... an extra point for his middle name... Yes, these are hard...'

Alice could see that the Clever Coves were writing away

and all you could hear was urgent, whispered conferring, or the scribbles of pencils.

After five questions on Russian literature, the topic was changed, much to Alice's delight, even though Max had written his answers down feverishly.

'Now, to our next round... and this time we focus on sport and leisure... not always a favourite with our brainboxes. Right, what is the name of the top scorer in the World Cup of soccer?'

'I haven't a clue,' said Becca.

'Nor have I,' said Alice.

But Conal was looking confident. 'I know it,' he said, taking the pencil from Max and scribbling down a name.

'The game of curling is played on ice but what kind of stone is used in the sport?'

They all looked at Conal to answer and he thought for a moment and then took the pencil again. 'I think it's granite,' he said.

'Right, to a leisure question next,' went on Professor Pauline. 'Ireland has many native birds, but what is the name of our largest native wading bird?'

'I think,' said Becca quietly, 'it's the curlew. My dad is a twitcher.'

And on they went, through the sport and leisure and to the next round.

'Geography now,' said Professor Pauline. 'Where am I? Where Engels trod and where...' she peered at the card, 'someone called Mrs Gaskell lived... no first name, which must be an error... Where is this?'

Alice took the pencil. 'Manchester,' she wrote.

'Next, where am I? It's named after a famous English poet but is now a famous surfing paradise.'

'I've been there!' whispered Alice, scribbling down again. 'Byron Bay.'

And so they continued all evening, not succeeding in every single question, but being able to answer more than they had imagined.

Eventually, the quiz drew to an end.

'Right, final round,' said Professor Pauline, 'and this is a hard one... Dinosaurs!'

Conal and Alice made eye contact, a smile playing on his lips.

'Right, can you name five carnivorous dinosaurs?'

Conal began writing five dinosaur names, and then put down his pencil and looked up.

'I've never wanted to win anything more in my life,' said Max. 'I had no idea I was so competitive.'

'What about breathing in the humiliation?' asked Alice.

'We haven't been humiliated *yet*,' said Max. 'We'll breathe it in when we are officially humiliated.'

Becca handed around the Rolos and they ordered more Old Seadog and waited while, in the corner, Kevin marked all the papers. Eventually, the results were in, and for a moment the professor and Kevin seemed to be engaged in quite an intense conflab.

Professor Pauline tapped her glass again. 'Right, well, we find ourselves in uncharted territory. Two teams have exactly the same score. With forty-six out of fifty are The Clever Coves and...' she looked again at her paper, 'The Old Seadogs...'

'That's us!' Conal punched the air as Alice and Becca hugged each other, knocking over their stools in the commotion.

'But!' The professor held up her hand. 'We will need a tie-breaker question to decide this once and for all. Right, Clever

Coves and Old Seadogs, the first team to shout out the answer wins the prize of a bottle of sherry. The question is, what is the square root of 361?'

'I didn't even know you could get square roots,' said Becca. 'If it's not something that grows, then I'm lost.'

'It's maths,' said Alice. 'That thing we did in school and then promptly forgot everything.'

Across the courtyard, the Clever Coves had fingers pressed so hard to their temples that their digits were turning white.

'Come on,' said the professor, 'I must rush you. Clever Coves?' One of them opened his mouth to speak but at that split second, somehow, from deep in the recesses of Alice's brain, a number appeared.

'Nineteen!' she shouted, knowing it was wrong, knowing she would be humiliated, but the number rang a bell somehow, from way back in a maths classroom twenty years earlier, and Mr Andrews and his greasy hair desperately trying to teach them.

Professor Pauline swept around. 'Yes!' She looked horrified. 'Yes, the winners are The Old Seadogs! Kevin! Bottle of sherry for the Old Seadogs! And €500 will be presented to the MS Society of Ireland. Runners-up are the Clever Coves. Everyone has an off-night and I am sure, next time, they will return to their triumphant selves.'

Kevin placed a bottle of sherry on the table in front of them. 'Please,' said Max, standing up, 'we would like to present this to Professor Pauline for running the quiz so well tonight.'

Professor Pauline blushed behind her glasses. 'Thank you,' she said, reaching for the bottle. 'That is very kind, very kind indeed, no one has ever... well, no one has ever... ever given me anything before. This is most kind indeed.' She smiled up at Max.

'It was our lucky night,' he said. 'Thank you.'

'Breathe in the success, Max,' said Conal.

'Breathe it in one ear and out the other,' said Becca.

And then the Old Seadogs danced around again and success did feel better than humiliation, thought Alice, even if it was just for one night. Sandycove, she thought, could still surprise. Who knew that such fun could be had in the strangest of places? However, she couldn't help thinking about Max and if he was going to call Breedge next week. But why wouldn't he? She was attractive. And what difference did it make to Alice? Absolutely none. Wasn't she leaving soon?

33

ALICE

The following morning, Alice and Eva were in the courtyard garden behind the shop. Ciara was serving, as well as holding a meeting with Mary-Marg about the following evening's disco. Ciara had been in and out of the shop all week, as though she had another life entirely, as well as the one in the shop. She had notebooks and was always writing things down and underlining several times. 'Check MIRROR BALL!!!' Alice had read.

But Eva had needed help tying back her amethyst-coloured clematis. Eva was wearing a faded sun hat, and brown sandals with socks. She'd had the sandals for as long as Alice could remember – the only thing that changed were the socks.

'Hold this,' Eva said, passing over her secateurs, as she wound twine around a tendril, and then twisted it behind the trellis. 'And snip here...'

Alice did as she was told.

'I hear you were out last night, at the pub quiz...'

'And we won, can you believe that?'

Eva smiled at her. 'I *can* believe that,' she said. 'My clever granddaughter.'

'It was as though the quiz gods had decided to shine on us,' said Alice, still marvelling at what had happened. 'Each round was something we knew about. Even sport and leisure.'

'Cut here,' ordered Eva, holding the twine-tied tendril up so Alice could cut off the excess.

Eva wasn't speaking for a moment, and although the two of them had spent many hours out here in the courtyard over the years, they had always talked as they worked. When Alice had thought of Eva in all her years in Perth, she'd imagined her in the garden, looking after her plants or filling her bird feeders with peanuts. She had a pet robin, or at least a little robin who, the moment the door was opened and Eva went outside with her bag of gardening things, would flutter down and hop along the wall beside her. 'Rory, my little birdyguard,' Eva would say.

Rory was hopping around on the small brick wall right this moment, one beady eye – it seemed – on Eva, the other on any worms that might be foolish enough to emerge from the soil just then. 'Robins are very lucky,' Eva went on. 'They bring happiness with them. Have you ever seen a robin and not felt happy?'

Alice had to agree she hadn't. 'They are so sweet,' she said.

'Ah, they are not sweet,' said Eva. 'That makes them sound ineffectual when in fact they are the kings and queens of summer, bringing good fortune to anyone who minds them.' She returned Rory's beady gaze. 'Isn't that right, Rory? And they bring messages from our loved ones who have passed on. We have quite the chats, don't we Rory?'

Rory seemed to nod his head and then fluttered to the gnarly rose branches, closer to Eva. 'So you're good friends with Conal Blake, then?' she said all of a sudden.

Alice looked up. 'He's so lovely... we get on really well. Not in any romantic way...' she said, wondering if this was what Eva was getting at, warning her needlessly that he was already taken with Becca. 'I'm not remotely interested. And nor is he in me.'

'Well, that's good, then.'

'Do you want me to find someone?' asked Alice. 'Do you want me to settle down?'

'We just want you to be happy,' said Eva. 'That's all. We want Conal Blake to be happy as well. Which he is. With Becca O'Hara.'

Alice nodded. 'But I haven't met anyone I want to settle down with yet. Sebastian was a non-starter... and...' For some reason, the thought of Max came into her head. He wasn't her type and she wasn't his. Except... there was something about him she liked.

'Life is full of possibilities and potentials,' Eva was saying. 'But what you have to remember are the sureties and actuals. What are you sure or? What is real? If you gather those, then you're on firm ground. It makes life easier.' Eva paused. 'Once, years and years ago, I was consumed with something which was just a possibility. And I thought that this was going to be my answer to happiness. But circumstances – or rather, another person – intervened, and all was swept away. And so I had to recalibrate. I had to work out what on earth I was going to do. I remember making a list of what I wanted and what I already had, and I discovered that what I was really looking for was right under my nose.' She smiled at Alice.

'Who was the person who intervened?'

'Oh, that doesn't matter, not now,' said Eva. 'But, just to say, when we are consumed with possibilities and potentials, we sometimes forget about what is real.' She paused. 'We love you. You're our light and our life... always have been. But you have to find your own path.' Eva was on her feet. 'Now, shall we go and make ourselves a cup of tea and drink it in the garden?' She turned to go back up the fire escape stairs that brought her to the flat. Alice sat for a moment wondering what her grandmother was trying to say. It was all rather mysterious.

34

CIARA

On Thursday evening, they shut the shop a little early and began to prepare for the wine and cheese gathering. By 6 p.m. they were all ready. Ciara had tidied the shop, set out chairs and benches, and she and Alice arranged the best of their cheeses – a beautiful Wicklow Blue and a Cratloe goat's cheese, all on the large wooden boards, along with Irish cured meats, including a truffle and fennel salami from West Cork and some smoked venison.

Conal had arrived carrying three cases of beer, and Willie Williams set up behind the counter. Willie was dressed in a bow tie and silk waistcoat, Conal in a loose checked shirt, sleeves rolled up. Becca stood close beside him. 'His assistant,' she explained.

Ciara came up to Alice. 'It looks amazing,' she said, stealing some cheese and crackers from the corner of one of the boards. 'We should have had events like this years ago... you've got such good ideas. And having you here over the last few weeks has made it all so much nicer. Sharing the shop and having someone else to think about it with you. It's like we're in business together.'

Eva came downstairs and was quickly accosted by Willie.

'You must be dying to try my wine as well, Mrs M. Senior,' he said. 'I will also be teaching the nostril twitch as you breathe in the wine aromas. And the mouth swirl... very important. It enhances all wine, so even if you spend very little on oenological delights, it will improve them.' He looked over at Alice and gave her a toothy smile.

'It's all very educative,' said Eva, placing her cardigan on the end of the front bench, closest to the counter, to guard her seat. 'And who doesn't like being educated?'

'Oh, you'd be surprised, Mrs M. Senior,' said Willie, sounding horrified. 'The amount of people who just want to drink the wine without tasting it... well, you'd be shocked, you really would.'

Alice placed the wooden boards on the counter. 'What kind of cheese do you have?' asked Willie, coming up behind her. 'I am partial to cheese but I find, having such a remarkable nose...'

'It's not so remarkable,' said Eva. 'It's a perfectly ordinary one...'

'My *nose* – not my *nose*,' said Willie, tapping his proboscis. 'My extraordinary sniffing ability means I am more bloodhound than human.' He turned back to Alice. 'What do you have, because I was too busy to eat dinner and I am what they call *starvatious*. I won't be able to eat until after the presentation, so it would be nice to partake in a slice or two.'

'I'll get you a little plate together,' offered Eva. 'Now, let me see... there's Cashel Blue, Corleggy goat's, a nice Durrus... and a St Tola... Would all of them work for you? And what about this nice Gubbeen chorizo and a fennel salami?'

'Yes please, Mrs M. Senior.'

Eva piled some cheeses and meats onto a plate for him and he put it beside the till for later, and then people began to arrive. Mary-Marg was there, of course, with Siobhán, Monica and Eileen. There was Bernadette O'Hanlon, wearing a T-shirt saying 'I run for fun – no joke', and there were Philomena and Sheila from the Forty Foot. Eva's pals were also there, including Edith Waters and her partner Sally-Anne Butler, and there was Fran from school and so many other faces that Alice knew.

Becca was handing out glasses of beer. 'Just an aperitif,' she was saying. 'Before the wine tasting. It's called Old Seadog...' And she introduced everyone to Conal and practically everyone asked the same question: *Are you anything to do with Blake's Beer?* And Conal would nod and say he was the son of Paddy.

'Of course, you are,' said one woman, 'aren't you the spit of your grandmother? Dol Blake. Now, she was a beauty. How is she doing after the stroke? Doing well, I hope?'

There weren't enough benches or chairs for everyone as so many had turned up, but luckily Willie had brought more cases of wine than were needed and Alice and Ciara raided the fridges to replenish the cheeseboards.

Everyone pretended to understand what Willie was saying when it came to tasting the wine.

'I can definitely get lemons,' Eileen whispered to Siobhán. 'But I'm not getting wet terrier, are you?'

'I'm getting menthol,' said Siobhán, 'but then I did consume a menthol sweet on my way here.'

'I'm getting armpit after a spinning class,' said Mary-Marg, wrinkling her nose. 'But I have the palate of a bonobo monkey. No sophistication at all.'

When they had tasted everything and had stopped having

to do the mouth swirl and the nostril flare, Willie just poured out all the wine, the benches were pushed back to one side and the shop was suddenly now a party.

Alice found Ciara. 'We should do this every Saturday evening,' she said. 'A bit of wine, a bit of cheese. Keep it simple. A glorified tasting...'

Later, when the last person had gone and the last bottle of wine had been taken to the recycling, there were just Willie, Max, Conal, Becca, Ciara and Alice left in Murphy's. Ciara and Alice began pulling a bench back into the stockroom.

'I'll help you,' said Willie. 'You can't carry that on your own.' He lifted up one end of it and they all shuffled backwards.

'Just here,' said Ciara. 'Thank you, Willie.' She smiled at him and walked back into the shop.

'Do you think it went well?' Ciara heard him say to Alice.

'Brilliantly,' said Alice. 'It couldn't have been more enjoyable. Everybody loved it.'

'Thanks so much for this evening, Ciara,' Conal said, as he was packing all the empty beer bottles away and everyone else was busy. 'Your support has been amazing. Since the beginning.'

'A pleasure,' she said. 'I'm only too glad to help.'

He was similar to Paddy in so many ways, but also different. Paddy at that age was so confident – Conal quieter, softer-spoken.

'Dad was telling me about the disco you used to put on,' Conal said, stacking his crates. 'It sounds amazing. And he said you've brought it back.'

'That's right... we've actually been booked throughout the autumn.'

'Dad was saying that they were the best days of his life...

apart from being a father, of course.' He hesitated. 'Did you ever meet my mother?'

Ciara stopped what she was doing and looked at him. 'Not really,' she said. 'She came to the disco a couple of times, but we never really talked.'

Conal nodded. 'I'm just wondering. I mean, I still see her... sometimes. But she's so different to us... And perhaps that's why she left?'

'Perhaps.' Ciara wished there were something she could say to him. 'What has your dad said?'

'He never talks about it. Any of it. He's never explained why she left.'

'I wish I could tell you,' said Ciara. 'I wish I could help.'

He nodded and looked away. 'I'm just a bit confused. Something doesn't add up. And I can't get to the bottom of it.'

'Talk to your dad,' said Ciara.

'I know... I know...' Conal turned away. 'Sorry for bothering you with it.'

'I really wish I could help,' she said again, her heart going out to him. 'I really do.'

Alice and Willie brought the last of the glasses to the back of the shop and began washing them up. Willie grabbed a tea towel and was on drying duty. Eventually, as they put the last glass back in the box, Willie cleared his throat.

'Perhaps you might like to go for a drink with me?' he said. 'Just the two of us. A date, I suppose, is what the young folk call them. Although I am technically one of the youngish folk, I feel old. But by date, I mean, everything would be on me. Dinner. Drinks. I think it is better to get all of that out in the open so there is no awkwardness or confusion. And perhaps a wine bar, or maybe you are fed up with wine?'

He was about to say more when Max appeared. 'Alice?

Where do I put the boards?' he said stiffly. 'Willie, shall I show you where the bus stop is?'

'Oh, I'm in the car,' said Willie. 'I never drink at a tasting.'

The two of them glared at each other for a moment. 'Max,' said Willie, 'I'm in the middle of *something* with Alice.'

Max hesitated and then, with another furious glare at Willie, he retreated back into the shop.

'So?' said Willie. 'Would you... perhaps, consider... even remotely – roll the idea around your cerebellum for a time – in other words, would you dare or care for a date?'

'Oh, Willie,' said Alice, 'that is so nice... and... flattering. It really is. But...' She thought of Max and his furious glare and felt strangely excited. 'I'm going back to Australia soon, and... well... it's too far for a long-distance thing.'

'Quite right,' he said politely. 'I don't know what I was thinking of. I am sure that perhaps, if you weren't about to descend under, then you might... I don't know? Consider it?'

Alice nodded. 'I might, Willie.' But she was thinking of Max and wishing she had more time here. Who knew what would happen if time were on her side? 'But as friends...?'

He nodded slowly. 'Better than nothing,' he said. 'I'll take that.' He grinned at her. 'Story of my life. Every woman I meet wants to be friends but nothing more. I will have to just settle for being a bachelor. You know what?' He perked up. 'Could that be a selling point? The bachelor wino?'

Alice laughed. 'Definitely not...'

'The single wine guy?'

'Better...'

'What about the unencumbered oenological-man-about-town?'

'Runs off the tongue,' said Alice. 'Go for it.' She smiled at Willie. 'Come on, we'd better lock up.'

The shop was empty, she thought, as the lights were off, but then she realised there were two figures sitting beside the door. One was Eva, and the other Conal. He looked as though he'd been crying, and Eva was patting his hand and speaking softly to him.

'All finished?' said Eva brightly, as Alice and Willie came from behind the counter.

'I think so,' said Alice.

Conal was standing up and trying to smile. 'It was a great night,' he said.

'It was...' said Alice, looking to see if she could work out what had gone on between the two of them, but Eva was as inscrutable as ever. 'Thanks to you and Willie.'

'Oh, but I am but a humble peddler of wines,' said Willie. 'What about the plonk peddler?' He looked hopeful.

Alice shook her head.

'Or... well, if I were female, I could be the spinster vinster?'

'Now that I love.' Alice smiled at him but was still thinking of Conal. He was such a sweet, open-hearted person, the kind of man easily hurt. She wished she could help him in some way. He was searching for answers and whatever they were and wherever they lay, she hoped he'd find them.

35

ALICE

BECCA

Conal has invited us to Landfall for a few drinks. I think he's feeling down about something.

ALICE

What's wrong with him?

BECCA

Not sure. He just said he didn't want to go out. But said we could go over there. He's being a little quiet lately. I hope he's okay.

ALICE

Did you ask him?

BECCA

Yes, but he says he's fine. But he either is about to dump me or there's something worse going on. Wish I didn't like him so much. So you'll come tonight? 8.30 p.m. at Landfall. We could walk up together.

ALICE

Definitely. Love you Becs xxx

> **MAX**
> Are you coming to Conal's this evening?

> **ALICE**
> Yes!

> **MAX**
> Just checking.

> **ALICE**
> Any particular reason?

> **MAX**
> Nothing... except...
>
> ...

> **MAX**
> I find evenings are nicer when you are there.

Was he flirting? If he was, Alice told herself, it was harmless. Perhaps Max was the type who threw compliments and charm about like confetti at a wedding? But still. It was nice. Even if she *was* going back to Perth so soon.

Something had shifted between her and Max. From being just the best friends of Becca and Conal, they had developed their own thing. They sought each other out and after her feelings of jealousy about Breedge and his about Willie, they had entered a zone which was not quite friends, not quite anything more. And yet...

She would miss him. He was so quirkily Irish, and so amusing. It was almost like a holiday romance, only without the romance. Maybe he and Breedge would rekindle whatever it was and maybe she would find another hot Jesus surfer. But she'd gone off them, the perpetually bare chest, the obsession with currents and waves, the way you could be in mid-conversation and suddenly, their eyes on the sea, they would start running towards the ocean and you would think someone was drowning and they were doing their hero bit, but it was just a wave that they fancied catching. Yes, she was over all of that.

But perhaps Max wasn't jealous about Willie asking her out, and perhaps he was just being nice in his texts and not remotely flirtatious? And it was best not to complicate anything – not now, not when she was leaving.

Becca called for her and they walked up to Landfall. The 'For Sale' sign made the house look even sadder, as though it knew the family were giving up on it. There was no music floating up from the house, as it had the last time they were there, and there were no lights on. Instead, looking past the house and down the long garden leading to the sea was a small glow from a fire, just outside the summer house.

Alice was clutching a prototype Murphy's canvas bag containing a selection of Irish cheeses, two bottles of rosé and one of elderflower cordial which was made by a local woman who had called in earlier to see if they would stock it.

'I called Conal an hour ago and he said he'd had some news...' Becca was saying as they walked up. 'So I asked what kind of news and he said didn't know where to even begin, or if he wanted to talk about it.' She gave Alice a look.

Alice nodded. 'Hope it's not serious. Perhaps Dol has had another stroke?'

'But if she had, he would just say, wouldn't he?' Becca frowned. 'This is far more mysterious, but I must show restraint and poise and not ask too many questions.' She paused. 'At least I think he's still into me and I'm not the problem. It's always so much better when people's problems have nothing to do with you. I love those kinds because I can just be a kind of Florence Nightingale brow-soother, you know?'

They kept to the left of the house, and towards the back

garden. Beyond was the shimmering sea, which glittered like a disco ball. On either side were densely planted trees, and at the top of the lawn were long beds planted with old-fashioned roses, and their scent hung in the warm evening air. Close to the bottom of the garden was the white wooden summer house tucked into the trees. A plume of smoke from a firepit curled upwards and there was Conal, a long stick in his hand with which he'd been poking at the fire – but he was gazing out to sea.

'Hey...' Max was behind them and had broken into a kind of jog, his linen blazer bunched over his arm, the cotton tote he was carrying clinking. 'Hold up!' He beamed at Becca and Alice as he came to a halt beside them. 'I'm celebrating. Bought us a bottle of champagne... well, *not* champagne but on the same paradigm, if you know what I mean. I've just been nominated for best new independent bookshop in the Bookies.'

'The Bookies?' Becca looked confused.

'It's the Irish book awards,' explained Max. 'I only got the email an hour ago.'

'That's brilliant,' said Alice, smiling back at him.

'Well, it's not exactly the Nobel Prize, but it's the only award I've been anywhere close to since I was given "most improved" during cycling week in Sixth Class.'

'I failed cycling week,' said Becca gloomily at the memory. 'I kept bashing into the cones.' She slipped her arm through Max's. 'You go the other side, Alice,' she ordered. 'Let's bring the champion through.'

'I haven't won yet,' said Max, but he didn't seem to mind Alice and Becca linking arms with him. Max caught Alice's eye and gave her another smile and she squeezed his arm in response. It *wasn't* flirting, she told herself again. It was just friendly banter, but she still felt a kind of giddiness as they walked towards Conal.

The summer house was an octagonal-shaped structure, half-trellised and open on four sides at the front, and facing the sea. There were two old, lichen-covered stone benches and four faded floral sun chairs positioned around a small round firepit.

'We used to play here when we were young,' said Max. 'It was our hideout. Conal dragged down an old gas heater and we just spent ages hanging around. But now Paddy is selling the house, it's the end of an era.'

'Thanks for coming,' Conal said when they reached him. He didn't look quite the same, Alice thought. He looked as though he were distracted by something else. 'I just wanted to have one last evening at the summer house...'

Becca had one hand on his back, rubbing him, in what Alice supposed was a Florence Nightingaley way. 'It's not easy to sell the family home,' she said.

They sat around the fire and chatted, and Conal seemed to be trying to make an effort to relax.

'How are the Irish breakfasts going?' he asked Alice.

'Great,' she said. 'We've already doubled the amount we serve and we're selling out by 9 a.m. Gran's friends are all making jam. Dorrie and Angela are making vats of it and Gran is collecting raspberries from everyone she knows who grows them. And strawberries and blackcurrants, I think. It's a bit late in the season, but some people have greenhouses and polytunnels. It will be plum season soon and we can move onto those. They are stockpiling them for winter, so we have enough to get us through.'

Max laughed. 'I think you seem to have found your purpose in life, feeding the citizens of Sandycove!'

'Oh, this is not my purpose... I'm only doing this to... well, help the business a bit. I'm going back to Australia soon.' She managed to laugh. 'My true purpose is being purposeless, I suppose. Anyway...' Being purposeless didn't sound as cool as it once had. Now, more than anything, she realised, she wanted a purpose, like Max and his books, or Becca and her dog-grooming, and Conal and his brewing. Being free had once meant nothing tied you down or restricted you, but it was nice to have responsibilities. She had *loved* waking up at dawn with a plan for the day, tasks to carry out and, better than anything, the feeling that you were in charge. If you wanted to change something, you could.

They opened the wine and the four of them sat in the old chairs, in a half-circle facing the sea. Conal sat quietly while the other three chatted.

'This cheese is very good,' said Max, taking some more of the Wicklow Blue and spreading it onto a cracker. 'I never liked blue cheese until I reached the age of twenty-five and, boom, I liked it. Same with red wine. Never my thing. Now, can't get enough of it. Same with writers. You read them and think, yes, okay, fine. But then, you read them when you are older and it's like they are writing just for you.'

Alice nodded. 'Things people did in novels were so perplexing to you as a teenager, but then, as you understand how complex people are and how confusing life is, you understand. My mum says life doesn't get easier as you get older, you just get better at accepting the fact.'

'I had a realisation the other day,' said Becca, 'about *Grease*.'

Max looked confused. 'The country?'

'The film!' Becca laughed. 'Don't tell me you've never seen it? Well, the T-Birds – they're the boys' gang – well, they are just as insecure as the girls, the Pink Ladies. I had literally never noticed that. You're right, you notice so much more as an adult.'

There was a noise behind them and they turned to see Paddy walking towards them. 'I thought I heard voices...' He was smiling.

'Yeah...' Conal said cooly. 'You don't mind, do you?' He seemed stiff and awkward with Paddy, as though they barely knew each other.

'No, no...' Paddy was smiling as broadly as always, but he kept glancing at Conal, a worried look in his eyes.

'Would you like a beer or a glass of wine, Paddy?' asked Becca, standing up, smiling.

'Wine, thank you, Becca.' Paddy sat down on the lichen-covered bench. 'Hope I am not disturbing anything.'

'No, not at all,' said Max. 'We were just talking about how life never stops getting complicated as you grow older, you just are less shocked by things...'

Paddy laughed as he accepted the glass from Becca. 'Yeah... it never stops... there's always another surprise around the corner.' He looked over at Conal who was still staring at the sea, as though Paddy weren't there.

Max caught Alice's eye and she gave a slight shrug as though she were as clueless as him.

36

CIARA

Standing in the near-empty function room of The Sandycove Arms, Mary-Marg and Ciara were feeling nervous. The bar staff were setting up, Jake and Josh were shifting tables and chairs. It was Friday night and another See The Stars disco.

'We *did* sell all those tickets,' said Ciara, worriedly. 'Didn't we?'

'I am almost sure we did,' said Mary-Marg. 'Or did I dream it?'

'Look, if it's just us, we'll just pack up and go home. Tell no one. Style it out. Okay?' Ciara looked at the time on her phone: 8.55 p.m.

Ciara was wearing a long, flowing maxi dress and trainers, Mary-Marg was in a silver mini dress and clompy boots.

'Too much?' asked Mary-Marg, anxiously smoothing down her dress. 'Aged disco queen? Miss Havisham does the seventies?' She turned to look at her reflection in the glass behind the bar. 'Brian said I looked as though the cryogenic machine had gone wrong and it had been pressed on future rather than past. It's his sense of humour. Never give a compliment if you can be funny.'

Ciara shook her head. 'You look amazing.'

And Mary-Marg did. There was practically no difference between Mary-Marg then and Mary-Marg now. The last three decades were nothing. And if they were nothing, then, if Ciara wasn't careful, the next thirty years could slip by and she would be eighty and she wouldn't have noticed.

'I'm ready,' she said. She thought of Paddy and his hand around hers in the dark of Newgrange. Her hand still tingled from where his fingers had entwined her own. It was almost as though an ancient energy had overtaken them both, imbued with the power of their ancestors, and they had returned to Sandycove in high spirits. It was only when he dropped her home again did their slight shyness around each other return. All she knew – and was so happy about and grateful for – was that she and Paddy were friends again.

'Ready for what?' said Mary-Marg. 'Ready to get down with the Sandycove forty-five-plus crowd? Ready to make shapes on the dance floor with the more mature crew?'

Ciara laughed. 'All that. I'm ready for all that...' She felt looser in every way, as though all the tension in her shoulders, the tightness in her chest which she hadn't really noticed because it was ever-present, were dissolving. She had spent years either nursing a broken heart or had her head down minding Alice and the shop. There had been zero room for anything else. She wanted the next thirty years to be filled with the kind of sparkle in Mary-Marg's dress. 'I'm ready for tonight,' said Ciara. 'And tomorrow morning. And I want the two of us to always be the last people on the dance floor, until they have to carry us off.'

Mary-Marg punched her arm in the air. 'The battle cry of

the ageing disco queen! Age will not wither us! Nothing shall defeat us because we will play music and we will dance... and we will be dancing with our zimmer frames...' She began dancing. 'All hail the mighty middle-aged disco queens!'

'*Young middle-aged* disco queens,' Ciara reminded her.

'Young middle-aged disco queens of the world unite!' said Mary-Marg. 'You know, I don't care about what Brian said. I feel amazing and if I *feel* amazing, then it stands to reason that I must *look* amazing.'

'Your logic is impeccable,' said Ciara. 'You can't keep a middle-aged disco queen down.'

'No, you can't...' Mary-Marg slipped a record out of its sleeve and placed it on the turntable. 'Not when there are songs like this to be played...' She carefully placed the needle on the edge of the record and then the opening lines of 'Can You Feel It' by the Jacksons began.

The two of them began singing and dancing, their own private disco. They danced the whole expanse of the room. Mary-Marg clambered up onto a chair as if to command the room for the chorus as Ciara danced as she had never danced before. In her head, she was nineteen years old again, and as she looked over at Mary-Marg, eyes closed, dancing away, she knew she was feeling exactly the same.

Mary-Marg opened her eyes, her face breaking into a huge grin. 'I feel amazing...'

'Therefore we are...' said Ciara.

'...AMAZING!' they both shouted, still dancing as the music filled the room, their heads and their hearts.

And then there were the sounds of voices and singing outside, and they raced to the window and looked down. From one side of the road came a group of over-forty-fives, strutting along with the attitude of a New York street gang, and from the other side came another group of their friends, shouting, cheering, skipping.

'They're here!' shouted Ciara, as Mary-Marg was now dashing back to the decks in a kind of comedy dancing-run, the look on her face one of joyfully panicked bliss, and for some reason it made Ciara start to laugh... unable to stop. She carried on laughing as Mary-Marg ran about, turning off the lights. She was helpless with laughter as the bar staff arrived to see a woman slumped to her knees who was either laughing or sobbing. And she was still laughing as Mary-Marg raced back to the decks to put on 'Stand' by R.E.M. And then, giving up on Ciara, opened the main doors.

On cue, people began to pour in, already dancing, jerky movements or smooth and lithe. The faces of Sandycove's over-forty-fives alive and alight with the anticipation of the evening stretching ahead of them, an evening of unknown delights.

The past does not matter, thought Ciara as a group of women she knew from the shop pulled her into their circle and she danced with them for a moment or two, shouting comments about the night, their outfits and the music. *Now is all we have!*

37

ALICE

The atmosphere outside the summer house at Landfall was strangely awkward. Conal was sitting looking at the sea, refusing to look at his father, while Paddy was shifting nervously on the edge of the bench. Becca, Max and Alice tried to keep the conversation going.

'It's so sad you're selling Landfall,' said Becca. 'It's a lovely place... the view of the sea is amazing. What kind of house are you going to buy next?'

'Smaller,' Paddy said, standing up and poking the fire with the same stick Conal had been using. 'In the village. Close to everything.'

Becca nodded. 'Maybe you could take down the summer house and rebuild it in your new place? If the garden were big enough. Obviously.' She looked over at Alice. 'Would you like a summer house, Al?' There was a desperate quality to her voice.

'I suppose,' said Alice. 'I've never thought about it.' She looked at Max, who accepted the baton.

'I would like a tree-house,' he said. 'I used to have one when I was young. Built by my grandmother – remember I told you about her?' He nodded at Alice. 'She was very handy with a hammer and a nail. There was nothing she didn't either hammer or...' He paused. 'Or nail.'

The three of them exchanged glances again.

'The disco is on tonight, isn't it?' said Paddy.

Alice nodded. 'Mum and Mary-Marg are both terrified that no one will come...'

'Ah, they will.' Paddy smiled at her. 'Everyone used to go to their discos. And there's been quite the talk about it. They were always the life and soul, she and Mary-Marg, and every disco they put on was special. They took it very seriously and saved every penny. They were going to take a year off before college and go to Central America, I think it was. And *then* college. Ciara had applied for Latin American Studies. There was going to be a year in Argentina, I think...'

Alice had had no idea Ciara had ever wanted to travel. 'I knew she wanted to travel but I didn't know how much...'

He nodded. 'They were both obsessed with it. Had a Latin American night a few times. Made everyone speak Spanish, served these amazing drinks. Another time they had an "Around The World in Eighty Countries" night and everyone came as a country.'

'What were you?' Conal was looking over.

Paddy smiled at him. 'Oh, I was Antarctica. I wore a dinner jacket that made me look like a penguin.'

'Antarctica isn't a country,' said Conal coldly.

'No...' said Paddy evenly. 'But I remember Lorcan...' He stopped, just as Alice looked up.

'Lorcan?' she said. 'Lorcan *Kennedy*?'

Paddy had a look on his face as though he knew he had said something wrong.

Alice could feel her face turning red, but she pressed on. 'You mean, my *father*, Lorcan?'

Paddy nodded. 'Yeah... we used to all hang out.' He stopped.

'What were you going to say?' said Alice.

'Lorcan came as himself. He said he was the United Nations. Representing all countries.' He gazed at Alice, trying to smile at her.

'Did you like him?' she said, feeling embarrassed but having to ask. 'Was he nice?'

'Oh, we all liked everyone in those days. It's so easy to be friends when you're young. It's the one thing that gets harder as you get older. Life is complicated.'

'But...' He hadn't answered Alice's question.

'I don't know if he was nice or not,' he went on, as though he knew she needed more. 'We all just accepted one another. Being nice wasn't something we thought about. People were just people. Your mother liked him, though...' He paused again. 'There was something magnetic about him, I think. I didn't see it at the time. But he wasn't like the rest of us boring fellas. He used to quote poetry and was slightly odd. I didn't understand it then, but you might call that *charisma*.'

'Charisma doesn't last,' said Alice. 'We met him once, years ago, and he was so...' She searched for the word. 'So *plain*.'

Paddy nodded. 'We're all plain, really. We're all just ordinary people trying to live the best we can.' He looked over at Conal, who had returned to staring at the sea, as though hoping he was listening. 'We all make mistakes and try our best and hope that we don't hurt too many people along the way.' Paddy stood up. 'I'd better go... leave you to your night. Enjoy the evening.' He paused. 'Bye, Conal.'

Conal grunted a reply and Paddy walked across the grass

and towards the back door of the house from where light was spilling out.

'Is everything all right between you and your dad?' asked Max.

Conal poked the fire with the stick. 'Not really,' he admitted.

'Is it selling the house?' asked Becca. 'That must be hard.'

'I was trying to renew my passport and... well, I was asking for different things and... he said my birth certificate was lost, so I said "no problem". I'll just apply for a new one...' He stopped. 'Well, that's when... that's when my entire existence blew up.'

Becca's eyes were like saucers. 'You don't mean literally?'

Conal nearly laughed. 'I mean, I don't exist.' He shrugged. 'And that's literally. I literally don't exist. I was born something else. To someone else. And there is nothing official about Conal Blake.'

'Did you see this on your birth certificate?' asked Max.

Conal shook his head. 'It hasn't arrived yet. It's on the way. But Dad... Paddy. Whoever he is. He sat me down and told me I was adopted. And it wasn't one of those official adoptions, but I was available and they said they'd take me. Like I was on Done-Deal or something.'

'You can get good things on DoneDeal,' said Becca. 'I mean, it's not a bad thing.' She faltered. 'But obviously, *humans* aren't on DoneDeal.' She pulled up her chair to Conal's and began rubbing his back again, and he leant his head on her shoulder for a moment, his eyes closed.

'So, he's not my father. My mother is not my mother. My grandmother isn't my grandmother. And they have all lied to me. All my life. All of them have been in on this massive secret and no one bothered to tell me. I mean, who just *gives* a baby away? Why would anyone do that?'

They all shook their head, shocked.

'They just took you? Or were you *actually* given away?' Alice asked.

'I don't know... Dad... Paddy... Dad says none of it matters and that I'm his son, which is the only important thing. But I don't *feel* like his son. Not any more. I want to leave, get away from them all. I feel like... I don't know... I hate him... Even what I do with my life,' went on Conal. 'My own brewing company. I mean, I wouldn't be doing it if it weren't for Blake's Beer. I feel like such a fool.'

Alice tried to imagine what that might feel like, to not know who you were. She'd always thought of herself as only being half there, the rest of her missing, but the bit she did know was actually more than enough. But poor Conal. He'd lost everything.

'What are you going to do?' she asked gently.

'I don't know,' he said. 'Maybe leave Sandycove, and start again somewhere...'

There was a cry of anguish from Becca.

'I have to try to make sense of this. Dad wants us to carry on as though nothing has happened. He said it doesn't change anything and he loves me and wouldn't change a thing. Except... except I would change everything. I would change being unofficially adopted. And them not telling me. And then waiting until I was thirty and dropping this bomb on me.'

'Literally a bomb,' said Becca.

'I mean, my mother has never been that bothered about seeing me. I never understood why. I do now...'

As they pulled their chairs closer to the firepit, they let Conal talk, allowing him the time and space to go over everything in his head, the unanswered questions, the lies, the secrets... and what he felt was his loss of identity.

'I don't even know why I made you come here this evening,' he said, as the embers in the firepit glowed. 'We should have met somewhere else... it's not my house... it never was. I'm not even a Blake.'

38

CIARA

She must have talked to *everyone*, moving around, thanking people for coming, accepting their gratitude to her and Mary-Marg for hosting the night.

'You keep this going?' shouted Eileen O'Connor into her ear. 'I always said that what Sandycove needs is a nightclub for our lot.'

'You can never stop these nights!' Dessie Desmond exclaimed, sweaty in a Sultans of Ping T-shirt, a face on him like a cat who'd fallen into a vat of cream, clutching Yvonne O'Callaghan's hand. 'It's the best thing ever! Better than a round of golf!'

'I feel like a new woman,' shouted Yvonne – and then, with a cackle, 'and a new man!' The two of them creased themselves laughing, arms around each other, while staggering off to the bar.

But Ciara caught sight of someone standing in the doorway and she stopped still, wrenched back into reality. It was Paddy Blake with an expression in his eyes that made her stop breathing for a moment.

His eyes met hers. And she knew. The secret was out.

Pushing past a group of women who were dancing in a circle, holding hands and singing Cher's classic 'If I Could Turn Back Time' at the top of their voices, Ciara made her way towards him. She grabbed his arm. 'Paddy,' she began. She wanted to ask him if he was okay and tell him how sorry she was, because perhaps she should and could have done more at the time. 'I'm sorry...' She had to shout in his ear.

'What?' he shouted back.

She pulled him by the arm, to the cool and quiet of the corridor outside.

'I'm so sorry for coming,' he was saying, his words tumbling over themselves. 'I'm so sorry. Look, I'm just going to ruin everything, I know. But I needed to talk to you. To someone. You see, Conal... it's all... it's all gone wrong.'

At the end of the corridor were two small armchairs and she pulled him over towards them and he sat down heavily, his long legs sticking out.

Rebecca O'Neill and her best friend Cora Doyle walked past them, swaying slightly. 'Great night,' said Rebecca. 'Fair dues to you and Mary-Marg. You two are just fantastic, so you are.'

'Great... great...' Ciara turned back to Paddy.

'It's unravelling,' he said, still that stunned look on his face. 'I've got something shocking to tell you. I'm not... I'm not Conal's father. I mean, I *am* his father. He's my son, he's my boy... but we adopted him.' He looked at her.

'I know,' she said.

'You know?'

She nodded. 'I've always known.'

He looked at her. 'Because of...?'

'Yes...'

'So you know whose son he actually is?'

She nodded again as, behind them, Elaine, Monica and Siobhán were noisily coming out of the function room, their arms around each other, still singing 'If I Could Turn Back Time' at the top of their voices. It was a screechy rendition but nevertheless heartfelt.

'Look,' Paddy said, 'this is not the place. Tomorrow?'

She nodded. 'Any time. Alice is minding the shop for me.'

He nodded. 'You should be enjoying yourself... this is your big night...'

'It doesn't matter.'

'It does,' he said, standing up. 'It really does. I'm sorry...'

'It's all right... Are you coming in?'

'Not tonight,' he said. 'Not ever... I don't dance any more... two left feet.'

'You used to love dancing...'

He shrugged. 'Well... there you go... Look, I'll see you tomorrow, okay?' He looked at her again. 'I'm so sorry... what a mess us Blakes made of everything.'

He turned to go.

'Stay,' she said. 'Come in. All your friends are in there. All of us.'

'I know I should,' he said. 'But all I can think about is Conal. I love him. He's my boy. He really is. And... I need to talk to him.' He paused. 'Next time, okay? If I manage to sort things out with him. Then I will.' He smiled at her. 'Thanks, Ciara. In Newgrange, I was happier than I can ever remember feeling. It was as though the blood began to run in my veins again.' He paused. 'I've missed you, you know. I missed you for years and years. I missed everything.'

She nodded, understanding him perfectly. 'Me too,' she

said. 'But I've got to work out how to talk to Alice. She'll be up early, and that's not the time. But later... I'll let you know.' He reached for her hand again, clutching it in both of his. 'I'll call you tomorrow,' he said. 'I'll be thinking of you.'

39

ALICE

Alice's alarm had sounded and she lay for a moment mulling over the events of the night before. Conal had seemed utterly lost and confused about all he had learned about himself and his family. Alice and Max had left Conal and Becca alone. 'I'll mind him,' Becca had promised them, after she had hugged Alice and Max goodbye. 'I'll let you know in the morning how things are.' And then, in a lower voice: 'I can't believe his dad did that to him! I thought he was nice!'

Alice and Max had walked back to Sandycove, their arms linked, their bodies close together as Max had told her about his maternal grandmother. 'She was one of those early feminists,' he told her, 'who went out on marches and always had women in her house painting placards and wearing dungarees. I became their mascot, and they would bring me to protests. There's a famous photograph of these women burning their bras outside the archbishop's residence and there is a pushchair with a chubby toddler in it wearing a knitted bonnet. That's me.'

Alice had laughed. 'That explains a lot.'

He had looked hopeful. 'In a good way?'

She'd smiled. 'I couldn't possibly say. But it makes a lot of sense.'

Outside her house, he had stood, his hands in his pockets. 'So, m'lady,' he had said. 'We say goodnight. Until the morrow.'

He turned to go.

'Sleep well,' she'd called.

He looked at her briefly, a half-smile on his face.

She'd gone in, her head full of Conal and Becca... and of Max. How was she going to leave them all? The thought was unbearable. She loved this little life she'd had here for the past few weeks. It was where she belonged. Leaving now would be like stopping reading an amazing book halfway through. She had to know how the story ended.

She looked at the clock on the bedside table: 5.53 a.m. Right. Time to get up and make the bread.

Downstairs, she weighed out the ingredients, enough to make eight loaves. She'd got used to sifting all that flour and oats, adding the bicarb, the buttermilk and a swirl of local honey. She mixed it quickly, flipping it onto the wooden board and slicing it into eight pieces which she shaped into round discs before cutting crosses into the top, and sprinkling oats on before putting them into the oven.

By 6.40 a.m., she was leaving the house, with the loaves wrapped in greaseproof paper in two big IKEA bags. A trolley, she thought – one of those little pull-along ones – would be useful. Something else for her to-do list. And they needed more loaves. An army of bread makers was required. She closed the door quietly behind her, wondering how Ciara's night had gone, and hoping she was fast asleep, enjoying her extra hours.

The village was always surprisingly busy at that hour of the morning. She'd learned over the last few weeks that, far from a sleepy backwater, Sandycove was a bustling hive at all hours of the day. This morning, there was a troupe of lycra-clad cyclists heading towards the seafront, she must have met five or six dog walkers, and Jimbo McAlister and Jessica Feeney were sitting on the bench outside the shop, holding hands and talking. Jessica had on a short silver dress and Jimbo wore a pair of smart navy jeans with a slightly creased striped shirt, but it was the kind of shirt that you saved for special evenings out. Surely they hadn't been up all night?

'Morning, Alice,' said Jessica. 'What time will the Irish breakfast be on? Not to hurry you or anything, but we're both a bit peckish.'

'She means we have a fierce appetite on us, that's for sure,' said Jimbo, giving Jessica a squeeze.

Alice quickly unlocked the door, flicked on the lights, made sure the fridges were on, and the heating and the coffee machine. To save time, she filled a kettle and stacked her loaves of bread on the counter.

Jessica and Jimbo had sidled in behind her.

'We were at your mother's disco last night...' said Jessica.

'Class it was,' said Jimbo. 'Like the old days, but better...' And he turned his rugged, life-weary face towards Jessica, his eyes melting caramel as he took her in, and they gazed at each other, her small hand in his big, rough one.

Alice sliced the bread, which kept crumbling.

'That's the way I like it,' said Jimbo. 'My mam used to always give me the first slice. Piping hot from the oven, the butter would run off it like Sonia O'Sullivan in the Barcelona Olympics...'

Jessica laughed. 'You can't have too much butter,' she said. 'There's no such thing.'

'I'll have to buy you a block of butter every day,' said Jimbo, kissing her hand gently. 'You're as golden as Kerrygold.'

Jessica laughed and smiled back at him. 'We've been walking and talking all night,' said Jessica. 'I've got to go to work in two hours...'

The shop's bell jangled as Eva came in, carrying her loaves. 'You're open already?'

'I'm just getting an Irish breakfast for Jessica and Jimbo...'

'Morning, Mrs Murphy,' said Jimbo.

'Morning, Eva...' Jessica was smiling, as though the whole world was a happier and shinier place today.

'Good morning, Jessica, Jimbo,' said Eva. 'Have you been for a swim already?'

'No, not swimming...' Jessica turned to Jimbo. 'But we could?'

'We could go together...' Jimbo gazed at her. 'Now we've found each other...'

Jessica smiled at Eva and Alice. 'We've known each other for years, obviously, but it was only last night that we got talking properly.'

'We haven't been able to stop.' Jimbo seemed to stand even taller than he normally did. 'I'd given up on romance and all that business. Fed up with those apps and the whatnots. I wanted to meet someone in real life.'

Jessica nodded. 'Real life,' she echoed. 'I love real life.'

'I feel like I'm about to take off.' Jimbo gazed again on Jessica. 'Like I have heels of helium, or my heart is so full I'm going to float away.'

'I'll hold on...' Jessica gazed back at him.

'Here we go...' Alice handed over two Irish breakfasts, breaking up their loved-up reverie.

Once they'd gone, Eva closed the door and locked it again.

'We can't be opening too early,' she said. 'Unless it's an emergency.'

'It *was* an emergency,' insisted Alice. 'They were starving. And lovesick.'

Eve nodded approvingly. 'I remember my dances, when it was my time. It was the anticipation of them all... I used to make my own clothes in those days. I'd run up a dress or a top in an afternoon and wear it that night. There used to be a big dance hall in Dún Laoghaire and everyone from around would be there. And I'd go with my date and my friend would go with hers...'

'You mean Granddad?'

But Eva seemed to be too far down memory lane, thinking of all those happy days.

When everything was ready, they leant against the back wall, drinking their cups of tea, ready for the morning rush.

'I was at Conal Blake's house last night,' said Alice.

Eva nodded slowly, her hands around her mug of tea.

'You won't tell anyone this, will you?' said Alice. 'It can't get around... promise me?'

'Best not to tell anyone's secrets,' said Eva, picking up a slice of buttered bread. 'If I don't need to know it, then don't tell me.' Eva was always like this when you told her something, but sometimes you just needed someone else's perspective and Eva was the one person who never shared any news or gossip about anyone.

'He says he's adopted,' said Alice. 'He's only just found out...'

Eva remained silent.

'He doesn't know who his mother and father are, but they aren't his mother and father...' went on Alice.

'The poor divil,' said Eva, at last. 'The poor divil.' She

sighed heavily, and closed her eyes, giving her head a little shake.

'He's really upset.'

'Of course he is. Of course he is... Well, they should have told him before. Secrets gnaw away at you.'

Alice agreed. 'I feel so sorry for him. It's awful, isn't it?'

Eva was nodding. 'The people responsible should be ashamed of themselves.'

'Do you mean Paddy Blake and Conal's mother? They didn't mean *not* to tell him... they probably thought it was the right thing to do.'

'Oh, I'm not talking about them,' said Eva. 'It wasn't *their* secret to tell.' She paused. 'The secret was the woman who gave birth to him. She should have told.' She glanced at the clock on the wall. 'Eight a.m. Time to open up.'

They both turned to the front of the shop and looking through the glass were several faces – the dog walkers, sea swimmers and weekend early birds.

'Come on.' Eva was smiling at her. 'Let's feed the masses.'

40

CIARA

Ciara was awake, thinking about Paddy and Conal and the godawful mess of it all, when her phone buzzed.

PADDY

> Sorry for turning up last night. Just needed someone to talk to. I hope you are okay. Let me know if you would like to meet this morning? But I completely understand if you don't. Take care, Paddy.

CIARA

> Up for a run? Meet you on the hill?

PADDY

> I could be there in 15 minutes.

CIARA

> I'll just get my runners on. See you then.

* * *

Bernadette O'Hanlon, in her special 'I survived the Mojave

300K' T-shirt, powered past Ciara, arms pumping. 'Lovely day,' she called as she overtook. 'Rain on the way...'

But she was already gone before Ciara could answer.

Ciara was feeling nervous, unsure of what more revelations Paddy might have, but she definitely knew there was no going back. It was Conal her heart was going out to more than anyone. Poor Conal. What a shock for him.

And there was Paddy, appearing from the other side of the hill, slowing down his pace, his hand raised in greeting.

'Are we running or walking?' he called as he came closer.

'Whatever you want?'

'Walk?' he said. 'That okay with you?'

She was hugely relieved. Being expected to run, think and react would have been too much. Her little jogs up and down the hill had fulfilled the purpose of clearing her mind a little, and she now understood what people meant when they said they actually enjoyed running. But today, she needed to walk slowly so she had time to take it all in. If indeed he was going to tell her what she thought she already knew.

For a moment or two, they walked in silence, taking their route across the meadow and towards the forest.

He smiled at her. 'I'm so glad to see you,' he said. 'I'm always glad to see you, you know that. But I can't tell you how much better I feel now someone else knows.' He stopped. 'I don't know why we went along with it. Why I didn't say no... for years and years, I've been trying to excuse my part in it...'

'Why don't you start at the beginning?' Ciara felt a little shaky.

'Can we start with Lorcan Kennedy?' he began. 'If you don't mind?'

'I was in *love* with Lorcan Kennedy,' said Ciara.

'I hadn't forgotten,' said Paddy. 'So, what was he... twenty, twenty-one when he left?'

'Something like that,' said Ciara. 'I've tried not to think about him much. He didn't want to have anything to do with me or with Alice...'

He nodded. 'He wasn't a good person...'

'Not really...'

'He was selfish, only concerned with himself... I never understood that, really. You always try to look for the good in someone, thinking that they must have redeeming features. But maybe people are just born without them...' He paused. 'Look, I don't know how to say this because I don't want to hurt you...' He looked at her, concerned.

'Go on...'

'Well... my mother was having an affair with Lorcan...' He paused again. 'I'm sorry... She was... what? At least twice his age...'

'It's okay,' said Ciara flatly. 'I knew...'

'Dol said you knew,' he said. 'But I didn't know whether to believe her...'

Ciara nodded. 'I've always known. I saw them together.' Ciara was lost in a world where Lorcan Kennedy swanned about, quoting poetry and blathering on about whatever pretentious nonsense he thought would impress people. The worst thing was, it obviously did.

Paddy pulled a face. 'I'm sorry... I mean, I'm trying to get my head around all this. I mean, it's not *ideal* that your mother is having an affair with a friend of yours, who is meant to be going out with the girl you... the girl you are friends with.'

'When did Dol tell you this?'

'Yesterday afternoon. I went to see her to tell her that Conal knows he's adopted. And I thought she wouldn't have much to say. You might remember that she's not a people person...'

Understatement of the century. 'No...' she agreed.

'Anyway,' went on Paddy, 'she asked me to sit down. She never asks me to sit down. Normally, she's got this look on her face, a kind of look of eternal sufferance. I saw it once in a painting in the National Gallery on someone who is just suffering the mere mortals of the world. And to Dol, everyone is a mere mortal. Anyway, she told me to sit down and she came out with it. *Do you want to know who Conal's father is?* She likes upsetting people and is only happy if someone is crying because of something she said. She treated Breda like she was nothing. Poor Breda couldn't stand it by the end, not after everything...' He sighed, his hands to his face. 'So, yesterday, she said that Eva Murphy's daughter knows who Conal's biological father is. That you saw her and Lorcan Kennedy in the summer house on the day of George Murphy's funeral.' He shook his head. 'It explains everything. I always wondered why *you* never spoke to any of us again. Why *he* left so abruptly. Why *my father* was so furious. Everything. My mother having an affair with her son's friend.'

They sat in silence for a moment. And then Ciara spoke.

'The whole village was at my father's funeral. Except for...'

'Dol Blake and Lorcan Kennedy.'

'Exactly,' said Ciara. 'So, everyone was making their way to the church hall... that's where we had the reception...'

'I had delivered a whole load of beer for it that morning,' said Paddy.

'And I needed to tell Lorcan I was pregnant. I'd found out two weeks earlier and I hadn't told him. Dad had been so ill and... anyway, I was determined to tell him. And I cycled to

Landfall... someone said they'd seen him heading through the gates.' She swallowed. 'And anyway...'

'You saw them?'

Ciara nodded. 'Your housekeeper was there...'

'Mags? She was a lovely woman...'

'She met me and asked me if everything was okay. She was probably wondering why I'd left my father's funeral... but anyway, I said I was looking for Lorcan and I went down to the summer house and there they were... your mother and Lorcan.'

Paddy was silent for a moment. 'I'm sorry,' he said softly.

'Anyhow, I ran away,' went on Ciara. 'Picked up my bike and went back to the funeral like nothing had happened. Made sandwiches and millions of cups of tea and never said a word. The performance of a lifetime. I couldn't stop crying for the first month or so after. Lorcan left straight away and I could only guess what was going on with all of you at Landfall...' She could feel herself becoming emotional. All of what she had packed away was still there. Not as bad, thankfully, because it had been overwhelming. Paddy sensed she was becoming upset.

'But there's more. Much more – and it's so much worse.'

Here we go, she thought, bracing herself. They walked along the mowed path through the shimmering green and wildflowers.

'So... my mother became pregnant...' Paddy stopped to look at Ciara, to gauge her reaction.

'You mean...?'

Paddy nodded. 'She told my father and, of course, he went mad. He'd put up with a lot by then. The affairs. Lorcan wasn't the first. He probably wasn't the last. But anyway, I was going out with Breda. Our fathers were friends. And... well, I hadn't met anyone in Sandycove who was interested in me. And Breda was. Or, rather, her father was very interested in my family's money, and vice versa. It was a match made in the bar of the Enniskerry Golf Club. God, I was a fool. Poor Breda...'

Ciara nodded. 'You were both so young...'

Paddy nodded. 'But this is where it gets worse. Well... my mother suggested that Breda and I take the baby, adopt it. Bring it up as our own. Initially, we thought it was a ridiculous idea, but my mother is clever. She knew about Breda's endometriosis and that she might never be able to have children... so Dol found the perfect way of getting her onside, as though this were a solution. But how could you say no to a baby, to your mother? Family pride and honour were hanging in the balance. I didn't want the whole village to know what my mother had done. And my father was threatening all sorts. Breda and I convinced ourselves that what we were doing was a good thing. We were married and she began telling people she was pregnant and then disappeared back to Wexford for the last few months. Meanwhile, Dol just went about her normal business. Big coats, stayed in the car. No one noticed anything.'

'She was a bit of a recluse anyway...'

'By that time, she was. She never had any friends. Your mother was her only friend, she used to say.'

Ciara nodded. 'Apparently. Mam never spoke about it.'

'I wonder if she knew,' said Paddy. 'Dol once said that Eva Murphy was the only person who could look at someone and know their whole life story...'

'She's definitely perceptive,' agreed Ciara. 'But I doubt she's guessed this.' *Only me*, she thought. *I knew and I guessed and now everyone will know. Including Alice.*

'We adopted Conal. And tried to pretend all this was normal. And I loved Conal so much. He was a delight. Still is. He's my son. As well as my mother's. God, it's so messed up, isn't it? And Breda loved him. But the secret began to gnaw away at her and she began accusing me of colluding with my parents and her parents. Eventually, Breda couldn't do it any more and she left. Packed up, barely said goodbye to me.'

'Poor Breda...'

'She tried to explain to Conal. And it was then that I should have told him. But I didn't.' Paddy looked shocked at his own behaviour. 'I mean, I should have come clean, explained everything. But he was upset about Breda leaving. He clung to me so hard. He wouldn't leave my side for weeks. I took time off work and we just played in the garden, frisbee and football and all that. We'd go fishing. And I could see he was doing okay...' He gave a shrug. 'You know? He still had me. And I remember thinking to myself that the moment had passed. Why would he ever find out? My mother was never going to tell him, Dad was dead. Breda gone. And I thought our secret was safe. Or I thought that if he ever did find out, it would be okay, and that our bond and our love was strong enough...' He had tears in his eyes, which he wiped roughly with the heel of his hand.

'Poor Conal.'

Paddy was nodding. 'I know.' He closed his eyes for a moment. 'I know...' He opened them again to fix Ciara with a look. 'I love him more than I could love anyone.'

'Of course you do. You just have to make it right.'

Ciara and Paddy had reached the cool of the forest and they made their way along the soft path, through the sun-dappled grove. 'What are you going to do?'

Paddy shrugged. 'Come clean. Be there for any questions... and more than anything, keep telling him I'm sorry and I love him.'

'At least...' Ciara struggled to find the words. 'At least he had you. If he hadn't, he wouldn't have had any father. Alice didn't.'

'But she had you and you are amazing...' He smiled at her and she found herself smiling back.

'I just hope,' he said, serious again, 'he's able to forgive me. If he doesn't, I don't know what I will do.'

'Well, we're just going to have to make sure he does,' she said firmly. They had reached the edge of the forest, where the grass gave way to a floor which was soft and yielding, covered in twigs and leaves and dappled with light. 'The light always finds a way in.'

He paused. 'You know it makes Conal and Alice brother and sister...'

Ciara breathed in. 'I'm going to talk to Alice today.'

41

ALICE

All that Saturday morning, customers talked about the disco. 'My WhatsApp group was going mad this morning,' said one woman, 'with all the stories from last night. Your mother and Mary-Marg played a blinder. Now, tell her I'll be at the next one.'

They were busy selling the Irish breakfasts and Alice found a rhythm of talking and serving, like some kind of tai chi master, moving around in some kind of efficiently perfect flow. It was exhilarating – a glow emanated from within, making her feel both calm and excited. Thinking of Conal last night and seeing how much he felt he was losing made her focus on everything she possessed. Her mother, her grandmother and this shop, and she now realised why her mother had never wanted to leave it. It was part of her, part of all of them.

She looked around; at the shelves that had been there since her great-grandfather's time, at the softened oak counter, at the floorboards which were polished by a million feet, at the doorway, where her grandfather George had carried Eva through on their wedding day. She could feel the history. And it wasn't just history, it was Murphy history. This shop was where she belonged, not some beach on the other side of the world. It was *nice* to wear flip-flops 365 days of the year, but it was so deeply satisfying to run a small shop on the edge of Ireland.

It was obvious, really. Her life was here. It always had been. She had nothing to prove by travelling and being away. She wasn't brave or free. She'd just been far from home. Having people who loved you, who wanted you, was precious. She was lucky. And she wanted to be here, she had always wanted to be here. And perhaps, if her mother agreed, she could stay and help run the shop. She was smiling, her mind full of everything she wanted to do in the shop, and where she might live. Perhaps she could take a college course in business and see which of her ideas they could really make a success of?

The bell above the shop's door rang. Max was slipping inside.

'Morning...' She smiled at him, thinking of their walk home and the look on his face when they had said goodbye. Perhaps he would be happy to know she was staying... perhaps...

But he wasn't smiling. There was a slight frown on his face, which he always had when he was thinking. 'I've discovered something,' Max was saying.

'Have you?'

'Remember I told you about the box of books I picked up at Conal's grandmother's house? There was a book in there that a customer was looking for. Well, there was a letter inside it, addressed to Dol Blake, and I put it to one side because I was so pleased to match the book up with the customer, and I thought I would give it back to her at some point. But I totally forgot. And by the way, I just noticed a first edition of *Light A Penny*

Candle in the box as well, which must be worth quite a bit. But anyway... for some reason this morning, I remembered the letter.'

'And you've read it...?'

'Not *read* it,' he said. 'But glanced at it. I was thinking about Conal... and about the Blakes and everything he told us last night. And I thought that perhaps the letter had some kind of clue to who he was.'

'And does it?'

He shook his head. 'It's from your grandmother.'

'My grandmother?' Alice was confused. 'Are you sure?'

Max nodded, patting the inside jacket pocket of his blue linen blazer. He took out a small, blue envelope. 'Look, addressed to Dol Blake...'

The paper was so thin, so insubstantial. But there was her grandmother's handwriting, stronger than it was now, Alice noticed. She hesitated before pulling the letter from the envelope.

Dear Dol...

I am writing this after seeing you off on your honeymoon. And I thought how beautiful you looked. And you turned and waved to us all and I could see you looking for someone and then you saw me. If you want me to tell you that you looked happy, you did. If you want me to tell you that I wish you and Patrick all the love and luck in the world, I will.

It was like waving at Grace Kelly, someone said, marrying her Prince Rainier. I wish your mother had bothered to turn up rather than saying that she was at the Galway Races and that her new husband didn't like her to be away from him. You borrowed my blue necklace, the one I'd bought in that fancy shop in town. You can keep it as a good luck charm.

It all fell into place yesterday at the wedding as I watched you and Patrick together in the church. Dol, I have so many memories of us growing up together, but I am sorry to say that I no longer want to be your friend. I hope you understand. I'm sorry.

Eva

42

ALICE

Alice put the letter back into the envelope and handed it to Max.

'You keep it,' he said.

'I should give it to Dol, I suppose,' said Alice. 'It is hers.' She looked at Max. 'We shouldn't have read it...'

'Well...' He shrugged. 'Could we call ourselves archivists? Does that make it better?'

'Historians?' She smiled at him. 'Except we should give it back. I'm going to walk down to Honeysuckle Lodge. I could leave it at reception.'

He nodded. 'I'm coming with you.'

'We could go now, if I could find someone to mind the shop? And what about your bookshop?'

'I can close for lunch, back in an hour...'

Alice tried to call Ciara but there was no answer and Eva wasn't upstairs. Mary-Marg was crossing the road with her two lumbering boys.

'Morning, Alice,' said Mary-Marg. 'Say hello to Alice, boys.'

'Hello, Alice,' they mumbled in stereo.

'Would you be able to mind the shop for an hour?' asked Alice. 'I'll pay you.'

'You will not pay them,' said Mary-Marg. 'They will be grateful for the experience. Yes, of course they will. I will supervise but of course they will mind the shop. Say thank you to Alice, boys.'

'Thank you to Alice, boys,' they said, cracking each other up.

Alice and Max walked through Sandycove, along the coast, past the big houses, the ones with the huge gardens and oak trees and multiple cars in the front.

'I feel like a member of the Famous Five,' said Max. 'I always wanted to join them.'

'A dream come true, then,' said Alice, smiling at him.

'But I used to think that if I joined them, we wouldn't be the Famous Five. We'd be the Famous Six... and that doesn't work.'

'Unless one of the Famous Five died...'

'Don't say such a thing!' He stopped in the street, in mock distress, crossing himself, making Alice laugh. 'We'll just have to be our own detective team,' he went on. 'The Tenaciously, Terrifically Talented Two.'

Honeysuckle Lodge was ahead of them as they walked through the gates and along the short path. 'We'll just leave it at reception, okay?' said Alice, as they stood in front of the door. 'We won't even say who we are...'

The door was opened by Abigail before she could even knock. 'Ah, Alice! How are you? And Max, what a pleasure. I've nearly finished *The Three Musketeers*. Thank you for your recommendation. It's kept me busy, I can tell you, I haven't been able to put it down. Now, are you here to see Dol Blake? It's so nice she's having so many visitors lately. Her son was in earlier and Conal the other day, and now you two... go straight up and just give a quick knock on the door. Okay?' She smiled at them both as they stepped inside. 'That's right, through there and up the stairs. Dinner will be ready in a few minutes so you won't be able to stay long.'

She beamed at them and The Tenacious Two found themselves making their way up the stairs and standing outside Dol's room.

'We could post it under the door,' said Alice, hoping Max would think that was the right thing to do. And luckily, he did.

'Go on then,' he said in a whisper. But the door was suddenly opened and a young woman dressed in a nurse's uniform was standing there. 'Mrs Blake, visitors for you. Go straight in.' And she nipped around them, making them have to step *into* the room to allow her to pass.

Dol was sitting in her chair by the window. She looked up at Alice. 'You came again?'

Alice nodded. 'We found a letter,' she said. 'Well, Max did...'

Max cleared his throat. 'Hello, Mrs Blake,' he said. 'I'm a friend of Conal's... your grandson... I mean...' He looked desperately for a second at Alice. 'Anyway, I'm a friend of Conal's. And Alice's... and well... we found... I found...' He dried up.

'Max had some books from your house...'

'Paddy... He said I could take some of your old books... I have a bookshop in the village...'

Dol was looking at the two of them as though they were both mad.

'We found a letter,' repeated Alice, taking it out of her jacket pocket, and handing it over. 'It's yours. From... well, we'd only know who it's from if we'd read it, which we haven't...'

'It's more of a note than a letter,' said Max.

They watched as Dol held it in her hand, reading the words on the front. 'I thought this had been brought with me,' she said. 'Not that I need the letter. I memorised the words.' She looked back at Alice. 'It was the cruellest letter I ever received. A bullet to my heart...'

Alice wanted to tell her that in all her life she had never known Eva to be cruel in any way. She put food out for birds, she rescued spiders, she was the woman who loved Alice and Ciara. She was the one who made their lives *work*. Without her, they wouldn't be who they were.

'She's not cruel,' said Alice. 'She must have had a good reason...'

A flicker of a smile played on Dol's lips. 'So you did read it?'

'Yes,' admitted Alice. 'I'm sorry.'

'My own fault for leaving it in that book. *Light A Penny Candle*, I think?'

'That's right,' said Max, smiling. 'A first edition. I am going to sell it and I will give you the money.'

'Oh, I don't need money,' said Dol, dismissively. 'Give it to charity... or whatever you want.' She looked back at Alice. 'I didn't blame her,' she said. 'Not for one second. It may have felt cruel to me, but I understood why. She'd taken all she could from me. She let me go.' There was a knock on the door.

'Dinner, Mrs Blake?' said a voice. 'Will you be taking it in your room or in the dining room?'

'Up here,' said Dol. She looked back at Alice and Max. 'Thank you for returning my letter.'

Alice and Max edged out of the room, just as a member of staff in a pink housecoat came in carrying a tray.

'You look just like her,' said Dol, just as the door closed behind them. 'The spitting image.'

Max and Alice raced downstairs. Alice's heart was beating

out of her chest and it wasn't until they were back on the main road and halfway to Sandycove again that they slowed down.

'We did the right thing,' breathed Max.

'I hope we did,' said Alice, thinking of Dol and finding herself feeling sorry for her. Why did Eva send that letter, what had happened?

'Are you hungry?' Max was saying. 'Perhaps... you might like...' He paused. 'Some food or something.' He laughed a little awkwardly. 'I mean, you're surrounded by food, so that's probably not ideal. But different food. Food you can't buy in Murphy's... like...' He paused again. 'Something like... fish and chips? The Tenacious Two have to eat. And there is a really nice van down by the harbour...'

They walked down to the shore past the people sitting on the sea wall, eating ice creams, the evening dreamers staring out to sea and the exercise class, dressed in lycra and sweatbands, who were doing sit-ups and lunges, their muscles glistening in the reddening light of the sunset.

Once they'd bought their fish and chips, they sat on a bench and opened the pile of hot chips, the crispy scampi and the mini pots of tartare sauce.

'You won't get this in Australia,' said Max, spearing a chip with a little wooden fork.

'No, I won't...' said Alice, looking out to sea and along the low stone wall to the wooden hut which housed the sauna. People were running out of it and shrieking as they jumped off the rocks, hitting the water. There was something about Irish life that she'd forgotten all about, the way everybody was to one another, the ease, the familiarity even with strangers, the teasing, the humour, the kindness... Just being back over these last few weeks had been transformative.

'How's Conal?' she asked. 'I've been worried about him.'

'He's not great,' said Max. 'He's really upset...'

'Understandably. Imagine finding out your father is not your father... and that everyone lied to you.'

'It's a lot to process.'

'I adore Conal. From the first moment we met, we just got on, you know? Same sense of humour... he's such a sweet person.'

Max nodded. 'He really is. He'd do anything for anyone.' He smiled at her. 'You get on with everyone...'

'Not everyone...' She thought of Dol and how Nelson Mandela wouldn't have found her easy.

'Willie liked you...'

'I like him...'

'I can't believe he asked you out...' Max pulled a face.

'Oh, he was just being nice. And anyway, he's going to come and do wine tastings on a few Saturdays.' But she felt suddenly so happy. Max was jealous and she was glad he was jealous.

'He's got a cheek. I mean, you're a little out of his league.'

Alice smiled. 'I don't think I know enough about wine for him...'

'I think there's such a thing as knowing *too much* about wine,' said Max.

'No, but it's nice to have a passion.' Alice looked at him. *He likes me*, she thought, and she felt a glow spread through her body. It was so nice to be *liked*, and to be liked by someone as nice and attractive as Max. She hadn't realised that she'd been lonely all these years, working abroad, teaching in short-term positions, not feeling she had a home. And yet, all along, she'd had Sandycove. 'I don't know if I want to go,' she said. 'I've been really happy here...'

He began to smile at her. 'You mean the thought of a life

without scampi and chips eaten on a bench is enough to make you want to stay?'

'Yes,' she said. 'And Mum and Gran. I don't want to leave them. Gran is getting older and I want to be around for her. She's practically my favourite person in the world and I've always known how much I love my mum, but I now know how much I like her. And we're watching this Swedish drama and we have three series to go and she can't watch it without me and I can't make her wait a year for the next episode.'

Max laughed. 'I think those are good reasons to stay.'

'And the shop... I love it. It's part of the family. My great-grandfather started it. My grandfather and my grandmother ran it and loved it, and my mother has put everything she can into it. It's a beautiful place, it makes so many people happy. And if I stayed and worked here, it would take the pressure off Mum. I could do mornings, so she could lie in. We could do it together.'

Max was grinning wider than she'd ever seen him. 'Sounds like a plan.'

Just then her phone pinged.

CIARA

Can you make a quick chat? What time will you be home?

ALICE

In ten minutes…

She put down her phone. 'Weird. Mum needs me home. I don't know why. Do you think she's angry I left Jake and Josh in charge of the shop?' She rang Ciara's number. 'Mum,' she said, 'I'm so sorry but I had to leave to do something and Mary-Marg was there...'

Ciara cut her off. 'Don't worry about that. The shop's grand.

Mary-Marg will close up for us. The boys enjoyed the responsibility, apparently. But this is... this is a little more serious than that.'

Alice felt sick. What could this be? She looked at Max, fear in her eyes.

'Come on,' said Max, sensing the urgency. 'I'll walk you home.'

43

CIARA

Eva was sitting at the kitchen table, her mug of tea untouched, when Alice came in. Alice glanced at Eva and then at Ciara.

'Everything okay...?' she began.

'I've got something to tell you...' said Ciara. 'Mam, do you know what I am going to say?'

Eva shrugged. 'Depends on what it is.'

'I suppose it does.' Ciara breathed in, unsure where to start. 'Well, I suppose I could start on the day of Dad's funeral...' She looked back at Eva. 'It was an awful day, wasn't it?'

Eva nodded. 'It was... it was a long day. I thought it would never end. There were so many people and I needed a moment to just try to think...'

'That's what I did,' said Ciara. 'Do you remember? I left. I said I needed air and a moment to myself, and I promised I'd be back in half an hour. We had the reception at the house and I would have to be on tea-making duty. But I needed to see someone. I had to tell him something.'

'Lorcan,' said Eva.

'That's right.' Ciara pressed her lips together. 'I'd found out

I was pregnant and I hadn't told him because Dad was so ill...' She looked at Eva. 'I hadn't told you, either. Not then.'

'It was quite the few weeks,' said Eva, reaching for Alice's hand. 'But look what we all got out of it in the end. George would have doted on you.'

Ciara nodded in agreement. 'He really would have,' she said. 'You're a lot like him. Practical. Clever. Head for business. Far more than me.'

'And me,' said Eva. 'I'm fine for the bread-making and chatting to customers, but no interest in profits and all that.'

'Anyway,' said Ciara, taking in a deep breath. 'Someone told me that they'd seen Lorcan going into the gates of Landfall. I didn't think too much of it. He was always trying to make money. Never spent a penny on anything. He'd pat his jacket pocket after Dad had paid him and say, "That's for my travels, that is". So I just assumed he was doing a bit of gardening or an odd job. He hadn't been at the funeral, but I wasn't thinking straight. I mean, I wasn't annoyed that he wasn't there to support me. I just must have thought he was too upset to be there. I thought he loved Dad and... Oh, I don't know. I was still giving him the benefit of the doubt back then.' She paused. 'I had to. He was the father of my unborn child. I thought he would be happy about it and we'd be a family, and the sooner he knew, the sooner I would be relieved that all was going to be well, and we could tell Mam, and tell all the village. It would be a happy ending to losing Dad.'

Eva was patting Alice's hand. 'Here's our happy ending,' she said.

Ciara smiled at Alice. 'She certainly is. So, I cycled up to Landfall and there I am, a slightly crazed, sweaty, hormonal mess. We had spent the last two weeks minding Dad *and* the shop, the two of us were exhausted, weren't we?' She turned to

Eva. 'And I was just fixated on telling Lorcan and then getting back to the reception. I remember thinking that perhaps he would come with me and we could tell everyone, make an announcement.' She sighed. 'So, I got to Landfall and left my bike on the ground, and after sweating all the way and after the weeks of being indoors, and holding Dad's hand, and the smell of the incense in the church and... Oh God, it had been suffocating but, finally, there was a breeze off the sea, and I could breathe again. So, I began to run down the drive and Dol's red sports car was at the front. And I was just about to go towards the front door and ring the bell when I heard someone behind me. It was Mags Higgins, you remember, their housekeeper, she used to work in Murphy's years ago?'

Eva nodded. 'They were lucky to have her. She had a phobia about dust. Wouldn't stand for it. And she waged war on germs, as well. A great woman for the Ajax, as I recall. Loved the stuff. Used to come in and buy a tub a week. Might explain the look in her eyes. Ajax is *strong*.'

Ciara continued. 'Mags was amazed to see me. "Oh, you poor loveen", she said. "Is everything all right with ye?" And she asked me what I was doing there. And I remember thinking that she had a funny look on her face. It's all a bit strange, but I was thinking that she just thought I was terrible for leaving my father's funeral, you know how people are with doing the right thing and all that. But there was a look on her face...' Ciara stopped, her brow furrowed, trying to recall exactly what that fleeting moment was on that day. 'She looked kind of panicky. "Lorcan," I asked, "have you seen him?" And Mags shook her head but also glanced towards the end of the garden, towards the sea. Towards the summer house.'

Alice glanced at Eva, whose eyes were fixed on Ciara's.

'It was just this fleeting look,' went on Ciara, 'as though she didn't even realise she'd done it. But I knew then what was going on. Don't ask me how or why. But I just knew… I started running around the side of the house, past the rose garden and onto the lawn towards the summer house. It had been newly painted, I remember. Perhaps this is the work Lorcan had been doing, I told myself. He was just painting. But I heard noises. Not speaking. Not talking. Dol Blake. And then a man's voice. I think I must have stopped breathing. My heart may have stopped also. I crept forward and I could see two people. A woman and a man, their arms around each other. Her hair messed up and on his face was her lipstick. Revlon's Pink Panther. He had his hands on her hips, pulling her towards him, her head back as he kissed her neck. Lorcan.'

Eva gasped. 'Oh my sweet Lord! I thought it was something like that!'

'Mum, you poor thing!' said Alice.

Ciara shrugged. 'I've never experienced shock like it. As though the blood left my body. As though from that moment on, I was not the same person. And I wasn't. Not really. I mean, we'd just lost Dad, hadn't we? And that was bad enough, but I'd been prepared for that, in many ways. This was like being electrified and left for dead.'

'What did you do?' asked Alice. 'Did they see you?'

Ciara nodded. 'Dol did. I remember those icy eyes, kind of triumphant. I staggered backwards and then ran… all the way back to the gate. Picked up my bike and began to cycle home. And just joined the funeral. And it was ideal, really, because no one wanted to chat to me, it was all people just saying how sorry they were…' She looked at Eva. 'If I could turn back time, I certainly would not have allowed that to affect Dad's funeral. I've always felt so bad about it. I always thought I had let you down.'

'Never. I'm just sorry that it happened.' Eva reached across and took Ciara's hand. 'You poor thing.'

'I got over it. And anyway, I had Alice to think of. And so I started making sandwiches, in this very kitchen. Do you remember? I just buttered loaves and loaves of bread...'

'I remember it,' said Eva. 'You wouldn't let anyone help you...'

'I was in a daze,' said Ciara. 'If I kept busy, I wouldn't have to think about what I'd seen.' She paused. 'We get through, though. It's amazing what we can withstand.'

'If you give it enough time,' said Eva.

Ciara smiled at her. 'Healing takes time,' she said. 'It takes ages for shock and pain to leave. Years, even. But, my God. Seeing Lorcan, who was twenty, with Dol Blake who must have been around forty-five... younger than me now. She was in her prime, wasn't she?'

'Always was,' said Eva. 'She hit her prime younger than anyone and held onto it for longer.'

There was silence in the room. Alice was trying to take it all in. 'So... Dol and Lorcan were having an affair?' she said slowly.

'That's right,' Eva said. 'Which means...' She looked at Ciara. 'Does it?'

Ciara nodded.

'Means what?' asked Alice.

Ciara and Eva looked at each other. 'I guessed that it might be possible,' Ciara said. 'But it was only when Paddy told me the truth. I mean, until now, I thought it could be. But what do you do if you don't know something is real. You can't go and ask. What if you're wrong?'

Eva was nodding.

'What?' said Alice. 'What did you guess? What is true? What did Paddy say?'

'That Dol became pregnant,' said Ciara. She and Eva now turned to look at Alice. 'She had a baby...'

'A baby?' Alice was frowning. 'So what did she do with the...' She looked up at Ciara, and then Eva. 'The baby...? She allowed it to be adopted?'

Ciara nodded.

'Conal?' said Alice slowly. 'So Conal is Dol and Lorcan's *child*...? And if he's Dol and Lorcan's child... that means that he's...'

Eva and Ciara were nodding again.

'My... my... what exactly?' said Alice. 'My half-brother?'

'Yes,' said Ciara.

'Conal is my half-brother? I have a *brother*?' Alice began to smile. 'Oh my God... but you two knew...'

'We guessed,' said Eva. 'Neither of us have ever discussed it. Your mother saw them and I... well, I knew what Dol Blake was capable of.'

'So what happened between the two of you?' Alice asked.

'I just realised that life was better and easier without her. She poisoned everything and I just became tired of being part of her life.'

'But you did grow up together? You were friends, right?'

'I'll start at the beginning,' said Eva.

44

EVA

'I've never worked her out, not in all these years,' said Eva. 'But some people are just born that way. In the beginning, we were never out of each other's houses, Dol in those flouncy dresses that she was under strict instructions never to muddy. We were babies together, then girls, then teenagers, but... it was strange, really, she became increasingly angry if anything good happened to me. It was as if she needed me to be in the background, so she could shine. Which was fine, I didn't mind. But if I had any other friends, Dol would become petulant and mean, calling them names, and telling me things about them that she'd heard. Or in school when it came to exams, if I was praised or did well, it made Dol so angry. She once took my history homework and hid it. I never did find it. But where Dol succeeded was where she'd always succeeded – the way she looked.'

Eva looked at Ciara and Alice. 'She was so pretty,' she said. 'Like a little doll, everyone said. When she was small, her mother curled her hair every night. Dol's mother, Mildred, was like a film star herself, and the only woman in the village who had *Vogue* on order. Mr Feeney who ran the newsagent's would keep it behind the counter for her. Dol's father used to work in the garment factories of Birmingham, staying away for months at a time. Now that wasn't unusual, many fathers worked away in those days, to send money home to the family, but Dol's father stayed away for longer and longer until he just didn't bother coming home again. And so it was just Dol and her mother... and she was a cold fish. I think doing her hair and dressing her up were the only times Dol's mother ever touched her. On a Sunday, when everyone in Sandycove gathered at Mass, Dol was always resplendent. Mildred would plan the outfits and she'd give Dol things of hers to wear, a little evening bag or a straw hat. On Easter, Dol would be all in yellow; on Christmas morning, she would be in red and white. A generation later, Mildred would have been some kind of designer. She *certainly* shouldn't have been a mother. She was bored to distraction, but dressing up Dol was her little bit of fun.'

Ciara and Alice made eye contact. 'I couldn't get you to wear anything nice,' said Ciara. 'You wore those brown corduroy dungarees on repeat for about eight years.'

'I loved those dungarees,' said Alice. 'I was so upset when they finally fell apart.' She turned back to Eva. 'Go on, Gran...'

'Well,' said Eva. 'I adored Dol, completely idolised her. To be a friend of Dol Duffy brought great social cachet. We joined the Girl Guides together and when we walked into the scout hall that first evening, the room went quiet. Dol was wearing *lipstick*...' Eva gave a laugh. 'We were all thirteen and the lipstick created a crescendo of excited hysteria. Dol became an instant celebrity and we were totally in her thrall. And as her neighbour and best friend, well, it was like being in the court at Versailles.' She shrugged. 'But as Dol grew older, her mother seemed to lose interest, and anyway, Dol didn't want to be

Mildred's plaything any more. She would spend more and more time at my house and my mother and father didn't mind at all because they felt a bit sorry for her. But Dol seemed invincible. After the hysteria caused by the lipstick, she began looking for other ways to shock and awe. She was the first person I knew to wear a mini dress. She sent off to London for a pattern and some fabric and she made a dress for herself, using her mother's sewing machine. And then we were all hooked, all of us girls, making our own dresses and skirts and belts. She would go as high and as short as she could, her eyelashes as heavy as possible, and drenched in so much perfume that your eyes would water. The nuns in school were driven crazy by her. When we were sixteen, we started going to the Top Hat dance hall in Dún Laoghaire. Every young person from Donabate to Delgany would turn up, dressed up to the nines. Shiny shoes, smart suits, the boys would all come from their different jobs in factories and car mechanics' and offices, the girls all looked like film stars, headscarves and sunglasses, legs on show, our mothers scandalised. But we were as innocent as they came. It was so much fun. Our gang of girls, dancing on a Saturday night at the Top Hat.'

'It sounds lovely,' said Ciara. 'Every generation needs its disco.' She smiled at Alice. 'Even us middle-aged.'

'There were signs, however, that all was not right with Dol,' went on Eva. 'She was known for getting angry, kind of fits of rage. To most people, she was as nice as pie, as though she were in a permanent beauty contest, her whole life one big Rose of Tralee, but with me she could rant and rave, give out, berate me for things I'd said or done. And other times, she'd cry about something and I would soothe her and tell her she was wonderful and how much everyone loved her. Or it might be towards some person in a shop who had stepped in front of her, and the language she would use! I didn't know anyone who swore like that. And Dol was like my sister, remember? We'd grown up from babies together and you don't walk away from your sister, just because she gets mad from time to time.

'Except it got worse. And she started raging at everyone for the slightest thing. Friends were staying away and I had two lives, one with Dol, and one with my other friends. She had a few boyfriends in those days, good-looking lads who knew how to dance and smoke and could drive cars. But it happened one evening in the Top Hat when someone tapped me on the shoulder.' Eva smiled. 'He looked... like a young George Harrison. Dol was off dancing with some boy somewhere, and so this young George Harrison type asked me if I wanted to dance. I said yes. And we danced all night, the two of us, laughing and talking, and between dances he would fetch us both a lemonade – not many of us drank in those days. Think of it, we were only seventeen or so. And at the end of the night, he asked if I would be there the following week.

'All week, I couldn't sleep. I slept in hard rollers. I put every cream I could find on my face – Astral, Pond's, some substance I found in my mother's dressing table which stung. And I made a new dress. Pink. Flowers. Short. I came downstairs and my mother and father – both of whom had become well used to the new style and even liked it –said how nice I looked. And the thing is, I did look nice. I knew it. It wasn't because I was a great beauty or anything – I wasn't Dol Duffy.' She shrugged. 'I didn't want to be Dol Duffy. I was perfectly happy being myself. And perhaps that's what she hated most.

'I remember Mam and Dad waving me off at the door, the two of them smiling at me. And there was Dol coming out of her house. She could sense something. You know when you know someone, when you have spent your life around them, and you know when something has changed, when something has shifted? She knew. She knew I was... well, not in love... not then, anyway, but she knew I was different. I was excited and confident. Happy. And she liked that not one bit.

'"The dress," she said, her nose wrinkling. "Did you make it?" "Of course I did..." "Looks like it. It's wonky. And the colour is the one on the walls of St Brigid's." St Brigid's was a notorious asylum where they put women who were wayward, hard to control. Fighters, in other words. Rebels. "Your hair looks like it's been electrocuted." She laughed at me. "Did you put your finger in the socket?" "Mam and Dad said I looked nice..." "I was only joking! God, no sense of humour."

'And on we walked. Now I hadn't told her about my George Harrison man. But she was looking at me, wondering. But I paid no mind. We handed over our money and in we went. And there he was. He looked up and had no eyes for anyone but me. I introduced him to Dol and you could see it, the penny was dropping. So *that* was what was different about me. A man. A good-looking, charming man at that. And then she started asking questions. Who was he, what did his parents do. And by the end of the night, by asking around, she knew everything. His family were rich, she discovered. They owned a big company. But I paid no heed. The man and I began going out for drives, up Killiney Hill, to the pictures, an ice cream on the pier and we enjoyed the summer. All very innocent. All very nice. We had such fun. He told me all about himself. He was only twenty-one and was already dealing with too much, with the pressures of the family business. And his father was cruel and unpleasant, his mother, a bit weak. But I liked him. Could feel myself feeling more than like for him. We even talked about what it would be like to be married, and he asked me if I would consider someone like him.

'I brought him home to meet Mam and Dad who both loved him immediately. And after that tea, I walked him out to his car and we kissed, just quickly. As I waved him off, I thought I saw something out of the corner of my eye. Dol was up in her bedroom, watching us.'

'Who was he?' asked Alice.

'Patrick Blake,' said Eva. 'Paddy's father. Conal's grandfather.'

'No!' said Alice.

Ciara looked grimly pale. 'Go on, Mam,' she said.

'Anyway, I never saw him again... Dol didn't come back to the Top Hat and neither did he. Nor did he call around to see me. I pined and moped, desperate for a phone call, a knock on the door. Until there was one. But it was Dol, whom I hadn't seen for weeks. "I'm getting married," she said. "Will you be my bridesmaid?" She smiled. "It's this Saturday... We have to get married straight away because I'm pregnant. But you're not to tell a soul, right? Because his parents are crazy Catholics and they don't want anyone to know. But it's either that or I go to a mother and baby home." She shrugged then, as though this were all a game. I was still catching up. "But who are you marrying?" "Patrick Blake, silly. While he's been courting you, he's been seeing me." She smiled. "I hope you'll be very happy for us, and anyway, you have to be – you're our bridesmaid."'

45

CIARA

Alice turned to Ciara. 'Did you know any of this?'

'Nothing...' Ciara looked at Eva who was sitting there, her two knees pressed together and her feet up on the low stool. She had carried all this around with her forever? 'Why didn't you tell us?'

'Because it was ancient history. Things happen in life, you can't dwell on them... you have to get on with things.'

'But did you go to the wedding? Were you bridesmaid?' asked Ciara, hoping she would say no, and that she set fire to the registry office or found some other way of sabotaging the event.

But of course, just as Ciara knew she would, Eva nodded. 'Yes, and it was a lovely day.' She almost smiled that wry smile of hers. 'And the bride looked magnificent. It was the biggest wedding that Sandycove had seen in years. In those days, everything was so much more modest. People didn't have the money. But the Blakes did...'

'That could have been you,' said Alice. 'Living a life of luxury up in Landfall.'

Eva didn't say anything, just looked out of the window for a moment, deep in memory. 'God knows how they turned it all around in a few days, but they did. Dol was brought into the city centre to a shop called Blissful Brides by Barbara. It was the most exclusive in the whole country. I was brought along too and dressed in pale lilac...'

'Your least favourite colour,' said Ciara.

'Don't think that didn't escape me,' said Eva with a smile. 'Dol knew what she was doing.'

'And what about Patrick Blake?' said Alice. 'So he's Paddy Blake's father, Conal's grandfather?'

'That's right,' said Eva. 'The very same. Charming, handsome... and I didn't really see him ever again. Well, except at the wedding, of course, where we didn't even look at each other... Mam and Dad, they were so good. They let me cry as much as I liked at home, but as soon as I left the house, they told me I had to have a stiff upper lip. "Don't let her see you upset," they told me. *Ordered* me, actually. Dad was furious. I remember his hands shaking at his side. God, they were both so angry, and these are two people who just never got riled, two very gentle souls. But this upset them. And I hated being the cause of it, so when I left the house, I was all big smiles, and at the wedding, there in my lilac dress, I smiled and smiled until I thought I'd used up all my smiles for life. I couldn't have been a better bridesmaid. At one point, at the reception, when I was rearranging Dol's train, and helping her with her bouquet, she was quite sharp with me. "What's wrong with you?" she asked. "Nothing!" I said. "Just want to make sure everything is perfect." I think...' Eva looked quite pleased for a moment, 'it drove her a bit mad. And then, after it was all over and I walked home from The Sandycove Arms alone at midnight...'

'You poor thing...'

'Not a bit of it,' said Eva. 'I remember thinking, *I am so glad that isn't me.* It was not a life I would have enjoyed at all. All that fuss and expectation. And the weakness of Patrick Blake. I didn't want a man like that at my side. And they went off on their honeymoon. Sorrento, I think. And I never saw either of them again. Well, Dol called round a few times, once to ask for the bridesmaid's dress back, which Mam gave her. And she wrote a couple of times. And I answered, to let her know that I wasn't really interested in being friends any longer. I just wanted to be clear. And it wasn't because I was hurt. But because I didn't like her.'

'So you went no-contact?' asked Alice. 'That's what they say now. You do it with the difficult relatives and narcissists in your life.'

Eva nodded. 'Yes, exactly. It was over. And the relief was tremendous. Dol brought drama to life, it was fun being around her. But I had stopped finding it fun a long time before Patrick Blake came on the scene.'

'And what about Dad?' asked Ciara.

'I obviously knew of him,' said Eva with a smile. 'He was about four years older than me and I thought him quite a serious person. But one day, we found ourselves side by side in a queue for an ice cream on a really hot Sunday afternoon, and we chatted about Murphy's which he'd just taken over from his father, and I told him about my work at secretarial college, and how I was hoping to join the typing pool at one of the newspapers in the city centre and all that. I remember thinking how nice he was. Steady. The kind of man you would like by your side. And anyway, he got to the front of the queue and he was asked to give his order and he turned back to me – and I'll never forget this – and he said, "Eva, what would you like?" And it was just that. And I thought to myself, *You.* But of course,

I didn't say that, I said "Just a plain ice cream". And he turned back with his order and then he said to the girl, "And an ice cream for Eva, please, with two chocolate flakes." And I remember laughing then, and I hadn't done much laughing in a while. I certainly hadn't been back to the Top Hat in Dún Laoghaire. But that was it for George Murphy and me. We started walking out together and then we even went to a few dances. We found another venue in Bray which was lovely. And we got married a year later.'

'Thank God for that,' said Ciara.

'And yours wasn't a shameful shotgun affair.' Alice gave a laugh.

'Oh, don't say shame.' Eva was emphatic. 'No shame, ever. This country had traded in the shame of women for the last century. Let's never shame anyone ever again. We all made choices and I thank God every day that what happened, happened.'

The three women sat very still for a moment.

Alice broke the silence. 'Did you confront him? Lorcan? Did you tell him you'd seen him and Dol? Did you tell him about being pregnant?' She paused. 'With me?'

Ciara could see the confusion and hurt in her eyes. Just like her, three decades earlier. She nodded. 'After the funeral...'

'I knew something was wrong,' interrupted Eva. 'My poor Ciara... she was devastated. And it wasn't just about George dying... I knew she was pregnant...'

'You knew?' asked Ciara.

'Of course I did,' said Eva. 'We spent enough time at George's bedside, you looking pale and not eating. I knew.'

Ciara nodded, slowly.

'And then you leaving the day of the funeral. You had a look on your face and I knew exactly where you were going... and then when you came back... It took me a while to work out what you'd seen...'

'So,' said Alice, 'you came back, served the tea at the funeral... and then...'

'It was later that evening when there was a knock on the door. He knew everyone would be gone by then.' She paused, as though realising something for the first time. 'I think Paddy might have *made* him come down because I saw Paddy's car driving away. So, Lorcan didn't come and see me because he wanted to or to say sorry...'

'*Did* he say sorry?' Alice had pulled her chair closer to Ciara and was holding her hand.

Ciara gave a laugh. 'Not a bit of it.'

'I heard her say she was going out for a bit,' said Eva.

'I remember the moon,' said Ciara, 'it was huge that night. A harvest moon. My God, it was incredible. I couldn't take my eyes off it. It dominated the sky. And I was just this mess of thoughts and feelings and emotions. But all I could think about was you...' She smiled at Alice. 'You were inside me and I had to make everything okay. I was willing to put up with anything so you would be all right. I was willing to forgive him...'

There was an inarticulate sound of derision from Eva. 'Jesus, Mary and Joseph,' she said. 'That man... how could you forgive him?'

'Because I had to,' said Ciara, matter-of-factly. 'I wasn't quite in my right mind and I was scared. A single mother. I was only nineteen...'

'Of course you were scared,' said Alice.

'Terrified.' Ciara smiled at her. 'And so I told him that I was pregnant and that I didn't care that he'd been... doing whatever he had been doing with Dol Blake, and that I needed his support...' She paused. 'I expected him to be grateful. I was willing to forgive him, but he told me that he had to leave. The Blakes were forcing him to leave. Patrick Senior was giving him £5,000 to go and never come back.'

'Paddy's dad?' asked Alice.

'He was a good man,' said Eva. 'I suppose he was just doing what he thought was right.'

'But Lorcan...' Ciara shook her head. 'He *took* the money. What a coward.'

'Well, we knew that!' Eva folded her arms.

'I was ashamed for him,' said Ciara. 'His cowardice was shocking. That was almost the worst thing. What a person. But I knew I was on my own from then on.' She looked at Eva and the two of them looked at each other for a moment, remembering that long-ago time when their world had upended and they had to remake it. It had been like starting all over again, both learning so much. Eva being solely in charge of the shop for the first time. Ciara dealing with pregnancy and then a brand-new baby. 'How did we get through it?' She turned to Eva.

'I have no idea.' Eva smiled at her. 'But we had this baby. She might be the reason.' And they both turned to look at their angel, their little smiling baby who somehow had made everything okay again, the person who gave them strength.

'And of course they discovered Dol was pregnant...' Eva reminded them.

'What a mess.' Alice shook her head, trying to take it all in.

'That's what Paddy said.' Ciara thought about poor Paddy, the distress on his face. Once she'd managed to deal with the shock and cope with the demands of a new baby, she'd been fine. Paddy and Breda had to live with the decisions they'd made – or rather had been made *for* them. 'He and Breda pretended to the world that Conal was theirs...'

'Secrets corrode, they really do.' Eva looked at Ciara. 'We were lucky.'

'We were. We really were,' said Ciara. 'Paddy was pressurised into it. And poor Breda.' She stopped and turned to Eva. 'How did you know about Dol and Lorcan?'

Eva just shrugged. 'Sometimes you know things and don't know how you know. But I kept my eyes and ears open and you notice things. I saw him with Dol once, talking on the street, and I knew her. Then it all fell into place the night of the funeral, you leaving the house and...' She shrugged again. 'I didn't know about the summer house, obviously, and I didn't think for a second that Conal was hers. But I knew Lorcan to be a foolish boy and I knew Dol's need to triumph. I should have guessed.'

Ciara turned to Alice. 'He had lots of good qualities,' she said.

There was that sound of derision from Eva again.

'He did!' said Ciara. 'He was intelligent and could be very kind. He was just mixed up. He hadn't had a happy childhood and he had to live with his aunt because his mother was too ill to look after him. He never spoke about his mother...'

'And when he came back that time... Why didn't you say anything to him? You should have shouted at him...' said Alice.

'Oh, I was past the shouting by then,' said Ciara. 'And anyway, I'm not the shouting type. And I had found myself again. I was beginning to like my life. And I loved being with you. I was at peace with it all by then. And, you know, I felt a little sorry for him.'

'Sorry? For *him*?' Eva pulled a face.

'Yes, for being such a coward, for running away. He was a little pathetic.'

'That's putting it mildly,' agreed Eva.

If We Could Turn Back Time

They looked at each other again and half-smiled.

'We had each other.' Ciara looked at Eva. 'I was lucky to have the world's best mother...'

'Ah, stop...' Eva was smiling.

'I did and I do,' insisted Ciara. 'And the world's best daughter.'

Alice and Eva grinned at each other. 'We'll take that, then, so we will,' said Eva. 'I'm in good company with our Alice. Now, what about a cup of tea? I think we need one, and a chocolate biscuit. Everyone okay?'

They all nodded. 'We're okay,' agreed Ciara.

'If you could turn back time,' said Alice. 'What would you do?'

Ciara shrugged. 'I would have stood up for myself more. I would still want you, of course. But I think I might have wanted to be more... I don't know...'

'Kick-ass?' suggested Alice.

'That's what *I* want,' interrupted Eva with a surge of enthusiasm. 'That. What you said. That's what I should have been. More kick-ass.'

Alice and Ciara looked at each other, laughing.

'You totally *were*.'

'Oh.' Eva looked quite pleased, smiling back at Alice. 'I didn't mean to be. I mean, I didn't set out to be...'

But Ciara and Alice were still laughing. 'That's why you're so cool,' said Ciara as Alice nodded in agreement.

'Yep, the coolest grandmother ever.'

And Eva sat for a moment, lapping up this new accolade, while Ciara thought to herself that actually, if she could turn back time, she wouldn't change a single thing. Not one thing.

'I think...' Alice stood up. 'I think I'm going to go and text Conal. You think Paddy has told him by now?'

Ciara nodded. 'Definitely. He said he would. And Paddy is one of those people you can rely on.'

'Then I'll go.'

She looked nervous, thought Ciara. 'Will you be okay?'

Alice smiled. 'It's about time I met my new brother.'

46

ALICE

> ALICE
> Are you okay?

> CONAL
> Are you?

> ALICE
> I think so.

> CONAL
> I'm in shock. Obviously.

> ALICE
> Me too. Massively.

> CONAL
> Shall we meet?

> ALICE
> Definitely. When?

> CONAL
> Now?

ALICE

Forty Foot?

CONAL

See you there.

* * *

Conal was sitting on the wall, facing the sea. Alice remembered the last time she'd walked towards him, at this very spot. The seagulls were flying overhead, the sky was a swirl of orange, the clouds like carded wool. She had a feeling in her chest that she couldn't quite work out. She stopped.

Conal looked around, his eyes met hers.

She felt her body start to move as she broke into a run, while he was on his feet coming towards her, and then his arms were around her and hers were around him, and she was hugging him, tighter than she thought it was possible to hug anyone, his face in her hair. Then he lifted her up, and swung her feet off the ground, and she laughed. 'Conal!'

Someone was looking over at them. Fran Egan, the one who had told Becca that she thought they looked cosy together. But she didn't care.

Conal's eyes were red and he was either crying or laughing. Or both. She was definitely doing both, as they gazed at each other.

'Hello, sister,' he said.

'Hello, brother.'

They grinned at each other.

'Wow,' he said.

'I know.'

She'd never had a brother before. And because he was a month younger, he was therefore her *little* brother.

'The whole thing is a bit of a surprise,' he said. 'But this is the best bit of it.'

'It really is. Come on,' she said. 'Why don't we go somewhere a little quieter?'

They began to walk away from the Forty Foot, past the sauna, past a bemused Fran Egan – 'Hi, Fran! How's it going?' – and along the seafront.

'I always thought something was off,' said Conal. 'But I never knew what exactly. So I thought it must be me. I was wrong. I was what made everything feel weird and off. We didn't act like other families. I mean, Dad... or... Paddy. Oh God. Anyway, he was nice to me. Loved me, I suppose. But it was just strange. Mum... Breda... well, she loved me as much as she could. And when she left, I thought it was me. And now I realise that it was the situation...' He paused.

'You were caught in the middle.'

'I was the reason for what happened. But now it's all making sense. The way Mum used to hide away all the time, depressed. Granddad used to drink. Dad tried to make everything nice for everyone. And then... oh God. *Dol.*' He looked at Alice. 'My grandmother is my *mother*. It's horrible.'

Alice nodded.

'Of all people,' he said. 'I mean, I'm terrified of her...'

Alice didn't want to tell Conal about what Ciara had seen that day. He didn't need any more shocks. Better to let him believe that Ciara had just been told, rather than witness what had happened in that summer house.

Conal opened his heart as they walked the full length of the seafront. 'I couldn't speak to Dad,' he said. 'Or Paddy. Or whoever he is.'

'He's your dad, I suppose...' said Ciara, feeling a little out of her depth in this new world of blended families on acid. '*And* your brother.'

He pulled a face. 'It's awful.'

'They should have told you.'

'I'm going for therapy. Max's dad knows someone and I'm meeting them tomorrow.'

'That's a very good idea.'

'I just feel as though I've lost my entire family...'

Alice cleared her throat. 'Excuse me?'

Conal half-laughed. 'You know what I mean...'

'You have me,' she said.

He smiled at her. 'Thank you. And you have me.' He paused for a moment, as the two of them sat at the end of the pier, their feet hanging over the sea.

'If it had to be anyone to be my brand-new sister,' he said, 'I would have chosen you.'

'My feelings exactly.'

Despite the craziness of all that had happened, finally they had landed on the truth and Alice knew for sure that this was where she was meant to be – she had a place to be, a future to be lived. And amazingly, she had a brother.

47

EVA

The following morning was a Sunday so there was no bread to make or a shop to think about, and Eva stayed in bed longer than usual, thinking about *everything*. This flat was where she and George had lived for the first few years of marriage, before they moved to Sea Road. Coming back here, the place of those happy, early years, had been the right thing to do. She felt safe in this little room, high above Sandycove's main street. Every morning she would wake to hear, down below, Ciara opening up the shop, and she would get out of bed and knock on the window, rattling it open. 'Everything okay?' she would whisper down.

'Grand, Mam,' Ciara usually whispered back. 'Get back into bed, it's freezing.'

And now, sitting up in bed, the church bells ringing, she thought about Dol Blake. Eva knew exactly what she was going to do. She was going to see her.

There were many times over the years that she had thought about it, wondering what it would be like and what she would say. She had guessed everything that Ciara had told her. At the time, she hadn't been certain of anything, but some things didn't add up. But the fact that Conal was Dol's was typical because Dol never took responsibility for anything. But giving him up was just shocking. Why would she have done that?

Shame, Eva supposed – one of the most powerful, self-defeating emotions.

* * *

Mid-morning, Eva rang the bell of Honeysuckle Lodge and stood there, a fizzing feeling inside her. Nerves, definitely. Adrenaline, most certainly. Fear, absolutely.

'Good morning, Abigail,' she said to the manager. 'How are you?'

'Ah, Eva, how are you? How's everything at the shop? How's Ciara? I heard the disco was only mighty. Tell her I'll be at the next one, okay?' She looked at Eva, waiting to see what she wanted.

'I've come to see Dol Blake,' said Eva.

'Dol, is it? Are you...? I mean, do you...? You're friends?' Abigail looked sceptical.

To save on complicating things further, Eva nodded.

'Well, isn't that nice. She's upstairs. Room six.'

Despite being a little fearful of her reception and despite feeling like the young teenage Eva, it was determination which powered Eva up those stairs and along the corridor. But what was it that she wanted to say? She wasn't quite sure.

She knocked on the door. There was no answer.

'Dol?' she said, her mouth close to the wooden door. 'It's me. Eva.'

There was a silence. And then, 'Eva?' Dol sounded almost shaky.

Eva turned the handle of the door and stepped inside. The room was clean and bright. Two large windows overlooking the gardens. There was a neatly laid bed and a fireplace and wardrobe. And there, in a chair by one of the windows, dressed in dark green trousers and a cream cardigan, was Dol, looking so much like her old self, that little girl with the frilly dresses and the ringlets, the beautiful teenager in the mini skirts, her blonde hair cut short and straight and with winged eyeliner. It was as though all those phases of Dol were still there, the layers of history, still so present, like sediments in a rock face.

I must look the same, Eva thought, *all of me still so present, and just this latest layer, the oldest layer on the outside. But I'm still here, every part of me is still here.*

They looked at each other.

'So you came,' said Dol after a moment. 'Finally.'

'So I did,' said Eva.

'If you're staying, there's a chair beside the table,' said Dol, waving her hand. 'You can set it here, in front of me.' Her hands had been her pride and joy, she was endlessly moisturising them and wearing plastic bags over them at night, or laboriously and perfectly painting her nails. She used to say that you could tell everything about a person by their hands, and would judge other women if their hands didn't meet her standards. 'Did you see her nails? Shocking!' Or 'Her hands were like sandpaper. You can tell she works for a living.' Dol looked down on those who had a job – which was the majority of the women in Sandycove, all of whom worked both in and out of the home – and few had time to moisturise or to manicure.

Eva dragged the chair over the carpet. She noticed Dol's face drooped on the right side a little, her mouth twisted. And her eyes, which once burned with fire and ambition, were once alive with possibility, were dull. However, they watched Eva's every move as she sat in front of Dol, her legs together, her hands in her lap.

'And to what do I owe this pleasure... are you here to pity me? To see if it is really true, that I am reduced to one room in this place? I'm actually quite content here, Eva. I do my own thing. The other women are always talking and doing crafts and there's even a choir. God, the singing is impossible to ignore. I've tried putting the radio on to drown out the noise, but my Lord, it gets under my skin... and in my ears, and worms its way into my brain until all day long, all I can hear is that infernal racket.'

Eva nodded. 'I wouldn't say there is much soundproofing here.'

'Soundproofing!' Dol gave a laugh. 'When I complain, I am told that it's only singing and that the choir is only one hour a day, so shut the hell up.' She winked at Eva. 'Imagine that.'

'Is that what they said?' Eva couldn't imagine Abigail using such a phrase.

'Words to that effect,' said Dol, pouting a little. 'They wouldn't be so blatant. But it's what they meant.'

Eva could feel her eyes on her, taking her in: her face and hair, her long-knitted jumper, the one she'd been wearing for years, decades even. And her jogging bottoms which had once belonged to Ciara, but which Eva had swiped before she'd thrown them on the charity pile, declaring them the most comfortable thing she'd ever worn.

'You shut me up,' said Dol. 'Again, not in so many words, but effectively you shut me up.'

'I suppose I did. My granddaughter calls it "going no-contact".'

'That's a succinct phrase. But tell me this, why did you disappear like that? Or "go no-contact"? Why did you send me that letter telling me you wanted nothing more to do with me? We were friends. You were my *best* friend.'

'And you were mine. When we were children. And then we both grew up.'

'But did you really let a man get in between us? I would have thought higher of you, Eva. I would have thought you were better than that.'

'I didn't let a man get in between us. I would never do that... Look, that's not why I'm here... I thought I knew everything,' said Eva carefully. 'In a small village, stories get told, and you hear things whether you want to or not. I knew about you and Lorcan Kennedy.'

Dol stiffened. One side of her mouth twitched. Her eyes remained fixed on Eva. 'Are you here to tell me off because I had an *affair* with a young man...? Oh, the scandal!' Dol laughed. 'A woman in her forties... sleeping with a man of twenty...' She paused. 'He wasn't worth it, anyway. Patrick found out. He was furious. And everyone made sure I was punished. The scarlet woman.'

'It wasn't that,' said Eva. 'That was none of my business...'

'Oh, your daughter, then. Ciara. You are here to tell me off about that. How distraught she was. Heartbroken. How it brought back your memories of Patrick. Yes? Am I right?' Dol's red-painted nails were now clutching the sides of her chair as she leant forward. 'How could I do that to you and then to your daughter...' Her mouth, when she spoke, was as twisted and awful as the words.

Eva said nothing.

'Well?' said Dol. 'Are you going to just sit there?'

Eva shook her head. 'Ciara is fine,' she said. 'I am fine. None of that mattered... but there's one person who does matter.'

Dol said nothing... her beady eyes glued to Eva's face.

'Conal,' said Eva. 'He matters. And yet his feelings have never been taken into consideration.'

There was silence in the room – only from downstairs, they could hear the choir singing 'Down by the Salley Gardens'.

And then Dol spoke. 'How do you know? Who told you?'

'I've always known. When Breda returned from Wexford *with* a baby... I guessed. Those kinds of things happened. It wasn't unusual. But when she left, I was certain...'

Dol pulled her eyes away and, for a moment, she squeezed her left hand with her right, massaging it, remoulding it. And then she looked up. 'What else was I to do?' she said. 'Patrick would have been appalled. I mean, he *was* appalled. He wouldn't have taken on another man's baby. It drove him to drink. Couldn't ever look me in the eye after that. I disgusted him.' She shrugged. 'But Paddy... well, *he* was willing to take on another man's baby. He would do that for me. And Breda... she had endometriosis or something like that and she was desperate to have a baby. And so it was perfect. A ready-made baby for the perfect couple.' She stared again at Eva, her nostrils flaring. 'And I did all the hard work, the being pregnant part. The hiding away part. The backache and breast ache and being like a fecking whale... oh God. And then I had to get the thing out of me in some place in the Midlands.'

'That's Conal you're talking about. He should have been told.'

'And what has any of this got to do with you?' Dol snarled suddenly. 'What gives you the right to come in here and tell me off? Oh, I bet you've been planning this for years. What you would like to say to me, how you can be so high and mighty...'

'You're right,' said Eva. 'It's got nothing to do with me. And I shouldn't say anything, it's just that I want you to know that what you did was wrong... maybe right for you, but wrong for him...'

Dol shrugged. 'It was wrong for all of us,' she sighed, as though defeated. 'Me, Patrick, Paddy, Breda... what a fool she turned out to be, running back to her parents... God, she hated us *all* by the end. Mind you, I always hated her from the first time Paddy, the hapless fool, brought her home... Then she went and left Paddy on his own.'

'With Conal.'

'Look,' said Dol. 'I can't pretend to feel *much* for him. I never would have, even if I had kept him. It's not my fault, I wasn't *maternal*. And anyway, he had a much better life with Paddy... Not with Breda – she was useless from the beginning. She kept crying...' Dol rolled her eyes and in that moment she looked exactly like that haughty Dol of old, her nose in the air, disparaging and charming by turns. 'And it was better that Conal was with Paddy because they are similar. So I did him a favour, really. He was lucky. It would have been worse had he stayed with me because he would have died of neglect...' She laughed, amused at the thought. 'The only reason Conal survived was because Paddy took care of him and made sure he wasn't completely forgotten.' Dol sat back in the chair, her hands clutched together. Her red-painted nails, which Dol would spend so long on, which would always be so meticulously and perfectly painted, were done badly, the varnish smudged on the fingers, as though done with a shaking hand. 'Look... why were we all meant to be mothers?' went on Dol. 'Why? We had no choice in this world. It was to marry well, or live a life of either poverty or hard work, or both. But being a mother was our punishment, it kept us in our place. I didn't want that. Why would I? At least now... as I near the finishing line, now I am finally left alone. Paddy visits, out of duty. Conal, occasionally, because he's a good boy. But I want to say to him, "You can stop now. Go and find your own happiness".'

'Well, I am happy to keep an eye on him,' said Eva, 'if that's what he wants. And Ciara and Alice will. He's a fine young man.'

'Oh, do what you want,' said Dol, dismissively. 'None of it matters now. I didn't *murder* anyone. Nothing I did was criminal. When you think about it, I did a good thing. The best thing. I would do it again.'

Eva stood up. 'Well, at least I have your side of the story.'

Dol watched as Eva dragged the chair back to the table. 'Will you come back?'

'Do you want me to?'

Dol nodded. 'Yes...' she said. 'I would... I would be...' she paused. 'I would be grateful.'

'You don't need to be grateful,' said Eva. It was funny, she thought. You could go no-contact, you could move on without someone, but it didn't stop you caring about them. *No contact* didn't mean no feelings. Human beings could never quite cut those umbilical cords of connection. 'I'll come again,' she said. 'I can bring you something you might like.'

'Sherbet lemons,' said Dol immediately. 'I haven't had one in decades but the other day I woke up with a taste in my mouth and I couldn't remember what it was. And then it came to me. Sherbet lemons. A quarter of them in a little paper bag from Mr Feeney's.'

'I remember...'

'God, they were good. Better than any man.' Dol gave Eva a look, one she remembered from decades gone, that insolent, audacious, cheeky look. She was still there. 'If only I had stopped at the sherbet lemons.'

Eva smiled at her. 'If only you had.'

'That's what I like about a sherbet lemon,' said Dol. 'The best comes last. The nice fizzy bit. With men, all the best bits are at the beginning and it's the rest of it that's a bit disappointing.'

Despite herself, Eva laughed. 'You haven't changed.'

'I can't... It's just the way I'm made.' They looked at each other for a moment. 'You will come back, won't you?'

Eva nodded. 'Yes, of course I will.' She smiled at Dol. 'I'll come next week.'

Dol nodded. 'And, Eva...?'

'Yes?'

'I missed you, you know. You're the only person I ever missed. I just want you to know that.'

Eva smiled. 'We had some good times, Dol. Those years of growing up. They were fun.'

'Until you decided you'd had enough.'

Eva nodded. 'I had to.'

'I know.'

They looked at each other, both full of a lifetime of memories, thoughts tumbling and crashing into one another. It was so hard to make sense of it all, thought Eva. She had always assumed one would naturally come to a wise and sensible conclusion about everything, as though, as you drifted to the end of life, your narrative was all neatly edited. But it wasn't. It was still something of a mess. The only difference was you were a little wiser. Human behaviour didn't alter radically. People still did dreadful things, still risked everything, took giant leaps of faith, and sometimes they worked out, but very often they didn't. But where would we be if we didn't act so foolishly at times? Life would be very boring indeed.

'Goodbye, Dol,' said Eva. 'I'll find some sherbet lemons. See you next week.'

Eva closed the door behind her and for a moment, in the corridor, she didn't know whether to laugh or cry. Conal was going to be all right, they would all make sure of that. Paddy too. It was about time the Murphys and the Blakes found a new future, together.

48

CIARA

Ciara was waiting outside the flat for Eva to return.

'Where have you been?' Ciara asked, following Eva in and up the stairs.

'Just visiting someone,' said Eva, pushing open her front door, and stepping inside the flat.

'Who?'

'An old friend...'

'Not Dol Blake!'

Eva nodded. 'I had to see her,' she said, hanging up her cardigan and bag. 'And nothing's changed...' She went to the kitchen and began filling the kettle.

'What do you mean? That she's still a horrible person?'

'She's not horrible. She's just... I don't know... she's sad, that's what it is. Wants everything other people have and wants nothing that she does have. And I think that's one definition of poverty. You have nothing, then. All the wonderful things that we have – relationships, a place to live, a garden... she doesn't value any of it.'

'Do you wish she hadn't run off with Patrick Blake?' asked Ciara, sitting down at the small dining table in the kitchen.

Eva laughed. 'Not at all,' she said. 'Because then I wouldn't have had you, and we wouldn't have had Alice. George was the right husband for me and the right father for you, and I have really liked my life very much. And the shop... I've loved the shop. Everything about it... being part of the village, meeting everyone and knowing you are happy there...'

Ciara nodded. She loved the shop too. She loved their customers, those faces which she saw every day. All the people who had come into the shop were like friends, she had seen them go through pregnancies and births, holding their toddlers by the hand. She'd seen them on their way home from hospices, as they said goodbye to loved ones. She had seen them losing jobs or celebrating finding a new one. There had been graduations and marriages, love and loss, and it had all happened in Murphy's. It was a privilege to run a shop in this lovely village.

There were footsteps racing up the stairs. 'Gran? Mum?'

'In here...'

Alice pushed open the door. 'I'm not going back,' she said breathlessly. 'I'm going to stay. If you'll have me. I want to work in the shop. I've been feeling so miserable thinking about going back to Perth. I love the shop. I love being part of the village. I want to come home. And we could share it?'

Eva and Ciara looked at her. 'You mean, we'd work together?' asked Ciara.

Alice nodded. 'I'll get somewhere to live. We could share the early mornings and do half and half, or you could go away... go on holiday or travelling and I could mind everything for you...' She was smiling at them, excited. 'What do you think?'

'But your life in Perth...' Ciara took it all in, trying to work out if Alice was serious and if she said yes, then was she trapping her daughter into a life behind the counter of a small shop in a small village in a small country? All she longed for though was to have her daughter right here by her side.

'I want to come home,' said Alice. 'More than anything. I don't want to leave. I love everything here...'

Ciara and Eva looked at each other.

'I think that sounds like a good idea.' Eva smiled at Ciara. 'What do you think?'

Ciara began to nod. 'But are you sure? What about your life there, the school, your pals?'

'I have pals here,' said Alice. 'And we need to keep our Irish breakfasts going... and Mum? Why don't you arrange a holiday with Mary-Marg?'

'Me and Mary-Marg?' Ciara felt the itching of a dream, the twitching of an idea, the green shoot of a plan. Inter-railing. Just like they had planned all those years ago. 'Okay... if you're sure?'

Alice was smiling and nodding. 'I can't leave Conal. He needs a big sister. And I need a little brother. And more than anything, I need you two.'

'Yes...' Ciara felt a lump in her throat. 'And we need you, don't we, Mam?'

Eva nodded. 'Of course we do. It's not the same without you, Alice. And Murphy's needs you both. Now, Ciara, what was it you wanted to talk to me about? Anything important?'

'Nothing...' she said. 'No, nothing important.'

There was so much to think about, and just as she was about to call Paddy, he called her. 'Would you like to meet?'

'Not for a run, though,' she said.

He laughed. 'A walk, then? The seafront?'

He was waiting for her on the low wall by the harbour, his legs stretched out in front of him, his head down. She quickened her step towards him and then he was standing up and before she knew, his arms were around her and he was holding on as though he'd waited all his life to let it out, all that pain and anguish, everything he had carried with him all these years. Eventually, he released her. 'Sorry,' he said.

'Come on,' she said, 'let's walk... I just saw Monica O'Leary drive past and she nearly crashed her Toyota Avensis trying to peer at us.'

They climbed over the small wall, towards the beach.

'I've needed someone to talk to for so long,' he said. 'I said I missed you and I meant it. And I missed being young and not having anything to worry about. I didn't go to college... remember?'

Ciara nodded as Paddy carried on talking.

'I had to grow up overnight. At the age of twenty, I had a wife, a son, and what felt like the world's biggest secret... but my God, I feel both worse and better. Worse because Conal is so upset and better because I feel I can start breathing again.'

'I am sure Conal will understand...'

'I hope so.' Paddy tried to smile at her. 'He's the most important thing in the world to me. He's the best thing about me. The only good thing about any of us Blakes.'

'What are you going to do?'

'Concentrate on him,' he said. 'Be there for him. Keep talking. Listening... and spend less time in work. And more time trying to live a better life.'

Ciara nodded. 'Why don't you go back to college?'

'I was thinking of that,' he said. 'I looked online at an application. And I was thinking of signing up for the Riviera Run. It's 100 kilometres from Nice to Toulon over five days. It's next month so shouldn't be too hot...' He looked at her. 'I was thinking that you might like to come... I mean, I wouldn't be running *all* the time. And we could have fun?'

She was already nodding. 'I would love to...'

He was smiling at her. 'Are you sure?'

'Yeah, you need someone cheering you on. That's going to be me. And I wouldn't mind a holiday... I've kind of forgotten what they are like...'

Just then her phone pinged with a message.

ALICE

> Conal is staying for dinner. Okay for you? I am making pasta. When will you be home?

CIARA

> In 15 minutes.

She turned to Paddy. 'Fancy some pasta?'

He nodded. 'I'm starving, actually...'

'You always were,' she said, laughing. 'And Conal is going to be there. And something tells me you two are going to be okay.'

CIARA

> I'm bringing another mouth to feed. See you in a few minutes.

MARY-MARG

> I just met Eva. Am in shock. I'm coming around.

* * *

And so it was Paddy, Conal, Becca, Max, Ciara, Alice, Eva and Mary-Marg for Sunday dinner. And it didn't feel strange or awkward, and they all talked, and laughed, and Ciara noticed that Conal and Paddy stepped out into the garden and were talking for a while and then they hugged, holding each other for a long time. When they came back in, Conal joined the others in the front room, where Alice had served the tea and the apple pie and cream which Mary-Marg had brought over – 'it's a supermarket apple pie,' she had said. 'Don't worry. I haven't become domesticated yet.'

It was just Ciara in the kitchen with Paddy and this time she held out her hand for him to take, their fingers entwined again.

'Everything okay?' she asked.

He nodded. 'I think so. Going in the right direction.' He smiled and then his arms were around her and Ciara found herself pressed up against him, his big body and her small one fitting better than she could ever have imagined. He kissed the top of her head. 'Thank you,' he said.

They rejoined everyone in the living room.

'By the way...' Mary-Marg was eating her apple pie, 'we've been asked to do the disco for Jessica and Jimbo's wedding... he proposed yesterday. And we're the entertainment. The See The Stars disco!' She beamed at Ciara. 'And Killian at The Sandycove Arms wants us to do every Friday night in the hotel for the whole autumn. He said the tills were ringing with the sound of over-forty-fives' cash. So, you on?'

Ciara nodded. 'When is the wedding, though, because I'm off to the Riviera for a week in September...'

'Who with?' asked Mary-Marg.

'Paddy,' said Ciara, smiling. 'It's the Riviera Run. I'm his support vehicle.'

'Well, then,' said Mary-Marg. 'I'm coming too...' she paused. 'Unless...' she smiled, 'you want it to be just the two of you?'

Ciara could feel her face getting hot as every eye in the

room lasered in on her. 'Paddy just needs his old friends around him. And that's us, isn't it?'

Mary-Marg nodded. 'Less of the old. But the Riviera is always a good idea. I'll bring Brian. And the twins will have started their first term of university.' She sighed. 'I swear, I have aged one thousand years while they have been doing their exams. Results are tomorrow and I literally can't sleep, can only eat chocolate and I'm in a permanent sweat. They are going to fail. I know it.' She paused again. 'Actually, maybe it's my HRT. I've run out. Note to self. Get thee to the chemist.'

Ciara turned to Alice. 'Would you be able to mind the shop while we're on the Riviera?'

'Of course!' Alice was smiling. 'I've already put out a call for the soda bread makers of Sandycove to apply to make bread every morning. The Irish breakfast is about to be turbo-charged.'

Ciara felt a kind of happiness and lightness she couldn't ever remember feeling. 'And, also, Mary-Marg and I are going to South America next year for a month, so perhaps you might be able to do that as well?'

'We are?' said Mary-Marg, looking pleased.

'A long-awaited trip,' said Ciara. 'And Paddy's coming as well. Backpacking for the over-fifties.'

'I'll be delighted,' said Alice. 'I am so happy I'm staying here. I mean, who else would you trust with the shop? And anyway, I need to keep an eye on my baby brother...' She grinned at Conal and, Ciara noticed, she also smiled at Max, who smiled back, and she couldn't tell which one of them looked the happiest.

'The only problem is,' said Mary-Marg, 'what the hell are we going to wear backpacking?'

49

ALICE

A month later...

Every morning, there was now a team of people making bread. Five women and one man had offered their services to make four loaves each, and drop them off at the shop by 7 a.m. All of them were delicious, Alice had thought when they had done a tasting in the shop, and it was Eva who had given the seal of approval.

The Soda Bread Sisters, as Alice thought of them, including Gary O'Rourke, a young man who was taking time off from the rat race for his health and had discovered the healing properties of bread-making. His soda bread had blown everyone away. 'My nanna's recipe,' he had explained. 'But I tried it with spelt flour. It's much lighter.' It was, they all agreed, and Gary's bread was in. So were Alice's loaves, for which she followed Eva's recipe exactly. Every morning when she made it, she thought of those who had come before her, mixing and kneading and slicing the cross into the top. It was strange and wonderful to taste something which she knew had been tasted by generations of her family before. This was true belonging.

She and Ciara were co-managing the shop now, and Alice was doing every morning, not only because the Irish breakfast was her baby, but because she also wanted Ciara to have a lazier start to her day, after all these years. And anyway, Alice was waking up full of beans, raring to get going, and by the time Ciara started, there was always more that Alice wanted to do. She had applied for a business course at the further education college in Dún Laoghaire, and she had wine tasting evenings to organize, and a new idea for Murphy's vouchers, and already had some prototype tote bags made by a local designer.

It was all sorted. Alice would stay with Ciara and then look for a flat or a cottage on her own. There wasn't much she had left behind in Australia but she rang her old flatmate, Grace, and told her she could have her books and anything else she wanted to take.

'You're really not coming back?' asked Grace.

'I've been away too long. I want to stay and work in the family shop.'

'We have a farm in Roscommon. It's crazy but sometimes all I can think about is the smell of that cow-shed and those early mornings when my hands were blue with the cold, and I'd just slipped in some mud. I used to hate it and couldn't wait to get away, but I am longing now for the smell of a cow, and the way their noses would bash into you, and the warmth of their bodies.'

'I think you might be homesick,' said Alice.

'And the kitchen, when you'd come in and put your hands on the range to warm them up and Mam would have made her brown bread...'

'Ah, brown bread...'

'I tried making it the other day, but it wasn't the same...'

Grace, Alice knew, would be back home in Roscommon before the end of the year.

'Stay in touch, Grace, I'll see you soon.'

She called the school to hand in her notice. 'I'm so sorry,' she said to the principal, 'but I've decided to stay in Ireland.'

'I was half-expecting it,' said the principal. 'The way you went on about Ireland, I knew your heart wasn't here with us. But we'll miss you. You brought a great liveliness to the classrooms.'

'I'll miss you all too. Especially the children.'

So this was it, she thought, her life had landed on the right path, and she didn't have to long for home, or miss her mother or her grandmother, and she had friends, a career... a brother.

And a lover. Max.

They spent most of their spare time together now, and at lunchtimes, when Eva and Ciara sat down with their sandwiches, Alice would take one over to the bookshop, and she and Max would have their lunch, sitting cosily on his two battered armchairs, surrounded by books. *All is well with the world*, she thought, hardly daring to believe it.

'I'm so glad you didn't go back to Australia,' he said, as they drank their tea and ate their sandwiches. 'Do you remember when I asked you if you were going to stay there forever? I could feel my heart beating so loudly that I was sure you'd be able to hear it, and I was desperate that you weren't going to say that you were definitely going back. I was already falling in love with you...'

Alice grinned at him, delighted. 'I thought you were just making small talk,' she said.

'Small talk? *Moi*? Never!' Max grinned back at her. 'And

then I tried to go on about spiders and koalas, trying to plant the seed that Australia was too dangerous to live in.'

'Well, it worked.' She held out her hand and he reached for it and brought it to his lips. 'I couldn't be happier,' he said. 'The best woman in the world, the best job...'

'And pub quiz champion...'

'I feel too lucky. And too happy.'

'Me too,' she said, smiling back at him.

Alice and Conal continued their sauna and sea swims and their walks and chats back to the village. He seemed lighter and happier, especially because he and Paddy were taking time to heal their relationship and had embarked on joint counselling sessions.

'He's right,' Conal told Alice as they sat on the stone bench at the Forty Foot. 'I am his son, he is my father. That hasn't changed... at all. I love him and he loves me. And that, surprisingly, is actually quite uncomplicated. It's everything else which isn't.' He shrugged. 'I'm just glad I know the truth.'

Alice nodded. 'If we hadn't, we wouldn't have found each other.'

'It was weird, though,' said Conal. 'I kept wondering why I found it so easy to talk to you. I am never like that, it takes me ages to feel close to people...'

'I thought you were really sweet...'

'Thanks...' he swiped her with his towel.

'I did!' Alice was laughing. 'I thought you were very sweet because you *are* very sweet!'

'I suppose it could be worse,' he said. 'At least you didn't hate me. That would have been awful. Imagine discovering your new brother or sister was someone you detested.'

'Well, then, aren't we lucky?'

He looked at her, smiling. 'We are. We really are.'

That evening over dinner, Ciara turned to her.

'I've whittled down my TV watching significantly...'

'You make it sound like it was an addiction...'

'Except... I've spotted a new series.' Ciara's eyes gleamed. 'It's called *Död*. Swedish for death. I have it on series-record already.'

'I can't wait,' said Alice, smiling back at her mother. 'We start tonight.'

50

CIARA

Over at the DJ booth, Mary-Marg was glittering in her dress, the lights making her look like the golden disco queen she was always born to be. She couldn't remember when she'd seen so many happy faces, either dancing or talking; men in large groups, their arms around each other just like in the old days, or slow-dancing couples (both the newly minted and the long-standing), and groups of women laughing and dancing. Happiness floated in the air, almost as though you could reach up and grab it. The atmosphere was one of relief and release. And joy. It was joyful.

Mary-Marg had been joined by her husband Brian, who was wearing a T-shirt with the slogan 'I'm With The DJ' and there was a look on his face of pure pride as Mary-Marg changed the records, hovering over the faders as the opening beat of the next song transitioned (was that the word? Ciara couldn't quite remember) into the current one. And then the whole place began jumping up and down, as though Sandycove were in the midst of its own glittering earthquake.

There was a tap on Ciara's shoulder. Paddy.

'You dancing?' he said, smiling at her.

'You asking?'

He nodded. 'Always.' He took her hand and they stood in front of each other and began dancing, and Paddy had a smile on his face that looked exactly like the Paddy they all remembered. Laughing, they mixed and merged into the swirling swarm of all these people who had grown older together, all of them a little life-worn, battle-hardened, but still essentially the same. And now it was time to have some fun. It was long overdue.

A circle had been created because Dessie had broken into a few breakdancing moves, and was spinning around on his neck. Everyone was clapping and cheering, including Yvonne. 'This had better go on past midnight,' she shouted in Ciara's ear. 'There's no way I'm going home!'

Paddy put his arms around Ciara's shoulders as Jimbo skidded past them on his knees, in a kind of football goal-celebration way, and as Ciara turned to face Paddy, she knew that she wanted to kiss him. Luckily, he felt exactly the same way and had the idea just as she was looking at his handsome face, those gorgeous eyes. The hair which was a little greyer than before, but the smile was the same.

He leant towards her, his lips on hers, and she felt something totally new, something which felt completely and utterly and perfectly right. And then after a moment or two, Ciara realised that the circle around Dessie had widened to include her and Paddy, and everyone was cheering.

'At long fecking last!' She heard someone say.

'Jayzis, took ye long enough,' someone else said.

Paddy was laughing, shrugging. 'Best things come to those who wait,' he said, his hand around hers, their fingers entwined.

EPILOGUE

Christmas was a much bigger affair than Ciara had been used to. For one thing, she and Eva had Alice home, so that was one more place setting. And then, of course, Paddy and Conal were coming. And when she heard that there was a gathering, Mary-Marg, Brian and the twins wanted to join.

'We'll roast the turkey,' said Mary-Marg to Ciara, 'and you do the potatoes.'

Becca wanted to come as well, as she said her parents would be quite happy not to have to cook a huge meal and, in the end, the celebrations began on Christmas Eve as soon as the shop closed at 4 p.m.

Murphy's had been busy all day with customers in and out buying last-minute – and, in a few very disorganised cases, first-minute – bits and pieces. Alice and Ciara wore Santa hats all day and over the door of the shop, Alice had hung a huge bunch of liberally berried mistletoe. And many of their over-enthusiastic customers took full advantage, including Jimbo and Jessica who lingered a little too long.

The village looked beautiful, every shop lit up, fairy lights hung from roof to roof, and Christmas trees at every corner. *If I were in Perth*, thought Alice, *I wouldn't have any of this. It would be warm, no one would be in big coats and gloves, exclaiming about the cosiness of the shop as they stepped inside.*

There were glasses of sherry for everyone and some of Dorrie O'Flanagan's excellent mince pies, as well as an open box of Quality Street which Alice had to replenish at least four times during the day.

Eva was too busy chatting to everyone to do much serving. She had assumed the role of grande dame since Alice had joined the firm, seeing herself in an advisory role. All of her friends popped in to see her and have a glass of sherry.

At closing time, Paddy arrived with a case of Taittinger, but he first pulled Ciara over to the mistletoe where he kissed her gently, and they lingered almost as long as Jimbo and Jessica. Ciara felt a little teary when they locked eyes. Everything they had gone through – separately. Thank God they'd finally found each other again.

'Sherry, Paddy?' said Eva who had made herself sherry-monitor.

She had been visiting Dol once a week throughout the autumn and was the first to visit her when she'd had her second stroke, just ahead of Paddy who had to race on his bike from Trinity College in the city centre. Dol was much diminished, but she was kept going by the team at Honeysuckle Lodge and a supply of sherbet lemons.

Paddy was in negotiations to sell Blake's Beer and had invested money into Conal's business, and was also volunteering as a mentor for the local enterprise group. He was, if not a new man, a man with a new life. He was loving his course, cycling into Trinity for his BA in Classical Civilisations as a mature student. He told Ciara that he sat in the front of the lecture theatre, and asked most of the questions in tutorials. Despite this behaviour, he had become very popular among the younger students who sought his advice on everything from love and relationships to the proper way to pour a beer. There was a lightness about him now that he'd nearly sold Blake's and invested in Conal's company. But being free of Landfall had had the most positive effect. He had bought a small cottage around the corner from Ciara's.

He and Ciara, and Brian and Mary-Marg, had travelled earlier in the autumn for the Riviera Run where they waved miniature Irish tricolours, and cheered Paddy as he ran by. Mary-Marg and Brian were celebrating the fact that the twins had passed their exams and had begun some kind of engineering degree at University College Dublin.

Ciara and Mary-Marg had organised a disco every Friday for the rest of the year and it had become wildly popular, with over-forty-fives coming from all over South County Dublin, and there were other similar discos springing up everywhere. The *old-skool* clubbers of Dublin had been mobilized – perhaps even radicalised.

Conal and Becca were still very much an item but Becca still regularly had crises of confidence and was convinced Conal was going to end it all, even though he showed no signs of being fed up with her.

They were about to head back to Ciara's for champagne, Connemara smoked salmon and Eva's soda bread, when they realised that Max hadn't turned up. The bookshop was due to close at the same time as Murphy's and it was now after 4.30 p.m.

Alice had been waiting to see him all day, her present for him wrapped and ready. She'd agonised over what to give him, but she had found a signed copy of the complete poems of

Seamus Heaney that she knew he'd love. The poem 'Scaffolding' was on the first page with the line, *'We may let the scaffolds fall confident that we have built our wall.'*

Just as she was about to get worried, Max arrived, his face red from the cold, his eyes shining behind his glasses.

'A droppeen of sherry, Max?' offered Eva.

'No, I just had to pick something up,' he said quietly, patting his coat pocket.

Eva nodded. 'You might need a *droppeen*, so.'

Max thought for a moment. 'You might be right,' he said, and before he knew it, his glass was charged and he'd knocked it back, smiling at Eva who was looking at him as though she approved heartily of this lovely man with the hair with its own mind, and who had enticed her wonderful granddaughter to stay in Sandycove forever.

At home, everyone agreed that the champagne was delicious, the smoked salmon and bread, delectable. Mary-Marg was in her silver trousers as she chose the playlist. 'I can't DJ and talk to everyone,' she said. 'Tonight, I'm off duty.' She put her arm around Ciara. 'What a year,' she said. 'I couldn't have done it without you.'

Ciara laughed. 'I wouldn't have done it without *you*! You made me do it.'

'The menopause made us do it,' said Mary-Marg wisely. 'The universe works in mysterious ways.'

Alice went into the kitchen to bring out another bottle of champagne when Max walked in behind her. 'I can't wait another moment,' he said. 'I was going to do it tomorrow... but I can't wait. I wouldn't sleep a wink and I'd just end up ruining Christmas for everyone, and I need to know now what your answer is because I literally am about to expire on the spot and I know I am babbling...' He pulled out a small box. 'I was going to make a speech about how much you mean to me and how much I love you and I want to be with you every second of every day. And how you make me happy from my toes to the ends of my ridiculous hair, how you have made the blood sing in my veins and the neurons in my cells dance. All I want to do is make you laugh and love you... and more than anything, will you marry me?'

Alice was laughing and crying and perhaps it was the sherry and the champagne, but more than anything it was love and happiness. It was, she thought, the best Christmas imaginable. With her beloved mother and grandmother, her best friend, her brand-new brother, and best of all, Max. Sometimes, she woke up in the middle of the night in a panic. What if she *had* returned to Perth and missed out on all this?

'Yes,' she said.

'Oh, thank God...'

'As long as there are books...'

He was smiling. 'Of course.'

'And pub quizzes...'

'Naturally.'

'And stories about evil koalas...'

'Kenny wasn't evil though. He was nice. It was the ones in Australia I was thinking of. But yes to more stories about koalas, evil or otherwise.'

They kissed. 'I am just so incredibly happy,' said Max gently. 'I am suffused with happiness.'

'I couldn't have put it better myself,' Alice said.

And they kissed again, without the need for mistletoe, while their family and friends talked, laughed and sang in the living room next door.

* * *

Murphy's – a Sandycove gem

The small grocer's has been in the same family for 100 years and has undergone a renaissance. Journalist **Shazza Keegan** *meets three generations of the Murphy family.*

On Sandycove's Church Street is something of a treasure, I always think. Every morning, as I queue up for my slice of soda bread, Irish butter and home-made jam, before having my cup filled with piping hot Barry's tea, I wonder what exactly we all did before? Why were we satisfied with a desultory pastry, always a little on the dry side, and a watery coffee? And now, like the proud Irish citizens we are, we line up for what Murphy's call their Irish breakfast.

The bread operation is overseen by the grandmother, Eva Murphy, who has commissioned others to bake and deliver fresh, warm loaves of soda bread to the shop by 7 a.m. The hordes begin arriving straight from dips in the Forty Foot or from their early-morning runs. I bumped into Paddy Blake, formerly of Blake's Beer, who was in the queue, dressed in his running shorts. He told me exactly why this has become part of his morning ritual. 'I like everything about it,' he said. 'It's not only the best and most delicious breakfast but it comes from the heart. And isn't that what we all need more of?'

Murphy's has always been a wonderful shop to buy some cheese and wine and other essentials, but over the last few months, it has undertaken what some in the retail trade might think of as a 'zhuzh'. This has been masterminded by Alice Murphy, recently returned from Perth, and full of Aussie can-do. She began the Friday night pack, which is a bottle of well-chosen wine and some delectable Irish cheeses, but she says equally popular is her 'picnic pack' which has been flying out the door.

Alice's mother is Ciara Murphy, who has been running the shop for the last thirty years, but she is taking a step back to focus on some of her other projects, including the See The Stars over-forty-fives' discos, which run in The Sandycove Arms every Friday, as well as organising parties and weddings. One nuptial that they have been asked to provide the entertainment for is that of Alice's brother, Conal Blake, of the Forty Foot Brewery, son of Patrick Blake, and Rebecca O'Hara, of Happy Paws dog-minding business.

Meanwhile, Alice and Ciara will be holding more wine tastings, Alice told me, and she and Max Williams from the bookshop next door have plans for a food and books mini-festival next year. Max's book boxes have become legendary. How he knew what books would be perfect for this writer, I have no idea.

Murphy's is possibly my favourite place in the whole wide world and to see a lovely shop go from good to stratospherically fabulous has been heartening in this age of online and monolithic megastores. Go and queue for your Irish breakfast tomorrow and return for the Friday night box. You won't be disappointed.

* * *

MORE FROM SIÂN O'GORMAN

Another book from Siân O'Gorman, *For Once in My Life*, is available to order now here:
www.mybook.to/ForOnceLifeBackAd

ACKNOWLEDGEMENTS

Thank you...

To my wonderful agent, Ger Nichol.

To my amazing publishers – Boldwood Books, Amanda Ridout, Nia Beynon, Jenna Houston... particularly to Caroline Ridding for all her support and guidance, and to Jade Craddock for her insights and meticulous editing.

To my friends, for being so brilliant – and for making me laugh.

And to Ruby for being everything I ever needed.

ABOUT THE AUTHOR

Siân O'Gorman was born in Galway and now lives just along the coast from Dublin. She works as a radio producer alongside writing contemporary women's fiction inspired by friend and family relationships.

Sign up to Siân O'Gorman's mailing list here for news, competitions and updates on future books.

Follow Siân on social media:

- facebook.com/sian.ogorman.7
- x.com/msogorman
- instagram.com/msogorman
- bookbub.com/authors/sian-o-gorman

ALSO BY SIÂN O'GORMAN

Friends Like Us

Always and Forever

Mothers and Daughters

Life After You

Life's What You Make It

The Sandycove Supper Club

The Sandycove Sunset Swimmers

The Girls from Sandycove

For Once in My Life

If We Could Turn Back Time

LOVE NOTES
LOVE IN EVERY CHAPTER

WHERE ALL YOUR ROMANCE
DREAMS COME TRUE!

THE HOME OF BESTSELLING
ROMANCE AND WOMEN'S
FICTION

WARNING:
MAY CONTAIN SPICE

SIGN UP TO OUR
NEWSLETTER

https://bit.ly/Lovenotesnews

Boldwood

Boldwood Books is an award-winning fiction publishing company seeking out the best stories from around the world.

Find out more at www.boldwoodbooks.com

Join our reader community for brilliant books, competitions and offers!

Follow us
@BoldwoodBooks
@TheBoldBookClub

Sign up to our weekly deals newsletter

https://bit.ly/BoldwoodBNewsletter